Also by Meagan Brandy

BRAYSHAW

Boys of Brayshaw
Trouble at Brayshaw
Reign of Brayshaw
Break Me, Brayshaw

BOYS OF AVIX

Say You Swear
Promise Me Not
Trust Me Always
Keep Me Never

STANDALONES

Fake It 'Til You Break It
The Deal Dilemma
Badly Behaved
Wrong for Me
Dirty Curve
Not So Merry Memories

FUMBLED FUTURES

Fumbled Hearts
Defenseless Hearts

GIRLS OF GREYSON

Tempting Little Thief
Bad Little Bride

LORDS OF RATHE (WITH AMO JONES)

Fate of a Royal
Fate of a Faux

BE *My* BRAYSHAW

MEAGAN BRANDY

Bloom *books*

Published by Bloom Books, an imprint of Sourcebooks
1935 Brookdale RD, Naperville, IL 60563–2773
(630) 961-3900
sourcebooks.com

Originally self-published in 2020 by Meagan Brandy.

Cataloging-in-Publication data is on file with the Library of Congress.

Printed and bound in the United States of America.
LSC 10 9 8 7 6 5 4 3 2 1

To the one who stands for those who can't stand for themselves and needs no praise, you are courage at its finest. Never change.

Trigger Warning

Please be advised that this list contains major spoilers for *Be My Brayshaw* that could ruin your enjoyment of the story as it's meant to be experienced.

Themes and topics in this book include, but are not limited to, the following:

- dubious or coerced consent
- weaponization of homosexuality
- threats of confinement/imprisonment
- past/implied sexual assault/trauma
- physical violence
- secrecy regarding a child

PROLOGUE
VICTORIA

The light knock of knuckles against old wood has my eyes popping open to meet the cracked ceiling, but my focus quickly snaps toward the doorway.

Maybell, the woman who runs the group home I've spent the last three years of my life in, enters, the wrinkles on her forehead growing deeper with every step she takes inside. She pauses beside the second bed in the room, tapping her shoe against the wood to get my roommate's attention.

She looks up from her magazine, pulling her headphones from her ears.

"Nira, why don't you take a walk, hm?" Maybell says, letting her know to get lost without having to tell her to.

It's her way of avoiding the backlash of rebellious teenage girls who don't do well with orders.

Nira glances from her to me and, with an overdramatic huff, rolls her eyes and walks out.

A scoffed exhale escapes Maybell as she drops beside me on the mattress. "All these girls, they'll be the death of me."

"Yeah," I agree. "But would you walk away from this place if you could?"

"Oh, trust me, child." She grins, her age showing in the heavy creases around her eyes. "I could go if I wanted, ain't nobody forcing me here, but to answer your question, no. I wouldn't walk away." She's quiet for a moment, a low, hopeful thought spoken in the next. "I'd like to help care for the next generation while I've still got it in me."

Next generation.

Right.

The boys of Brayshaw, the power behind this town. Brothers who share no DNA but are connected in every way that counts. The boys Maybell has spent the last eighteen years caring for, and their fathers before them.

The "next generation" Maybell is referring to, though, isn't the three she's already helped raise but the newest members to the Brayshaw family, one not yet born but healthy, growing inside his or her mother, and the other, just shy of three years old.

A little girl who, as of this moment, only a handful of people know exists—the daughter of Captain Brayshaw. The little girl who was not only hidden from the world she belonged in but from Captain himself. He learned of her months after she was born and went on a mission to find her.

He did, but their world is not a simple one, and threats from too high up to ignore kept her from coming home the moment he met her, but nobody could keep a Bray from their child forever. And after several decades' worth of battles between power families—the Brayshaws and the Gravens—the right one won.

Zoey Brayshaw is finally home, where she belongs. Permanently.

But I'm not supposed to know any of this.

Not that she exists or is home or the struggles it took to get her here.

Not yet anyway.

Not until later today when Maddoc and his new bride, the true, long-lost blood heir to the Brayshaw name, Raven Carver, get home.

Raven, who just learned she has a sister.

Me.

A secret that was given to me when I was a little girl, and only because I had no one to share the knowledge with, but then I did.

I found my sister, met her, spoke to her, lived in a group home alongside her, and chose not to say a word, but six weeks ago and with a little help, Raven discovered the hidden truth on her own.

She and I, we share a father, one neither of us would ever claim, as he's the enemy to all who proudly represent the Brayshaw name and was the head of another family, Donley Graven of the Gravens. A bastard of a man who tried to ruin this town and the people in it, people who once trusted in his name.

Eighteen years ago, he took our mothers with purpose but decided they weren't worth the trouble when neither baby was going to be a male heir. Donley tried to force them both to have abortions, but they ran away. Their disappearances were still a win for him, as nobody would learn the truth.

A lot has happened since then, though. His lies were exposed not long ago by Raven and he was killed—with his end, both his name and empire fell.

Everyone pays when they piss off a Brayshaw.

Cross one, cross all.

A heavy sigh leaves me.

I'm expected to move out of this group home today and into the Brayshaw mansion at the back of the property line, hidden and protected by thousands of tall trees that cast huge shadows, a blanket of darkness to shield the black in their souls, or maybe it serves an opposite purpose—to hide the light they don't want others to witness.

There are light, tenderness, and care, but nobody would ever guess that, as they don't share them with the world.

It's, in part, why their home is reserved for them and them alone. Those on the outside aren't allowed near, can't see, and could never enter.

I have been inside many times now…because they allowed it.

First, it was at Raven's demand, and they weren't happy, but then things shifted.

The strong four became a loose five. I wasn't *in*, but I was present, accepted.

Will my foot even cross the steps this time?

I swallow past the lump forming in my throat, looking at Maybell.

Her dark eyes move between mine, a knowing glint in them as she stares back and she confirms what I assumed—she knows. She even knows things she isn't told.

"You put it off long enough, girl," she scolds, but there is no anger behind her words.

My shoulders fall.

A seriousness takes over her, a hint of tenderness she typically reserves brimming the surface. "Go on, Tor. The sooner it happens, the sooner it's out."

"The sooner they send me packing."

"The faster they can forgive," she counters.

A humorless laugh escapes and I drop my head back.

"Uh-huh, yeah." I stand. "'Cause they're known to forgive outsiders."

"You're not an outsider."

"I'm not *her* either." I look at Maybell, referring to Raven. "I might not be just 'the blond from the group home' anymore, but I'm not her. They don't… They won't understand."

They have no real reason to try.

"Raven will want to understand," Maybell says. "And slowly, they'll follow."

"What if she doesn't?"

Maybell stands, stepping right in front of me. "Then you make her."

Make her.

I can't even laugh, though I want to—as if anyone who has

ever tried to make Raven Carver, Raven *Brayshaw*, do a damn thing has ever been successful.

Yeah right.

With a deep breath, I hold Maybell's gaze a moment before I force my feet into the hall, out the front door, and onto the dirt road that leads to the mansion, venturing deeper into the trees and off the path once it's in view.

It's been a month since Raven and Maddoc got married and decided to take a mini-vacation to breathe after all the shit they went through to get to where they are now—on top of the town.

During that time, I've gone back to being who I came to this place as, the overlooked loner I worked hard to create.

Before, it was easy. I've always been a watcher, a listener, and I've never been social, so I purposefully avoided useless conversation, which helped block out unwanted friendships. The fact that the few others from the group home were mixed into Brayshaw High already meant I wouldn't stick out like an ugly duck among swans; they were used to seeing less "pristine" females around.

I knew and appreciated quickly no one would bother with a bitchy blond mess with winged eyeliner and red lips, not when prissiness and perfection and mirrored personalities were so sickeningly desired.

Now, though, being who I convinced myself I wanted to be when I first arrived here took effort I didn't even want to give.

Living the loner life was no longer appealing.

Realizing this was like granite to the face.

It was only days into hiding myself that I started to grow restless and couldn't stay away, no matter how hard I tried.

That's when I knew for sure there was no going back. I've always had self-control, but it seems to have slipped.

What started out as righting wrongs I'd helped create turned into more, and without permission.

My little wonder grew to want, want morphed into need, and there was no going back from there.

Possibility bloomed, grew richer roots, and clawed its way into the ground around me.

I couldn't stay away, so I compromised with my own damn mind, and it was back to hiding in plain sight, like before.

Like now.

But Raven called. She's home and very unlike Captain.

He looks for me, scans the yard when he passes the girls' home, and I have no doubt he'd stop if he spotted me, which is why I made sure he didn't.

He's patient, or he forces himself to be anyway.

Raven is the complete opposite.

She'll get out, walk right inside the group home, and drag my ass out the door herself, if even just to hang out on the porch.

I fill my cheeks with air, puffing them out as I attempt to calm my nerves.

Out of everything—knowing who attacked Raven when she was young, the news of my being there when it happened, the truth about Donley being our biological father, Raven's mom being a complete fucking psychopath, and everything in between—this is where my real fear lies.

This is the part I've dreaded the most: the disclosure of a secret so devastatingly complicated.

"Standing in the shadows again?"

The sultry, crisp voice wraps around my ribs and squeezes the air from my lungs. My heart beats double time as I spin.

Messy blond hair, clear blue-green eyes, and a small tip of his lips, Captain stares.

Shit.

Twigs snap beneath his feet as he comes closer, the crack of each one spiking my pulse higher.

My spine straightens, and I shuffle backward until my shoulder blades meet the tree I tucked myself into, allowing no room for an escape should I need one.

"Hi," I manage to force out after a long moment.

The corner of his mouth slowly lifts higher, his gaze roaming across my face as if he's refreshing his memory of me, and my teeth clench tight.

"Hi," he mimics. "Why you hidin' in my orchards?"

"Maybell told me Raven was home," I say.

He nods, humor lining his features. "She tell you this today or a week ago?"

"What?" Shit.

A low chuckle leaves him, and he takes another step forward, his chest now brushing mine.

"You thought I didn't notice?" His words are a slow whisper. "That I'd let you keep hiding in the shadows, watching?"

Shit. Shit.

Captain's eyes fall to my lips when my tongue sneaks out to wet them.

"You've been avoiding me," he accuses, his stare flying back to mine. "Why?"

"I haven't," I lie.

"You're lying."

It's what I do…

"Captain—" I bite back my words when he jerks in even more.

His hand finds my neck, and he uses his thumb to help lift my chin where he wants it, his lips now only a breath away from mine, thick and full and so, so tempting.

"You lay in my bed, touched me in your sleep," he rasps, the blue in his eyes darkening, almost covering the green completely. "Dreamed out loud." A slow smirk appears, and his tone drops to a playful roughness that stirs deep in my stomach. "That was my favorite part."

I swallow, my body growing lax against the tree.

I should push him away.

He stands perfectly still for several seconds before he says, "This is the part where you tell me to kiss you, Sleeping Beauty."

I frown, my palms flying forward to plant against his pecs,

fully intending to shove him back, but my body betrays me, my hands not doing as I willed and instead pulling him in.

Greedy, heated lips fall on mine, and I forget how wrong this is of me, my mouth answering his tongue's demand and opening farther.

Anything for him, my subconscious screams.

His teeth lightly scrape my bottom lip, forcing a low groan from deep within his chest, and he pulls back when I'm positive this was him having not even started.

He tilts his head to the side, a heavy, raspy chuckle escaping.

"I knew it," he confesses, his tongue peeking out to tease the corner of his mouth.

I clear my throat, officially dazed. "Knew what?"

"You want me," he states with confidence, drawing back, but only by an inch, and his knuckles skim down my neck. "Same way I want you." His eyes find mine again, a calm command front and center. "Say it."

Reality slams back into place, pulling at my muscles until I can hardly breathe.

What did I just do?

We've had a simmering attraction for weeks, months even, but it's never been spoken of.

We've talked, but not about anything outside of what we've needed to.

We've hung out, but never alone, except for the night at the Brayshaw cabin, when Raven married Maddoc.

Neither of us could sleep, and we both ended up out on the balcony, looking up at the stars and old sugar pine trees. It was comfortable, the silence we sat in, so when he said he was going to watch a movie, I took that as an invitation and followed him to his room.

I did sleep in his bed.

I *didn't* realize I'd touched him, and while I have been known to talk in my sleep, he never mentioned it. Not that he had a chance.

Like he said, I'd been avoiding him, but not for the reasons he's thinking or one he'd ever guess.

I swallow, shaking my head as I answer his question in a cop-out way.

"I hardly know you." The lie is easy, the truth that follows even more so. "And you don't know me at all."

Captain isn't deterred. His gaze is sharp, focused, and sure. "But you want to know me, like I need to know you."

My body warms.

Like he needs…

The soothing heat quickly shifts to a burning flame, and I dig my nails into my thighs. "You won't like what you find."

"I like enough already, and I'm not asking you to tell me all your secrets *yet*…even though you already know my biggest one."

Fuck.

He keeps going, a hint of a smile on his lips. "You've been out here every day, Beauty. You've seen her, my daughter."

My jaw clenches, and I consider lying for the hell of it, but he saw me, right? I have no bar to balance on, no rope to grip.

This is it.

I knew it was coming; it's why I delayed as long as I could.

This is it.

I give a jerky nod.

"You want to meet her?"

My brows slam together, the hope in his eyes causing my stomach to turn.

Captain Brayshaw. The strong but guarded brother. Quiet and logical, fierce and loyal to his core is standing in front of me, inviting me into his entire world, having no idea I'm woven deeper than he knows.

He'll hate me.

They all will.

"Come on." He steps back, while I remain frozen in place. "I was only supposed to be grabbing her ball from the car. Let's not make her come looking for me."

"Too. Fucking. Late." Raven's chuckled words float from behind me, and the tension in my body doubles. "We found you."

We? Oh no.

"Daddy!"

No, no, no.

Not like this.

Captain's eyes instantly cut over my shoulder, and he moves away, beaming at the little girl I can now sense behind me.

He bends down, and as he does, two new sets of footsteps shuffle closer.

His brothers.

They're all here now.

"Come here, Zo." Captain crooks his finger. "Come meet our friend."

My chest begins to ache as I try for a deep breath.

I catch Raven's stare, and her frown is instant, query blanketing her features as she attempts to understand the panic etched across mine.

This isn't how this was supposed to happen.

I needed a chance to talk to them, to say the words out loud rather than spit it in their faces, as I imagine this is about to feel.

In a world led by loyalty and trust, a heated blade to the gut burns less than learning of a liar.

Raven takes a half step toward me, but then Zoey bursts past her and her eyes follow the little blond who throws herself against her father's chest.

"Find you, find you!" Her laughter lightens the air, allowing me a small breath, but only for a moment as my lungs run dry once again.

Cap's smile bounces to me, his eyes tightening at the sight.

He keeps his grin on for Zoey, reluctantly pulling his gaze back to her.

"Zoey." He spins her around, and her little head lifts. "This is—"

"Rora!" Zoey shouts in excitement, a sound that both settles and stirs everything inside me all at once.

Her eyes shoot wide with her smile as she jerks from Captain, running right for me.

I drop to my knees just in time for her to wrap her arms around my neck in the tightest grip she can manage.

I can't help the tender laugh that escapes.

It's been too long, baby girl.

I hug her back.

My eyes close on their own, but I quickly force them open, and it's Captain's they collide with.

I hold his stare as he pushes to his feet in slow, methodical movements.

The air surrounding us shifts, growing heavy, threatening, as Royce and Maddoc step closer. Raven, though, she remains frozen, frown stuck on me as she attempts to work her brain over what she's seeing.

Zoey finally pulls back enough to gaze up at me, but she doesn't let go. "I miss you, Rora!"

I swallow, forcing my smile to match hers, while tension threatens to knock me on my ass. "I miss you, too, ZoZo."

She laughs, eyes the exact shade of Captain's and focused solely on me.

"Hey, uh, Zoey Bear," Royce calls, clearing his throat. "Let's go get some ice cream, huh?"

"Ice cream!" she shouts and starts to rush off, but not before pausing and running right back to rub her nose across mine. "Baby kisses!"

I force the moisture threatening to creep into my eyes away and respond as I would any other day. "And butterfly hugs."

She giggles as she follows her uncle. "So much, Rora!"

So much, ZoZo.

A deafening silence follows Zoey and Royce's retreat, and I know they're waiting for whatever my next move will be, but their guess is as good as mine. It takes me a second, but I meet the impenetrable eyes not four feet in front of me.

Captain's jaw clenches and he takes a measured step back, away from me.

My hands lift as his stature does, and slowly, I push to stand, my gaze bouncing between the three.

Maddoc's glare is locked on me while Raven continues to glance in the direction Zoey headed and back.

Cap, though, he doesn't look away for a second.

His eyes turn to glaciers, the harsh edges of his jaw growing more profound as his chin lowers closer to his chest.

"There was no right time to tell."

"My daughter knows who you are," Captain rumbles as if I hadn't even spoken. "How?"

I cut another quick look to Raven.

"Maria." I say the name of the woman who posed as a social worker and cared for Zoey while it was too dangerous for her to come home. "She's my mother."

Raven's brows snap together. "You knew?"

"I told you before." My face twists. "Discovering secrets was my purpose, remember?"

"How long," Captain barks as more of a demand rather than a question.

My eyes fly his way.

When I don't respond, he pushes closer, driving words past clenched teeth, "How. Long. Have you known about her?"

I admit, "Long before you."

You'd think I slapped him. I'd even go as far as to say he was hoping for a different answer, that maybe there was one that wouldn't cement a wall between us, not that an *us* existed.

"What does *so much* mean?" he asks, now completely detached, no emotion to be found, not even anger, which is somehow even worse.

"Exactly what you think," I tell him. "It's how she tells me she..." I trail off, unable to say it out loud with his focus on me.

It's how she tells me she loves me.

She's the only person who ever truly has.

"I'm sorry." My shoulders fall. "I don't know what else to say." I turn to Raven. "Don't hate me. I'll go, won't bother you guys..." I trail off, and my eyes cut to Captain and back to her. There is so much I should say, nothing that will make it any better in this moment, so I don't bother to try.

"Go." Raven speaks through a locked jaw, her glare slicing to Captain. The two, already connected on a deeper level than I have had the chance to earn, share a silent, unspoken but understood message before she looks to me. "And make it quick, Victoria."

With a slight nod and a heavy dose of self-hate, I back away. "I expected this. My bags are already packed," I admit. "I'll only be minutes."

I get a few feet before Captain says, "Well, in that case, we'll have Maybell send someone with your things."

My eyes cut over my shoulder, and I frown.

"You'll be moved in in less than an hour," Raven tells me as she reaches for Maddoc's hand, a sharp scowl covering her true thoughts.

I spin to face them once more. "You're asking me to stay?"

She scoffs, glancing from Cap to me. "I'm telling you to."

Maddoc and Captain share a look, and then he and Raven walk away, leaving me and Captain behind. Alone.

I wait until they're out of earshot and attempt another apology. "Cap—"

"Don't," he cuts me off, stepping into my face, but I don't cower.

I can't show weakness; he'd hate that just as much.

He looks ready to say something, but I couldn't guess what. His eyes give nothing away. The second the ice within them begins to thaw, he jerks away, stepping from the trees before turning to me once more.

"Welcome home, Beauty." His words are delivered in a cold and unfitting manner.

Maybe I pushed the rational brother too far?

Captain spreads his arms out wide, the Brayshaw mansion taunting me in the distance behind him. "Might wanna sleep with one eye open."

My forehead tightens as my pulse spikes.

Does this make me the enemy?

The tension written across his face screams no, that he doesn't want me to be, but he's gone before I can be sure.

In the next moment, I consider running, disappearing—only the thought is gone as soon as it hits because the cost of leaving this place is too high.

If I run, I lose everything I never had and always wanted, risk having the only people who've ever made me feel as if being myself was enough, in turn hating me forever.

Allow them to push me away when I've only just grown closer?

I don't fucking think so.

They pulled me from my hiding places, and I'm glad.

I'm tired of dark corners, tired of the background.

Tired of losing before I've gotten to compete.

It won't be easy, and I'll have to claw my way in when he—when they—try to force me out, but I know them enough to understand that if there was a chance to gain their trust, that's the way they'd want it.

They'd never respect someone who would roll over and take it, change who they are and allow the broken parts inside to win.

They want the challenge, proof I want it.

They want the strong, proof I can handle it.

They want the truth, confirmation I belong.

I *do* belong.

They'll see.

Raven is my sister; this is my new home.

It won't be easy, but I'm ready to fight for everything that comes with it.

If I'm lucky, a blond Brayshaw included.

CHAPTER 1
CAPTAIN

I should have known.

My last name is Brayshaw, and while those on the outside looking in may believe being a member of this family means all things come easy, the reality doesn't come close.

More than anything in our lives, we fight.

Me, my brothers, Raven. Shit, anyone who is tied to our name, really.

We fight for our people, what we believe in and what we want, what we feel we deserve. Outside of the love and loyalty for them, not a damn thing has ever even come close to easy.

That right there is exactly *why, when a long-legged, strong-willed, stubborn-ass blond with pouty lips and a bratty little blink slid into our world, I should have taken four steps back for every one she drew me forward.*

And fuck me, did she draw me forward.

I resisted.

I fought against her.

I caved.

I took her mouth like I'd wanted to for months, tasting what became my new favorite flavor.

But our town is a twisted place, and no move is as simple as making it, so I shouldn't have been surprised when not two minutes after, I learned of a lie.

A lie too big to forgive.

Two and a half years ago, I found out I had a daughter who was already born and hidden from me. She was two months old by the time I discovered her.

Today, I learned the blond I planned to keep for myself knew of my little girl before I did and never said a word.

This blond, she was a stranger to me then, so did she owe me any loyalty? Not even a little bit, and I want nothing I haven't earned.

That's the solid truth.

So why the fuck does her betrayal sting like a cut to the chest as if she already holds a place there?

She doesn't.

She won't.

Because while she might not have owed me then, she sure as fuck does now.

I slam my notebook shut and toss it to the floor with a huff, my glare flying to the dark, empty hallway. The hallway that now leads to her new bedroom.

At first, she was afraid to move in—only a fool would lie where the wolves sleep, especially when one has been left starved and angry, right?

At least, that's what common sense would tell you.

So why did the little liar take the stairs two at a time, and how, after being warned to keep one eye open, did she fall asleep with ease?

Running my hands down my face, I let my head fall to the headboard, blindly reaching over for my Brayshaw item—heavy brass knuckles given to me by my father at the age of seven.

I pull them close to my face, inspecting the anchor symbol etched along the curves, a perfect match to the ones tattooed across my knuckles, and read the words scrolled beside them.

Family runs deeper than blood.

Words all Brayshaws live and breathe by, another way of saying *never trust blindly or give loyalty to those who haven't earned it.* You don't have to come from the same line to form a solid and strong one.

If only the treacherous blond understood such a thing.

I close my eyes, pulling in a deep breath to try to relax, but not two seconds later the quiet click of a knob turning has them flying open. I focus, listening to the silence stretching across this wing of the mansion, and for a moment I think I imagined it—three a.m. will do that to you—but then soft thumps sound.

Footsteps.

I bring my eyelids as low as I can without shutting them completely, and not a moment later, she tips her head around the corner, only one of her eyes showing as she hides as much of herself as possible.

She was expecting me to be lying down, sleeping, or absent altogether, so the sight of my body sitting up against the headboard has her freezing in place.

I hold as still as a hunter while she searches for a sign of lucidness.

She finds none and tiptoes a foot farther, peeking into the open room across from mine.

Peeking in on my daughter as if she has any right to go near her.

Brave or stupid?

She leans forward, her hand resting loosely on Zoey's doorframe.

I jump up as swiftly and silently as possible, and right before she tries to take a step inside, I cage her in, my body forcing hers flat against the wall.

Her gasp is quiet and quickly swallowed.

She knows who's behind her, which is why she doesn't bother looking to confirm.

Her grip on the white molding tightens, even more so when I place my right hand beneath hers, my left planting on the opposite side.

I don't say anything and neither does she.

Tension builds around us, thickening the air as heat and hatred meet, she as aware as I am.

Her shoulders rise higher, fall faster, her quick breaths fanning across my hand and causing my jaw to clench.

I shift closer, not missing the curl of her toes against the floor.

Is she scared? Nervous?

Turned on?

My dick twitches without permission.

She should be uneasy at the very least.

We opened the door for her, something we don't normally do, and she stepped right through, hard lies buried beneath a baggy hoodie.

She was a master of hiding—herself, her thoughts, her truths.

I bring my lips close to her ear.

She's maybe five five to my six two, so I have to dip my head to get where I want.

I let out a slow exhale, a sick satisfaction flaring in my groin when her fingers twitch.

Every little thing from me stirs a reaction inside her.

I wait a long moment before speaking. "What do you think you're doing?"

"I woke up and couldn't go back to sleep," she whispers. "Thought I'd check on her."

Anger boils beneath my skin—from her words, from the way they fuck with my head—but I hold it back, moving my hands to her hips and reminding myself they don't belong there. That I shouldn't touch her at all.

She tenses but doesn't resist, allowing me to spin her around, still blocking her in with my chest.

It takes her a second, but then her eyes, a brown, almost-golden color, the same shade as brown sugar, lift to mine.

I grind my teeth together as I bring a hand up, running my knuckle against the edge of her curved jaw, flexing mine when her pupils dilate before me. *For* me.

She'd be so easy to please, I can nearly fucking taste it.

Her lips, perfectly pouty, forever rusty red in color, part.

I swallow a growl and allow my fingers to trail lower.

Victoria gives a subconscious tilt of her head, granting me easier access to her neck as she stares, a little unsure and a lot hopeful.

Once I reach her collarbone, I slip a piece of her silky blond hair between my fingers and force my gaze to soften as much as I can control.

Every inch of her settles.

Just like I wanted.

"I want to fuck you, Beauty," I whisper, anger causing my pulse to jump because damn if it isn't as true as it is false. "So bad."

Her eyes widen; she's completely caught off guard.

"I've been thinking about it for weeks, can't stop," I admit, tugging on the smooth strand a little. "I wanna lay you on my bed, run my hands through your hair, and pull your body close." I slide my arms behind her back and do just that.

She melts into me as I drop my face into the crook of her neck, and her grip flies to my biceps.

"I wanna kiss your throat, like this." I run my lips across her skin, and she shivers.

The hold she has on me tightens as I glide my mouth higher, back to her earlobe, and I have to bite into my tongue to keep it from sneaking a taste.

"I wanna strip you bare," I rasp. "Have you…bare."

Her hard swallow brings a smirk to my lips.

She tugs on my arms, trying to bring me in more, but I'm already flush against her.

I remove my hands, placing them back on the wall while keeping my body pressed to hers. She's not wearing a bra, so her pebbled nipples are felt on my naked skin through her sleep shirt, and I clench my thighs as a way not to focus on the feeling.

"Wanna know what I'd do next?"

Her answer is a whispered moan.

"I'd flip you over, fill you from behind."

She nods, breathless.

"And once I'm inside..." I drop my palms to the curve of her ass and she squirms. "Smashed between this tight ass and your slick spine is arched and begging, I'd run my hand up your back until I reached your hair so I could wrap it around my fist and pull. And, Victoria, baby..." I breathe, and she shivers, leaving marks on my biceps as her nails dig in. "I'd stare right at the back of your head...imagining I was fucking an entirely. Different. Blond."

She turns hard as fucking stone.

She doesn't breathe, doesn't dare move, and neither do I.

I keep her there, trapped, a long moment before I slowly push away, letting my hands fall as I take a backward step, eyes icy and on hers.

"In case you weren't aware, my daughter's blond didn't only come from me." I speak with no emotion.

She stares, still stuck with her back to the wall, palms planted flat against it.

"Her mom's name was Mallory, and her hair was just as long as yours." I tilt my head, regarding her with a coolness I hope gives her frostbite. "Just as blond. Maybe a bit shinier," I callously add.

She's good, though, has the whole "hide what's real" thing down well, and recovers quickly, a mask sliding over her dark eyes.

"If that's what you need to do, do it." She steps forward, shoulders held high as she places herself directly in front of me. "You wanna play pretend, need me to be her for a night or two, I'm game. Use me."

A dark chuckle escapes me, and her fingers anxiously tap at her upper thigh but stop when she realizes I've noticed.

"Use you, huh?" I take my time bringing my eyes back to hers. "That what you want?"

"I'm used to it."

"Not from me, you're not."

She fights not to let her frown free, the muscles in her cheeks twitching as she prepares to snap at me. "I said I don't mind."

I move toward her, and she doesn't budge when I reach out to tuck her hair behind her ear, my gaze locked on hers. I leave it there for several seconds until, yet again, her guard slips the slightest bit.

This girl has little to no control of herself where I'm concerned.

Won't take much to erase it completely.

I lean in, stopping once I can speak against her lips.

"Victoria Vega…" I breathe, and her chest rises with a deep inhale. "Such a pretty. Little. Liar."

CHAPTER 2
VICTORIA

Little liar.

Captain's words have been on repeat since they were whispered into the dark.

Am I a liar?

The simple answer is yes, but who runs around sharing secrets so easily?

I might have grown up in a different world with different rules than they did, understood trust in an entirely singular way, but I know better than to share my soul with others. I saw firsthand what happened when you did, and it was never good.

Even the strongest are rendered weak against their greatest enemy, and the smart know exactly where this lethal threat lies—deep within your own mind.

Nothing is more dangerous to a person than what's hidden inside them.

Secrets steal your humanity, rob you of your riches, hold you back from living your life, yet still, secrets are what make worlds like these, the Brayshaws' and the other families' out there just like theirs, go 'round.

Every so often those hidden truths leak, and down goes the weakest link.

Not that there is one of those living inside these walls.

These boys, these brothers, they're equally strong, but oh so different in so many ways.

Maddoc, the oldest, is the most intimidating, both visually and mentally. The green glass of his eyes and dark hair make for a menacing allure—and he's even more dangerous than he looks. A simple stare from him gets in your head, forcing you to question everything you're thinking.

Royce is the tatted, teasing party boy who never calms enough to pause and moves without thought, yet still, somehow, every move holds purpose. He's a hardened heart and harder fists, smiling through each hit. The dark in his eyes never brightens, though he grins as much as he glares.

And then there's Captain.

As if built from the deepest desires of my own mind, ones I didn't know existed until I laid my brown eyes on his Caribbean-colored ones, a perfect mix of green and blue and ever-shifting. Tall and broad, wide shoulders and sculpted arms, his strength needs no added flare. Combine those things with his sandy-blond hair, and he's a perfect Ken doll.

If his body wasn't enough, his person radiates a deeper pull, one I tried to run from the moment it was felt but couldn't escape.

He's inquisitive, like me. Sees with his mind, processes with reason, and commands without further force. But as much as he's all these things, he's just as threatening and untouchable as his brothers. His ability to think before acting makes him the most dangerous, at least for me.

Maybell has been with them since the beginning, helped guide them along the way, watched as they grew into who they are now, strong and unpredictable.

Brayshaw.

They may have a few months left as high schoolers, but they've never been summed up so simply.

They're much, much more.

Young men of power they both inherited and earned, showered with respect for the good they do for their people, and feared for the bad they eliminate.

They've brightened nightmares.

And they've just taken official reign of this town. Their town.

My lungs expand with a deep breath as I drop my head against the plush patio pillows behind me.

I couldn't sleep for shit, have been staring out at these monstrous trees surrounding the property for hours now, thinking, but it's been a complete waste of my time. I haven't come up with a single way to keep things smooth and simple that won't bring a whole new set of issues with it.

If it were the four of them and no one else, it wouldn't be a problem. They'd push, and I'd take it in stride while working toward fixing what I—sort of accidentally—broke.

It's intimidating, sure, knowing it's not one person I have to prove myself to but four, but I knew this from the get-go. There is no other option, no one or the other.

The Brayshaws are a package deal, and I'm the current stray.

Those simple facts I could handle with ease, but Zoey being home changes everything.

There is no way I would even consider forcing myself on them when she's around. Not only would it be fucked-up, but they'd never allow it, and they shouldn't. I understand that fully, so I'll need to find another way or use the time we'll have once we go back to school to show them I belong, that this isn't some power kick of a random girl wanting into the family that leads this town.

It's fated—I can feel it in my bones.

I'm not sure if they realize it or not, but the next few months are going to be tough in some ways.

I have no doubt Zoey found instant comfort here with her family, in the home she was always meant to be in, but there will still be some sort of adjustment or learning period for all of them. Especially since they function as a unit. Not only is Captain going to be faced with new trials as a dad, but the others will as well. They'll grow in ways most eighteen-year-olds don't, and quickly. Not that they've ever really been teenagers.

It's part of the Brayshaw way, to grow into manhood young, marry right out of high school, and produce an heir just as quickly.

Maybe because of this, they have an upper hand here, as running this town has prepared them to be strong men all their lives, but it's hard to say for sure.

All I do know is while Zoey's shy of three years old and definitely won't comprehend every little thing, she's smart as a whip and picks up on things fast. It won't take long for her to realize her new home is mine as well, and she'll seek out my attention.

What am I supposed to do when she does? Walk away?

Yeah right.

I'm the person she saw the most, outside of Maria.

Maria.

I haven't spoken to her since before Zoey came home. Not that she and I talked about anything other than Zoey, but she did care for the youngest Brayshaw for years, and now it's only her and acres of land.

I pull out the cell phone Raven had sent to me when she was gone and scroll to Maria's name, hitting Send, but after a few short rings, the line goes to voicemail.

I don't leave one.

She may have given birth to me, but I never had a mother, or love and affection for that matter, as I now know a child should.

Back then, though, I knew no different.

You don't miss what you never had, and I had nothing.

At least, not until my tenth birthday when a man showed up at the door with news—or at least it was news to me.

I had a sister—Raven.

The man who came to share the information was Mero Malcari, the biological brother of Rolland, the boys' dad, who was believed to have died the night the Brayshaw family was attacked eighteen years ago, the night Rolland chose to save his friends over his own blood.

Mero was a sick man, and the day he dared to roll up to

the Graven estate—the home of his family's enemy—he strode in with a smirk, head held high and all, prepared to barter.

I'll never forget it.

The bushes shake and I pause, tilting my head all the way back to look up at the tip of the wall.

The deep-green leaves cover the heavy stone, the strands braided over the top to hide the thick, spiked metal wire beneath it, but they don't rustle.

There's no wind today.

A smile breaks free, and I jump to my feet, promising the new lilies I'll be back to give them their home, just beside the female that had offered them life.

I wipe my hands along the cool blades of grass near my thighs, peeking through the small sliding door to make sure the lock's shadow is still seen beneath it, indicating it's bolted in place, as normal. I'm locked inside.

I scoot over to the wall, tug on the brush twice, and wait.

It takes a moment, but then it's tugged back.

A low laugh leaves me as I lean forward, reaching inside the thorny bushes, meeting a soft pair of fingers once I've stretched as far as I can go. I drop my head down, peek through the tiny opening, and there are his eyes, peering into a small hole he created, the rest of his face hidden behind bricks that separate me from everyone else.

"You're back!" I grin even though he can't see it. "And just in time. It's almost midday. The bird will be flying by soon."

Or maybe he can see my smile, because even though all that is visible are his eyes, I spot the fear and sadness clouding his.

"What's the matter?"

"I can't watch the vulture fly with you today."

My excitement falls, bringing my shoulders down with it. "How come?"

He doesn't answer right away, and then, "There's a man. He's come for you."

"A man… What man?"

His gaze leaves mine a moment, but then it comes back, and the sadness is gone. "You'll see. He's on his way, and your father is with him."

My eyes widen. "Now?"

"Now." Strain pulls at his eyes and he sighs. "Be brave, do what he says, and you'll be okay."

"You're scaring me."

He hangs his head, whispering, "It'll be okay, Garden Girl. I don't know if he's a good man, but if you listen, I know he'll try to be."

"What do you mean? Why would I have to listen? Nobody's allowed to talk to me."

"They're coming!" he hisses. "I can't wait to see you."

"See me how?"

"I'll be with you soon," he rushes out.

Something blooms in my chest, my hand sinking farther into the ivy. "Promise?" I whisper.

"I promise you. It'll be you and me forever one day, no matter what."

Voices sound in the distance.

"Go!" he hisses again.

I quickly glance behind me, and when I look back, the only friend I've ever had—but never even seen—is gone.

I quickly stand and rush back to the flower bed, but the door is thrown open the moment I reach it, so I jump back to my feet, lowering my head as my father's shiny shoes come into view, another pair planting just beside them.

"Eyes."

I look up, forcing my gaze not to travel to the man at my father's right, but then my father steps aside, and suddenly the man is before me.

He's handsome, tall and trim, and wears a smile, one that meets the corners of his pretty green eyes.

"Hello," he says so softly that the muscles in my body relax.

I swallow. "Hello."

His gaze falls to the dirt on my fingers, and I quickly hide them behind my back.

He glances beyond me at my garden. "You enjoy flowers?"

I push my hair over my shoulders as I nod, and his strong stare follows the movement.

"Then I will give you all the flowers in the world." His smile spreads and he turns to my father. "You have yourself a deal, Graven." He hands him an envelope. "You'll find your other daughter's location inside."

My eyes widen and I take a half a step forward. "I have a sister?" Hope, if I had to guess, is what expands in my chest, making it hard to breathe.

But the hard, empty glare of my father swings my way, and it's gone as quickly as it comes.

I freeze, shuffle back, and lower my head.

He scoffs, turning to the man. "Walk out with her, and you don't get to bring her back. She'll be your burden from here on out, Brayshaw."

Brayshaw?

Is that his name?

"No," the man responds gently as he steps toward me, his fingers sliding beneath my chin, bringing my eyes to his. He smiles. "She'll be my savior, and one day, my bride. Speak to or of her like this again, Graven, and I'll be forced to make sure you regret it."

My heart beats like crazy as I try to make sense of their words, but all that clicks is *bride*.

He bends so we're eye level and grips my hands in his. "Never lower your eyes when a man's meet yours. Never look away." His gaze roams mine. "Never cower, sweet girl. Your eyes, a deep, daunting…perfect brown, are your power, and I'm going to teach you how to use them."

Not five minutes later, I was in a car for the first time, with nothing but the clothes on my back and shoes on my feet.

Mero had given up Raven and her mother's location, something Donley Graven had been searching for since the day her mother disappeared, and in exchange, my father gave him me.

Just like that, I went from the worthless, ignored, ghostly girl in the gated garden to a golden puppet, the highest valued, most precious tool in a strange man's world.

I developed early and never looked my age, always older. I never had a chance to play with other children when I was young, though I knew more existed, the sounds of their laughter echoing on the other side of the wall, and then there was the boy who dared to look beyond it. Because of this, I was too mature for my own good, nothing but guards and a tutor to learn from, and once I turned eight, I was given a television.

Mero must have seen it in my eyes at ten, a child who never lived as one, a girl desperate for more.

He was proud of his new "property," and quickly, I became his pawn, did as he asked, found ways to trick who he instructed until secrets spilled from the mouths of some of the most powerful men he could find. Men who held high positions, men who were forced to leave Brayshaw, traitors to the family and pure outsiders. Jobs for purpose and some simply for payment.

We had ruses, ways of gaining the truth, and I always wanted to give him what he asked for, so I was extremely inventive. I studied people, trained myself to see more than the average person's eye, hear what wasn't said. It became a game, something to focus on, a way to earn the affection I came to crave.

Secrets were my purpose.

I was blackmail.

It wasn't until I turned my back on the man who freed me from the prison that I wasn't aware I had been living in that my life changed.

I know I'm strong, I know I can handle this place, but I want more than that.

I can't go back to being the little girl I once was, completely dispensable.

Knowledge—it gave me purpose, power.

It's ironic, how the only thing to ever offer a shred of color is the exact reason my world's been painted gray.

Holding on to secrets in a place like this has done the opposite of what I've understood them to.

I hold no leverage, only lies.

I feel no pride; I'm buried in shame.

I hate myself more than I hate the man who molded me this way.

How weak you are to become what someone else asks of you?

I can be different here, an asset instead of a threat.

I want that: to be useful.

Worth something.

I sigh, licking my lips as I pull a full breath through my nostrils.

The shuffle of feet catches my attention, and I roll my neck against the chair cushion to find Rolland, the man who helped me hide in plain sight, walking up.

I never told him who I really was, daughter of the man he hated, only how I grew inside the walls of the Graven estate until I was traded—I never told him to whom.

Rolland slides his hands in his pockets, looking across the orchards in front of us. "You don't have to stay out here."

"Yes, I do."

"This is your home too."

I nod. "It will be."

A small smile finds his lips, and he slowly lowers into the seat beside me. "I'm glad you feel that way."

The cloud of uncertainty surrounding me must be suffocating him, as he says, "I assume you realize now."

"That you knew I was a product of the enemy, Graven, by

dirty blood, all along?" My eyes slide his way a moment, but I quickly look away.

"I'll admit, I wasn't positive, but I had a feeling, maybe even a bit of hope, you were the child of the woman I tried to free."

"What does that mean?" I ask him, having never actually held a conversation worth anything with Maria. I learned bits and pieces of this, but nothing means a damn thing if it doesn't come directly from the person who knows the full truth. "Free her how, exactly?"

"Your mother worked as a maid for the Gravens, and Donley threw her out like garbage when he learned she was pregnant with a girl. All he was after was a son. Maybell brought her to me, and I offered her a home, a safe place to make a living and raise her child—you, once you were born." He looks at me. "Unfortunately, she never had the chance. I believe you know why."

"He took me from her at the hospital." I shrug. It's not sad; it's reality. "Why'd you let her back in your home after that?"

His forehead creases and he glances away. "Guilt, maybe. I'm not sure anymore."

"And that was enough for you to slip me in past your sons?"

"I gave them your file, as I do for every person we add to the group homes. All I did was simplify yours."

Simplify… Right.

As if "abusive home" and "absent parents" even come close.

I watch for a sign of a lie as I ask, "Do you have a real file on me, Rolland?"

He shakes his head. "Not for the lack of searching," he admits. "You're not in the system, Victoria. You don't even have a birth certificate. It's why I suspected there was more to you than you shared. Technically, you don't exist, but we can change that if you'd like."

A long moment of silence stretches between us, and when he realizes I have no comment on his last statement, Rolland inhales deeply, dejection clear as crystal in his tone. "I knew the risk I was taking allowing you into the Bray house. You came as a secret, and that meant you must have had more. I assume we've only brushed the surface."

"You only learned what I've allowed you to and nothing more," I tell him bluntly, my eyes connecting with his and holding. "Many of the things I know hold no weight on this place…but many do."

There is so much the boys don't know, things the Brayshaws likely thought they'd long buried, but that's the thing about secrets: It takes two to have one.

Or so the naive believe.

The only way to bury the truth is to bury the man, the manipulator, and the predecessor.

How they forget, I don't know, but…

For every burning king, there's a boy who rises from the ashes.

That's how kingdoms work.

That is the exact reason I haven't dropped to my knees and let all my secrets pour from my mouth.

This family's strength, while unwavering and unparalleled, wasn't built on loyalty as most believe.

It was built on blood and betrayal.

My truths will hurt some, will break many, and might just lead one Brayshaw to the grave, but greed is a cunning bastard, and I'm its newest victim.

I could leave and take my secrets with me, but I won't.

I want in, and not just for Captain—for me too.

I'll tell them when they're ready for more and let the chips fall where they may.

I drop my head back. "Did your PI really find nothing on me?"

He fights a smirk. "Nothing. I thought Mero died long ago, so I never would have thought to look for clues that could lead to him. They hid you well—both my brother and your father."

I nod. "Mero was careful, sure, but it was Donley who gets most of the credit. I would spot people trailing or watching us, and I knew who they were sent by. Mero knew too, but he didn't care. To him it was like free security. He pretended never to notice, but he saw everything. Donley pretty much cleaned up any crumb he might have left behind. He allowed no room for chances."

Rolland regards me for a long moment. "There was a price."

"There's always a price, Rolland, and his was high. Wanna know what it was?"

"Do you want to tell me?"

"Raven's life," I rush out, having never shared this before, and a heavy ache twists in my ribs. "If Mero lost me, no matter how it happened, he would kill her. If I stayed his, stayed hidden, she got to live."

Deep lines form at the edge of his eyes and he shifts his body to face me better. "Victoria—"

"The threat wasn't even meant for me but for Donley. What kind of girl would care to protect some random girl who shared her blood, right? After all, family runs deeper than blood."

Rolland's eyes narrow. "He shared that with you?"

"More like drilled it into me, made sure I'd never forget those words, never turn my back on him for my father. Guess he had some fear I might care for the man."

"Those words are sacred in my family." Rolland's lips press into a firm line.

I shrug, knowing full well the weight the Brayshaw sentiment holds on your soul, and refocus the conversation.

"Mero tossed out the threat on Raven's life knowing Donley planned to leave Raven right where she was—the last thing he wanted was for her to end up here and people to find out what he had done, raped the virgin who was promised to his own successor out of greed and need for a male heir. He brought his own family down, but it took an eighteen-year-old, five-foot-six chick's fearlessness for him to realize it."

"He was a weak man in more ways than one." Rolland studies me.

"I could have walked away," I tell him. "So many times, I could have left, just…ran. It would have been so easy."

"Yet you stayed with a monster."

A sad scoff leaves me, and while I keep my head facing forward, I shift my eyes to Rolland. "To protect a sister I didn't even know."

"Why?"

"Because even though I'd never met her, never saw her, my gut told me her purpose was bigger than mine," I answer instantly. "I was right."

Rolland inhales as he stands, and when he offers me his hand, I take it, allowing him to pull me to my feet.

He stands there, staring straight on with his shoulders high and eyes bright, a vibrant green like his only biological son.

"That is honor," he says. "That is loyalty without purpose or personal gain. That, Victoria Vega, is Brayshaw."

Warmth-wrapped guilt starts under my ribs, slowly spreading throughout my chest as unease drives my eyes to the second floor of the Brayshaw mansion, to the window that leads to a certain little girl's room, and what do you know…

He's watching.

CHAPTER 3
CAPTAIN

She releases my dad's hand, her eyes remaining locked with mine.

Her existence is infuriating.

Intoxicating.

Fucking troubling.

I don't know what it is or why it's there, but there's a fiery pull between us, one that's been brewing since the beginning, and with her under the same roof as me now, I suspect it'll only grow.

My eyes narrow of their own accord, and she tips her head, not willing to look away first.

I hate how my body senses hers, but worse, I hate what the little fact confirms.

She drives me fucking mad, but goddamn how mad I could drive her—

"Whatcha lookin' at, Packman?" Raven cuts into my thoughts.

I glare at the girl in our yard. "She looks nothing like you, polar opposite, in fact."

I glance behind me, taking in Raven's long, sleek, jet-black hair with purple-colored strips and her stony gray eyes. Even her skin tone is different, a lighter creaminess, a contrast of her curved, pink lips.

Victoria is more bronze toned, a flawless summer tan she carries all year long, dark eyes and plumper lips, like she keeps them constantly pursed.

Their styles, though, are slightly similar—thick black liner stays on their eyes and they both sway toward a scrappy rocker chick with a wild side, but where Raven screams recklessness, Victoria's straight cynicism.

Raven doesn't think; she acts. And Victoria forever has something working through her mind.

Raven laughs. "That's because I was cursed to look like my mom, may the devil keep her soul burning in hell."

I scoff, shifting to face her better.

It was only months ago she dumped her mother's ashes in the creek out at our family cabin, giving the vile woman a familiar place to rest, even though Raven didn't even think she deserved one.

"You been thinking about her?" I ask, my eyes falling to her stomach.

She shrugs, a slight frown taking over as she focuses on the flower stencil covering Zoey's wall. "If worrying I'll suck as bad as she did at the whole mothering thing counts, then yeah." A heavy sigh leaves her. "With every couple blinks," she admits.

"What's Maddoc say?"

"How I'm not her and would never allow myself to be."

"He's right."

Raven scowl deepens. "She was a drug addict, Cap. I smoke weed, or did before I got knocked up. She sold her body for quick cash. I let people beat on mine for the same."

"You didn't let people beat on you." I shake my head. "You found a way to take care of yourself, got in a ring, and earned some money with your fists by winning. That's nowhere near the same thing."

Her lips pinch and she gives a jerky nod.

"Trust me, Brayshaw, you'll be more than she ever could have."

She looks to me with a small smile. "Or die trying."

No doubt in my mind she'd do exactly that.

We eye each other, and with each passing second, her features soften.

She tilts her head, always knowing when I have something to say but never forcing it from me.

I ask her what's been on my mind. "Why do you think our dad did this for her? Why hide a Graven with the girls in the group home?"

She nods as if she was expecting this question at some point, proving me right when she speaks.

"I worked this shit out in my head so many times," she admits. "I thought for sure it was to keep an eye on her, track trouble, you know?" She takes a deep breath. "But now that I know he's not a total dickhead," she says, making me chuckle, "I think he wanted to give her a chance in hell at a life." She looks my way. "Who the hell knows what it was really like for her before this place. You saw the scars on her stomach, same as me. We can't even pretend to know how she got 'em."

My lips flatten at the mention of the markings on Victoria's skin, something we were never meant to see but did when her shirt was torn without her knowledge a few months back, giving my brothers, myself, and Raven an accidental clear view of the markings carved into her. She never offered an explanation and we never asked for one.

I've turned over every possibility in my head, but in our world, it could be the result of a million things. My thoughts could be tame compared to her reality, not that I have any way of fucking knowing.

"I think she has a lot to tell," Raven says.

"Then why the fuck hasn't she?"

A soft chuckle leaves her, and she shoves to her feet. "Asks the guy who shares his life with us but his deepest thoughts only with a paper and pen."

I frown, pushing from the windowsill to stand in front of her.

"Why hasn't she?" she teases as she pats my chest, her gray eyes meeting mine. "How about, why would she? She might be living in a big fancy mansion, but with space doesn't come comfort for girls like us, and we've given her none."

"What does that mean?"

"It means we're fucked-up rejects, and we know it. In case we ever start to forget, society is always game, set, and ready to remind us. We're well aware of the dangers hope can bring, so... we have none."

With that, she moves toward the door, and my gaze follows, knowing she'll pause to add something before she walks out.

She does.

Her hand plants on the doorframe as she shifts her body sideways to look at me. "Trust is normally a two-way street, Cap, but in our case, it's a four-lane, one-way highway. Imagine being on the outside of that."

"You were at first."

"And I made mistakes."

"You made selfless choices."

"I made reckless decisions."

"For us," I stress.

Raven shrugs. "Who's to say she didn't do the same? Your dad brought her here, put her in the safety of your group home, on your property, in your town. Maybe she felt a sense of loyalty without realizing it. Or maybe she does and admitting it is the hard part. All she knew of Brayshaw was the man she was raised with. Can't be easy to suddenly hurt for one Brayshaw when not long ago you wanted to hurt another."

Unease lines my throat, the thought having never crossed my mind.

Victoria had no clue what it meant to be Brayshaw; all she knew was what Mero told her, taught her.

Raven is right—that's a hell of a change in mindset.

"If she's serious about her place here, she'll talk to us eventually, and she knows what follows once she does. We hide nothing from each other." The corner of her mouth lifts into a grin. "Other than the saucy stuff."

A chuckle leaves me, and she laughs, walking out.

I drop onto Zoey's bed, knowing damn well Raven is right.

Both of us are aware I won't ask what I want to know—that would make it easy on her.

She wants to stay; she needs to be brave.

She needs to come to me.

She—

"Daddy!" Zoey yells from the media room. "Hu-mon!"

"Yeah, Daddy, come on or Imma press play without your word!" Royce's shout follows hers.

I chuckle, grab Zoey's blanket like I came in here to do before getting distracted, and head to watch a movie with my brother and my little girl.

As soon as I step out of Zoey's room, Royce is at the top of the stairs.

I nod in question, a frown following.

He jerks his head, indicating for me to follow him.

In the living room, Raven sits on the couch, Maddoc right beside her with a hand on her thigh.

There's no sign of Victoria. She might have gone to her room while I was putting Zoey to bed—anything to avoid passing me in the hall.

"What's goin' on?"

Royce sets a Hot Wheels on the coffee table, a little blue sports car.

"That's not Zoey's." I say what they already know. "Where'd you find it?"

"After the movie, I went for some playtime. It was on my hood when I came outta Tracy Parks's pool house." He wiggles his eyebrows. "Don't worry. Didn't tell her when we were coming back to campus, not even when she came at me with some good-ass incentive."

Raven chuckles and Maddoc flicks a glare her way.

"It was just the toy?" I ask, knowing he's already filled the other two in while I was busy with Zoey.

Royce nods. "Sitting on a torn piece of blank paper." He tosses it down. "So I wouldn't hunt the fucker down for scratchin' my shit, I'm guessin'."

Raven leans forward, picking up the item and inspecting it. "This is how people tell you when someone's fucking up and shit needs fixing? They drop puzzle pieces and make you work for it?"

"They trust us to read between the lines."

"And," Royce adds, "we figure it's 'cause nobody wants to be a rat."

Raven's lip twitches. "Now that makes sense."

Maddoc frowns. "We haven't heard shit in a minute, nothing more than the petty bull Mac handled on campus while we were gone," he says.

Mac is one of the few we can depend on. He's been doing work for us for several years now but only recently slipped in as our go-to man. Before that, though, he was a trusted friend.

"Day Royce goes out, suddenly there's shit going down?" Maddoc leads.

"It's not like people are allowed here," Raven says, looking his way. "Maybe it was the first chance they had."

I eye Maddoc, and while his brows dip lower, he doesn't say anything, looking at the car in Raven's hand instead.

She passes it over and his gaze meets mine. "Only one blue sports car I can think of."

"Jason Rowe."

He nods, looking to Royce.

"Who the hell is that?" Raven's head tugs back.

She looks at Maddoc, her eyes narrowing slightly when a hint of a smirk finds his lips.

Royce chuckles, catching her attention. "'Member a few weeks after you got to the Bray house? When that guy asked to go to our stoplight party and you showed up in green when Madman told you to wear red?" She smiles wide. "The night Maddoc wigged out and laid claim on your ass…and puss?"

She laughs, pulling her feet up on the cushion. "It went down a little differently, but yeah. I remember."

"That was Jason Dickbag Rowe from our basketball team."

"You don't like him?"

"Come on, RaeRae," he teases. "We don't like anyone."

"Right." She grins, dropping back with a yawn. "So what now?"

"Season ended a few months back," I say, glancing to Royce, knowing they're thinking the same thing.

His phone is already in his hand. "I'll call Mac."

Maddoc turns to Raven with a grin. "Time we get the boys together for a game."

"Yeah—" I cut myself off when my spine shoots straight, and not a second later, the reason reveals herself.

"Zoey will love that."

Our heads jerk in the direction Victoria's interruption comes from.

Immediately after she's spoken, Royce is on his feet and creeping toward her, but that doesn't stop her. She steps from the billiard room, headed right for us.

Raven takes the car from Maddoc's hand and slips it in her hoodie pocket, her eyes on Victoria, who doesn't so much as flinch at Royce's advance.

"You're either smart as shit or dumb as fuck, girl, and I gotta say I'm going with the second one." He pushes his chest against her. "Maybe Maybell pretended not to see you hidin' in corners at the group home, but this ain't the place. You'll be gone as quick as you came, and I'm not talking 'bout your midnight thoughts of Cap."

Victoria gives a lazy blink, unaffected and already accustomed to Royce and his protective, pounce-first ways.

Her eyes slide to mine. "She'd love to watch you play."

My blood runs hot beneath my skin and I move forward.

"Well, that was mighty fuckin' brave, VicVee." He glares, calling her by the dumbass nickname he came up with for her as he backs away, knowing full well I'm ready to take his place.

She tips her head, brown eyes waiting to see what they'll find in mine.

"I'm not sure you understand the situation here," I draw out. "You're not in this house because you earned it; you're here because we can't trust you outside of it. We can't allow you to go around running your mouth about things the town isn't aware of yet, but if you try to come in here and tell me what to do with my daughter like you know better than me, I will toss you out so fucking quick, your head will spin." I get in her face and she pulls her lips in. "And I'm not talking about out of this house but out of our town."

"You can try."

My head tugs back, and in my peripheral, I spot Maddoc pushing to his feet.

I crowd her but she doesn't budge, her chin lifting to keep our stares locked. "And what will you do, hm? How will you stop me?"

Her hand lands on my forearm, in a warm, strong hold, attempting to soothe with her touch, with her eyes…as if she has the right.

My jaw flexes.

"I'm not being hateful or spiteful or anything else you're working to convince yourself of," she says for only me to hear.

Fuck me if that's not worse than if she would have screamed it in my face.

I lower mine to hers. "Have you learned nothing, Victoria?"

When her eyes tighten, I continue.

"You want to stand here and act like you know us, yet still you whisper, hide your voice from my family? Have you not realized yet we don't work like that? We talk, we fight, we fuck where we need, when we need. We don't hide from each other." My eyes begin to twitch. "You lied about knowing my kid, and you dare tell me what the fuck to do with her like your opinion or thoughts or wasted-ass whispers matter?" I toss her hand off me, taking a step back. "They don't."

She licks her lips, her focus shifting behind me for a long moment before snapping back. Stronger, more determined. "They will."

My eyes bulge before I can stop them, and damn if I'm not struck.

She's fucking insane.

To my left, Maddoc slowly drops back into his seat as Royce shuffles a few feet away, but Raven, she leans forward on the couch, watching.

If Victoria notices they've let up a little, she doesn't let it show.

She closes the gap I put between us, her hand shooting up to grip my chin so she can tip my head, but I don't budge, and she doesn't let fucking go.

My pulse pounds heavily in my throat as I glare down at the girl who ruined everything.

Hate to want you, Beauty…

"I'm not going anywhere, but I have a feeling if I tried… you'd stop me."

A heavy strain tugs at my shoulder blades, but I cover it well. "If you think I'd chase you, you're wrong. I said I wanted to fuck you, Victoria. I never said a damn thing about wanting you."

"Oh, but you did, Cap." She speaks slowly, anger darkening her cheeks. "Minutes before that little girl ran up to you in the orchard, you were clear about what you want."

She calls me out, but I blanket her words with a mocking chuckle, almost missing the slight pinch at the edge of her eyes.

"Want." My grin is far from playful. "I said I wanted you, Beauty." I lick my lips, forcing my eyes to flick over her carelessly. "Not your mind, not your heart, not you. My want is groin deep, satisfied by a warm body I can play with."

"Now who's the liar?"

I smirk through my anger. "Hold on to that bit of confidence. It'll feel good when I shred it to pieces."

Something dims in her gaze, but it's gone as quick as it comes. "I didn't know you were such a dick."

"You don't know me at all." My glare intensifies and I jerk my chin from her grip, lowering my face to hers on my own terms.

"Don't touch me. Don't talk to me. Don't look at her."

That gets her, a heavy strain tugging at her features instantly, and for the first time tonight, unease stares back. "You want me to run from a three-year-old? To deny her? Ignore her if she calls my name?"

"She's two. And yes."

"She'll be three in three months, and that's not fair," she says.

I growl, shoving closer and forcing her to trip over her own feet until she stumbles back a step. "Fair is an opinion, and yours is as worthless as your word."

She clamps her lips shut before saying, "What happened to being the logical of the three, the Brayshaw who sees what anger shadows?"

My lip curls. "I was blinded by a blond for the last time."

She runs her tongue across her teeth, nodding lightly as she looks off. "Right."

I stare at her, knowing I can't have her roaming the halls of this house, as my little girl freely will. Spring break began on Friday for Brayshaw High, so she has no place to be over the next seven days until the five of us return to BHS.

I'm not okay with that.

So when she walks past me, I let her, waiting for her foot to hit the first step, letting her think our conversation is over, and then add, "Don't come out of your room this week unless it's to leave before we wake. There should be no sign you exist."

She hesitates a second before slowly climbing the stairs and disappearing from sight.

Not until I'm sure she's gone do I blow out a long breath, turning to the others.

Raven grins, while my brothers fight laughs.

They know I bald-faced fucking lied, but she needs to sweat, and I need a sign she gives a damn. A real move, not one wrapped in an agenda or dipped in fear.

The problem is, in our world, it's hard to tell the two apart. The truth always comes at the worst possible moment…like right after I forced myself to push aside the betrayal from the last female I let in and reopened a part of me I swore I never would.

Mallory messed me up good.

It's fucked-up, but Victoria's betrayal, it should have been expected.

My brothers and me, we know the drill.

With truth comes trouble.

It's why we exist in the first place.

We were born with purpose, warriors from the womb, leaders at birth, adopted into this family by a man who cared for our real parents, who weren't lucky enough to live and watch what we would become.

Unstoppable, unbreakable.

Brayshaw.

"So, uh, anyone interested in seeing the pic I got of Tracy Parks's tit job tonight?" Royce asks, easing the tension and earning a laugh from each of us.

Twenty minutes later, I'm showered and lifting my baby girl from her bed, carrying her across the hall into my room, and lying her down beside me in mine.

She doesn't so much as flutter a lash, hugging her little stuffed train as tight as ever. I tuck her blanket around her, laying mine on top, and stare at the most perfect little face.

I will love you with all I am and protect you with all my might, my little Zoey.

No matter what.

CHAPTER 4
VICTORIA

There should be no sign you exist.

I'd have begged for such an order not long ago, when the last thing I wanted was to look a Brayshaw in the eye and risk them seeing the truths in mine.

Now, it's annoying and everything I used to strive for but no longer want, at least not when it comes to them—invisibility.

Oh, the irony.

Over the next four days, I do as asked, leaving early and returning late. When they do see me, they don't speak, giving only side glances and blank stares I'm left to decipher, but I don't care.

I do as instructed without so much as a frown, head held high and all.

I'm still sleeping under their roof, aren't I?

Besides, I'm almost positive they're having me followed. I've been going to the same park in the mornings, hanging out and keeping myself busy by picking the weeds from the planter boxes around there, and today when I went back, there was a pair of new gloves sitting right on top of the next bed in line to be worked on, tags still on and all.

"Heads up, Brayshaws coming in hot," Nira, who happened to be walking the same way I was this morning, whispers into her cup as she leans back in the chair.

I turn to look, and there they are, rolling up in a black Denali, one of three in this town.

I always thought it was odd all three brothers drove identical vehicles, but it makes sense now. You see one, you know a Brayshaw is coming, and each is as important as the other. It doesn't matter which is inside: Brayshaw is Brayshaw.

Further proving my suspicion, Royce needs not a moment to roam the area, his smirk instantly landing on me as he hops from the passenger seat, Captain moving a bit slower to exit the driver's side.

Royce saunters over, way too much confidence for his own good, not that he doesn't deserve it—he's hot and he knows it.

He flips one of the extra chairs around, straddling it, and reaches out to snag a fry from my tray, stuffing it in his mouth.

"VicVee." He grins and then looks to Nira. "Group home girl."

She offers a tight-lipped smile but focuses on her soda.

"So what up, girl?" Royce leans forward, elbows planted on the tabletop. "Catchin' some rays?"

"Killin' some time." I lift a brow, and his smirk grows.

"Good girl."

I roll my eyes, dropping back in my chair.

My gaze cuts over his shoulder as Captain approaches, but his eyes slide past mine, and he walks inside the small burger place we just came out of.

Nira nudges me in the elbow, cutting a quick glance around, but I don't have to look to know what she's stressed over.

This is the downtown strip, and during off-campus hours, it's overtaken by students, specifically the picnic area, where we are now, where two of the three Brayshaw boys have just been spotted.

Of course they're staring.

They haven't laid eyes on the boys of Brayshaw in weeks, and their blue-blooded selves could hardly take it, so this? Confirmation with their own eyes when all they've had was word of mouth and speculation?

This is golden.

Long live their kings.

"Watch 'em flock, like the starved ducklings they are." Royce scans the area using his peripheral vision, not once moving his eyes from mine. "Ten minutes and there won't be an empty seat near this bitch."

Right as he says it, a guy comes from behind me, adding three more chairs to my—our, I guess—table.

Nira wastes not a second, hopping to her feet and rushing off. "See you around, Tor."

I frown after her, nodding even though she's not looking at me.

"Yeah." Royce chuckles, pulling his phone from his pocket. "We have that effect on people."

I roll my eyes, my head snapping left when the back door of the SUV suddenly opens and a smiling Raven climbs out, tugging on her man's hand.

She laughs loudly when he growls, glaring at her.

"See that, VicVee?" Royce starts. "That's the face of a half-cocked fucker."

"What does that even mean?"

"That means he only got half of what his cock wanted, which was to fuck her. Get it?" He grins.

A light laugh escapes right as Captain makes his way outside, a tray in each hand.

He glares at his brother but quickly drops it to the drinks he's slowly setting on the tabletop.

He, of course, chooses the seat a space away from me, leaving Nira's vacated one empty.

Raven lowers into one on my left as Maddoc takes her free side.

"Hey." She briefly meets my eyes and then looks at a grinning Royce. She leans back in her chair. "What?"

"Little Big Man gettin' in the way of the real one? No more back-seat lovin'?"

She fights a grin while Maddoc shoves at Royce's chair, making him laugh.

"Shut up, fucker," Maddoc tells him quietly. "She's wearing my hoodie for a reason."

My eyes fall to her stomach.

That's right.

They haven't shared she's pregnant with the town yet.

I guess the hoodie helps but not much.

"Man, word spread quick."

We look over to find Mac and his girlfriend, Chloe, heading our way.

Great.

A huge smile takes over Chloe's face as she advances, her five-inch heels clinking with each step.

"Holy shit!" Chloe rushes toward Raven. "You're show—"

"Shut up."

Chloe's glare meets mine, and I grin as Raven smacks her hand away the second it reaches for her stomach.

Chloe's eyes widen and she lifts her palms, whispering, "Sorry. No one from here has left and come back carrying a mini watermelon."

"She likes to call it a basketball," Royce throws out.

"It's not an it." Maddoc glares.

"You just said it," Chloe sasses, crossing her arms. "And what did you expect, Rae? I won't be the only one attempting to, you know, so maybe be better prepared for that."

"You need to chill."

Chloe's blue eyes fly to mine, and her lips form a bitchy smile. "Nobody was talking to you."

"And nobody asked for your opinion." The words fly from my mouth, and I lean forward in my chair. "You think because you weaseled your way to the wedding because of who your man is and added a Brayshaw to your bedroom after party that suddenly you're allowed to tell her what she should and shouldn't do? It was only months ago you were trying to turn your little entourage against her and she gave you that fancy little haircut you've now got goin' on. You're lucky anyone at this table even speaks to you."

Chloe was Brayshaw High's queen bee before Raven got here and took this place by storm. Two months ago, Chloe hated Raven for stealing her spotlight while Raven didn't give a shit about any of her petty games. She isn't one for trusting but has given Chloe a break—one I don't think she deserves.

Chloe's eyes narrow. "Water under the bridge."

"Because it's that easy, isn't it?"

Raven's eyes meet mine, but I only briefly look away from the girl who thinks she's going to slither into a spot she has no idea I slipped out of. Sure, it was Royce she had a three-way with, not Captain, but still.

No.

And then Raven speaks.

"Vee's right, Chloe," she says, her head still angled toward me before she looks up at her. "I couldn't handle your shit before, so I sure as fuck can't handle it while I'm permanently irritated."

"Hate to break it to you, Rae, but that's nothing new." She shrugs, then her eyes widen, and she laughs it off. "Sorry. I'm working on the whole bitch thing."

I scoff and she purses her lips.

"Maybe keep your guard dog close," she says, mocking me. "If you don't want hands near you."

Raven fluffs the hoodie out more so it doesn't form to her shape. "I'm pretty sure my face screams *don't fuckin' touch me*."

"It's just what people do when someone—"

"Keep it the fuck down," Maddoc snaps, his tone low but threatening.

"Fine, sorry," Chloe whispers. "It's true, though—they want to feel the baby move."

"I haven't even felt the baby move," Maddoc and Royce say at the same time.

Their heads snap toward each other, Maddoc with a glare, Royce with a wide grin.

Captain and Raven chuckle, sharing a look, and I force my eyes away.

That right there, that's when shit's hard to handle.

I admit, it's the subtle, simple things between the four of them that I envy the most—the quick glances and side grins. Conversations without words and selfless decisions.

When the chair across from me scrapes the ground, I turn my head back.

Mac drops into the seat a space from me after Chloe takes the one at Captain's side.

Why wouldn't she offer that spot to her man?

"Somethin' sour coat that filthy little tongue, VicVee?" Royce calls me out.

I leave whatever the hell slipped over my features and shrug, not bothering to take my eyes off Chloe's.

Chloe looks from me to Captain, her head tipping in question as her eyes brighten. "Ohhh…what drama did I miss?"

I give a slow blink, sitting back. "Please."

Her head draws back, and I know she's ready to talk some shit, but then Mac leans over, whispering in her ear, and she clears her throat, offers a tight smile, and then announces she's going inside to grab a drink.

And conversations ensue as if this wasn't my table they chose to take a seat at.

As if I'm not even here.

As if I don't exist.

If there was a punch line here, I'd go as far as to say the joke would be on them because being ignored doesn't affect me as I assume they had hoped.

I'm not new to blackouts, have gone weeks at a time without so much as hearing the voice of another person, let alone laying eyes on one.

The quiet treatment is hardly a punishment, especially when my Brayshaw speaks so loudly with his eyes, his touch, his calm.

It's like they say: Silence speaks the loudest, and his is deafening.

I hurt Captain Brayshaw.

You have to be inside someone to have that kind of power, and that's a damn good place to start.

As if sensing my thoughts, his eyes skate my way, but then the words that were just spoken catch my attention, and I look to Mac.

"Fourth table, two to Victoria's left," Mac says, keeping his eyes trained on Royce. "This is the fourth time this week they've come across the bridge."

Across the bridge, as in into Brayshaw territory.

These are Graven Prep students they're talking about, guys who followed the family that's now fallen. Assholes without a leader to set them straight…or knock some sense into them when they're feeling too brave.

"Bold little fuckers." Royce's jaw ticks.

"They're standing." Raven speaks into her cup.

"They know why we're here." Captain licks his lips. "Shriveled up like punks the second I fuckin' parked."

Royce nods, slowly setting his phone down. "Grew a half a fuckin' pair to try to play like mice."

A sheath drops over Captain's eyes as he falls into the situation; his mind is racing, running through every possible scenario second by second, and then his hand discreetly slides beneath the table.

My pulse ticks heavily in my ears, an unexpected thrill tightening my stomach as I wait for what I know is to come, the shine of the sun as it meets a heavy, solid piece of metal that has now slipped over Captain's fingers. He closes his fist once, testing what he already knows is a perfect fit, his brass knuckles now sitting ready as he keeps his arm loose at his side.

Royce's fingers wrap tight around the top edge of the chair he straddles, his eyes lasered in on nothing, yet he sees everything, body bouncing as his leg jerks in anticipation.

These boys, they've been caged for too long.

"Raven." Maddoc's voice is deep and low, warning.

"I know, Big Man." Her hand comes up to cover the keys on the table, her eyes popping up to mine.

That's when they come forward, a group of six guys I've never seen, weaving through the crowd, forced to round our table—that or get trapped inside our circle.

Royce waits for the exact second their feet plant in the spot he wants them and is on his in the same second, chair already spun and lifted, shit-whipping the front two with the ass of the cheap plastic.

The impact sends them stumbling into the next few behind him, blood pouring from their faces, and every person at our table is on their feet at the same time.

Captain moves, blocking me completely as his shoulders seem to bow, his height with them, and suddenly I'm locked in a cocoon of his shadow.

And then the shadow grows, and I turn in time to witness the solid unit standing tall and bold, but they're only still for a split second.

Fists fly, but all I see are Captain's.

He shifts with swift, clean movements, his back bending as he dodges a punch, an elbow flying to knock another asshole back while the one across from him creeps closer.

Captain's fist flies out so quickly that by the time the guy realizes he's been hit, Cap's already pulled back and has his right hand swinging around.

The crack of bone against metal seems to echo around us, blood droplets flying through the air and splatting on my sleeve as the guy's head whips to the side, but Captain doesn't allow him to simply fall. He catches him with a high knee on his way down, and it's lights out.

He goes for the next right as the table is jolted in front of me, Royce's back hitting its edge as he's blindsided, but he uses the fall for momentum, bouncing back harder, quicker.

Raven curses at my side, and panic spreads through me, my eyes flying to hers.

The table's been shoved closer to where she stands, meaning the fight has too.

She quickly looks from the boys to me to her, and a thick strain pulls over her, anger fused with so much more. She hates to walk away, but what's hidden beneath her hoodie trumps everything else, and it could get wild and bumpy quick.

I glance back at the scene and at her.

She nods, keys scraping against the tabletop as she dashes by, and as if sensing her, Maddoc's head snaps her way, following her form as she jumps inside the SUV.

It's as if that flipped a switch, seeing her locked away and safe.

His entire body grows lax, an eerie calm taking over, but before he can refocus on the fight, a right hook comes down across his jaw. Maddoc simply grins, spits blood from the corner of his mouth, and gets right back in it.

I jump when a body lands on the table, my eyes popping up and meeting Royce's.

They're dark and empty. "Raven?"

"In the car. Watch out!" I shout.

Captain's entire body shifts this way when I scream, and he catches the arm of the dickhead who tried to get Royce back with a chair of his own.

Captain blindly throws it over his head, yanking the guy in and headbutting him in the same second.

With his jaw clenched tight, he glares at me. "Get out of here."

My eyes fly left, at the guy attempting to stagger away, to leave his friends behind like a complete dick. So instead of listening to Cap's command, I flip the table over, tripping the guy and sending him right into Royce's fist.

All at once, the boys inch closer to each other, the six across from them slowly wobbling to their feet, helping each other balance by sharing their weight.

"This is Brayshaw, motherfuckers," Royce throws out as they allow them to hobble away.

Not another word or threat is needed—they know they don't belong.

Then, as if nothing at all happened, Captain picks up the table as Royce grabs the chairs. Maddoc moves for the SUV to get his girl while Mac disappears inside the burger joint, and not five fucking seconds later…up walks Jason Rowe, his girlfriend, Tisha, tight under his arm.

My muscles tense, and I chance a glance at Captain.

He takes his sweet time acknowledging their former teammate and his girlfriend.

There's a new shift in the air, but it's unlike the one that just took place, and you would never know by looking across the three.

These guys, they're Brayshaw, and issues among their own are handled a lot differently.

Always the calmest bravado.

Talk about a test of endurance—they've still got blood on their knuckles.

"Damn, Brayshaws," Jason teases, having caught the entire fight. "You handed them their asses."

"They knew it was coming," Royce says with a grin I'm not so sure Jason realizes is vindictive. "We know and see all, my man."

Jason chuckles, making eye contact with Maddoc. "Almost didn't believe you were back when Mac called a game."

"Only a fool would question our boy. Ain't that right, MacMoney?" Royce tips his head toward his friend, his thumb coming up to dab at the cut on his lip, giving a nice slow show of the busted and bloody ones that make up his fist.

"Yup," Mac shouts from behind me somewhere, having come back outside.

Jason grins, but it's forced, the arm around Tisha tightening as he bounces his shoulder. "So, Saturday, yeah?"

Captain nods, looking to Maddoc and Royce.

"Hell yeah, bro." Royce reaches out, knocking knuckles with him, but his chin has dropped low, and he watches him through his lashes. "Been too long since we knocked elbows."

He couldn't hide the intensity behind his dark eyes if he tried.

He doesn't try, but that's Royce, purposeful so nobody can read him right—rage or rager. All you can do is take him as he is and teeter on edge until he's gone. Right now, he's nothing but a ball of adrenaline, waiting to let loose again.

He hides it well, though.

They all do.

"You bringin' yours?" Jason asks Maddoc, nodding toward Raven.

Maddoc eyes him, unblinking, and Jason licks his lips.

He tries again, degrading his girlfriend for all to see. "Trying to decide if I should bring my piece or not."

Piece of shit.

Maddoc lifts his chin, making a shift so subtle, no one may notice he's moved to block Raven's belly.

"Yo, you want your piece there, bring her." Royce shoves his phone in his pocket with a shrug. "The more, the fuckin' merrier."

"Yeah, for sure. We'll see." He looks to his girlfriend, nods his chin, and walks away.

All four silently stare after him, Mac too, but to the average eye, there's nothing to see but a couple guys having said bye to their friend.

They have a unique ability to put off whatever vibe they want without so much as a twitch flashing across their faces. Right now, their query is hidden behind a sheath of nothingness.

Just like that, light chuckles leave each one, grins slipping in place with ease.

Couple of boys who just had some fun.

I suppress a smile, shaking my head.

Like nothing, Royce flips another chair around, once again straddling the seat as the others settle into theirs, and within less than a minute, we're all sitting around the table again.

I glance at Captain as his knuckles brush along the splatter on my top, and his eyes meet mine, but as if he hadn't realized he reached out to touch me, he looks away.

I spot Raven's gaze traveling along the onlookers, so mine follows.

With every ounce of caution, they begin returning to their seats as we have, not a soul daring to look this way.

Raven leans over, whispering into my ear, "Another day in Brayshaw."

I nod.

One thing's for sure: If anyone had even an inkling of a doubt their boys had grown weak while they were absent from school, they don't anymore.

I look back to Captain and then the others, at the smirks playing on all their lips, and realize that's exactly why they showed up here in the first place.

They knew they'd be here, and they knew Jason would be too.

Two snakes, one stone.

Chloe finally comes outside with a tray full of new drinks.

She sits down, grinning across the group. "Now that was a Brayshaw homecoming."

Everyone laughs, and I can't help it when my own follows.

CHAPTER 5
VICTORIA

It's been hours since my boring afternoon was lit up by a Brayshaw plan I wasn't privy to, hours since we all stood from the table, they slid into their SUV, and I headed the opposite way.

My feet hurt from mindless walking, and I'm exhausted from having nothing to do but think as the minutes ticked by.

Thank hell the sun has finally faded, the moon now taking its place, indicating it's safe for me to make the walk back home.

At least that's what I thought, but as I grow closer, the smoky flavor of an evening firepit coats my throat and my steps slow.

In the distance, off to the right of the mansion, a flicker of a flame lights the orchards.

They're outside.

Maybe it's only them?

My hope is crushed when I reach the end of the dirt path.

The most precious laugh fills my ears, a laugh I've missed more than I can explain, more than anyone would understand.

I tense at first, but then I close my eyes, taking a full, deep inhale, allowing her to breathe air back into my lungs and calm me in a way only she can.

Zoey laughs harder, a loud "and one and one" following.

A chuckle bubbles out of me, but I still don't open my eyes. I lean against the tree and listen.

She has no idea what "and one" means, but that won't stop

her. She repeats what she hears, as many toddlers do, and I know she's at least connected it to sinking a basket.

Captain's laugh floats across the yard right then, and my lungs quickly deny the full breath its exit, a heavy pressure forming at the base of my throat and holding.

"I think Royce was right."

My eyes fly open, locking with Maddoc's.

He stands beside his SUV, arms crossed over his chest, head cocked. "You must be dumb."

I swallow, but my voice still comes out raspy. "Or following orders."

Another round of laughs reaches us, and my brows cave at the sound, the knot in my stomach tightening, driving my shoulders forward as the pain settles beneath my ribs.

Maddoc narrows his gaze, licking his lips as he steps toward me.

He studies me a long moment, and I'd dare say surprise is what has his glare sharpening as his jaw sets tight. "You love that little girl."

If he expects me to respond, he has to ask it as a question.

He knows what I know, how powerful people find pleasure in taking what you cherish. To give a piece of you is to place a shock collar around your own neck and give the controls to another.

Maddoc comes to stand directly beside me, his eyes trailing in the direction I know the others are but can't bring myself to look.

"This game on Saturday," he says, easing in. "It's the wrong fuckin' place for her, yeah, but more than that, it'd mean revealing her to the town when he's not ready to share her yet." Maddoc's head snaps my way, his frown meeting mine. "You should have realized that on your own."

"I only meant she'd love to watch him play—"

"Changes nothin'." He shifts his body to face mine. "Don't

talk without thinking; don't move without understanding. You should know this shit already. Don't make us ruin you."

"Is that not what you want?"

"Here you go again, playin' dumb." He gets in my face, an angry irritation written across his. "You think it didn't tear at his insides to walk away from you today, knowing you were out there alone after the shit that went down? No protection, no one to have your back?" He shakes his head. "You know we're stubborn, hardheaded, and untrusting. Shit don't come easy for us, and it might not be fair, but that means the females in our lives have to work twice as hard to break through, be twice as fuckin' strong. There is no other way."

"I'm not looking for a pass."

"Then sink your claws in deeper," he growls. "And don't flinch when the blood pours out."

Fight harder.

That's what he's saying.

That's what he wants from me.

His eyes narrow, and he pauses a moment before speaking again. "I can be everything Raven needs, give her anything and every-fucking-thing she'd ever want, but that's not good enough. I want her to have more. She decided a long time ago, before she knew you shared her blood, before she knew you hid things from us, that it was you. She's never had a friend. We were her first. Be her next, be what my brother needs and wants, be here for my family in full, or get. The fuck. Out."

Maddoc takes several steps backward, and my eyes slide over his shoulder, landing on the others who play around in the cool night air. Tension hardens his jaw as he looks at me. "He has to see what you mean to her… We all do."

My brows pull in in question as he shifts in my line of sight once more, before quickly turning around. He shouts across the long driveway, gaining the attention of every single one of them.

Three smiles fall in an instant, but the fourth…it spreads wider and wider with each passing second, and my heart sighs.

Hi, baby girl.

Maddoc covers his mouth, giving a hushed, "I didn't do this for you, and I won't do it again."

He walks toward the rest of his family, each standing frozen and wide-eyed, but the shock quickly morphs into rage when Zoey drops the ball they'd been playing with, her feet carrying her right toward me.

She breaks into a run, a blinding smile on her pretty little face, blond curls bouncing all around, and she doesn't slow her pace.

Captain demanded I deny her, but I don't, can't.

I quickly step from the shadows and onto the grass, holding my arms out so she can jump right into them.

"Rora! Rora! Rora!" She laughs, rubbing her nose against mine excitedly. "You see me? I did it!"

Tears threaten to fill my eyes, so I nod, pressing my tongue hard against the backs of my teeth to try to hold everything in. "I didn't, ZoZo, but good job," I whisper.

"Daddy said, 'Way to go, Zoey!'" she says, a beautiful shine in her voice.

I laugh lightly; she still can't say her name quite right.

"I bet he was so happy," I manage to croak.

"Uh-huh!" She smiles, kicking to be let down.

The second her feet hit the grass, she grips my finger, and I try not to tense.

"Hu-mon, Rora!" She attempts to drag me along.

Having no choice, I force my eyes to Captain's.

If it were humanly possible, steam would be rolling off him—he's fuming.

It takes everything in me to grab ahold of her little hand and steady her.

She looks up, confusion swimming in her blue-green eyes.

I swallow, lowering to my knees in front of her, breathing through the ache in my ribs.

"I don't feel so good, ZoZo." Lie, lie, lie to the one person I was always able to be honest with. "I have to go so I can feel better."

"Oh no." Zoey tugs her hands free, placing her palms on my cheeks. "You got owies?"

"Yeah," I admit quietly, my hands coming up to cover hers. "I do."

"Daddy fix it?"

My throat grows thick, and I'm unable to swallow, unable to look into the eyes waiting for mine to lift.

Why did Maddoc do this?

I glance his way, but he watches Captain as Raven focuses on Zoey. Royce, though, his glare is directed right at me.

I release Zoey, but she's reluctant to let go, and a small frown forms across her forehead as I push to my feet.

"Daddy fix it," she says a little firmer.

"No, ZoZo. I have to go."

"No." She shakes her head, gripping my hand again and tugging. "No, no. Daddy do it. Hu-mon."

Shit.

"I can't." I gently pull free, and she stops in her tracks, pushing the loose hairs from her face. "Rora has to—"

"Come here, Zoey," Captain gently calls her, cutting me off. "I have your ball."

"No ball!" she shouts, the teeniest trace of a cry in her tone.

Captain's fist clenches at his side, but still, I can't look up.

His anger has already wrapped around my ribs, pulling and tugging and twisting.

Royce tries next. "I feel like some Fruity Pebbles." He walks closer, reaching out for her. "Let's go get some, Zo—"

She jerks away from him, running behind me to wrap her hands around my legs. "No, no, no!"

I freeze, dropping my eyes to hers, and when her little lips start to tremble, my heart shakes with them.

Four sets of eyes burn into my skin, all waiting to see what I'll do.

What the fuck do I do?

Piss them off or break her spirit?

How is that even a question?

I shift, ready to pick her up, but Captain beats me to it, clutching my arm to stop me, while leaning down to swoop up Zoey.

He keeps his focus on her, but his firm hold gives more than he'd like—his hand twitches against my skin, tightening just to loosen in the same second.

"Let's head inside now, Zo."

To everyone's horror, and dare I say surprise, Zoey starts to cry, kicking her feet and throwing her body over his arms until she's half hanging from his arms, attempting to land in mine.

With her arms out, she opens and closes her hands, wordlessly begging for me to grab her as her tears take over her sweet little eyes.

Sweat builds at the base of my neck, and I lift my arms the tiniest bit.

Within seconds, I'm surrounded by the other three, and while the moon is bright above us, all I see is a thick cloud of gray.

It takes everything I have to shuffle backward, away from her, and it's like shredding myself in half.

They don't get it, but how could they?

My lips have stayed sealed.

I lift my eyes, meeting a pair of turbulent blues, the light shade of green they normally hold absent altogether.

There's so much happening within them, rage being the clearest, but that's not what gives me pause.

Conflict, pure and simple.

To deny his baby girl is to break his own heart, but to allow someone he can't trust near her is against everything he is—the nurturing, fierce protector he prides himself on being, traits that have only strengthened with Zoey's homecoming.

I can't allow him to battle himself; it's not right.

I'm the bad guy in this story.

I drop my eyes to the grass and rush around the group, but I don't head for the house, not when Zoey will see and possibly come looking.

I hustle toward the driveway until I get to the orchards, where I take off in a full sprint down the dirt road—but I don't make it to the end.

Heavy arms wrap around my elbows, and I'm ripped from the ground, spun, and slammed between long, thick tree branches.

A hiss escapes, my eyes darting forward and connecting with Raven's.

"Are you fucking stupid?!" I shout, attempting to steady myself.

Raven doesn't allow it and nudges me back, her forearm coming up to lock off my throat. She's shaking, furious, gray eyes burning.

"You shouldn't be running like that," I rasp, attempting to swallow past her hold. "What if I acted out of reflex and knocked you down?"

"Shut the fuck up," she forces past clenched teeth, not flinching as heavy, hasty footsteps grow closer. Her nostrils flare, jaw clenching.

She pushes harder.

"You ever gonna come out and tell him whatever the hell it is he needs to know?"

"No."

She slams a hand down on the old wood near my head, bending to bring herself closer. "You really think you're in a position to play like this?"

I flick my eyes between hers. "They haven't earned it."

A scoffed laugh leaves her, and her frown begins to fade, but she puts it right back. "Are you for real?"

"What kind of Brayshaw would I be if I made this easy?"

"You aren't one."

"Yet."

Her eyes fly between mine, a heavy dip forming between her brows.

Trust me, Raven.

Her hold lets up the slightest bit, and I look to the side. Royce and Maddoc are rapidly approaching, vicious scowls on both their faces, but their anger is likely for Raven.

A sudden sting races across my neck as she twists her forearm against the stretched skin there, purposefully creating the burning sensation and regaining my attention.

"You better fucking hope you're redeemable," she hisses. "I'd hate to have to show you what'll happen if you're not." She swallows, jerking her hand away, and with it goes every shred of emotion. "But I won't hesitate to either."

She steps away right as the others arrive.

Maddoc glares down at her, but she only places her palm on his chest, her free hand gripping and forcing him back down the dirt road with her.

I cough, clearing my throat as I watch her walk off, but Royce quickly slides into my view.

A hard edge lines his face and he stares directly into my eyes for a long, quiet moment. "It's so much more than knowing she existed, isn't it?"

I tell him what he already knows, what all those connected to the world of Brayshaw have either heard or experienced firsthand.

"Nothing is ever as simple as it seems."

He scoffs, a hateful, disgusted sound, and spins on his feet, but he doesn't start to walk, instead shifting his cold eyes over his shoulder to meet mine once more. "Get back to the house, now."

He walks away.

CAPTAIN

I'm sitting on the edge of my bed with my elbows on my knees when my brothers walk into my room.

"Zoey fell asleep?" Royce drops his shoulders against the wall.

I nod, frowning at the floor. "Dad home?"

"Yup," Maddoc answers.

Good.

I lift my head, locking eyes with Royce.

"I need a body tonight."

His smirk is slow, his phone already in hand. "Warehouses?"

Maddoc nods with a frown. "The new inside spot's all set up now too. Raven's been wanting to go check it out."

"Fuck, bro. You sure you want her out there?" Royce's eyes widen.

"What's she gonna do?" Maddoc snaps. "Jump in the ring with my kid in her stomach?"

"She might." He laughs. "She only needs a solid right hook."

Maddoc reaches out, punching him in the arm, making Royce grin. "She's good. We'll have them clear a path so she don't get bumped and shit by the crowd walking through."

"Fuck yes!" Raven comes around the corner right then, huge grin in place.

I chuckle, sitting back. "So we're good, then?"

"Oh, hell yeah. One Bray girl buffet coming up." Royce pauses a moment before adding with a hint of a grin, "Should we stick to brunettes?"

Raven and Maddoc chuckle, and I can't help but join.

Fucker.

CHAPTER 6
VICTORIA

As if he knew exactly where I'd be, Captain's glare finds me instantly, quickly traveling over my body as I lie here in the grass with my head at the edge of the flowers.

"What are you doing?" he questions.

I shrug against the ground. "Waiting for Monday."

The corner of his mouth twists. "Why?"

"Because I hate being here like this."

At least at the school I don't have to hide anymore.

His eyes widen the slightest bit.

Why does that surprise him?

"If you hate it here, why the fuck are you?" he snaps.

With a sigh, I push to my feet so we're standing face-to-face but still a few feet apart.

"I said I hate being here like this, not that I don't want to be here, but don't forget I was 'ordered' to stay."

He pushes closer, so I square my shoulders. He's angry, but so am I. Why won't he ask me what he wants to know already?

"Yeah," he rumbles. "And what if you weren't? Would you have left?"

"Why ask if you don't care, Cap?"

His lips clamp shut, the cords in his neck bulging as he watches me with hard, heated eyes. Always so closed off.

I wish he'd scream and yell, demand or force me to do something I don't want.

Anything to get him to surrender to whatever is going on inside him.

Maybe that's what I have to do: piss him off, bring him to his breaking point.

Does he have a breaking point?

"I wouldn't have left," I admit, and his eyes narrow. "Even if you tried to make me."

They pinch even more as he tries to gauge me. "You'd disobey a banishment from a Brayshaw?"

"Yes."

"There're punishments for that."

"Not one worse than having to go when I want to stay."

Another step closer. "Stay where?" His chin lowers.

Mine raises. "Stay here."

"Why?"

"Because I belong."

His knuckles come up, and I hold perfectly still as he brushes my hair from my face. "Belong…to who?"

A hushed chuckle escapes, and I shake my head, looking to the grass. "You want me to say it out loud, and for what? So you can throw it in my face in some way?" My eyes pop back up to his. "I don't think so. Only when you're ready to hear it."

Not until you're brave enough to ask.

His entire face morphs, nothing but rage to be found as he encroaches. "You think I give a shit about anything that could possibly come from your mouth?" he questions, disgust tightening his words, mockery woven within them. "You're nothing but an added figurine."

"So play me like your favorite toy."

"You couldn't handle it if I did."

"There is nothing you could do that could cut deep enough to make me bleed. I'm hollow, Cap. Torn apart, depleted, and restitched with a whole lot of nothing."

He's slow in his movement, brushing his chest across mine as he lifts my chin. "How fun it will be to prove you wrong." He steps around me. "Go inside, brush your hair, and be on the porch in fifteen minutes. We're leaving and you're coming."

"Where?"

"Fourteen minutes."

Ass.

A familiar heat burns against my skin, but I pretend not to notice for as long as my body allows, which happens to be no more than a minute or two.

I meet his eyes.

Captain gives no expression but pointedly looks in the direction I was staring, where Chloe and Mac sit chatting with Tisha, and back to me with a raised brow.

Of course, no words follow, so I look away.

He hasn't said a single thing to me since we got here an hour ago, not that he's spoken at all, but still.

If he wants attention, then he needs to give it. I'm not playing his staring games tonight.

I take a long drink of water and stand, walking closer to the entrance of this place, and lean against the inner frame. There are crowds of people all around, from one end of the warehouses to the next.

Nothing but giant iron rods surround this place, large sheets of tin woven between them to keep those on the outside from peeking in—if they don't want you to see, you never will. There are guards out front and scattered all around to make sure of it. Being on the outer edge of town, closest to nothing, it leaves no excuse for passersby who don't belong having "just been in the area."

It's growing louder by the minute out there, several people now crowded around the smaller makeshift rings, watching the opening match while others wait by the larger one, securing their spots for the fight of the night.

A small smile finds the corner of my mouth as I glance around.

My kind, their kind, all together for some late-night debauchery—not that it's any different from normal out here, but I haven't had a night out or away in a long-ass time. It's rowdy and wild, yeah, but it's a good-ass place to chill out, people-watch.

A great place to find leverage.

My features tighten at the thought.

That's the kind of shit that got me into the trouble I'm currently in, but my brain won't stop. It's what I'm good at.

Movement to my right catches my eye, and I shift to find Royce stepping up.

He winks, but it's ugly and malicious as he pushes the sliding sheet-metal doors open all the way, allowing those outside to see into the newly remodeled building.

Only months ago, all that was in here were a couple chairs and crates lining the walls. After bets took place, the guy who used to run this place, Bass Bishop, would slip in here. Maybe to count or store the money, I don't know, but it was a wasted space for sure—dust and cobwebs, unused.

Maddoc, though, he knew how much Raven liked this place and wasn't okay with her being out in the open constantly, so he had it redone.

While the outside is still old and beatdown looking, stepping inside is like entering some sort of Black Cards Club.

Walls have been put up, thick, black-and-white stripes covering three of them, a large wolf head painted across the center, black where the white stripe is, white where the black is.

The fourth, the longest back part of the building, is rich royal blue, thick white lettering above it reading *The Wolves Den*.

There's a bar stretching along it, leaving about five feet at each end, where matte-black curtains are hung. They curve outward, forming a crescent-like shape, hiding whatever is beyond them.

Each corner of this place holds something different: couches that match the color of the back wall are grouped to the farthest right, surrounding a giant TV mounted high, ESPN playing across it, while the outer left has a poker table set up and ready to go—Captain sits at one of the tables, must be where he plans to spend his night.

The front left is plush leather chairs and mini tables, another TV, while the front right, where I'm standing by the door, is a long row of lockers. Where they expect people to leave their shit, maybe?

I glance back when I notice Raven stand, an oversized jacket swallowing her small frame, to hide her stomach still, I'm guessing. Maddoc is already on his feet, leading her behind the hidden area on the left.

Royce's phone pings in his pocket, and his eyes slide back to mine. "That's the church bell, VicVee. Time to be kings for peasants."

My mind spins, but I don't have to wonder what he's talking about for long.

"Royce!" a bubbly voice squeals.

I'm almost knocked back when long, thin arms fly past my face to wrap around his neck.

"Ladies, come in." He shifts to the side. "Victoria here is channeling her mama tonight," he says, and I grow stiff.

As far as everyone around here knows, I'm nothing but a handout kid, parentless and living in a home for "free," a group home girl.

Thankfully, these girls are more interested in Royce himself and not his words at the moment.

"She's playing maid lady tonight. Whatever you need, she's your girl." He smirks like a dickhead. "Put your phones in one hand and purses in the other."

Wow.

"Oh, boo, but I wanted to get some pics tonight," one girl

says, her voice coming out completely whiny and desperate, but she sticks her lip out like it's supposed to be cute and flutters her lashes as if he cares.

He doesn't, and he doesn't do desperate.

He nods at the tall, intimidating dude with braids who stands just outside the entrance.

Dude slides in, wraps an arm around her shoulders, and spins her on her heels.

"Hey, wha—"

"Don't make it worse, girl," he whispers as he leads her out.

Royce turns to the others, all three standing wide-eyed and unsure.

"Trash is out. Ready to party?" He grins, unfazed.

Three words from him, and their fourth friend is forgotten.

They swiftly pull their phones from their bags as instructed and step toward me.

I roll my eyes, holding my palms out without so much as a pause, and Royce steps back with a smirk.

The last chick takes forever to pass off her stuff, applying what must be a fifth coat of gloss to her lips.

"Oh my God, Amber, hurry up!" her friends complain.

"What?" She shrugs, finally handing her bag over. "I need to be all shiny and plump. I heard Captain likes that."

My muscles lock.

Royce was waiting for it, and his grin grows a little deeper, a lot nastier.

So these girls are their entertainment for the night—this is why Captain wanted me here.

A sick burn races up my stomach and into my ribs, but I'd never show it.

"Ladies, let Victoria know what you want to drink. She can deliver it to us." He wraps an arm around two of them. "Make it quick, Rora. We'll be behind the right curtain."

Asshole.

I take a deep breath and walk to the bar, ignoring Chloe and Mac, who are relaxing with drinks on a set of barstools.

Chloe watches me as I slip behind the counter, instead of giving the orders to the grunge dude taking them.

I quickly pour the stupid champagne but leave some room and top it off with a little less than a double shot of gin. They'll never know, and they won't dare complain after their girl got kicked out for thinking her wants mattered.

Let's see how well they can perform later when they can't even walk.

Brayshaws don't do sloppy.

Chloe chuckles, and then a stir stick is pushed into my line of sight.

I eye her a moment, then take it and give a light swirl, tossing it to the granite top after. I lock my fingers around the edges to support my weight, holding her gaze.

She leans over, grabs the gin, and signals for the guy, who drops an empty glass in front of her.

Mac eyes us both as she fills it to the brim, the contents spilling onto her fingers as she slides it my way. "I don't know what's going on or why you're on socialite duty, but something tells me you can handle your liquor and that you might need that." She doesn't make me ask, which is good because I wouldn't have, and offers her explanation anyway. "The chick in there, the one with the pink shorts, is Amber, and she's wanted Captain since sixth grade. This is her first invite."

I tap my fingertips along the rim of the glass, then lift it, allowing the sweet yet piney liquid to warm my throat. I look to Chloe. "Why are you telling me this?"

She grins at the empty glass a moment before looking at me.

"Because I know a scorned Brayshaw when I see one. Clearly you fucked up. I can see it, even though it's not common knowledge to others how bad he wants to screw you…in both ways." She places her elbows on the countertop, dropping her chin atop her interlocked fingers. "And because she's a competitive gymnast and you're just…you."

"You couldn't help it, could you?"

She shrugs, hiding her grin in her drink as I hold mine back.

Mac chuckles, shaking his head, and offers to help me carry the drinks, but I ignore him and walk to the end of the bar, squaring my shoulders before I slip behind the black curtain.

The second I'm on the other side of the expensive material, strong, fluorescent eyes demand mine and hold, but I force my gaze over his shoulder, and I'm met with my own reflection across the room.

Mirrors all around.

There are no walls to be seen—only myself and everything surrounding me, and more than one of each. Soft, tranquil music comes from every direction—how it's not heard outside this room, I don't know.

A black velvet couch curves along the edges, and it takes me a second to realize I'm raised higher than the seating area, higher than the others in the room.

A stage.

I take the three small steps to the floor level, a sparkly black tile, maybe even marble. There are a few end tables here and there, ice buckets sitting atop them.

Royce reaches out, taking the two drinks closest to him without a word, so I move one from my right over to my left, now holding a flute in each hand.

Finally, I look to Captain again, his stare still stuck on me.

It takes some masking, but I don't acknowledge the two girls who have planted themselves at his sides, at least not until they turn to see what's stolen his attention.

Both stick their hands out, demanding with actions instead of words like bratty children that their drinks be brought within reach.

Captain tips his head back the slightest bit, waiting, so I walk closer, surprising them all when I use the space between Captain's open legs as my delivery location.

They wouldn't notice, and I'm betting it was completely subconscious, but his shoulders lift off the cushion the teeniest, tiniest bit, bringing him a fraction of a hair closer.

To me.

My chest is in his reach and positioned right about in his line of sight. Sure, my tits don't spill from my bra and my top is tucked tight into my jeans, but I've got shape and it's a shape he happens to like.

He inhales deeply, holding his breath as I lift my arms out at my sides, my chest pushing higher as I do, and slowly, the girls grab their drinks.

Captain's gaze quickly drops only to come right back just as fast.

In my peripheral, the girls' stares move from Captain to me, their pretty little minds spinning, I'm sure.

My focus falls to Captain's mouth when his tongue sneaks out, licking across his full bottom lip, but he catches himself and hastily pulls it back in. The thick veins of his neck throb against his golden skin as his eyes angrily jerk left—to the girl Chloe mentioned, the one with the heavy lip gloss who wants what's not free for the taking.

She leans into him, speaking in a low, seductive tone that makes me want to vomit. "This is my favorite champagne. I can't believe you have it stocked."

I scoff, and her caked-over lip coils, her beady eyes slicing to mine. She takes a second, making a public show of assessing me and deciding I'm less than her.

"What?" She pushes her lips out, her free hand curling over Captain's shoulder as she tucks herself closer. "Jealous, group home girl?"

I pop a shoulder, letting my hands fall to my sides; the move has my fingertips skating across Captain's jeans. "Not unless you've got a box of dye hidden in your vag."

That gains the attention of Royce and his little toy.

Amber, as Chloe called her, tugs back. "Ew, what?"

Royce chuckles but quickly buries his face in the girl's neck to hide it.

I place a palm on Captain's knee, not missing the way his muscles clench as I do, and lean forward, getting in the girl's face. I flick her hair with my middle finger, and she jolts.

"He's got a ban on blonds," I whisper, and Captain twitches under my touch. "Your friend will have a better chance than you…but I'm pretty sure she's calling dibs on the only other Brayshaw she's allowed." I slowly stand, keeping my brown eyes on hers, not much of a shade different. "Guess you're out of luck unless he wants to take you on too." I look to Royce, who is now paying close attention.

He shifts in his seat, spreading his legs farther as if to invite her between them.

Awesome, so he's gonna fix her little Bray-less problem?

"But, uh, good luck with that," I add, and all their eyes slide to mine. "I hear he only goes for three when it's another dick involved."

Royce's frown is instant, and he moves the girl from his lap as he glares at me, but when I smack the bottom of the drinks of both girls that are in reach, sending the alcohol into their laps, he cracks a grin.

They shriek and jump up—away from my man.

I move toward the stage and up the small steps.

Amber's arms are in the air as she looks at her soiled clothes in horror. "Who the hell do you think you are, trash?!"

"Watch it," flies from Captain before he can stop it himself, but he quickly hides his frown in his drink.

My tongue slips between my teeth as I tip my head at her. "Guess I'm not just the 'group girl,' huh?"

I put up two middle fingers, dragging each arm out and across the room, turn on my heels, and walk the fuck out of the area, across the floor, and to the lockers. I take the girl's shit and slip from the damn building, quickly getting lost in the middle of the chaos outside.

I toss her bag and phone in one of the blocked-off firepits and find a corner on the farthest end of this place. I climb up a few crates, planning to watch the weaklings fight until the main event begins in the next couple minutes.

I prepare to settle in, closing my eyes for a quick, deep breath.

He defended me without meaning to and to a girl he was hoping could distract him tonight.

A small smirk finds my lips only to fall right off when a voice I could never forget but hate to hear calls out from below.

"There's my girl."

Oh.

Fuck.

CHAPTER 7
CAPTAIN

I tried.

Real fuckin' hard, I tried to ignore the fact she stormed off, reminding myself over and over again I had all I needed for the night right beside me, but I only made it three leg bounces before Maddoc flew in here with a glare that meant one thing—she's outside.

Royce is on his feet as quick as I am, waving the girls out into the main room as we follow behind.

He gets Mac's attention, and Mac flies from his seat, letting us know he's got eyes on the few we allowed in here tonight.

Raven steps up next.

"Andre was trying to watch where she went," she says, talking about our recently promoted main man out here. "He didn't know if he could leave the door since we were inside. Lost her."

Of course he did; she's not under Brayshaw protection.

I haven't put her there.

To everyone around, as proved by the chick now covered in champagne, she's simply a girl from our girls' Bray house.

"The fuck, man? She gonna be like you?" Royce frowns at Raven. "Taking off and shit all the time? This is bad for the heart; we'll be on meds by the time we're done with you two."

Raven grins, shrugging a shoulder.

"She might have walked out, but she won't leave."

Maddoc and Royce scoff while Raven smiles wider.

I know what they're thinking: We said the same thing about Raven before, and she took off on us more times than we can count, but Victoria isn't Raven.

I pissed the girl off, yeah, but she's here.

Raven looks to me. "Cap's right. She's just mad 'cause you guys had girls in there. She'll never allow that."

My lips form a flat line and I glare at her.

"What?" A laugh bubbles from her. "It's true. No matter what you think, in her mind, you're already hers." She smirks. "She'll push when she feels she has to."

"Girl already did," Royce scoffs. "Talked some shit, spilled some drinks, and, according to the text Mac sent me before she even stepped foot in that room, spiked their shit with something heavier."

Raven laughs. "I would say make her sweat, let her think you're in there with the girl still, but I guarantee you she's not stressin' on that. She knows what we all do."

"And what's that?" I frown.

She shrugs, leaning against Maddoc's chest. "Those girls were never gonna get beyond your belt, Packman. You're past the point of a night's entertainment."

Royce and Maddoc chuckle while I groan, looking off, and the assholes laugh harder.

"Fuck it," I cave. "Let's get set for the fight. Let her come to me."

Royce goes for a quick refill of his drink while Raven and I wait near the door, Maddoc having slipped out first to speak to one of our guards.

A few minutes pass and he steps back inside, and heads begin to turn our way as an aisle clears, a straight path that allows us to move toward the rings with ease.

Clemmons, one of the new guys we've offered work out here, pulls back the chain and we step through, climbing into the new stool-like seats Maddoc had cemented into the ground. We're lifted a solid three feet above the floor level and perfectly ringside. Close enough to get some blood on you if it gets wild enough but protected by a barricade and height.

I glance at Raven and the smile she can't erase, at the way Maddoc watches her and how his hand tightens against her thigh.

His eyes meet mine, a small grin twitching at his lips, and I nod.

He did good—she loves it.

Andre walks toward us, tipping his chin as he grips the megaphone. He spins on his feet, looking across the crowd that has started to cram closer, and begins announcing the fight.

Both guys step into the ring, listening to the rules—no weapons, no outside help.

Their tape is checked, and then Andre dips under the chain and the crowd goes wild.

"That guy looks familiar," Raven says, squinting.

Maddoc tells her, "They both went to Brayshaw a minute."

She nods, then she and Royce start betting.

"Fifty on the shorter guy." She sticks a hand out.

"What? Nah," Royce whines. "I want the short guy."

Raven laughs. "It's the flightiness, huh? He's quick."

"He's 'bout to creep in and knock that tall fucker out."

"Join bets, and I'll take the payout."

Our heads jerk left to find Victoria trying to slip under the chain, but the guy guarding it blocks her.

She rolls her eyes at the dude, moving closer, and his hand comes down on her arm, seizing and twisting her back, but mine flies out, gripping his neck between my fingers in the same second. His shoulders hunch up tight, hands flying into the air just as quick.

"Sorry, man," he rushes in a whisper. "I didn't know she was with you. Andre said no one in, no one near, no one stares."

My jaw clenches as I release him, and he turns to me, waiting for whatever's to follow, but I only nod my head at him. He did what he's paid to do: keep others away and in line.

I frown at Victoria, but she grins at me, climbs into the seat at my side, and leans her upper body closer to mine.

"Can't help it, can you?" she whispers, but she's not mocking me in any way.

That's the second time tonight I reacted in her favor, without intention.

It's fucking frustrating.

"Don't run around acting stupid," I tell her. "You wanna take off, don't expect to slide right back with ease."

She looks from me to the ring. "Maddoc had this built a couple weeks ago, with six seats. Let's not pretend one wasn't added with me in mind."

I clench my teeth, annoyance heating my chest.

On one hand, she's got some fuckin' nerve; on the other, her confidence over her place here thrills me when it shouldn't.

She looks past me. "You guys want the bet or not?"

Raven's gaze narrows. "You want to put money on the tall guy?"

"He's going to win," she says, but the way she flicks at her fingernails gives her away.

She's anxious, nervous.

Something's off.

"My pick always dominates," Raven reminds her.

"Then what do you have to lose?" Victoria shrugs.

"Fifty bucks," Raven snaps. "That's like, what? Thirty-seven meals from the dollar store."

Maddoc groans, shaking his head. He hates when she talks like she's still broke and fighting to feed and clothe herself, but at the same time, he knows it's a part of her and will likely never go away.

Victoria's chuckle is tight. "Or a hundred-plus packs of ramen."

Raven grins but rubs her lips together when the crowd starts screaming again.

"Royce," she says, "you got a bill on short guy?"

"The fuck? You're going with VicVee's bet?" he asks her, wide-eyed.

Raven shrugs while Victoria tries to hide her smile, facing forward to avoid my eye.

I'm half tempted to ask her where the hell she went, but the fight begins, serving as a good distraction.

The tall guy is slower than his opponent, like Raven and Royce had guessed, but he's instinctive, that or studied the other guy before taking this fight. He knows what the other dude is going for before he even moves.

The short one gets him with a right jab to the jaw, but the guy grins, shaking it off.

Victoria shakes her head beside me, a heavy sigh following, and my frown slices her way.

It takes a minute, but she gives me her attention.

Her brown eyes roam over my face and she offers a sad smile.

My chest muscles constrict, my scowl deepening, and she drops her gaze to her lap before focusing back on the fight.

The dickhead continues to circle the ring until they're right in front of us.

Raven leans forward, only for Maddoc to tug her back, while Royce glares at the scene.

"Wait a minute," he says slowly, turning toward me, but his eyes wait to leave the ring until the last second. He glares, then looks back. "RaeRae, ain't that the asshole who dropped you off the night you were jumped?"

Her head snaps to Royce, eyes flying to Victoria and back to the guy in the ring.

"What the hell?" Raven drags out.

I squint to get a better look, and Royce is right.

Six or so months ago, Raven was jumped when leaving here, and Victoria and this fucking guy ran up on the scene, scaring the pussies away. They picked her up and brought her home to us—that was the first time Victoria was close enough to see the mansion beyond the trees.

I remember locking her against the car, questioning her about what had happened, and the girl wouldn't budge, kept glaring at me.

That was also the first night I went to bed with thoughts of this bratty, little blond.

All I remember about the dick in front of us is he was a nomad—not tied to the Brayshaws or the Gravens. He stood back, saying not a fucking word, and when Royce scared the piss out of him, he couldn't get off our property fast enough.

Why the fuck was she with him that night anyway?

The tall dude comes in with a sudden uppercut, and screams fill the air.

He looks around, scanning our people before his eyes land on the girl at my side.

The muscles in my back tighten when he grins, his right hand coming up to hit the ugly-ass, red-necked, matted-feathered bird tattoo taking up his entire torso. The guy fuckin' winks at her.

Raven leans forward, looking to Victoria. "I thought you said he left town?"

"Yeah, well," she says, sitting back in her chair, a tense smile at her lips and slight pull at her brows. She drops her head back, looking up at the sky. "Guess he's back."

"Who is he to you?"

She frowns, closing her eyes a moment, only to bring them to mine in the next.

She shakes her head but doesn't get to answer because suddenly the tall fucker is leaning over the chain that separates us from him.

He pushes his hair back, smiling at Victoria. "How's that for a win, baby?"

My jaw locks as Royce chokes on his drink, hopping off his seat to view us better.

Did he just dare call her *baby*?

She doesn't look his way, keeping her eyes locked on mine all the time, and says, "Captain, meet Mike."

Mike sticks his sweaty-ass palm out. "Her boyfriend."

I'm on my third drink when the others make it back into the Wolves Den, not that it took them long. I poured three straight doubles.

Raven is the first to reach me, a heavy frown in place as she steps around the bar to grab herself a glass of water.

"I asked about this guy a while back. She said he helped her pass the time and time was up. Said he left." She speaks into her cup before taking another drink.

I down mine, slamming the crystal on the countertop. "She's a liar."

Raven scoffs.

Mac joins us, pouring and handing drinks to everyone but Raven and Maddoc, who is driving tonight.

As soon as Victoria's ass plants on one of the stools, I jerk from where I stand and move for the couches surrounding a flat screen.

The annoying blond from earlier spots me and makes her way over, but Victoria stops her in her tracks when suddenly she's dropping right beside me with a glare.

"You walked away before I could even talk."

"Oh, you wanna talk now?" My eyes widen mockingly, anger front and center. "All of a sudden? Thought secrets were your game?"

She glares. "You gonna listen or not?"

"What makes you think I'd care what you have to say?"

A single brow rises. "You storming off like a toddler pretty much said enough."

I growl, but then the door is shoved open with a loud bang,

and in comes Royce with a smirk I know all too well, arms open wide as he plays it up and pulls in attention.

"The man of the hour is here to join us," he calls flatly, tipping his chin when I meet his eyes, the dickhead right behind him, his shirt still off and in his hand, cheap-ass bird tattoo on full display.

Victoria tenses at my side.

"Servant girl," Royce snaps, and her eyes slice his way. "Make the man a drink, hm?" His glare hardens in warning.

One she ignores.

"What the hell is he doing? He shouldn't be in here," she says, a hint of panic in her tone as she trails the two with her eyes. "Mike's done nothing wrong. He's always… He stayed away." Her fingers grip at the collar of her shirt, brows caved.

"Victoria."

"He shouldn't be in here." She shakes her head, waiting until the last second to drag her eyes to me. "Make him go."

My fingers clamp tightly around my glass as I study her, noting the anxious flare of her movements. My stomach muscles tighten as I cock my head. "Make him go," I repeat.

Why?

Does she want him away from her, or is this her way of keeping him away from us?

Is she protecting him?

Anger builds inside me as she thoughtlessly adds, "He's done nothing wrong."

An instant dark chuckle leaves me, and her tension-filled eyes pull to mine. "Nothing wrong?" I ask, leaning forward until our lips are damn near touching.

Her eyes widen, but then a layer of fog covers them just as quickly.

How easily I can steal your attention…

I know he's watching—everyone is—so I lean a little more, pulling at all my control as I brush against the thick velvet of her lips, while reminding myself I can't take what I should, what I know she'll give.

Instead, I whisper, harsh and slow, "He thinks you belong to him, and that right there, Beauty…so fuckin' wrong."

"You need to open your eyes, Captain," she hisses, a strain to her tone I can't quite interpret, and my mouth twists. "And when he called me his, you should have done or said something that showed otherwise."

I push my frustration down and attempt to spin this in my favor.

"Did I confuse you?" My smirk is as measured as her scowl. "I said you're not his, but you're sure as fuck not mine."

Her scoff is easy and mocking as she pushes to her feet, my eyes rising with her.

She rubs her lips together. "Fine," she forces out. "I'll play maid, like your brother wants me to. Serve the man, and then, I don't know…" She trails off as she shrugs, shuffling backward a few small steps. "Serve the man."

I'm on my feet, tugging her into me in the same second. My glare is heavy, fingers twitching against her spine.

And she giggles, freezing me on the spot.

It's a soft, open sound I've never heard, one that reaches deeper than it should, driving even further as, ever so slowly, rich brown eyes, almost a brassy, bright copper, lift to mine.

I'm struck, stuck standing powerless as every part of her dives beyond the surface of me.

A small smile finds her lips, and she melts against me, the room around us falling away.

I tell myself to let her go and walk away, get some fuckin' space between us, but my muscles won't move.

She's gorgeous and I hate it.

"You can try to deny me with your words, Cap," she whispers. "But your body knows the truth, and your mind will never allow such a lie."

My stomach twists, a hollowness taking over and making me nauseous, 'cause, fuck me, she might be right.

She shuffles her feet, and my hand falls to my side.

My eyes follow as she walks away, each step heavier, more forced than the last. She doesn't want to go to him.

I should bring her back.

To me.

I stand there staring as she begins making a drink for some asshole when she's the one who should be served. I glance at the dickhead who watches her every move, a frown written across his forehead as he waits for her to meet his eyes, but she doesn't.

She shifts with lax movements, but she's on edge. Unsure.

Why?

He gives a subtle shake of his head when she gives him her back, reaching for a bottle of something.

Raven walks over, but I can't look away. She steps up beside me. "Cap."

"I gotta get the fuck outta here."

She's getting in my head…or maybe it's the alcohol.

Dickhead says something that has her pausing, and ever so slowly, her palms plant on the countertop, and she lifts her eyes to his. A small, fuckin' tiny grin forms on her lips, and my blood boils.

Yeah. I gotta go. Now.

Maddoc and Royce spot me cutting across the room and beeline for me, their quick steps gaining Victoria's attention.

She sets the bottle down, boldly staring.

"I'm out." I keep walking. I don't have to tell them to keep her in line; they already know.

I make my way to the door, and just as quick as my feet carry me, Victoria is at my side.

"I didn't ask you to come with me."

"I live with you. I don't need an invitation."

I spin quick, forcing her back into the doorframe. "No, but you do need permission," I snap.

"So give it to me," she damn near begs, dropping her head to the metal behind it. "I don't want to be here, don't need to be if you aren't. Take me home, Captain."

The double intent in her tone has my groin heating, but I fight against myself to push it away. It would be so easy to give in, but easy is for pussies, and she doesn't deserve the power of rendering me weak.

In my peripheral, I spot Mike focused on us, so I turn to face him head-on, leaning in close and refusing to inhale her scent.

My fingers stretch wide at her side, and I slowly slide them up her ribs. Finally, his eyes lift from where I'm touching her body, meeting mine.

He's a bold fuck, holding my gaze for a solid five seconds before he finally cuts his gaze away.

I bring my mouth to Victoria's ear.

"No," I snap. "You stay; he's your mess. You think you're strong enough to be Bray, let's see it. Make him disappear." I pull back, glaring down at her. "But touch him, and I'll shatter his knuckles. He touches you, it's a bat to the kneecaps."

Her lips pull to the side, and she pushes against me, causing my frown to deepen.

"You want him gone?" she whispers, leaning in only to slip away in the same second. She cocks her head, walking backward as she gives a single, hard blink. "Handle him yourself. He wouldn't listen to me anyway, Brayshaw or not, but believe me when I say, Mike? He doesn't belong here."

She walks away, and not back where we came from, but out the fucking door and straight for Maddoc's SUV.

And I'm not sure what I hate more: how much I like when she fights me or how I crave her submission.

Something's got to fucking give.

CHAPTER 8
CAPTAIN

"And this one and this one—oh!" Zoey runs to the windowsill, grabbing a small stuffed bear. "This one too!"

She shoves the three into her backpack, sticking her tongue out as she tries to make them fit enough to zip the thing closed.

I laugh and crouch beside her. "Why don't we leave some home so you have room for new stuffed animals, huh?"

She gasps, looking to me with a smile, but her eyes quickly fly over my shoulder, and she pushes to her feet, running over to my dad as he steps inside the room.

When Zoey cried for Victoria, I'd have sworn my fucking chest plate cracked. The only time I have ever seen her cry that way was when I visited her and my time to leave her came.

So to see those emotions from her for a girl who doesn't deserve her attention was hard. If I'm honest, it was the most unsettling experience I have ever fucking had.

A sick, twisted knot formed in my stomach, but I held my ground.

It only lasted a few minutes before she forgot why she was upset and started playing again, but I haven't been able to erase the picture of her pink, tear-streaked cheeks from my mind.

I look from her to my dad.

"Ready, Zo?" he asks, opening his arms so he can lift her.

She smiles at him. "Yes! I want to see aaaall the animals." She stretches her arms out as wide as she can. "All of them, 'kay?"

I squint as I stare at my dad.

I've never known him to be an emotional guy, the opposite in fact. He was kind and caring with us, sure, but a seriousness always followed.

We were only months old when my and Royce's biological dads were murdered, and he took us in, along with our moms, to live with him, his wife, and Maddoc, who was only a couple weeks older than we were.

Our fathers were his best friends, men of Brayshaw, equals at his side as the three of us are now. Their plan was always to have us grow to take their places, so he felt no hesitation when he took us in…and then our mothers were killed.

Murdered by his very own maid, his wife dying right alongside them.

That's the day he became a father to the three of us, rather than the father figure he had planned to be. He's loved us equally all our lives, but he's made mistakes, as all do.

He took a sentence that wasn't his to take, in a courthouse he could have paid off with ease but didn't, in order to protect our world and the future he planned for my brothers and me. He gave eleven years of his life, working and connecting with us behind steel walls as Maybell filled the role of mother for us. He's hidden things he shouldn't have, the hardest truth for me being the day I learned the man I thought to be my biological father wasn't, even though he saw me as his own.

Despite the bullshit along the way, though, we've always trusted in our dad, even when he pissed us off. We know his every move made was to protect us in one way or another.

I understand that more than ever now.

The last couple months, we've gotten to see a side of him we never have or don't remember—a softer, gentle side that Zoey has drawn from him.

I swear his eyes grow glossy as he looks down at her and nods. "Okay, Zo. We'll see all of them."

She claps her hands and darts out the door. "Uncle Bro! Where are you?"

I smile, stand, and hand her pack over to my dad, giving him an extra empty one along with it just in case. "She insists on bringing all this shit."

He grins but quickly sobers. "You don't like having her out of your sight, and you go back to school the day after tomorrow. Should I be concerned?"

I raise a brow. "This is Brayshaw."

He nods, leading us out of the room. "Of course."

"We got a tip we're feeling out, set it up a bit already," I tell him, looking away. "She can't be there for that."

"No, she can't."

Zoey spots us coming down and starts to run for us but pauses mid-step, going back to Royce to take another bite of his donut.

He laughs, lifting her up, and they follow us outside. "Told you, baby girl, Uncle Bro's got you covered."

I grin, shaking my head as I open the back door to our dad's town car, finding Maybell already inside.

Royce sets Zoey down, and she climbs across the seat with a smile.

"Hey, little miss." Maybell helps Zoey onto her lap. "You ready to go to the zoo?"

"And Papa too!" She looks back to our dad.

He nods, a softness covering his face. "I'm coming, Zo. Climb in your seat, okay?" He turns to me.

My lips press in a firm line, and I look off.

"There's nothing wrong with a little girl spending a few hours of fun with two people who love her," he reassures me. "This is normal."

"We aren't normal."

He laughs, his palm coming down on my shoulder. "The fact that this even makes you pause says enough. You've got her for the rest of your life, you can share her with us from time to time," he teases.

I hold my grin, dipping my head inside the car. "Ms. Maybell."

"Boy." She smiles as Zoey grabs her hands, clapping them for her as she sits in her lap. "Go on."

I nod, leaning farther in to kiss Zoey's cheek. "See you in a little bit, okay?"

She nods but looks past me as she climbs into her seat. "Uncle!"

"Right here, Zoey Bear." Royce laughs, stretching his arm past me and setting the rest of the donut in her hands.

"Bye, Daddy!" She carefully slips her arms into the straps of her seat, kicking her feet as she bites into the donut, both of us forgotten.

We step back so our dad can slide in, and then they're off.

Raven and Maddoc are coming down the porch as we turn around, an ice chest in Maddoc's hand, blanket in Raven's.

"Ready?"

"She wants to stop for ice cream on the way," Maddoc grumbles, sliding a frown toward Raven.

"I need to stop for ice cream," she corrects him.

"Like you needed the chocolate and chips and shit this morning. We're barbecuing. Why not wait until after you give my kid some protein first?"

"You might not like sweets, Big Man, but this thing inside me is half mine, which means it has half my appetite for snacking."

"Not an it, and you're dead wrong, baby." He quickly pushes his lips against her hair. "Sometimes kids don't share shit with their mamas."

Royce chuckles beside me, and Raven smirks, looking away.

Maddoc's eyes narrow on her, quickly shifting to our brother. "What?" he snaps.

"Growin' a puss on us, bro?" Royce teases.

Maddoc shoves him. "Fuck's that mean?"

"It means Royce owes me a stack of twenties." Raven wiggles

her eyebrows. "Told you he secretly read the books Maybell gave me."

Royce laughs harder, but Maddoc doesn't say anything. He smirks as he makes his way to the back of my SUV to put the ice chest inside.

I glance up at Victoria's window as Raven stops beside me. "She take off?"

"Nope." She shakes her head, jerking her chin toward the side of the house. "Heard her go out the back door when we were gettin' out of the shower."

I nod, open my door, and slide in, but I only get as far as putting the key in the ignition.

I growl and slip right back out.

I walk around the front-right side of the house, jolting to a stop when I spot her on her knees. Her hair up on her head as she feathers her fingertips along the flower bed we had put in for Zoey before she came home.

It's identical to the one she was used to seeing when she lived with Maria, long parallel lines of every shade of purple in existence, a thicker, heavy curve in the middle, wide-open sky behind it, allowing nothing to block the sun from beaming down and giving them life.

Victoria sits back on her heels, scanning over the twenty-foot-long garden. She closes her eyes, inhaling a full breath right as a heavy crease covers her forehead. I jerk around and move back to my SUV.

I slide inside, slam the door, and peel out of the driveway, loud enough to interrupt her thoughts but not loud enough to drown out my own.

Why is she touching the flowers, and what came to her mind, bringing pain with it?

Does she like flowers?

Why the fuck do I care?

I lift my palm, slamming it against the steering wheel, only to tighten my hold on the cool leather.

Nobody flinches or is caught off guard, and nobody questions me.

It's how we work.

I feel, they feel.

I hurt, they hurt.

I get angry, well…that's when it's bad for everyone involved.

One's anger is what drives another's rage.

If there is one thing that pisses us off more than all else, it's to witness pain from one of our own.

I'm not in pain, but I'm sure as fuck in something.

From there, it doesn't take long to get to the courts, and once we do, we jump straight into a game.

I'm lost in my own damn thoughts the first half, only managing to focus toward the end.

Mac finishes up with the main part of the barbecue right around then, so everyone takes a minute to breathe and eat, but I'm done.

I wipe the sweat from my brow with the bottom of my T-shirt, my eyes sliding to the end of the court where Jason stands with Mac, Chloe, and a few other girls. He laughs as he throws away his plate before picking up a ball and heading back out onto the asphalt.

None of us picked up on anything outside the norm with him today, like we hoped. He's acting like his usual attention-seeking self.

Royce nods his chin, tugging his shirt over his head as he takes slow steps toward Jason.

The girls start whistling and laughing, causing Jason to turn around.

His dribble slows, but then his eyes tighten some and he starts crossing the ball between his legs.

Royce crouches the slightest bit, his fingers drumming the air at his sides, and then the two both move.

Jason darts forward as Royce shoots right, anticipating his exact motion, and steals the ball from him with ease. He continues down the court, jumping and dunking before Jason can attempt to catch up.

Royce grabs the ball, chucking it hard against Jason's chest.

He catches it easily, a light chuckle escaping him as he attempts a three-pointer, but Royce hops and is in the air, slapping the ball away.

Jason laughs and comes forward with his hand out, so Royce gives him props.

His eyes slide our way but don't hold.

No aggression from him toward one of us.

Maybe the little blue car's got nothing to do with him?

"Fuck's next?" Maddoc says behind his towel before swiping it across his head and draping it around his neck.

Royce makes his way over when someone else jumps up, ready to go one-on-one next.

"Let's see how things look at school, go from there?"

He and Royce nod in agreement.

"Aye, Raven loved that shit at the warehouses, huh?" Royce grins at Maddoc.

"Fuck, man. She did, but now she keeps talking about it."

"She miss the fighting?"

A strain pulls at his forehead as he watches her shift from foot to foot in an attempt to get comfortable. "She's feelin' useless. I think our fight the other day made it worse—that shit was hard on her, having to sit back like that." His eyes swing our way. "She's getting fuckin' restless. Gotta help her find something she actually likes, not some shit she came to crave out of survival. She's never been able to chill enough to know what she'd even want to try outside of what she had to do to get by or clear her head. She wants to fight still, after, so I'm looking at some trainers that I won't have to kill along the way. Legit boxing, not the savage shit like out there." He frowns. "Gotta keep her outta that ring."

"Concert?" Royce throws out. "Still has those earbuds in more than not."

Maddoc nods. "I'd fuck up anyone who came within four feet of her."

"We'll get floor seats or a box suite."

He licks his lips. "Yeah, let's find somethin' quick."

Royce's head draws back. "Gettin' blue balls?"

Maddoc's glare flies his way. "Fuck you, yeah right. My Snow's real good to me. I'm the only thing she can put all her pent-up energy into." His smirk is slow. "I'm not mad about it."

Royce laughs. "Aye, that's what I like to hear. The real Snow White took on seven men. Keep her ridin', baby on board or not."

Maddoc wraps him in a quick headlock, one Royce escapes just as fast, and the two mock box for a second before laughing.

"I'm out," I announce. "Mac giving you guys a ride home?"

"Yup," Maddoc says.

I nod and start toward my SUV as Royce moves over to Mac and Chloe's group of friends, and Maddoc drops on the blanket behind Raven, pulling her to his chest so she can relax against him.

I head to the zoo to spend the rest of my Saturday with my daughter.

Zoey passed out the second we got on the freeway, like I knew she would.

Once I confirmed I was on my way, my dad gave his driver the rest of the night off, so it's the four of us in my SUV for the hour ride home.

Maybell being Maybell, she uses the time to her advantage.

"She reminds me of you, you know," she says from the back seat as she runs a hand across Zoey's head. "So lively, always smiling and the first to share."

I scoff, and my dad chuckles beside me.

"Now don't you go thinkin' nasty with me in this car, boy."

I laugh a little louder and my dad shifts his smile to Maybell.

"I'm pretty sure none of my boys are the sharing kind nowadays," he teases.

This time it's Maybell who scoffs. "Go on and ask your other son."

I grin, switching lanes. "Yeah. Royce is all for shares."

"Ain't nothin' wrong with that, for now anyway. Give him time. He'll find someone he won't..." Maybell trails off, making sure to catch my eyes in the mirror. "Takes a lot for a Brayshaw to get to that point."

"You sure about that?" I frown at the road.

"I'm not saying it's easy. I'm saying the second it clicks, it's over, instant and eternal. Endless."

"Real reassuring, Ms. Maybell," I grumble.

My dad laughs, and while I glare at him, Maybell reaches forward to smack his arm.

"Now none of that. You know the story of the raven and the wolf," she says.

Of course I do—we all do.

One mate, one mission: love and honor and protect your home. The raven will lead the wolf; the wolf will destroy all who threaten. A solid, everlasting team.

I thought it was fate for my brother and Raven, but clearly, she thinks more.

"We Brayshaws," Maybell begins again, "we're wolves. When we decide we want something, that makes it ours. There is no going back, no changing our minds. It's sealed in the heavens and etched along the walls of hell."

"I've made no decision," I tell her.

She nods, but nothing is said the remainder of the drive, and thirty minutes later, I'm pulling up at the Bray house.

My dad climbs out, opens Maybell's door, and helps her to her feet.

She comes around, stepping up to my window, and levels me with a stern expression. "You might not have made a decision, but that girl has."

"Why's that matter to me?"

She eyes me a long moment before saying, "I said what a Brayshaw wants, a Brayshaw gets."

I frown. "Victoria is no Brayshaw."

Ms. Maybell smirks, pats me on the cheek, and walks away.

"Why does she do that?"

"You mean make you think, force you to step back and consider what you haven't?" He raises a dark brow. "It's what mothers or grandmothers do."

I nod, looking away.

She's the closest we've ever had to either.

CHAPTER 9
CAPTAIN

The knock on my door has my muscles stiffening, but Raven's laugh floats from behind me in the next second, and my body relaxes the tiniest bit.

"Yikes." She slides farther in.

I glance over my shoulder, my head following as she moves around me, sitting on the edge of my bed.

"Tense, Packman?" she teases.

I scoff. "Let's go with that."

She smirks. "Zoey still sleeping?"

"Yeah." I sigh. "Can't decide if I should be waking her up to say bye before we leave or let her sleep in. She's gotten used to having me every morning. Think she'll be confused or something when she gets up and only my dad and Maybell are here?"

"Your guess is as good as mine, Cap." She laughs, but there's a nervousness to it.

I reach out, and she slips her hand in to grasp mine, tension surrounding her.

"Stop," I reassure her. "We're gonna figure this parenting shit out. Me and Zo, you, Maddoc, and the baby."

"And Royce and Rolland and Maybell," she ticks off each name.

I chuckle. "And them."

"Pretty sure Royce thinks Zoey and the mini-basketball I'm carrying around are equally his."

"Pretty sure that's exactly what he thinks."

She smiles, looking around my room. "I think it's good for him. He's been a little out of it ever since we got back from the cabins. Glued to his phone and shit."

Agreed.

Out of the three of us, I'd say Royce is the hardest shell to crack, but Zoey slipped by his shield in an instant, and with his soft spot for Raven, her and our brother's baby earned his love by existing.

I think it's the innocence of a kid he prefers. He can trust their little souls and doesn't feel he has to be on high alert like he is with everyone else.

Raven pulls her hand away, leaning back on her elbows. "I say let her sleep. She's little. Can't hurt, right? I'm sure Maybell knows what to do about naps and stuff. Wait, is she too big for naps?"

I laugh. "No, I have the full schedule Maria had her on, so I've been trying to stick to it, but she's been sleeping longer than Maria said was her normal since the day she came home."

"Maybe that's because she is home when before she wasn't."

I nod, and Raven looks off, the shadowed mood she found me in now creeping over us both.

Before, as in when Zoey was being cared for by Maria and kept from me while my family fought for its place against Graven and the assholes surrounding them.

I can't fucking believe Victoria never even let on that she knew I had a kid, let alone that she'd met her. She hid it until she was forced to admit it, even after we put faith in her to stand with us.

That's the shittiest part. She could have come clean along the way but chose not to.

Raven asks me the exact question I've been rolling around in my head since the decision was made to keep Victoria here ten days ago. "What are we doing, Packman?"

I sigh, glancing around as Maddoc steps in, dropping beside her.

She leans her head on his shoulder, eyeing me.

"No fuckin' clue," I admit. "Maybe this was a bad idea."

"Nope." Royce bounds in next, flopping on the other side of the bed and reaching out to put his hand on Raven's little belly.

Maddoc slaps him away while Raven smiles.

I pull my computer chair up and sit in front of them.

"Moving her ass in is how we keep an eye on her. She's gotta be here," Royce says.

"It's past keeping an eye on her and we all know it." Maddoc looks to me and admits what we've tried to ignore. "We've already let her in."

I nod, sitting back against the cushion. "And now we know she's lied to us."

"About big shit," Royce adds.

"Life-changing shit."

"Broke our trust." Maddoc stares.

I tip my head. "Her loyalty is questionable."

"She's Raven's blood." Maddoc looks to her.

Raven licks her lips, eyes moving between the three of us. "And family runs deeper than blood."

"Based on that, she's everything opposite of what it means to be Brayshaw," Maddoc points out.

"Fuck me," Royce sighs as he pushes to his feet, the three of us following. "Still feels like she belongs, don't it?"

"She does," Raven says with unmistakable certainty. "I can feel it. She's stubborn, yeah, but she's—" She cuts off with a heavy frown when I lift my hand.

Movement in the hall confirms what I somehow knew—she's stepped out of her room.

Victoria walks by, pausing in my doorway when she spots the four of us. She hesitates, and then her footsteps carry her down the stairs.

I look back to my family.

Maddoc smirks, tugging Raven closer to him.

Nobody speaks, but the consensus is there.

We believe she does, but belief is not enough; there's an order to be followed, and no one gets a pass. She'll need to prove beyond reason she deserves her place.

She'll be gone if she doesn't.

"Gotta remember we have no clue what she's capable of." Royce looks at the three of us.

"Then we need eyes on her, always," Maddoc adds.

Raven chuckles. "Did we just deem her the newest Bray girl?"

We smirk.

Raven shakes her head, fighting a smile. "This could backfire on you so hard."

"So how do we play this?" Royce asks, the question directed at me since she's mine to handle.

Fuck, not mine, but mine to decide what to do with.

"In public, she's ours, protected. Untouched. In private—"

"Still ours, aye, Cap?" He rubs his hands together, one corner of his mouth tipped up.

Raven laughs, glancing between us both.

My chest thumps at the thought, and I start to tell him to fuck off, but the words don't come, and my frown smooths out.

Maddoc narrows his eyes but doesn't say anything while Royce's grin grows.

"By the way, douchebag Mike is handled," Royce tells me.

I frown. "That easy?"

Maddoc frowns. "You sound surprised."

"She was acting odd, edgy. Told me to send him away."

"Prolly didn't want him putting her on blast, shit from when they dated or whatever."

I shake my head. "I don't know. I don't like him."

They both laugh, and my frown deepens.

"Course you don't, bro. He's had what you want." Royce grins. "But for real, he said he thought she was waiting on him, understands now she wasn't, won't be, ain't his." Royce bounces his brows. "Painted a real pretty, flesh-colored picture for him, drove the point home a bit."

I scoff, shaking my head, and Raven grips Royce by the elbow, laughing as she tugs him out the door, but Maddoc holds back.

"You can want to kill her and keep her at the same time, you know." He levels me with a glare. "You saw it with me and Raven in the beginning. Don't share what's meant to be yours."

I say what he already knows: "I don't trust her. And if I don't trust her, I can't keep her."

He lifts his chin, tipping it to the side a bit. "So send her on her way."

Now it's me who glares.

A hint of a grin edges Maddoc's mouth. "That's what I thought, brother. You don't trust her, but you want to. You don't think she's worth it, but you need her to be. Ain't nothin' wrong with that." He steps closer. "Only thing to do is wait her ass out."

"Brayshaw lockdown."

"Nice and tight."

"If she fucks up?"

My eyes move between his as he slaps me on the back and walks toward the door.

"Then we throw away the key, my man." He meets my stare. "With the chain still around her ankles."

He walks out and down the stairs, giving me the minute I need to shake the tension wrapped around my shoulders, and then I step into the hall.

Quietly, I move into Zoey's room, kissing her on the forehead, and then make my way downstairs.

Victoria's eyes lock onto mine the second I'm in view.

She's propped against the wall by the door, her long blond hair lying over her shoulder in the messy way it always does, not quite curly, more a windblown wave. Brown eyes blinding and bare, she stares at me with what I'm betting she thinks is a show of indifference.

It's not.

Small creases frame her eyes, lips are pinched tight, and her thumb repeatedly flicks at the black nail polish on her ring finger.

She's anxious, as she should be, as most liars are.

Whatever the hell that was Friday night, my body's reaction to her, I have to fight it.

I can't afford to ignore the risk she brings, not when I have Zoey to think about.

What I didn't say to my brothers, but they understand all the same, is it's more than wanting to trust Victoria—I get the sick sense I'm supposed to.

I've always been a good judge of character, able to see what others couldn't—it's part of my role in this family—but my vision of her is blurred, and I'm not sure what to make of it.

Royce hits me on the shoulder as he walks by, swinging the front door open. "Back to Brayshaw High today, assholes and ass-ettes. Three months till graduation and shit's about to get even more interesting."

Victoria pushes off the wall. "Too bad none of you will be graduating without summer school," she says before disappearing onto the porch.

"Ah, shit," Royce says, loud and mocking. "She is capable of speaking some truth." He follows after her. "Hey, VicVee, you're ridin' bitch."

My dad and Maybell step inside right as the others disappear from sight.

Maybell nods. "You ready, boy?"

The three of us quickly go over everything for Zoey, even though we've done this a solid dozen times in the last week, and then I'm sliding into the driver's seat of my SUV.

We stop at the donut shop on our way to school, getting right back to our regular routine.

"Two chocolate sprinkle donuts for me, large hot choc," Royce says, his face in his phone.

"Coffee, lots of creamer," Raven tells me.

I look to Maddoc, who eyes me.

He told me last night to swap her out for decaf if she asked—she'll kick his ass if she finds out, and he'll gladly take it.

"Black," Maddoc says. "And grab her a maple bar."

"I don't want one today." Raven shakes her head.

"You will the second you smell Royce's."

"No, I won't—"

"Get the damn donut, Cap."

I fight a grin and turn to Victoria, but she doesn't bother looking my way, keeping her head dropped against the seat, eyes pointed out the window, so I slam my door and head inside to get everyone's orders.

Not ten minutes later, we're turning into the parking lot of the school, and just like that, head after head snaps our way, conversations dying on people's lips as they turn, unable to control their stares as they normally would when they spot the familiar SUV.

It's been almost two months since we've been here, and a lot of shit's changed.

Thankfully, our boy Mac helped keep things in line best he could in our absence; still, though, people pulled their shit.

The assholes at the promenade were the perfect example—the Graven Prep dicks who are looking for an in they won't get. We would never trust someone who flip-flopped so fast, and all because the head of their little world will never be allowed back here. That's not how loyalty works.

Mac did good, held down what he could, and did well, but no matter how you look at it, the perfect little world the students of Brayshaw High felt they lived in has been shaken and stirred, and they have no clue what to do with that.

They don't know how to function without order and rules and expectations. They were born into it, into this town run by power and respect, so when it was disrupted, they panicked.

This is Brayshaw, and it's the head of our name they need to feel safe, that they want to look to.

Me, my brothers, Raven—the queen they were promised.

Rumors spread like wildfire when we first allowed Collins Graven, the next in line for the Graven empire and our family enemies, into our school this past winter, and they only got worse when he and Donley Graven disappeared not long after his estate was burned to the ground.

Mac told us dozens of kids flipped out and stopped showing at school, so we had to give them something, let them know we weren't hiding but building our strength.

They know now the town is ours without question and the Gravens no longer have a leg to stand on to challenge this.

They know Raven is both Brayshaw and Graven blood and holds more clout here than anyone before her and that she married my brother to fulfill a decades-old contract made by men before our time. Not that she wouldn't have on her own later; the contract just sped the timeline up a bit.

But that's it.

They don't know about my daughter.

They don't know Victoria is Raven's sister.

They don't know the sudden departure of their principal was our doing—Connor Perkins, the man who helped hide Zoey's existence from me by hiding her mother. They also don't know he was the man who got my mother pregnant with me, giving her the son her husband couldn't—my biological father, who I would never claim.

Rolland is my dad, period.

There is a lot they're clueless about, but the shock they'll be let in on first is what will be obvious the second we step from this vehicle.

I glance at Raven, who frowns out her window.

"I'm a fucking statistic," she grumbles.

"And anyone who points that out will get their tits punched or balls chopped." Royce glares, sitting forward in his seat.

My eyes fall to her top, a stretchy material that forms to her frame perfectly, leaving her small bump on full display for the first time.

She shrugs, looking at Royce. "Why? It's the truth."

"Yeah, and so is the fact that Victoria here is a sneaky little snake." I look in my mirror in time to see him point a malicious grin toward her. "But we still won't allow others to say it to her face."

"I don't need you to look out for me," Victoria tells him in a monotone voice, eyeing the chaos in the parking lot with annoyance.

She's so used to hiding in the background, but she won't get that anymore.

"If you haven't figured it out yet, VicVee, lemme break it down for ya. We don't give a fuck what you need, not yet anyway." He pushes his door open the second I put the vehicle in park and steps out, quickly tucking his head back inside. A deep glower covers his face. "Or instead of 'not yet,' maybe I should say not anymore, huh?" He slams the door.

She scoffs, drops her head back on the seat, and lets her gaze flick past mine.

"Fuck it," Raven huffs. "Let's go."

Maddoc and I step out, simultaneously pulling the girls' doors open before they have a chance to do it themselves.

Victoria stares at me, blindly snagging her backpack off the floorboard as she climbs out.

I allow my eyes to travel the length of her.

She's small compared to me. Where my shoulders are wide, hers are narrow, almost petite, as is the rest of her body, but she's got shape, subtle curves that make it impossible not to wish for a closer look. Even more so with the way she tries to hide it, always with the least amount of skin on display as possible.

She never openly flaunts.

Not that she has to—she's got a natural allure she's aware of and, if I'm guessing right, hates.

Her toned legs are constantly covered in cheap jeans, and she only wears tops she can tuck into the waistband. Most of the time, she has a little jacket on, but it's getting warmer, so today her flannel is tied around her hips. Still, her long sleeves hide every inch of her.

She's left her hair as it falls, a little messy but still full and shiny; by the end of the day, it'll be thrown in a ball on top of her head. When I've seen her out, she has dark shit on her eyes, deepening the brown of her gaze, but on most days, like today, she wears little to no makeup. Her high cheekbones, dark lashes, and brows make it seem otherwise. Mix that with the natural swell her lips constantly hold and the shaded rosy red they tempt me with daily, and she's too fucking much, wakes up with that pouty baby-doll look.

A legit sleeping beauty.

I draw my eyes back to hers, and her chin lifts the slightest bit.

"Ready?" she asks, and I'm not sure if it's a mask of bravery or stupid stride of confidence she shouldn't hold on to.

I move a step closer, lifting my knuckle to her jaw, knowing dozens are staring and telling myself that's the only reason why I want to feel more of her.

She's as aware as I am that others are watching, but instead of fighting, she allows me to tilt her head back farther.

"Better question." I trail my knuckle down her throat, and her head slowly rights itself. "Are you?"

Her eyes narrow. "Based on how you're acting right now, I assume I'm the new pet, so I'll ask you again." She whispers, "You ready for this, Cap? 'Cause you're the one who 'has' to touch me today, then go home and convince yourself you didn't want to."

A dark laugh leaves me, and I shuffle closer.

"Oh, I want to," I rasp, the honesty of my own words getting my blood pumping. "Pretty fuckin' sure I made that clear."

She looks away only to come right back.

"So, yes. I want to touch you in ways you couldn't imagine if you tried, in places the sun's never seen," I admit, and her features pull. "But I have self-control."

I take a few steps back, allowing her out of the doorway, but grip her upper arm before she's fully free. "Don't do anything stupid."

"Like tempt you?" she throws back instantly.

"You could try."

"Should I?"

Annoyance flares inside me, and she discreetly yanks free.

"I won't play games, Captain. I did that for years because someone told me that was my purpose, and I'm not up for it anymore."

My frown is instant. "What the fuck does that mean?"

She eyes me but then shrugs and changes the subject. "I'm not going anywhere, so you'll either come to understand who I am or you won't."

"Who are you, Victoria Vega…Graven?"

Her lips smash together before a low chuckle leaves her. "Just a girl, capable of mistakes and living with regret like everyone else in the world—not that I regret all things I'd bet you want me to," she says unapologetically, taking a small step away. "But I am human, no matter how much you try to convince yourself I'm a monster."

"I don't think you're a monster," I tell her. "But I know you're a liar. I can't trust you, and that is the issue."

"Yet I'm sleeping down the hall, only feet away from the most precious thing in your world, and you're allowing it. Demanded it, even." She calls me out, eyes bold and daring as she brings her body flush to mine. "Strange place for someone you can't trust to be…don't you think?"

My anger boils, a heavy tug stretching across my chest. "Don't test me, Beauty."

She steps back, flipping me off with both hands. "Wouldn't dream of it, Beast."

Raven's light chuckle has my eyes flying over my shoulder and narrowing.

She gives a small smile, shrugging as Victoria walks away from me, and my eyes decide to follow.

This weekend was a bust.

Feelin' out Jason was a waste, but that wasn't the worst of it.

I tried to curb my appetite only to be forced to face what I was trying to deny—I only want her.

I could have at least fuckin' hid it a little better, not let her in on my inner issues, but then a punk showed up and my possessiveness bared itself without permission.

If he thinks he can come in here and claim what he apparently believed to be his when he left, he's wrong.

He can't.

No one can.

Maybe not even me.

CHAPTER 10
VICTORIA

At the hood of the car, Raven scoots over, offering me a place beside her with a small, hard-fought grin.

This morning when I walked by during their little chat, I had a moment of uncertainty—to run, quick and fast, or to pause, hide, and listen.

In the end, I'm not dumb.

I'm more than aware eavesdropping doesn't exist in a place like this.

If you're standing back and trying to snoop, they know and say what they want you to hear. Between the four, there are no gaps to slip through, no holes left unfilled, and no way around.

I don't want around.

I want inside.

It's been ten days since Cap moved me in, caught me peeking on Zoey, and caged me against the wall.

I kept myself locked away, hidden by some means as much as I could, but we all know my forced absence solved nothing.

The air surrounding us is more power charged than ever, the tension between us growing every day.

So far I'd say it's in my favor, but that can change in an instant.

If Mike sticks around, it might.

I need to find him before he comes to find me, and I have no doubt he will.

I sigh, glancing around the parking lot and back at the boys.

Today will be the most time I've spent with them and Raven in months, and truth be told, I've been waiting for it.

Forming friendships I never meant to ended up being something I had no clue I was missing. Yes, lies were buried beneath the surface, but as a person, I was never fake.

The boys know and approve of all the stray teens they take into their group homes, and if you stay quiet, they leave you alone, sometimes even offer jobs like helping out at the warehouses and things. That's usually for the boys' home, though, because the girls get catty and let attention from the boys go to their heads.

For three years I was silent, invisible, nothing but one of the half dozen ever-changing girls in the group home on the front edge of their property because they allowed me to be, but then winter came, and Raven showed up, and everything transformed overnight. Literally.

She gained their notice within minutes of her arrival, held it, and, only days later, couldn't force them away no matter how hard she tried. And she tried like hell.

Like me, she didn't want their attention, but it didn't matter, and later everyone learned she was born to hold it. Her arrival forced me to rethink everything, and that meant stepping from behind the shadows.

It was subtle at first, but then she got jumped, and since I had been following her, I was the one there to stop it, which also meant I was the only one who could get her home, back to them…with the help of Mike.

I'll never forget how Captain looked into my eyes with curiosity swimming in his own. Of course, there was anger there too, but still.

He saw me that night.

Demanded a response, and after it, he never stopped.

I'd catch him observing me, straight on or behind his shades.

He wasn't shy about it, but the Brayshaws never are.

They see what they want, and they stop at nothing until they get it.

Raven told Chloe something not long after that, and it had a positive effect on her. She later shared the conversation with me, and it's been playing on repeat since they left me standing in the orchard the other day.

You don't need a Brayshaw to become one. All you have to do is earn it.

That's my goal.

I glance toward Captain, standing not three feet away, eyes on me.

Before I had this group, I had nothing.

My time as part of their fold, while short-lived, was long enough for me to grow greedy and want more.

Becoming a Brayshaw isn't enough, but it's where I'll start.

I'll earn their trust, prove my loyalty, and earn my token of acceptance as they all have theirs.

After I'm one of them, truly and completely…

I'll earn him too.

Anyone who gets between me and what I want will be dealt with in true Bray fashion because that's who I am supposed to be. I feel it.

Captain Brayshaw is mine. Period.

He just doesn't know it yet.

A slow, dangerous smirk crosses his lips right then, and the blue in his eyes flashes a deep, midnight ocean.

Or does he?

Suddenly, Royce is wrapping his arm around my neck, dragging me forward as our group begins to move.

"What—"

"Shut that pretty little mouth, VicVee. It's all part of the process."

I don't think so.

I dig the heels of my combat boots into the pavement, and

Royce jerks to a stop, his eyes slicing my way in warning, but I'm not backing down.

"I get it, you want me to fill the role of the new toy passed between the group, but that's too bad."

"Yeah?" Royce gives a menacing growl for only me to hear, but there's no power behind it. "And why's that?"

I stare into his dark eyes, allowing him to see the purpose in mine. "I have a point to make, want it clear from the start, and I can't do that under your arm."

His glare holds as his head dips closer until his face is hidden in my hair and neck. He allows his smirk to spread across my skin, where no one else can see, as he whispers, "That you fuckin' do, VicVee, but watch your step, 'cause every other motherfucker will be after today."

He shifts, looks past me, and nods his chin. "Take her off my hands, yeah?"

Royce's arm falls, smacking my ass on the way down, and then he catches up to the others chuckling from a few steps ahead.

I turn to Captain, who makes no move to come closer, so I do as he wants.

I go to him.

"My brother not good enough for you?" His gaze is sharp and angry, but I know him better than that.

"No, he's not," I answer rapidly.

Captain's frown deepens. "You'd be lucky to have him."

Instant and complete support.

I want that.

"I'm sure you're right, but someone else will be luckier. He's not the one I want."

Frustration drives him forward. "Having these people see you as my Bray girl doesn't make me yours. You get that, right?"

"Let me handle that part."

At first, he just stares, a question he refuses to ask written in his eyes.

He doesn't blink, doesn't speak, and he stays that way for several seconds until his arm finally drapes across my shoulders, and I'm yanked into him, his hold far more possessive than I'm betting he realizes. His spine even straightens with me tucked at his side.

We head up the steps of Brayshaw High, the others, including Mac and Chloe, waiting near the door for us to arrive and walk inside.

Maddoc and Raven lead, every eye around lasered in our direction, on their king and queen and their equals at their sides, but no one dares to whisper.

They will, but later and in private.

The boys do their little bro claps with a few others from their basketball team, and I wave at one of the girls from the group home when she nods her chin at me, but other than that, no one approaches.

Mac and Chloe break off first, heading wherever their classes are as we stay standing dead center in the hall.

Royce doesn't wait around but struts right into class while Maddoc takes his time with Raven before he too walks off. She glances our way and then slips through the door, leaving only me and Captain.

He slides his hand into my hair, bringing his lips to my ear, and I hold my breath, but no words come. His grip tightens only to fly from me in the next second as he takes a step back.

And then he takes another, all to rush forward in the end and slam his body into mine.

"If this is some trick, you will lose," he swears.

"Didn't I already?"

"Is that how you feel?"

"Yes."

His face twists, and he rumbles, deep and low, "Good."

With that, he's gone, but I've got a feeling a piece of that control he mentioned earlier broke off somewhere between the parking lot and here.

I give myself a second to breathe, then walk into class and drop into my desk.

Sensing Raven's eyes on me, I turn toward her, and she shifts in her seat to face me full-on.

"I can't trust you." She frowns, confusion etched across her face. "So why the hell am I rooting for you?"

My shoulders ease, and she shakes her head.

"Fuck this up, Vee, and I can't help you, even if I decide I want to. These boys..." She trails off, knowing she doesn't have to say it.

"They're your family, Raven. I get it." I lean toward her, quickly glancing to her stomach and back. "But so am I, and I'll do whatever I can to make sure you choose me too."

She glares before a small smile ghosts her lips and she faces forward to hide it. "You better."

From his seat on the other side of Raven, Royce makes sure to catch my eye. "Don't forget, our bite?" A dark brow rises. "It's much worse than our bark."

"I thought wolves howled?"

"Don't be cute." He flashes. "Be smart."

In other words...

Be Brayshaw.

The heavy thud of the door slamming against the wall as it's thrown open has everyone's attention snapping toward the front of the room.

Every muscle in my body locks, my neck likely burning a bright fucking red as Captain comes strolling in, in no particular hurry, a little glare teasing across his forehead.

The teacher pauses, saying not a word as he walks in, knowing if she did, it would only mean trouble for her.

I don't have to look to know every eye in this room has shifted this way.

Captain plants one firm palm on my desk, leaning over until I'm forced to look up.

He knows I hate this…which is exactly why he's doing it.

He grips the back of my neck, bringing his mouth to mine so he can speak against my lips, quiet and only for me. "You asked to be mine. That means you don't look at, talk to, touch anyone else. Do you understand?"

"No one else…" I whisper, intentionally ignoring his entire point. "Does this mean I've got the golden stamp to touch you?"

"My knuckles are brass, Beauty. I've got no use for anything golden."

I don't miss how his eyes cut to my hair as he says it, and his comment about Mallory flashes in my head.

He pushes to his full height, a sick satisfaction gleaming in his blue-green eyes as he gets set to push his point, making me the center of attention.

To piss me off.

Captain's command is purposeful and clear and loud enough for all to hear.

"Behave."

Shithead.

CHAPTER 11
CAPTAIN

"I'm fucked." I plant my ass onto the bleacher beside Maddoc.

"Let me guess, you wanna wring her fuckin' neck, then lick the bruises?" He gives me a quick side smirk, laughing at my expression.

Because yes, exactly fucking that. "I don't know, man. Thought she'd fight me, not—"

"Fight for you?" Maddoc lifts a brow.

I nod.

"Why don't you lock her ass in a room with the fake file we have on her and force her to talk?"

I scoff. "I lock myself in a room with that girl and there will be no talking."

"That bad?" Royce drops beside us, nodding for a towel.

I toss him one. "I caged her in the first fucking night, ready to just—"

"Go to pound town?" Royce laughs.

I chuckle. "Ended up telling her I wanted to bend her over."

Both grin, only for their jaws to drop when I add, "So I could picture Mallory while I fucked her."

The shock hits but wears off quickly, and they bust up laughing.

"That's cold, my man." Royce grins, proud, reaching out for a fist bump, but I leave him hanging. "Genius but cold. I think I'll take credit for that one."

Maddoc shakes his head, then shrugs. "Still say if you want her, have her. You don't have to trust her to fuck her."

"Damn if that isn't a true-ass statement." Royce grins. "Only chick I trust is Raven, and she's 'bout the only one I can't fuck," he jokes, shoving at Maddoc with his elbow.

Maddoc pushes him off the bench, and Royce hops up, laughing.

The bell rings, so we stand with him, gather our shit, and head to the locker room. As we step through the double doors, James Carpo, our former head of security for all Brayshaw operations, comes around the corner in a crisp, black suit.

"Boys. I'd heard you were back today, but I didn't have time to say hello this morning."

"Lookin' good, James." Royce nods.

He scoffs. "If I had known becoming principal of a high school was harder than managing the entire town's safety, I'd have never agreed to this."

"Hey, it's a good compromise. You have to stay involved; we need you," I tell him.

"I'm pretty sure my daughter doesn't share your sentiment." He chuckles. "She's not so happy I'm here."

"Ah, she'll come around. Doesn't take much to please Chloe," Royce adds with a smirk.

James levels him with a stern look. "I'm gonna pretend you didn't say that."

"Nah, my man." Royce pats his shoulder, stepping around him. "You mean, you're gonna try to forget I did. Good luck with that, James!" he shouts from inside the locker room door.

I fight a laugh while James looks ready to puke.

Maddoc watches Royce go before turning back to James. "You got eyes on Raven?"

"Am I tracking her every move like you asked me to?" James lifts his brows.

My eyes snap to Maddoc.

"Yes," he says.

"No," James responds.

I quickly put my shoulder between them, knowing Maddoc's advance is coming.

"That wasn't a request." Maddoc speaks slowly.

"I can't invade the privacy of the head of this town without her permission," James tells him calmly.

"I put a fucking kid inside her. That is permission enough." Maddoc's shoulder begins to push against my back.

James, though, he smiles at him, used to his aggressive nature and proud of his fierce protection over his girl. "I'll talk to Mrs. Brayshaw and see what I can do. See you guys later."

Maddoc shoves into the locker room with me on his tail.

"You know she's gonna tell him to kiss her ass, right?"

"Yeah, I know. I'm working on the doctor, need her forced into bed rest, so I can keep her ass locked at home until she's stronger."

I laugh. "She's pregnant, not broken."

"Then why's everything hurt her?" he shouts.

"She say that?"

He scoffs, giving an incredulous glare. "Yeah, fuckin' right, Cap, but I can tell. She's exhausted, makes all these faces when she moves, like she's stepping on thorns and shit. It's her feet, her back, her fucking tits." His eyes widen. "Swear to God, if her puss—"

"Cut it, brother." I lift my palms and walk away, but the second I get under the warm spray of the shower, an unexpected and unwelcome question begins to swim inside my head.

I try to refocus, force my thoughts to anything other than where they've suddenly taken me, but it's no use.

The things he's describing in Raven, the things we've all begun to notice—the swell of her stomach as her child starts to grow, the little cravings and mood swings, the added sentiment behind her eyes and lost look she gets when she's quiet—I wonder...are those things Mallory experienced while pregnant too, but alone?

And if she did, how the fuck could she go through all that and still walk away from our baby girl in the end?

Was it easy for her or hard?

Did she give a damn at all?

Did she ever even hold her?

Did my baby girl lie alone, uncomforted and unwanted her first days in this world?

A deep, crushing ache falls on my chest, and I fight for a slow inhale.

The pain has nothing to do with the girl who picked a different path than the one I gave her and everything to do with the little girl waiting for me at home. For a love that was foreign but felt the moment I knew she was out there somewhere.

I didn't have to see her to love her.

I needed no convincing to keep her.

The second I found the hospital birthing records with Mallory's name all over them hidden deep inside my gym bag, it was as if an invisible weight lifted, like somehow deep down I was aware something was missing, and learning Zoey was out there filled a hole I never knew had been dug.

Mallory lost out on more than she'll ever know, but Zoey never will.

I'll adore her enough for us both, as will my family.

She'll lack no love.

I'm stuck in my own head the remainder of the day. I don't remember speaking to anyone or even eating at lunch. All I've been doing is waiting for the bell to ring so I could get the hell out and home.

I round the corner, headed toward the main entrance, and a grin pulls at my lips.

Guess the others felt the same, as they're waiting in the hall, ready to get out of here. With basketball season over, we've got nothing forcing us to stay after school.

We head straight for the truck, but when I spot Victoria

eyeing Chloe and her friends across the parking lot, head tipped with a slight pinch of her dark brows, I pause beside her.

"Leave it alone. She's with Mac now."

It takes her a long moment, but then she glances my way, her expression blank, and shoulders past me until she's sliding into the back seat with Royce. Raven tries to slip in after her, but Maddoc beats her with a glare.

With a playful eye roll, she climbs up front as I walk around and get in the driver's seat.

"Was it as bad as you thought?" I ask Raven.

She shrugs. "I don't really care, but even so, nobody said a damn word about the two extra stomachs attached to me."

We chuckle, and I catch a small grin on Victoria's face, but she wipes it away quickly, anxiety blanketing her features the farther down the street we get.

Minutes later, we're pulling onto Bray grounds, past the group home and into the clearing that allows us a view of the mansion.

The tension in my chest eases as I spot her.

My little world.

"Look at her." Royce sits forward in the back seat, smiling out the front windshield.

Zoey starts stomping her feet, trying to tug free from our dad's hand as we roll closer to the porch, but he doesn't free her quite yet.

She starts waving, and even though I can't hear it, the sound of her little laughter fills my ears, and an unexplainable warmth flows through my veins.

This is it.

This is what I've dreamed about for so long, coming home to my baby girl waiting for me. I didn't realize it would be as hard as it was to leave her here today. When I'd go visit her, when Maria cared for her, an overwhelming sense of guilt weighed my every step. I thought it would be different when she was home, but it's not. I felt her absence all day.

As soon as the engine is off and my door is open, Dad lets her go and she comes charging down the steps, right into my open and waiting arms.

"Hi, Zo." I hug her to me, quickly pulling back so I can look at her. "Did you miss me?"

"Uh-huh!" Her smile is wide, her little feet kicking. "You're all done now?"

I squeeze her tighter. "All done for today."

I know she might not understand what I'm saying fully, but she throws her little fists up anyway.

"Yay!" She laughs, then shifts to look at the others climbing out.

I tense, but my muscles relax when Victoria keeps herself sitting inside.

Zoey wiggles in my arms, so I set her down, and it's Royce she runs to first.

"Zoey Bear!" he shouts as he dips down, lifts her up, and tosses her in the air.

"Uncle Bro!" She laughs back, kisses his cheek, then kicks again to be let go.

"You tryin' to ditch me already?"

"Baby's turn!"

Royce tickles her, and she throws her head back laughing.

"Fine." He pretends to pout. "Baby's turn." He puts her down, watching as she runs over to Raven.

Raven pulls her lips between her teeth and slowly lowers herself onto the porch steps so Zoey can drop beside her, same as she does for her every day, getting on Zoey's level.

Zoey smiles, tugging her shoulders up to her cheeks, then reaches out and gently pats Raven's stomach. She leans forward, thinking she's whispering, but her little voice is loud enough for everyone to hear.

"Hi, baby." She giggles at herself. "Hi, bestest friend. Are you sleeping?" She lifts her eyes to Raven. "Is baby sleeping?"

A gentle smile, a new one for her, graces Raven's lips. "Do you think baby is sleeping?"

"Yes!" Zoey shouts, making us all laugh.

It's the same exact question every day, and Raven plays along each time.

"Then I think so too." She winks, raising her eyes to Maddoc.

Of the three of them, Maddoc is the most timid with Zoey. I'm not so sure it's nerves as it is maybe he's afraid.

Outside of us, Raven is the first person he's ever loved, but every time he looks at my daughter, at his niece, it's not hard to spot the tenderness there.

I'm almost positive it terrifies him, makes him fear how hard he'll love his own baby, and I get it. It's the most powerful feeling I've ever known, but I can't help but wonder if he's fearful of loving someone more than he does Raven.

I can't answer that for him, though, because I have no clue how it works, the love of your woman in comparison to the love of your child.

I imagine it's different but just as strong.

I look to our dad, who pointedly shifts his eyes to my SUV only to bring them right back, a heavy, disapproving frown carved across his forehead.

"Son."

"Don't," I warn. "She deserves no part of this and she knows it."

"You saying she wasn't warned to drag behind?"

"Does it matter?"

His eyes narrow as he attempts to read the thought behind mine. "I'm thinking, yeah, it does. It's a sign of respect."

"Or fear of what we'd do."

"It ain't fear." Royce steps up with a shrug. "If she was afraid, she never would have hid shit from us, and when we found out, she'd have tried to run. The girl lived on our property, in our group home. She went to our school, walked up in our house, lies and all. Someone afraid wouldn't do any of that."

"I have to agree," our dad says, sliding his hands in his pockets.

"Maybe she's a master con artist and you're both wrong."

"Maybe she is, Son." He nods. "But maybe not."

Royce frowns at our dad, but I shake him off. Now is not the time for this shit.

I waited all day to get home to my daughter. I won't allow a deceiving blond to take a second of my time.

I turn away from them both, kneeling in front of Zoey. "Daddy's hungry, Zo. Wanna help me make a snack?"

"Me too?" She smiles.

"Yeah, you too." I laugh.

"And Uncle Bro too!" Royce adds, scooping her up and helicoptering her into the house, but not before pausing and turning to Maddoc. "You wish you had a cool nickname, bro."

Maddoc scoffs but with a grin. "My kid's gonna call you Uncle Dumbass."

"Nah…your kid's gonna call me daddy," Royce throws out right as he runs off.

Raven laughs, gripping Maddoc by the arm before he can chase after him.

We step inside, not one of us bothering to glance back at the girl left alone in the back seat.

I unbuckle Zoey from her car seat, and she hops right out, dashing across the driveway until she reaches the porch steps.

"Oh no!" She freezes, turning back right as I begin following. "My train!"

Maybell walks out right then, and I smile from her to Zo. "I'll get it, baby girl. Go inside with Ms. Maybell."

"Okay!" Zoey grabs her hand, and Maybell laughs as she's dragged into the house.

I walk to the vehicle and open the back to grab her stuffed

train when a streak of blond catches my eye around the right side of the house.

Victoria must have seen us pull up and went out the back.

I close the door, tracking her movement, and instead of sticking by the flowers this time, she searches across the mounds, picking one that looks ready to die and carries it to the farthest side of the pool. She chooses the only spot with the little bit of sunlight left and lies back, placing the flower on her chest right as her eyes close.

I head inside, make sure Zoey is good with Maybell, and take the stairs two at a time toward Victoria's room.

The door is shut, but I had her lock removed, so I push it open with ease.

A quick, resilient burn fires down my throat as my senses are assaulted, a heavy mix of lavender and mint, sun and fucking sin, the only proof she lives inside these walls.

I had the room completely remodeled for her when I thought her place here was starting a lot differently.

Fresh paint and brand-new furniture, a bright chandelier to match.

I wasn't sure what her style would be, but satin seemed fitting, and the colors are soft with some royal blue around the room, the crystals hanging from above offering a ray of light throughout where the sun or moon can't reach.

Annoyance flares when I look in her closet, finding her small selection of clothes still neatly folded inside her bags, the hangers and drawers all empty, bed pristinely made as if she's never even slept in it.

The two small blankets lying over the reading chair lead me to believe she hasn't. The computer is off, curtains still drawn up the way they were the day it was prepared for her—before we found out she purposely withheld information from us.

She hasn't settled in the slightest fucking bit.

I should be happy about that, her understanding she's got no guarantee.

So why am I more pissed off than I was walking in here?

I grab her backpack and unzip it, pulling out her notebooks and binders before stuffing them back in and looking into the small front pockets.

I glare at the near-empty baggie of weed stuffed inside, a half pack of Zig-Zags beneath it.

I zip it up and toss it back in the corner she had it in, kicking over the small garbage can, but there's nothing in there but pencil shavings. The bedside drawers are empty too.

What the fuck?

Next, I move into her private bathroom.

At least this area is being used. There's a towel hanging over the rack and a small, open makeup pouch sitting on the counter. I glance inside, but it's all normal bullshit.

Faded jeans sit on the top of a small laundry basket, so I grab them, checking the pockets. My brows lift as I feel something inside, but all I find is a sucker wrapper, a couple quarters, and a dollar receipt for a school newspaper.

I stuff it back and drop the jeans, making my way to the window. My hands stretch across the frame as I stare out at her.

What other secrets do you hold, Beauty?

"You know, when you were small, you were full of questions." Maybell's voice floats inside the room, but I don't turn, her footsteps indicating she's moving closer. "You'd hear a word or see something in passing, anything, really, and you'd hold on to whatever it was. Hours would go by and then you'd ask what it was or what it meant, how it worked. Something. Anything."

She perches against the frame, holding her long dress in her hands. "You had this tick where you couldn't focus on anything until you broke down what was on your mind in a way you could understand it, and then you'd move on to the next." She eyes me. "When you were twelve, you stopped asking. You trained yourself, developed a natural ability to see things for what they were, to comprehend without asking, to speak without a word."

My frown deepens and I follow her gaze to Victoria.

"Now you're in the dark, feelin' blind, can't understand, can't even form the question in your own mind, and it's frustratin' the heck out of you, but remember, boy." She waits for me to look at her. "Closed mouths don't get fed."

"You act like she'd tell me the truth if I asked for it."

"You act like you know she wouldn't." Maybell lifts her brows, making me chuckle. She grins. "She's just like you, you know. Her mind works the same."

I repeat what she said: "Closed mouths don't get fed."

Maybell pulls her lips to the side in a soft smile, patting me on the shoulder. "And that, my boy, is why you both sit starved."

CHAPTER 12
VICTORIA

"The person you are trying to reach is not available. Please leave a message after the tone."

I hang up, dropping my phone in my lap as I look out over the empty field.

Why do I keep trying to call her?

"Gotta say, Friday night was interesting."

My muscles grow taut at the intruder's voice, and I squeeze my eyes closed a moment.

Damn it.

Right as I open them, Mike comes to stand in front of me, and while his smile is easy, his stare weighs heavy with a critical squint.

My shoulders fall, a heavy exhale leaving me as I look him over. I spot a few small scrapes and already fading bruises, but they're too subtle to have been given by a Brayshaw, so they must be from his fight.

"Can I sit?" he finally asks.

"Should you?"

His lips twist as he looks away briefly. "Come on, Tor."

As much as I don't want to have this conversation, I know I have to.

I pat the metal bleacher at my side, and he drops down, sits back, and stares out at nothing, as I am.

"Bell don't ring for another hour. Why you at school already?" he leads, having already come to his own conclusion.

"Needed some air."

He scoffs, and I hold in my frown.

"I take it Royce didn't threaten to cut you at the belt the other night?"

"You mean after you ran out?" he throws back quickly, but I don't respond, so he answers my question. "He took a different approach."

I can only imagine.

Mike's quiet a moment and then gets right to the point. "Big change from when I left."

"Yeah…it is," I admit.

No point in denying, he saw with his own eyes, and I have no intention of hiding what I want from anyone, not even him.

I finally glance his way. "What was that 'my boyfriend' shit, Mike? Why'd you do that? Why come into their zone, draw attention to yourself?"

He pulls a cigarette from the pack in his shirt pocket, offering me one as he does, but I shake my head, so he delays, lighting it and pulling in a long drag.

He slowly blows the smoke out. "I was fucking around."

Tension builds in my gut as I ask, "Were you?"

His eyes swing to mine, resentment front and center. "I could sense something was up with him and you. He was…watching you watch the fight, didn't see him look away once, noticed how he got angry when you smiled." He leans his elbows on his knees, eyes now glued on the burning tip of his cigarette. "He was angry at the entire situation."

My stomach curls as I stare at his profile.

His jaw ticks beneath his caramel skin, giving away his true thoughts.

"I don't know," he keeps talking. "Guess I wanted to test him out, see if you were a plaything or, fuck…" He frowns. "More."

It takes him several seconds to meet my gaze again, and when he does, his is full of confusion, indecision, prompting me to ask what I don't want to.

"Why did you come back here? First the warehouses, now the school?" I whisper, shaking my head. "You made the decision to go. I told you I wanted to make a life in this place. You said you understood. I thought you did."

"Yeah," he snaps. "Thought I did too, Tor."

"Mike—"

"Stop." He cuts me off as he glares across the field. I eye him, and after a moment, he swings an easy grin my way. "I just… wanted to see you."

It settles something inside me.

I run my fingers along his jaw, only to snatch the cigarette from his mouth to lighten the mood.

It works—he chuckles, a shred of light coming back into his eyes, but as quickly as the atmosphere shifts, it shifts again.

The cigarette is slapped to the ground.

My head snaps to the right, and I squint as the sun meets my eyes, only for a heavy shadow to block it a moment later.

Captain stands there, face blank, but that's not what has me slowly rising to my feet.

His fingers begin to disappear into his pocket.

"Cap—" I cut off as his chin lifts, his hand now at his side, brass knuckles already on and firmly in place.

"Get out of here." Captain's eyes slowly lift over my head, locking onto Mike as he adds, "Now."

"You don't have to do this."

Captain's glare slices back to mine, and at first, annoyance flares, but then it's gone and a mocking glint takes its place. "What, you thought he was brave enough to try to sneak his way to you?" A taunting laugh leaves him. "Come on, Tor. I thought you knew more about this place than that. Clearly he does."

I whip around, looking at Mike.

He approached the Brayshaws?

When?

Where?

Shit.

I shake my head, and he shrugs, anger making the movement stiff.

"You know how it goes." Something flickers across Mike's face but it's gone just as quick. "Bray girls are off-limits."

And I've been deemed one.

Mike licks his lips, stretching to his full height. "The price is worth it," he says, daring Captain and shifting closer.

Captain understands what he's saying, sees his challenge, and moves an inch in as well.

He narrows his eyes on me, and while I shouldn't, I can't resist using this moment in my favor, to bait him, wishing he'd bite as hard as he's able.

"What all did they give you permission to do?"

Captain's jaw flexes, and he slides forward right as a garbled sound leaves Mike.

I whip around to find a long, tatted arm wrapped around his neck.

Royce grins, tightening his grip as he kicks Mike's feet from under him, causing him to fall to his knees. "Hiya, VicVee. Doin' stupid shit again, I see."

Suddenly, I'm gripped around the thighs, my body lifted into the air, and I yelp, trying to reach for something to hold on to, but the move has me almost falling forward, so I lock my knees straight and growl, hoping not to fall flat on my face as Captain takes the bleachers two at a time.

"Is this necessary?"

"Shut up, Victoria."

I'm passed off, now stuck in Maddoc's hold like a child as Raven laughs at his side.

I flip her off, making her laugh even harder, quickly looking toward Captain as he rushes back to where Mike is being held in place by Royce.

Not that he tried to fight free.

Not that he'd get free.

I relax, and Maddoc allows my feet to hit the ground but spins me so my arms are wrapped around myself, wrists in each of his hands at my sides.

"Nice to be on this side of the grab-and-go game for once." Raven grins, sipping on her coffee.

"Shut up." I roll my eyes, and she smiles wider, quickly jolting back as Captain appears again.

I expect him to pause in front of me, yell and scream, but he doesn't.

He dips, lifting me from the front this time, leaving me no choice but to wrap my legs around him or be a pencil in his arms.

With angry, jerky movements, he carries me across the grass, past the cement, and doesn't pause for a second until we're entering the side building that leads to the media rooms in the school.

Once inside, his arms fall, and I'm dropped to my feet.

I stumble backward, forced to use the desk to catch my fall, but shove off as quickly as I hit it.

"Why the fuck is he so interested in you?"

"Why the hell would you give someone permission to come to me if you didn't want them to?"

"I'm asking the questions," he booms.

"Oh," I mock like an asshole. "All of a sudden you're about asking what you want to know?"

"Goddamn it," he growls.

He grips me and tugs me close, our bodies now flush and heated for more reasons than one. His heavy glare falls to my lips, his hand flying up in the same second to grip the back of my neck. He drives me backward until my spine meets the cool wall, but before either of us can speak another word or give in to the heavy, desire-coated tension we're falling headfirst into, a tearful shriek fills the air, and we freeze.

Captain's eyes grow sharp, and he lifts a finger to his lips.

I rush toward the door to gauge the sound better, and Captain's right there to grip my arm.

He yanks me back, but then a broken plea follows.

"Please, I'm sorry."

Captain flies out the door, me on his tail.

Right as we round the corner, Jason Rowe's hand comes down across his girlfriend's face in a hard, open-handed slap.

She cries out, but it quickly turns to a shrill scream when Captain suddenly slips into her sight. He has Jason by the neck, lifts and slams him to the marble at our feet in seconds.

Jason's head bounces against the hard flooring, eyes fluttering as his body fights to stay conscious.

Captain pulls out his phone, lifting it to his ear. After a moment, he says, "Get in here." He shoves it back in his pocket.

Tisha, his girlfriend, tries to run off, but I dart forward, gently gripping her wrist.

She whips her wide eyes to me, tears pouring down her face as she tries to work through her shock.

"It's okay," I say gently, my muscles settling. "This is what they do."

"He'll—" she starts, but cuts off when Captain looks up at her.

She swallows, dropping her eyes to her toes.

Royce and Maddoc come charging around the corner in the next second, and when Maddoc looks over his shoulder, Raven steps to his side.

Royce's gaze wildly snaps along the scene, and a sheet of rage blankets his entire being. A visible tremor shakes him where he stands, and with it, the brown of his eyes grows black. It's as if he leaves his body completely. He opens and closes his right fist at his side, and I can't help but notice the blood already spread across his knuckles.

Mike's blood.

Captain takes his knee off Jason's chest and stands.

Jason coughs, half rolling on his side, his first sign of consciousness since he was laid on his ass, but Captain doesn't let him find comfort by shifting his body.

He pulls his leg back, kicking Jason straight in the side, and Jason gasps, panic in his eyes when he realizes he can't get air into his lungs.

Royce moves forward as Captain slides back, an eerie, black cloud surrounding him.

He picks up Jason's foot, hooking it over his shoulder.

Jason's eyes widen, moisture filling them as Royce begins to walk forward in slow, unnerving steps, Jason's head scraping against the ground as his body hangs over Royce's back.

He doesn't stop until he's kicking open the door at the very end of the hall and stepping through it, the heavy metal coming back to slam against Jason's limp body as they exit.

I look to Raven, who stares in the direction Royce went.

Maddoc looks to Captain and then pins Raven with a stern look that can only mean for her to stay put right before he charges in the direction Royce disappeared.

The girl finally comes out of her shock and begins to cry, her body shaking as she lifts her hands to hide her face.

My pulse races and I step away from her, looking to Raven to find the same uncomfortable expression on her.

She meets my eye and then focuses on Captain.

Captain wipes the sweat from his brow with the hem of his shirt and then steps toward her.

"Tisha," he calls, a tenderness in his tone that has not only her shoulders falling but mine. He shuffles closer, gently reaching out to wrap his fingers around her hands.

She flinches, hesitating, but slowly allows him to pull her hands down. She can't bring herself to look at him, though; her eyes are focused on the floor.

"Can you turn your head for me? Let me see?"

Slowly she does, and her hair falls to the side.

A thick welt stares back, the perfect shape of a hard hand, as if she didn't cower away from the slap but stood there and accepted what she knew was coming.

"How long?"

She shakes her head as more tears build. "No, he, um…" she cries but tries to laugh it off. "It's track season, you know?" she rushes out, sniffling. "Mr. Carpo asked me to interview the team, and when he found out I was meeting a couple at lunch today, he…he didn't mean…" She swallows. "It's just—"

"Look at me, Tisha," he cuts her off.

Her nose grows red, and finally she meets his eyes. Something inside her breaks then, her cries growing uncontrollable.

Raven turns around, taking a few steps away.

He pulls her hands into his chest, whispering, "How long?"

"Couple months," she breathes. "I…tried to break up with him, but he…" She shrugs.

Captain nods, letting her go and stepping back. "He's gone."

Her eyes slide toward the door he was dragged through, and she asks, "What will he do to him?"

"Everything he could have possibly done to you but worse," Captain answers honestly.

"Will he kill him?" she asks.

"He might." Captain shrugs. "There is no stopping Royce when it comes to something like this."

"He was accepted into Brown," she hesitantly offers. "For basketball. Made me accept their offer too."

Captain glares. "We'll take care of it, break both his legs."

Her lip twitches and she nods, pulling her hair over her left shoulder to try to help hide the markings on her face. "I, um…"

Captain shakes his head, stepping back more, and she offers him a tight smile before hustling off.

My chest settles as I watch her walk away, imagining the weight she must feel has lifted.

This is why their people love and listen to them.

A small smile finds my lips, but it's quickly erased when suddenly I'm the one caged against the wall.

He glares down at me, but the longer he looks, the more his gaze narrows, and then he jerks away. He takes slow steps toward where his brothers are and then spins on his heels, rushing out.

Raven scoffs, stepping up beside me.

"What?"

"Everything is what. You're an idiot and cruising along like nothing. He's being stubborn and allowing you to. Royce is…I don't know yet, but something, and Maddoc thinks I'm made of glass."

"You're fragile."

"And you're running out of time."

"Are you pissed at me or not, 'cause I can't tell anymore."

"Me either!" she snaps, and I have to hold back a laugh at how frustrated she seems with herself. "And that's the fucking thing. I want you here—don't make me say I need you here. I'm having a fucking baby, Vee, and yeah, it's gonna have a damn army behind it, but I want it to have more. Love from something tied directly to him or her like I never had. Like you never had." Her shoulders fall and she shakes her head. "So stop fucking around. There is no way you're not still hiding things you haven't told us yet. Talk to him, make him understand."

I frown. She has no way of knowing this for sure—none of them do.

Still, I say, "He's still too angry. He's not ready for more."

"Whatever you say, Victoria. Just remember, a week of hate for them burns like a lifetime."

She slowly moves closer, as if she's got more to say, but walks right by instead.

I stand there, staring at the door they all four exited from, not moving until students begin to show up, letting me know it must be getting close to the start of school.

Today sucks already.

CAPTAIN

Royce runs the towel through his hair, draping it across his neck as he drops onto the bench.

After he handled Jason, we had Mac get rid of him and opened up the locker room attached to the gym, one only used during games so we could give him some time to recoup.

He leans back, knocking his head against the locker behind us, his eyes meeting ours as he tries to snap out of it.

"I'm good," he rasps, a small grin appearing next. "Him, not so much."

Suddenly the locker room doors open, and Victoria rushes in, Mac behind her.

"We said let nobody in."

He lifts his hands. "I know, man, but she—"

"Where's your phone?" Victoria cuts him off, moving closer. "Where are any of your phones?"

I frown, patting my pocket to find it empty.

Royce digs his out, waving it around. "Broke or dead." He shrugs, his arm flopping back to his side.

Maddoc glances at Raven as she pulls his from her hoodie. "I didn't hear it ring."

He grabs it, looking at the screen. "Missed calls from Dad and Maybell."

Panic sets in, and I jump to my feet. I snag it, glaring from it to Victoria.

My dad answers on the first ring. "She's okay."

My shoulders fall, and I slouch against the locker, but then I hear her little whines in the background and turn, my hand coming up to rub at the back of my neck.

"What's wrong?" My chest constricts. "Was she crying?"

Royce tosses his towel and quickly finishes getting dressed while Maddoc stands, grabbing his and Raven's backpacks off the floor.

Suddenly Maybell is on the phone. "Boy."

My heart beats wild in my chest, and I squeeze my eyes shut. "Talk, Ms. Maybell." I dig my keys from my pocket.

"She's all right, but she's fussin', wants her daddy now."

"Daddy!" Zoey begins to cry.

My stomach turns, and I nod, already rushing out, my brothers on my tail. "I'm…I'm on my way."

I start jogging but freeze, looking back to Raven, taking quick steps to keep up.

She jerks to a stop, shaking her head with a glare. "Go. Now. We'll get there."

My eyes slide to Victoria, just behind them. "She stays."

Mac nods, and I take off in a full sprint, Royce at my side, school forgotten.

Daddy's on his way, baby girl.

CHAPTER 13
VICTORIA

"She stays." Captain's tone is hard and leaves no room for argument, but nobody could miss the heavy air of worry surrounding him.

He and Royce run off, and not a minute later, they're peeling out of the parking lot.

Mac nods his head to the others, pushing the alarm button on his car.

Raven slides in front of me. "Don't piss him off. Stay here. I'll find you if it's serious," she promises when she doesn't have to.

My mind spins as I consider if I should listen, behave as he wants me to.

I squeeze my eyes shut, a small growl escaping as I spin on my heels and head back inside the school. Maddoc, Raven, and Mac drive off behind me.

My steps slow when I spot Chloe leaning against the doorframe, her eyes following Mac. "We'll never be on their level, will we?"

When I don't respond, she looks my way.

"Come on, Victoria." She tilts her head. "I know you fucked up somewhere, and it's no secret I tried to fuck over Raven when she first came to Brayshaw." She sighs and looks off. "I love Mac, but I'd be lying if I said I wasn't jealous of his position with this family. My dad ran their security all my life, was their most trusted man, and he isn't even allowed to answer his phone if I'm in the same room. Every call, he steps out…away from me." She meets my gaze only to look away again. "Worst part is it's no one's fault but my own."

I eye her a long moment, not understanding why she'd open up to me but somehow knowing she has no one else to admit this shit to.

Her dad embodies Brayshaw, she was born to be a part of it, and she fucked it up.

I get it.

I try to walk back inside, away from someone I don't trust, who doesn't trust me, but my feet don't move me.

I hold in my groan and dig into my backpack, pulling out a half a joint.

I already ran out of second period. What's the rest of the day?

It takes Chloe a second, but then she looks over.

A grin twitches her lips, and she shrugs, pushing off the wall.

I follow the brunette Barbie to her little convertible and slide inside.

She adjusts her mirrors as the top goes down and puts the car in drive. "In three, two…"

Her phone rings, and she laughs, answering with a wink.

Mac's voice comes through the speakers, deep and gravelly. "Baby."

"Baby," she mimics, turning out of the parking lot.

I pull a lighter from my bag, holding the flame over the end of the joint while rolling it in my fingers to make sure it's equally lit.

"Don't make me spank that ass, gorgeous."

Chloe laughs. "Is that supposed to convince me to go back, because talk about a rebound?"

I want to roll my eyes, but a small grin forms instead.

She laughs silently when Mac growls. "Meet me at my house in a couple hours. Daddy isn't home until six."

"Done."

The line goes dead, and we both laugh.

"Only good thing about my dad working at the school is I've got more alone time at home." She looks over with a grin, holding her hand out, so I pass it over. "So I heard you stole Amber's shit that night at the warehouse?"

I shrug. "She tried to steal mine."

"I guess she did, didn't she?" A loud laugh leaves her, and she smiles. "You should pawn the purse. It's a limited-edition Cartier. Worth bank."

"It's not worth shit now."

She looks over.

"I tossed it in one of the bonfires with everything in it."

Her jaw drops, but a giggle quickly follows. "Man. It's almost cute how clueless you group home girls are." Her eyes pop back to mine. "I didn't mean that like a total asshole."

I can't help the small grin that escapes, and an easiness settles over us.

Chloe drives a little longer, pulling over at a small park, and we sit silently for a few minutes, smoking and thinking, when she asks, "Do they know?"

She wears a tight smile, and unease creeps over me.

"Do they know what?"

"My dad was head of security, Victoria," she says softly. "If there's one thing I know how to do, it's snooping without getting caught. I've seen shit the boys never have. How do you think I stayed on top before Raven showed up? I'll give you a hint—not because they liked me, but because I was aware."

"Out with it, Chloe."

"Mallory," she says instantly.

My pulse hammers against my temples, and I shift to face her full-on to try to hide it. "What about her?" My voice comes out raspier than I intended.

Chloe offers a sad smile, as if she knows I'm doomed to the end. "Do they know what you did?"

Oh fuck.

"Chloe…" I trail off, shaking my head. "You—"

"We all have secrets, Vee. Some are just bigger than others."

"Yeah?" I snap, pushing past the pressure in my chest. "And what's yours?"

"Did you notice how I kept grabbing the joint from you, twirled it around my fingers, and passed it back?"

I frown.

"I didn't take a single hit." Her eyes fall to her steering wheel before coming back to mine. "Threesomes are fun, but now I'm pregnant." She gives a small side grin, and tears fill her eyes. "And I have no idea who the dad is."

Oh. Shit.

The rest of the day is a blur of nothing, and before I know it, it's dark out. The moon's shine wants no part of this night and hides behind a heavy set of clouds, making the tree-covered dirt road even blacker, so I navigate it in the darkness.

I keep moving forward, surprised to find Maddoc pacing the driveway as my feet meet the concrete. He's so out of it, he doesn't hear me step up.

"Hey."

He whips around, a hard glare in place, but his eyes are a little wild.

"I thought everyone would be in bed."

He runs a hand over his mouth before throwing it to his side.

Okay…

My shoulders fall. "Is it safe to go up to my room or not?"

His lips clamp shut, and he curses under his breath before looking me dead in the eye and giving a curt nod.

I can't help but take it as a warning.

The second I open the door, I hear her, and my foot freezes only a step in.

My head snaps back to look at Maddoc.

The creases across his forehead deepen, and he quickly walks off.

With slow steps, I make my way up the stairs, Zoey's cries growing louder and louder with each foot closer. She wails, and then little mumbles follow, only for another heavy cry to leave her.

Sweat beads across my neck as I move closer.

Maybell is suddenly coming down the long hallway; she offers me a small, sad smile and then disappears into the bathroom, coming out just as quick with a wet rag in her hand.

I continue toward my room, pausing as I reach my door.

"Daddy, go, go away," Zoey weeps, exhaustion coating her little voice as she gasps through her tears.

My eyes widen, and I freeze.

Captain stands a few feet away, anguish painted across his face. His shoulders fall, and he looks off, helpless. "She, uh…" He swallows. "She has a fever."

My body instantly settles some, but I don't show it.

This is huge for him, new.

"It happens," I whisper, and his eyes slide back to mine.

Zoey cries behind us, and he stiffens. "She won't stop."

Royce rushes out right then. "Cap, hurry the fu—" He cuts off, his lip curling when he spots me there, but Zoey's tired sobs have him shaking his head. He looks to Captain. "I have tried every movie. She doesn't want any of them."

Movie?

Captain sighs, running his hands over his face. "Okay." He slips by me, into his room and back out quickly, stuffed animal in his hands. "I tried to call Maria."

A sense of resignation seeps from him and creeps right inside me, his misery weighing like the finest of steel.

"You did?" I know that was hard for him.

He hangs his head a moment, and then angry eyes come back to mine. "My daughter won't let us, won't let *me*, give her medicine, and I have no fucking clue what my own little girl is asking me for," he hisses, storming off down the hall.

"Maybe I do."

He jerks to a stop, half his body in the media room at the end of the hall, half in view. His hand curls around the doorframe and he hesitates a moment. He licks his lips and looks to his brother.

Royce eyes him a long moment and then turns to me as Captain disappears into the room. "Go, but don't do anything stupid."

I take a deep breath, running my hands over my jeans, and then move forward.

I spot Raven inside first; she sits at the end of one of the couches, her hair wrapped around her wrist as she watches Maybell try to comfort Zoey.

Rolland paces the back of the room, freezing when I enter.

Maybell seems to breathe a sigh of relief and slowly shifts from Zoey's view.

Her little head tips back, tear-streaked face looking up at me, cheeks red and puffy. Spotting me, she cries even louder.

She lifts her arms, but I only move a step closer. "Rora! Daddy movie. Please," she cries.

Daddy movie.

Oh shit.

I swallow, giving her a little smile. "Okay, ZoZo. Just a minute, okay?"

I turn toward Captain, who glares at me, unsure. "She wants to watch your videos."

"We tried every movie in that thing." He nods his chin toward a small box near the screen. "Whatever she wants isn't in there."

I shake my head. "She wants your videos."

"Wait." Raven shifts, looking at me. "Maria said she watches your games."

I nod. "Where's her tablet?"

Zoey starts to cry louder, and all eyes turn to her. Each blink is slower than the last. Baby girl is fighting her sleep. She sniffles, turning her head into the pillow.

I turn to Captain. “Her tablet?”

Royce slips past him, moving a blanket on the couch and picking it up.

He gives it to Captain, who hesitates a moment longer, but when Zoey starts crying again, wiping at her hair with her hands, he holds it out.

I take it and open the files, moving toward the TV stand. I look around, but all the cords are hidden in the wall, the giant TV stretching from one end to the next and mounted in.

Shit.

“I need something to plug it into.”

“I can hold it.” Captain rushes over to Zoey, helping Maybell up so he can slide in. He lifts her, sitting back with her at his side, but Zoey fights him, crying and throwing herself onto the cushion to his left.

Every inch of his face is pulled tight, and he can’t look up.

It’s as if this makes him feel incapable, shameful.

Unworthy of caring for her.

Raven stands, moving closer.

“She’s just tired, not feeling well,” I whisper, and a shred of hope seems to seep into him. “It happens.”

He holds my stare a long moment and then gives a curt nod. He wants to believe what I’m saying.

Zoey is restless, moving all around beside him.

I turn to Royce. “Your laptop—can you get it and a cord? It’ll be easier so he can hold her if she wants.”

He glares but slips out, and Raven moves to lean in where he’s just vacated.

Royce returns quickly, and I plug the laptop in, loading the videos on the screen, but I don’t click play.

Zoey pushes herself up, but she’s too sleepy to sit and falls against Captain’s shoulder.

"Daddy movie coming, Rora?" Zoey tries to catch her breath.

I smile softly, not looking across the room as I slip around the coffee table.

I lower to my knees in front of her, nodding. "It's coming, ba—" I clamp my mouth shut. "But if you want to watch, you have to take your medicine, okay?"

"I don't want to."

"Then no movie."

Captain's back shoots straight, and I know he's glaring at me, angry that I dare deny her, angry that I dare sit here and say a damn thing at all—but if she has a fever, she needs it. Not only to bring it down, but to make her feel okay enough to sleep, but then Zoey's little cries soften, and she scoots herself to the edge, her feet now dangling in front of me.

"It's yucky?" she asks.

I nod, lifting my fingers up to indicate a little bit.

Suddenly Maybell is there holding it out, but Zoey doesn't look at her; she starts tugging at the strings hanging from my zip-up.

"Rora do it." She scoots closer to me, still fighting for a normal breath.

I blindly grab the little plastic dispenser, reaching out for her sippy cup that she must have kicked over.

"Ready?" I ask.

She tips her head all the way back, opening her mouth, and I pour it in, quickly handing her her water.

She makes a face, whining a little, and then takes a drink as she scoots back again.

"Good job, mama."

She smiles, drags her stuffed train into her chest, and climbs into Captain's lap.

He quickly opens up to let her settle in, kissing her head as he wraps his arms around her, his eyes closing a moment as he does.

I quickly look away, feeling all the attention in the room now focused on me.

I press play, and within seconds, the boys' laughter fills the room as the videos of them practicing basketball play on the small screen.

Right as I stand, Maddoc is sliding into the room with a tense expression. His eyes go straight to Zoey, and his shoulders relax some. He tugs Raven from Royce, and all three step closer, glancing at the screen from behind the couch.

"What is this?" Royce asks.

Nobody speaks, though, the answer obvious.

It starts with them practicing at the park, but it'll switch to their game soon.

"Ms. Maybell," Rolland whispers, finally having stopped pacing. "I'll drive you back to the house. I think we'll be okay through the night now."

My shoulders tense, and I go to walk past Captain and Zoey, but she kicks her foot out, blocking my leg.

"Hu-mon, Rora. Wanna watch him?"

My mouth opens, but nothing comes out. I force my lips together and begin shaking my head, but then Captain's foot slides forward, hitting mine, and my eyes jolt up.

I guess to deny her right now is too much, as tension weighs in his gaze, a silent plea he shares only with me. There's a warning there, too, indicating I better not tell her no, even if I want to.

My stomach turns as I look her way and nod.

"Heck yeah, ZoZo." I drop onto the plush carpet several spaces away but where I can still see the screen.

On the video, the boys goof around, trying to make trick shots and dunk on each other.

When Zoey's tearful voice says, "And one," right as Captain does on the video, soft chuckles fill the room.

Something inside me settles, all while a knot forms in my chest as I remember my place, or lack thereof.

Another minute or two passes, and in my peripheral, I see Royce slowly make his way out as Maddoc moves closer, his hand coming down on Cap's shoulder.

Captain nods, and they too leave, the lights dimming as they exit.

And then it's just us.

I chance a glance at Zoey, who seems to be wide awake now, eyes glued to the screen.

She catches me looking and smiles, lifting her head.

Captain freezes when she climbs off him and crawls across the cushion, laying her head right where my elbow is pressed.

She doesn't say anything, just lies there, and I drink her in, knowing I might not have another opportunity to be near her like this.

I drop my arm, placing my chin on my hand, and stare at her.

She giggles, stretching in to rub her nose along mine.

"Baby kisses," I dare to whisper.

"Butterfly hugs," she tries to whisper back.

I chuckle lightly at her pronunciation and horrible whisper, and then my eyes slice toward Captain.

He watches her, a heavy strain in his brows, defeat in his demeanor, and I feel like a complete asshole.

He was finally able to comfort her as he's fought to find a way to all night, and here I am, taking this from him—another first of hers he's missing, holding her when she's sick.

I risk his anger, should he give it to me later, and turn back to Zoey. "Can you move over for me, ZoZo?"

She does, so I climb on the couch beside her, and as I had hoped, she chooses her daddy's lap to lay her head on.

I don't glance at Captain, but I can sense the relief slowly settling into him as Zoey's breathing grows steady, her eyes glued to the screen as she watches her favorite show.

CAPTAIN

Me.

I take a deep breath, running my hand over Zoey's hair.

Her eyes flutter heavier as she begins to fall asleep, but every time my voice is heard on the screen, they fly open, and damn if an overwhelming sense of calm doesn't spread through me, taking every ounce of tension and uncertainty with it.

For the very first time since I learned I was a dad…I believe it.

I believe, deep in my core, with every thread of my soul, every inch of who I am, I was meant for this.

For her.

For the beautiful, smart, courageous little girl who is half of me but owns every piece.

All my baby girl wanted tonight, while I stood convinced this was the proof I feared would show itself—that I wasn't enough for her—was to watch videos of me. To feel close to me in a way she must have become accustomed to.

This. These clips are how she felt me, came to love me, grew close when I wasn't within her reach.

She must have watched them often, to have our phrases memorized.

She had me with her all along.

The videos aren't clean—you still get our slang and some cussing here and there—but it's not vulgar or anything too bad. It's us.

At the park, at the school, even in gym.

It's as if it was purposely filmed this way, left true and honest, so Zoey, while away, could get to know the real us, unfiltered, unedited, and in our element.

My eyes close and I inhale deeply, pulling every bit of this moment into myself I can, when suddenly, the cushion dips beside me.

My eyes fly open and look over.

Victoria has her gaze locked where Zoey's feet lie in her lap and gingerly begins to slide away, freezing when my hand shoots across to capture her kneecap.

Weary brown eyes hit mine, searching. "I… She's sleeping," she whispers, unsure, as if I might not have noticed.

I did. Still, for some reason, my hand moved to stop her.

Hers suddenly falls on top.

I frown at the contact. "I told you not to touch me."

"Yeah," she whispers. "I know."

Something in me stings.

I don't know why I reached for her, to help keep Zoey sleeping, maybe, but that doesn't explain why it takes more effort than I'd like to admit to let go.

I do, but she doesn't move right away.

Victoria hesitantly reaches over to drag the back of her hand over Zoey's forehead. Deep-brown eyes lift to mine. "Her fever is gone."

I nod, my brows furrowing. Noticed that too.

She manages to stand and begins walking past but freezes when the video changes to one of us playing on the school courts.

It's more recent, toward the end of the season.

"Should I turn it off?" she asks.

But I just keep staring at her, unsure of what to say, torn between commanding her to stay and wanting her to want to.

Does she want to?

I say nothing, instead focusing on the screen as I shake my head.

She hustles from the room.

Several minutes go by, and I find myself chuckling when Royce dances across the court, having dunked on Maddoc, completely unaware he's flipping him off as he comes to me for a high five.

And then Raven's voice is heard saying, "I don't give a shit."

I grin, wondering if she'll be in this one, but then the screen is fumbled around, now facing the grass, a whispered, cut-off "fuck" following.

My body jolts forward, and Zoey stirs in my lap, so I quickly steel myself as the video ends, rolling right into the next one.

Wait.

I stretch my arms forward as much as I can, keeping my body in place as best possible, and grip the edge of the laptop, lifting it up.

Thankfully, the cord attached to the tablet is long enough and it doesn't fall, so I set the laptop on the cushion and tug the cord until the tablet is in reach.

I rewind the clip, listening carefully.

And I do it again and again until my shoulders fall.

I turn the volume up higher, playing it one more time.

"I don't give a shit." Raven chuckles.

Her voice isn't close, some scrambling follows and then…

"Fuck."

Fuck…

Victoria.

CHAPTER 14
CAPTAIN

Scooping Zoey into my arms, I slowly make my way to her room, laying her on top of her comforter and covering her instead with a thin sheet.

I feel her forehead once again and slowly step out, pulling the door shut.

I go to step into my room, but for some reason I toss the tablet onto my bed and keep moving forward, straight down the hall until I'm outside Victoria's door.

I glance over my shoulder to find Royce's is closed and then face forward.

Hers isn't—at least not all the way.

My palm flattens on the wood, and I push, my breathing growing more labored as it slowly sways open, revealing darkness inside.

But I see her.

So she does sleep in the bed, but not under the covers…

Her hair somehow glows against the deep-blue pillowcase.

I know she's awake; I hear her swallow.

I step inside, coming to stand at the foot of her bed as she pushes into a seated position.

Long blond hair spills along her shoulders, falling all around her.

I make my way to the left side of the bed, and her neck cranes to follow.

My knuckles come up, but I don't have to guide her—her head lifts on its own.

The darkness complies with my unspoken need, granting me vision and allowing me a glimpse of her face.

Hope and horror.

Such a deadly combination on you, Beauty.

She slowly slides her legs over the edge of the bed, the smooth sound of satin brushing skin sending an unforgiving zing down my spine.

Her posture shifts as she rises from the bed, body begging to be closer to mine.

She's the reason Zoey took the medicine, the reason she calmed enough to fall asleep.

She shouldn't know how to do any of that.

She shouldn't know my daughter at all.

But she does.

She made those videos, gave my baby something I couldn't.

Gave me something…

My knuckle stretches out, my hand sliding down so I can grip the hollow of her throat, and she pushes against my palm.

My fingers twitch against her warmed skin, and she shudders, her broken breath reaching my lips.

My shoulders curl a bit, bringing me in more, and her hand comes up to grip my wrist.

Her hold is tight, but she shakes.

My pulse beats heavy in my palm…or maybe it's hers that I feel spiking, growing faster and faster, louder and fucking louder. It's all I hear, and it drives me closer.

Her spine straightens, torso stretching to erase more distance, and suddenly those baby-doll lips are in reach.

I dare the tiniest of tastes.

Big fucking mistake.

My eyes close, my forehead tipping forward to meet hers as I fight a growl.

She shivers—hard.

Every fucking inch of her shakes before me.

In need.

In want.

In fear?

But not of what I'll do, of what I might not…

I lean forward, bringing my bottom lip between hers, and then drag it down until hers is nestled in mine, and I bite, gentle but firm.

Her eyes close in pleasure, and my cock is pleased, twitching and flexing inside my jeans.

She gasps, and it takes all I've got not to swallow it.

So I play with her neck as I would her mouth and crush my lips to the base of it, gliding along to the hollow of her throat.

Fuck if a heavy need doesn't fly through my veins, sending zings through my fingertips and toes. A need that grows deeper when Victoria doesn't only take what I give but sighs on contact.

A deep, heavy exhale that has her back arching high, driving her chest into mine, opening up her neck even more for me, and my tongue glides along, tasting and taking—and it's not enough.

I don't know if she lies back or if I nudge her myself, but when my eyes open, she's under me, my shirt's on the floor, her heated hands are running up my sides.

So smooth, so foreign.

So fucking familiar, like my soul already knows hers.

The thought settles, digging deeper, and I lower my body, holding myself up with my forearms as I bring my leg between hers.

I apply the slightest of pressure, desperate to feel and angered when I do.

Her eyes roll closed as her excitement coats my kneecap, and I slide against the wet spot of her underwear.

Her breathing grows heavy, and I bite the inside of my cheeks.

"You ruined everything," I tell her, sliding my mouth to her ear and down her neck in a torturously slow manner. I kiss her there, my fists tightening in the blanket as I pull back to look her in the eye. "And I hate you for it."

Her chest rises and falls in quick spurts, each second dragging into the next as she stares, waiting. Knowing.

It's even more infuriating.

Intoxicating.

Reckless.

I slide from the bed, and she's quick to fly up with me, her eyes widening in want when I grip her knees as I drop to mine. She lowers her chin, studying me through her long, dark lashes. With one quick tug, I've got her legs hanging over the bed.

She gasps, her head tipping back, exposing the skin of her neck, but I grip her chin and hide the tempting area. She leans in, but I yank away.

Her legs part, and all I can think is how perfectly I'd fit between them.

Fuck.

I growl, gripping her upper arms, and her tongue slides along the backs of her teeth, drawing my attention to the devilish red determined to take me to hell should I allow it, leading, forcing me near when all I want to do is fucking run and run fast.

She's taking power without permission.

Proof is when my mouth reaches for hers, but I somehow freeze there, a lick away, my eyes snapping to hers.

"I don't think so, Sleeping Beauty," I whisper, and her legs open farther, sending a tremor down my spine. Fuck. "The lies on your lips burn too deep to meet mine. Keep them away."

A small crease forms on her forehead, but she doesn't fight me.

I place my hand on her chest, spreading my fingers across her collarbone, and she pulls in a long inhale. I push.

It takes her a few seconds, but she finally gives in and falls back, tilting her head so she can look at me on my knees between her open thighs. Her brown eyes darken, eyelids lowering, and she lays her head back, her fingertips brushing the edge of her face.

A light breeze blows through the open window then, and goose bumps spread along her thighs, making her shiver. It's almost enough for me to tear away from her.

Fuck me, the sight, her on her back shivering and shaking in front of me, and all from the wind.

She's gonna lose her fucking mind.

I bring my hands to her panties, not looking away from where my fingertips dip into the cotton material, and tug. I chance a quick glance up when she lifts her hips but quickly focus back on what I want to see most.

What I need to see, taste—drive wild.

As wild and fucked in the head as I feel tonight, everything burns like a lie.

What she did and didn't do.

What I did and didn't do.

What she should have done but hasn't.

What I could but won't do…

I feel like a fraud in my own life, weak and unsure, and I hate it.

But this, her in front of me, terribly gorgeous and wanting, is no lie.

It's real.

And right now, tonight, that's what I need.

It's selfish and stupid, but it's happening…

I want her and can't fight it. No matter how hard I try to convince myself to stay away, it only serves as a bid to get closer.

Her bottoms slide past her hips, but I use all my control not to peek yet, forcing my gaze to the floor as I tug her legs in enough to slip them off completely, and she drags her legs right back where she wants them.

Wide the fuck open, but still, I don't cheat myself by looking.

My fingers begin at her ankles, my eyes following the left one as I trace along her calves, up over her knees until my palms are flat on her thighs. My hands twitch, squeezing into her soft skin, and a harsh exhale escapes her.

What a body you hide, Beauty.

Tanned and toned.

I push higher, my brows crashing together when a heavy, shadowed ink catches my attention. I lean closer, my heated breath now a gift to her skin, and she jerks in response.

A tattoo.

She has a tattoo on her upper thigh that stretches up under her shirt.

Purple petals, both frozen and falling, curved and cut, bleeding an icy blue, and hanging from a curved barbed wire designed to play as if it's ivy, giving the flowers life while taking it just the same.

Ruined but resilient.

My heart pounds heavily as I push the thin material of her top up to see the rest, but her hand flies down, clamping around mine in a death grip.

Her nostrils flare, a heavy frown taking over her face, and fuck if a pressure doesn't fall on my chest, no matter how hard I fight it away.

What…

Oh shit. Her scars…

I relax my hold, and slowly, hers falls away as she shifts her attention to my hands as I trail them across the image, ready to take both our minds to one place and erase everything else.

My fingertips test the skin at her hip bones, kneading and rubbing. I grip her there, nice and tight, and squeeze—a perfect fucking fit.

I lick my lips and, as slow as I can manage, slide my eyes to the prize in the center, pink and perfect. She's not bare as I imagined but precisely trimmed, shaped to mirror her body, and curved just right.

She's not shy, doesn't try to hide, but lies there offering me a seat at the king's table.

I bring my pinkie up, sliding it against the deep center, and I'm met with slick, warm proof of her arousal. My blood runs hot.

My eyes fly to hers. Her teeth come down to punish her bottom lip right as my finger glides across my own mouth, my tongue greedily following to get that first, fevering fucking taste.

Oh fuck.

My head falls back some, and I groan, my dick now fully hard and straining in my sweats, pushing tight against my boxers. Too tight.

I reach down, quickly shoving them to my thighs to free it, and an airy moan leaves her, sending a jolt through my body.

No, no. Can't have her taking control of my body's reactions.

I quickly grip her by the wrists, locking her palms on my shoulders, and squeeze.

A quick and heavy pounding fires within my chest, growing stronger with each beat as every nerve in my body wakes, wild and wanting. I lower until my breath is fanning across her, right over her swollen little clit.

She shakes, and I'm not even fucking touching her.

I pointedly move my eyes to her grip on me and slide them back to her gaze.

"Not a sound…"

Talk with your touch. Your moans will be my ruin.

Her head lifts as mine falls, my mouth closing around her clit, and her knees glide higher on the mattress, pushing her closer to me.

She buries my face between her legs, begging for all I've got, and tonight, I've got a lot.

I nip at her, licking and sucking, and when her body starts to quake, my tongue vibrates with it as I slip my left hand into my pocket, pulling it out just as fast, and press the cool brass against her slit, her body a frenzy of sensations—my heated tongue, the cool of the metal, the night breeze flowing through the window, and the dirty darkness we're playing in.

She gasps, flying off the bed, her hand slamming over her mouth in the process.

"There you go," I breathe. "Hide from me."

I fucking need you to.

"You're going to come for me, right against the brass."

She does, her pulse beating through her pussy.

"Mm," I moan, placing the edge of the pinky knuckle at her opening, and rolling my fist, coating my token from one end to the other with her cum.

With my left hand still playing along her center, I grab my cock with my right and pump. Slow to start, but as her legs fall open with satisfaction, I go harder, and her head lifts, her eyes falling to my arm she can't see the end of as my lower half is hidden by the rise of her mattress.

Her gaze snaps to mine, and I hold it, staring right in her eyes as I work toward my own release, thoughts of her heat in my head, her flavor on my tongue.

Her body slick on mine.

Her lips part as I pull my fist to my mouth, my tongue coming out for a heavy sweep along the brass, cleaning her from it completely. I groan, long and loud, my cum following the sound. I shift quickly, catching it with my palm.

I don't look back at her, don't wait for my body to settle or my heart rate to drop.

I pull up my sweats, place my knuckles back in my pocket, and walk out, but I freeze right outside her door, when her whispered words reach me, and I'm not even sure if they were supposed to.

"Hate me today, Cap," she says to herself. "But careful. You might just love me tomorrow."

Fuck.

CHAPTER 15
CAPTAIN

I fucked up.

I tested and tasted the deceiving forbidden fruit when I should have stomped it beneath my feet—a flavor so sweet I want more, a sight so gripping I'll never forget.

She was accepting, greedy.

Gorgeous.

Fucking dangerous.

It should make this easier, fighting and denying, knowing there're parts of her she doesn't want to share—what a story the marks on her skin must tell—but it doesn't.

Somehow, as sickening as it is to admit, it makes it worse.

She doesn't trust me either.

What's worse is the way the knowledge makes me ache.

I want her to give me all the things a woman gives her man—her faith, her heart, her heat.

For what, though?

What will I do with those things once I have them?

Even more frightening, what will she do when she realizes she's stolen parts of mine?

I close my notebook, tucking it back into the drawer at the side of my bed, and lift my laptop from my comforter, rewinding and pressing play for what must be the hundredth fucking time, each replay making her voice clearer and clearer.

"Cap. Yo," Royce shouts from the stairwell. "You up there?"

I let the rest of the video play out, then hit pause, and toss it aside. "Yeah," I call back, swinging my legs over the side of my bed.

He comes around the corner as I run my hands through my hair.

He frowns, nodding. "What's going down?"

I hang my head a moment before slightly lifting it and glancing up at him. "She recorded the videos."

At first, he frowns, tilting his head a bit, and then his eyes widen. "Wait, what?"

I sigh, letting my arms fall to the keyboard.

When I made my way back to my room last night, I did so after having snagged Zoey's tablet from the media room so I could copy all the files to my hard drive.

"Listen." I rewind it a few seconds and press play.

Royce hesitantly looks from it to me and back, nodding.

He steps closer, watching us fuck around on-screen. Like me, a hint of a grin finds his lips as Raven talks, but then his shoulders straighten, and the video cuts off. I pause before it can move into the next one.

He turns to me with a frown, looks me over, easily spotting my lack of sleep. "I'm guessing you already watched it a solid dozen times to be sure?"

"It's her, Royce. Raven must have been walking up this time, and she cut off before she was seen."

"And she had to hide it 'cause we didn't know she knew about Zoey."

I nod.

He licks his lips as his hands find his hips. "Huh. That explains the back-and-forth footsteps in the hall last night."

A scoff leaves me, but a groan quickly follows, and I drag my hands down my face. I let them fall to my sides and look to my brother.

"What if she weren't here? I wouldn't have been able to make Zo happy, help her feel better."

"Stop." His forehead tightens and he steps in to grip my shoulder, his eyes firm. "None of us have ever felt more worthless or weak or any other fucked-up thought you could possibly have than we did last night. You were alone in none of it. We fucking felt it. Shit, we feel what you're feeling right now. She's ours too, brother. She hurts, we hurt."

A heavy sense of comfort weighs on me, mixing with the ache of helplessness and overwhelming me to the point I have to look away.

Royce steps toward the door, and I nod, moving with him.

"Let's go tell the others."

We make our way down the stairs, through the billiard room, and out the back door.

As we step around the large pergola and into the grass, Zoey's animated voice reaches us, and Royce swings a grin my way. "Thank fuck she's feelin' a little better, and it's cool enough out."

I nod. "She was sweating pretty bad this morning, so I'm hoping tonight won't be a repeat. Not sure I can handle that."

"Yeah, brother. You can." He nudges me with his shoulder. "But I sure as fuck hope you don't have to."

As we get to the curve of the yard, my family comes into view, and I quickly throw my arm out to stop Royce's advance.

His head snaps my way with a frown, but then he looks out and a light nod leaves him.

Maddoc sits in the grass with his legs bent, feet planted on the ground while Zoey sits on her knees between them.

She has something in her hand and slowly opens it.

Maddoc darts his out, attempting to take whatever it is, but she quickly yanks it into her chest.

She laughs loudly, her little head tipping back. She falls to her butt when Maddoc reaches out to tickle her. After a moment, she pushes the little loose curls from her face and smiles at him.

Her mouth is moving, but I can't hear what she says.

I look to my brother, watching as a smile grows, one I've

never seen. It's soft and gentle, but there's a strain at the edge of his eyes.

Raven stands, having spotted me, and tiptoes behind him, so we move forward until we reach her.

She spins, leaning into me as she pulls the sleeves of her hoodie to her mouth.

She watches Maddoc through tender eyes. "Last night..." She shakes her head. "I've never seen him act that way. He was terrified, fully. Completely." She glances between us, and I'd swear her eyes gloss over, but it's hard to tell, they're already so light. "I think, for the first time, he realized there're gonna be situations where he'll be completely powerless."

She looks back to Maddoc, who lays his hands in Zoey's as she places her palms out for him, not taking his eyes off his niece for a second.

"He hadn't spoken a word all day. Not one." Her lips twitch, and she meets my gaze. "Not until she came charging into the kitchen, blew past me and Rolland, and walked right up to him, asking if he wanted to go play."

I blow out a long, heavy breath, a light chuckle following.

"It's like she knew what he needed," Raven gives voice to my exact thoughts.

She's intuitive.

Zoey latches her thumb around the edge of Maddoc's hands and stands, only to let them go so she can grab his face between her hands.

She smiles as she leans in, rubbing the tip of her nose to his.

Baby kisses...

A glare takes over, and I look away, officially brought back to the issue at hand.

Victoria.

"Daddy!" My head snaps forward again, Maddoc's having now jerked our way, but he doesn't move. Doesn't tense or draw away from her.

In fact, when she climbs over his legs, he looks about ready to reach for her.

That has me smiling again.

"Daddy!" Zoey bounds forward. "Uncle D says I'm a wolf!"

I laugh, bending down to pick her up. Her eyes are a little tired, but she's got some color back. I kiss her cheek, checking her head as I say, "You tell Uncle D you're no wolf. You're a raven."

She gasps, smiling, and kicks her feet to be let down, running right back to Maddoc. "Daddy said I'm a raven!"

In time, Zoey will grow to understand what that means—the raven will lead her wolves.

Maddoc chuckles and waits for Zoey to run back to him, but she spots our dad coming around the opposite side and darts past.

"Papa, I'm a raven!" she yells as she goes.

Royce chuckles beside me, wrapping an arm around Raven and kissing her temple only to let go and move toward Maddoc.

He doesn't bother standing, so we lower beside him, Raven gripping his bicep as she drops into the grass, only to be moved onto his lap.

Maddoc looks from Royce to me, and the switch is flipped. "What is it?"

"The videos from last night."

Maddoc's frown mirrors Raven's.

"It was her; she recorded them."

"What the fuck?" Raven snaps.

"You're sure?" he asks.

I nod, looking between them, explaining how I figured it out, and they jump up, ready to watch the video for themselves, so I nod at my dad across the yard, and he lifts his hand, letting me know he's got Zoey.

We make our way to my room, and I play it for them.

They sit there, glaring at the screen.

"That's the one and only mistake I was able to find on all hundred-plus videos," I tell them when they finally focus on me.

Raven's brows jump. "Hundred-plus?"

I nod.

"How far back do these go, Cap?" Maddoc asks, his tone dark and low.

"Sophomore year," I tell them.

Maddoc and Royce jump up.

"Hold on, back the fuck up." Royce lifts his hands, shaking his head. "Sophomore year." He dips his head forward slightly. "Sophomore fucking year?"

"Zoey was a newborn..." Raven trails off.

I pull my lips in, looking at my brothers. "I want her," I throw out without pause. Sure.

"We know, brother." Maddoc eyes me.

"What do I do?"

"We're not real good at leaps of faith." Royce licks his lips, pulling his bottom one into his mouth.

"It doesn't matter." Raven shakes her head. "Look what's in front of us, what we have seen. What we do know," she stresses. "I mean, shit, you guys, why would she do this and never ask for a fucking thing? Never use it to get paid or blackmail or any other reason?"

A tremor shoots across my shoulders, and I look to the door right as she appears, saying exactly what I need to hear.

"Because I didn't do it for me."

The others' heads snap toward the door, heavy, hard glares in place.

She doesn't cower but slips inside. When she licks her lips, I force my eyes away a moment.

"Why the fuck should we believe that?" Royce crosses his arms, unable to hold back his protective nature.

She lifts a single shoulder, letting it fall back to her side. "I don't expect you to, but it is what it is."

I move toward her, and her head tips with my advance.

Heat builds in my chest at the way her eyes soften when met with mine.

"Why? Why'd you do it?"

I had no intention of whispering, but for some reason my words are low. Heard around the room but low nonetheless.

"Because she deserved it."

"She should have been with me," I force past clenched teeth, unable to swallow beyond the ache in my throat.

"But she wasn't," she breathes, sorrow woven in her words. "So I did what I thought was right, or as right as right could be then."

"You spied on us," Royce spits.

She nods but doesn't look away from me. "Yeah, I did. Every single day until Raven finally arrived, and I'd do it all over again, even if I ended up right here in the end."

Her deep-brown eyes beg me to ask, and everything inside me fights not to, screaming we can't trust her answer anyway, but closed mouths don't get fed—I want to believe in the girl in front of me.

"Why?"

Her chest falls with a silent exhale, and she says, "Because Zoey deserved to have you when she couldn't, to know you when she didn't yet. To hear the sound of your voice, to picture your face, to picture all of your faces." Her hands twitch at her sides, and I know she wants to reach out and touch me, but that's a comfort she's unsure she'll get. "You have always been her favorite show, and she's the little girl she is because of you." She looks across my family. "Because of all of you."

My eyes fall to the carpet, and I take a deep breath.

My baby girl, a healer by nature, sweet and innocent and kind, nothing like us in that sense yet everything we needed—and dare I say, at the perfect time.

Royce needed someone to love him purely before he lost all hope in himself.

Maddoc, approaching fatherhood, needed affirmed proof of goodness in our dark, twisted world.

Raven needed hope, a reason to believe she's worth the life she now lives.

My dad needed a second chance.

And me, I needed help fulfilling my purpose.

I've always felt like the father, even though my brothers are the same age. Like we're witnessing more often with Zoey, my brothers and I each have natural instincts, whether we were born this way or our lifestyle demanded the skill, I don't know, but for as long as I can remember, mine was to listen and learn, to teach and help guide. I think each of us has felt something missing at one point, and my missing piece was Zoey.

A lot happens in the course of a lifetime, and for whatever reason, becoming a father at fifteen was what I was meant for.

My eyes flick between Victoria's.

The comfort Zoey felt so easily wasn't simply because she's young and unaware but because she already loved us, each of us.

Victoria gave this to me, to my daughter, to my family.

"You said when I finally arrived." Raven steps closer, pulling my attention to her.

Victoria's brows crash together, and she licks her lips.

"It was you..." Raven lets it trail off. "You're the one who told Collins Graven, the chosen grandson of the man who raped our mothers, the person who tried to tear me away from this place, take over this town, and leave this family bleeding, who I was and when I'd be here."

"The fuck?" Royce shouts, he and Maddoc hopping to their feet.

I jerk back.

She doesn't deny it, shocking us all when she unapologetically admits an even bigger secret. "I was the one who convinced them to bring you home in the first place."

Shock flies through me, stiffening my body as I try to make sense of her words.

Raven lurches forward but freezes in place when Victoria adds, "I knew you'd be taken care of, at your own hand or theirs. I could only protect one of you."

Raven's jaw is clenched tight as she glares at her sister.

Victoria lifts her hands. "I picked her…just like you would have."

"Fuck you for what you did," she whispers and, without warning, punches a hole through the wall at the side of Victoria's head.

"Raven!" Maddoc barks, bounding toward her.

"And fuck you even more for being right," she growls, rushing out.

"Goddamn it," Maddoc hisses and chases after her.

I stare at the empty doorway, slowly swinging my eyes back to Victoria.

All the trouble we dealt with the last several months, the pain she caused my family, almost cost us my brother when he disappeared as Raven slipped from his grasp, both of us landing ourselves in the hospital…

My baby girl being safe and away from it all…

A heavy weight descends on my chest, and I can hardly fucking breathe, can't look at her.

I know I'd cave right here, right now, if I did.

I'd fall to my fucking knees, grab and pull her close, and maybe I should, but I don't have to decide, and the struggle only gets worse when Victoria proves to understand me, walking out before I'm forced to face her.

Royce glares at the empty doorway.

It takes him a minute, but he locks his gaze with mine. "Maybe I'm more fucked-up in the head than I even knew, but if she did what she just said she did, protected my niece like that, your daughter, then we owe her our respect if nothing else."

My heart beats uncontrollably against my ribs. "She lied to our faces."

He shakes his head, his eyes dark and tortured, angry. He walks for the door, pausing just outside it to glance back at me. "She lied, yeah, or more hid shit—don't ask, don't fuckin' tell type. I'm fuckin' pissed about it too, brother, believe that, but, man. That lie…who was it for?"

Who was it for?

My brows dig in, and he nods.

Fuck.

CHAPTER 16
VICTORIA

It's six in the morning, the sun just beginning to show its colors above the trees when Raven drops in the chair beside me.

I didn't sleep for shit, so finally I stepped in the shower, and here I am.

My eyes slide her way, spotting that her hair is as wet as mine, so she must have had the same issue—a mind that won't shut up.

She knows I'm looking at her, but she's stubborn and holds still for a solid minute before finally facing me head-on.

"You were right yesterday."

"You already said that."

She glares. "Yeah, but there's still a big-ass difference."

A sourness coats my mouth, making it water. I don't want to know what she's thinking, but I ask anyway. "And what's that?"

"I risked myself for them once I knew who they were; you did it having never spoken to them in your life." Her frown deepens and she looks away. "I'm not sure I would have done the same for strangers."

I scoff, not having expected anything remotely close to that to come from her. "Please, Rae." I shake my head and stand.

"I'm serious," she snaps, but there's a hint of vulnerability mixed with her standard fuck-off approach.

"So am I. You didn't risk yourself knowing who they were, Raven. You did it because something told you you should." While she continues to face forward, her eyes find mine. "You saw what

I did. We felt it, the pull toward them, deep in our gut, beneath our bones like nothing ever before."

After a quiet moment, she whispers, "Why did we feel it?"

"Because this is where we belong. We were born Graven, Rae, born part of this town, but this is where we belong."

Her lip twitches the smallest bit. "You're a leg out, Victoria."

I chuckle despite myself and nod. "Yeah, but that means I've still got one in, right?"

"An optimist."

"A survivor."

Her features smooth, and after a moment she nods, a faraway look in her eye as she faces forward. "That's all we do, isn't it? One thing we'll never escape, no matter where we are…or end up," she adds for my sake. "We just…forever keep trying to survive and hope we don't fuck up everything along the way."

Raven looks at her wedding ring, a black band with a purple crown she wears on her middle finger instead of the traditional one, three tiers, three jewels, each representing the guys who gave her life meaning. Her hands then fall to her little bump and stay there.

I don't respond, and she doesn't say another word, both of us likely lost in thoughts of all the times we were forced to do just that.

We sit until the boys come searching for her, but they don't speak, leaving her where she sits.

It's not until Captain's engine roars to life and Maddoc steps around the house with her backpack draped over his shoulder that she stands. She turns to me, her eyes lifting over my head a moment before bringing them back. She holds her hand out.

When I don't instantly slide mine inside hers, she rolls her eyes. "Grab it, Victoria."

I do, but I don't give her any of my weight, pushing to my feet. "Pretty sure I'm the one who should be helping you up."

"Yeah, well." She lets go, backing away. "Maybe you owe me now."

I turn to find Royce and Captain standing there, the loop of my backpack wrapped around Cap's middle finger.

They move closer, so I reach out to grab it, but Cap's frown deepens as he pulls his gaze from mine, and the two walk right by me.

So I follow, and off to school we go.

We're sitting in the cafeteria during lunch hour, my eyes pointed where Tisha and Chloe talk quietly, Mac chatting with his buddy across the table from them, when warm, calloused knuckles slide along my neck, causing me to jump.

Captain pulls my head toward his, lifting my chin.

"This isn't the first time I've caught you staring their way. I'm starting to wonder if you're looking to party like Royce," he says, face blank.

I pull my lips to the side. "Wonder or worry?"

"Don't play," he whispers, his fingertips sliding along my skin, watching me closely.

"I'm not the one playing," I tell him. "Not sure how much clearer I can be, Cap, but I don't want anyone else."

"Get up," he says.

My head pulls back. "Why?"

"Because I said. Get. Up." The tone in which he gives his quiet command causes a hot ache to form in my throat.

I tap my fingers along the tabletop to delay and then push to my feet, spinning to face him. I'm tugged into his lap.

His arms instantly come under mine, palms flattening on the inside of my thighs and nudging them the slightest bit open.

He kicks a leg out, settling in, and goes right back to talking with Maddoc at our sides.

I chance a look at Raven and the others, but they don't acknowledge his move in any way. Raven continues to lean over

Royce's shoulder, pointing at the screen of his phone while he laughs, and Maddoc is focused on Captain.

"Breathe," Captain whispers in my ear, leaving his mouth there to tickle against my skin.

My ass cheeks clench against him, and he squeezes my thighs in warning, but an accidental chuckle leaves me and his head jerks toward me again.

I pull my shoulder in, meeting his eyes over it.

"Something funny?" he rasps.

I shift, swinging my legs over so my side is against his chest now.

That gets Royce's and Raven's attention.

"No, Cap. Nothing's funny, but if you're gonna play show-and-tell and put me on your lap, I'm gonna take full advantage of it," I say as I run my palm up his chest, knowing he won't stop me, that he can't stop me now that he's frolicking in public.

For the public.

It's a show—I know that.

He wants to make sure I'm watched, tracked and trailed by the many eyes of Brayshaw, and for that to happen with precision, he has to show the need for it.

Captain, being a guy of few words, of course has chosen the visual.

He might have deemed me a Bray girl, but for everyone to believe it, action has to follow.

I know him, though, and that's far from the only reason I'm sitting where I am.

He's caving, and I'm so ready for it.

He glares, but all that drives it is heat. "Be smart, Beauty."

I ignore him, hiding my grin as I tuck my face beside his. "Did you wash your face before you went to bed the other night, Cap?" I whisper, and this time, it's him who clenches against me, his dick flexing along with his hands on my thighs. "Or did you roll over through the night, waking to taste me all over again… over and over…again?"

"Stop," he hisses.

Damn, that strain in his voice…

My grin spreads. "Give me your answer, and I'll tell you how I spent those last few hours that night, but so you know, the answer isn't sleeping…"

His fingers wrap around my bicep, and he tugs me back, a wild eagerness in his eyes as they move between mine. Around us, his brothers fight their laughter, only to cough when he gives them hardened glares.

They come back to mine a full shade of deeper blue. He studies me a moment, frown deepening by the second. "Touch yourself again, Beauty. I dare you."

"And if I do?"

"You won't. You need something, say it."

"I need something." I raise a brow.

Surprise has him falling back.

And then he jumps from his seat, and once again I'm hanging half over his shoulder, hiding my face as I'm carried from the cafeteria on the shoulder of the gentle giant.

Captain doesn't stop until we've reached the gym. He throws open the door and charges right inside, shouting "out" to the few inside playing basketball during lunch.

They drop the ball on sight, grab their bags, and go, not one batting a lash or even giving a questioning glance at the dude with a chick hanging across his body.

In the next second, I'm flipped into his arms.

I yelp, grabbing on, but just as quick, I'm laid on the freezing-cold gym floor. I gasp, and Captain's hand quickly comes up to catch it.

He glares, his eyes darkening. "No sound."

I lick his fingers and he jerks away, but he can't keep the groan in.

He starts unbuttoning my jeans, and my eyes shoot wide, flying around the room.

"Anyone could walk in."

He freezes, his wild eyes coming back to mine. "Are you telling me to stop?"

I open my mouth, my heart pounding like crazy in my chest. I shake my head. "Never."

His jaw clenches, a heavy crease forming along his forehead.

Suddenly my pants are at my knees and my hand flies down to hold my shirt in place.

He tenses, but only for a moment before his finger slides along the seam of my underwear. "You touched yourself when I left, thought of me," he rasps, slipping the tip of his ring finger through the thin cotton. "Tell me what you did."

I lick my lips, and his focus falls to the contact. "No."

His glare reluctantly lifts from my mouth. "No?"

I shake my head, pushing against his touch and clenching to try for more. "You'll have to guess."

His eyes narrow. "Might take a couple tries…"

It takes a second, but then a grin slowly curls his lips and he chuckles, dragging a hand across his face. His finger leaves my underwear and suddenly he's on his back beside me, staring up at the ceiling. After a few long moments, his eyes close. "Go."

I tense, ready to speak, but he knows it's coming and cuts me off before I can.

"Now, Vee," he says quietly. "Please."

There's something in his tone, a hint of self-doubt, relief, and regret, maybe.

I nod even though he can't see me, tug my jeans up, and exit the gym.

CHAPTER 17
CAPTAIN

We're driving down the dirt road, the mansion now in view when my brother meets my eyes in the mirror.

He's with me—they both will be, no matter what move I make or when.

I spent the rest of yesterday and all fucking night trying to work through my own head, and each time I came out even more unsure—a rarity for me.

I'm supposed to be the positive brother, the one who breaks down each scenario and helps his brothers see what their anger and defiance hide, only now I'm on the opposite side. I'm full of blurred rage, craving defiance, and ready to risk all that I am.

I want to let go of all we are to uphold—respect, loyalty, trust—and gamble everything for what might be...my everything.

For *who* might be my everything.

Zoey will always be the most important person in my life, but Maddoc will soon have both—a child to love and protect and a woman who was made just for him.

Is it wrong to want both?

Is it wrong to want her despite her lies?

The more I'm around her, the harder it gets to remain angry. I thought I could bury everything under the sheets, focus on the physical, and the rest would fade away, but I'm learning I'm not built like that.

Sex has always been about the moment, the sensations involved, a mutual night of fun.

I can't do that with her, and it's frustrating.

Today, when she pushed the exact button she meant to and I carried her ass to the gym, I had every intention of getting her off, curbing her appetite and mine, and then she teased.

Victoria looked me in the eye, hair spread all around, arm bent and fingers barely teasing at the edge of her face. Through her words, she smiled, words that indicated a future or, at the very least, more.

More of me.

More with me.

More of us.

A strange fullness spreads through me, tightening and weighing my arms and legs. It takes effort to turn the wheel so I can curl around the driveway.

I'm losing it, my control.

Royce tips his chin, and my hands tighten against the cool leather. It's a switch, me being the one unwilling to see and him pushing me. I'm anxious and I hate it.

We were taught to trust our guts, but mine is split in fucking two, no part of me leaning any further one way than the other.

She didn't tell me she knew of my daughter, never shared Maria was her mother, never told us about the videos she recorded—all things that relate somehow to my little girl.

What else could she be hiding?

Royce's words come crashing back, forcing me to wonder if there's even a negative piece to her. Nothing I've learned tears at who she is.

Who was the lie for?

I let out a long exhale and put the SUV in park.

All my concerns fade into the background when my daughter's little hand lifts to wave even though she can't see through the windshield.

Like every day, Zoey is on the porch waiting, this time with a Popsicle in her hands.

Once our doors start to open, she begins climbing down the steps.

I glance over my shoulder, and one of my eyes is aligned perfectly, able to meet Victoria's through the small gap the opening allows.

Her face is pinched tight, flying from the open door and back to me, but light footsteps are where my focus lies, so I spin back around and move forward the last few spaces until I can pick up Zoey and toss her in the air, catching her on her way down.

She laughs and wraps one arm around me as she brings her Popsicle back to her mouth. "Look it." She licks it. "It's orange."

"It is orange, good job." I bounce her and she giggles.

"Papa said I can have it."

I chuckle and then Zoey is reaching past me.

"Uncle Bro!"

Royce roars and snags her from me, running a few feet and swinging her around.

She laughs, looking back this way.

There's a light shuffle behind me, letting me know Victoria is climbing out, but I hold my breath, forcing myself to focus straight on.

Maddoc and Raven walk around the hood, and I'd bet we're all curious to see what Zoey will do—go to them as she has every day or go to her.

"Baby!" she shouts next, and while I thought I'd feel relief, I'm no less edgy than I was five seconds ago.

I glance up at my dad on the porch, nodding lightly when he tips his chin, disappearing inside.

Zoey cups her mouth and starts talking to Raven's belly, while Maddoc bends on one knee to listen, his eyes glued to Zoey's face.

Victoria quietly closes the door and slowly steps beside me.

I don't move my eyes to hers, and she doesn't say anything,

not until Zoey notices she's there, and damn if a big, bright smile doesn't cover her face.

She drops her Popsicle and runs over.

Victoria stiffens, maybe unsure of where Zoey is headed—to her or to me—or maybe it's of how we'll react. I can't be sure, but the second it's clear, her entire aura changes.

Victoria laughs, a soft and airy sound, and throws her arms out.

"Hey, Mama!" Victoria calls with excitement.

Zoey claps and runs right up for Vee to lift her.

I can't not look.

My entire body turns to watch as Zoey's forehead falls to Victoria's.

Her hands come up to her cheeks next, and Zoey giggles.

"Look at you, ZoZo." She smiles, squeezing her. "You're all better."

She nods and, like second nature, gently brushes her nose with Victoria's. "And you're all better too?"

Victoria inhales deeply, her eyes closing, a smile I can hardly handle directed at my little girl—the most honest smile I've ever witnessed.

Real, loving.

Fuck.

She loves my daughter?

My mind races, panic flaring, and I'm ready to snag Zoey away, but Royce comes up, clamping a hand on both of their shoulders, and both their heads move his way.

"Oh, yeah, Zoey Bear. VicVee's real good. Daddy made her feel all sorts of better."

"Oh my God." Raven shakes her head, her hand coming up to hide her smile.

My muscles lose some tension, and I too fight a chuckle, but then Victoria's eyes slide to mine briefly, and I'd swear a hint of color rises on her cheeks.

"Yay!" Zoey, completely oblivious, shouts, kicking her feet

until she's set down and runs back for the house. "Hu-mon, guys! Ms. Maybell maked cookies! Chocolate ones, Uncle Bro!"

Light chuckles float across us, and slowly everyone moves for the house, but Victoria only makes it a single step before she pauses, glancing at me over her shoulder.

She doesn't say anything, and when she walks away, she doesn't go into the house like I thought she would. As far as I can tell, her smile never falters as she steps around the property, disappearing from my view.

And all I can think of is how I want her back in sight.

Victoria smiled at Zoey as if Zoey was all she saw.

All she needed.

All she had.

I will never unsee the sight.

Never.

As if that was all I was supposed to write, the ink in my pen dies, leaving me to stare at the half-blank page.

So I push to stand, slip from my room and down the hall to hers.

Victoria sits on her windowsill, and as her head lifts to mine, I'd swear she was waiting for me.

I walk inside, closing the door behind me, and she stays right where she is, her eyes locked on mine across the room.

Tonight, I'll try something different; I'll write the memory inside my head, for only me to reread and interpret.

Lust or more?

It's an unnecessary question.

I want more than what her body can give, this much I know, but am I ready to admit this to her, to act on it?

I don't know, but neither of us need that answer tonight.

I grip my shirt by the collar and tug it over my head, letting it fall to the floor as I make my way toward her.

Her hand shifts, now gripping the framing, and she stretches her spine, her chest inflating with her full inhale.

My fingers slide across her throat, eyes falling to the contact when she swallows, as I knew she would. I let my hands glide farther down, until the stretchy material of her top is hooked around my fingers.

I tug, and slowly, she rises to her feet.

I trace along her collarbone, down the edges of her breasts and ribs, until I'm wrapping them around her ass. I bend, gliding my hands along the underside of her thighs, and lift her from the floor.

Her arms and legs lock around me, and she tugs herself closer, her lips now right above mine, but I quickly dip my head into the crook of her slender neck.

My cock swells as I bite at the softness there, and her head falls back, her hair grazing my arms wrapped tight around her frame.

I open my lips, sliding my tongue along her satiny skin, and a heavy groan escapes.

Her muscles clench, hands gliding into my hair.

I take the few backward steps needed to sit on the mattress, leaving her to straddle me, legs still wrapped and locked at my back.

Victoria wastes not a second, seeking out the pressure she needs by grinding her pelvis against me with slow, small shifts of her hips.

My head falls to her shoulder, and her nipples grow hard beneath her cotton T-shirt.

I bring a hand up, lightly dragging my thumb across the pebbled peaks, and her shuddered inhale has my groin burning.

"Mm," I groan.

Fuck.

She unhooks her legs from around my body and nudges me back until I cave, falling flat onto her mattress, her knees pressed near my thighs. Nothing but my thin basketball shorts and her thinner pajamas keeping my cock from her entrance. I don't even think she's wearing underwear.

Victoria stares intently, with a heavy desire I couldn't possibly miss.

And not for herself, but what she wants to do to me, for me.

She wants to ease me, please me, and my heavy, tormented groan is all the encouragement she needs to start.

She begins riding as I imagine she would if I were buried deep inside her, filling her to the brink, fucking her the way she wants to be fucked.

When her hands fall to my chest, I close my eyes, seeing hers behind my lids.

Right now, our clothes are still on, but she's got me lined up just right, so the friction forces my groans from my lips and helps my mind paint a perfect fuckin' picture of flesh on flesh.

Me and her.

She's far from hesitant, boldly touching and tracing every inch of my exposed skin, pushing and scratching where she wants. The roll of her hips grows deeper, harder, but not faster, and her fingers freeze where they lie, flexing and twitching.

She likes a slow ride.

My cock loves the newfound knowledge, jerking at the realization, and suddenly my shorts are tugged down. Goose bumps cover my skin as my dick meets the power-charged air around us, hard as a damn rock and so fucking ready for more.

A soft hum leaves her and my head wrenches up, overtaken with a need to witness her expression, but I hold off.

The fight only lasts five seconds, as in the next, the mattress dips, warm breath fanning across the head of my cock, and my eyes fly open.

She's not looking at me, though, not waiting for approval. She has no plan to ask for any. She simply stares, with eyes dark and lips parted, her breaths growing quicker, thicker, as she moves in.

Her tongue flicks out as she drops her stomach to the mattress, her legs crossed behind her, feet in the air. Her hand glides along my abdomen until it reaches the base of my dick, and slowly, finger by finger, she grips it tight, aligning me with her mouth.

Those thick, red lips open wider, her eyes closing as her mouth teases around the head.

My chest rumbles, and she sucks as she pulls back, but she doesn't let me slip from her mouth, instead opening wide and, without touching the length of me, takes me fully into her mouth, got to be damn near to her throat when her lips finally seal over the base of my cock.

My fuckin' lips part, a heady exhale following as she sucks, gliding all the way up, her slick tongue flicking along the tip when she releases me.

My toes curl, and I lift my hips, not missing the small smile she gives, and she goes in again, more urgent, driven.

She sucks me, massaging me with the inside of her perfect fucking mouth, and I moan. Her mouth vibrates around me in response, giving away her own as she tries to swallow, and suddenly I'm fucking famished.

I slide my hand along the mattress, blindly gripping her leg and spinning her with a quick yank.

She gasps, now in position to sixty-nine, but doesn't pause or protest. She drops back down, pumping me with her mouth.

I push her hips in the air so I can tug off her pants, but she freezes, lowering her body, and I tense.

Her stomach.

Shit.

Thinking quickly, I grip her shirt, tucking it into her panties, and she settles, her licks slowing and driving me mad.

My head falls back, and I thrust into her mouth a few times, savoring the tight squeeze when she hollows out her cheeks.

When my body begins to tense, my orgasm growing closer, I snap out of it, fight the feeling as I rush her pants the rest of the way off.

I drag one leg over my head and wrap my arms around her ass, lowering her pussy to my face.

Fuck me, if she isn't eager to have my tongue, her legs practically fucking fly down the satin sheets, begging for what she knows I'm about to give.

A deep rumble fights free from within my chest, motivating her even more.

She speeds up, sucking harder, bobbing on me faster, so I push the thin line of her thong aside and drive my tongue inside her, vibrating my bottom lip against her clit.

She whimpers instantly, her thighs clenching, and it acts as a fucking stimulant.

Suddenly I'm harder, my need to taste her cum on my lips growing at an obsessive, uncontrollable rate.

I massage her with my tongue a moment, but then dip my head a little more, putting all the focus into her clit. I suck and roll and suck some more, and her hands leave me, slamming into the mattress as she shakes.

She moans, and it's not quiet.

It's loud and intoxicating, but she swallows it as quickly as she can, cutting off the sound I earned, likely remembering it's not allowed.

No sounds.

Suddenly I'm tearing myself from her mouth and tossing her to the edge of the bed.

I hook her feet flat on the mattress and push her thighs open, massaging as I work her faster and harder. I dip my thumb in her pussy, coating it with her excitement and, with the knuckle of my pointer finger, push at the edges of her asshole.

She gasps, her back flying off the mattress, and instantly clamps around me, so I push a little more and damn, if she doesn't push back, driving the tip inside the slightest bit.

She shakes, her fists flying to my hair, knees locking around her grip and my head repeatedly, whimpers caged at her lips. She tries to tear my head away only to grind a second later and hold me in place, but I don't let go.

I keep her in my mouth, slowing the stroke of my tongue until she finally stops twitching, and as soon as her hands fall, her legs relaxing with them, I speed up and take her there again.

Her gasp is a desperate, breathless, perfect fucking sound, one that she hides behind a pillow she scrambled for, hiding her face and noise from me.

She comes in my mouth again, reconfirming it's a flavor I need more of.

Now.

Tomorrow.

Fuck.

I tear myself from her floor and move into her bathroom, closing it behind me as I flick on her shower. I don't wait for it to heat but jump right inside, my back falling against the wall, cock already in my hands.

I start stroking, my chin dropping to my chest as I lick my lips, tasting her on me, recreating the feel of her lips around me as I squeeze and jerk and my muscles tense.

Fuck, Beauty.

My eyes pop open when a hand covers mine, halting my movement, and my dick throbs furiously in my palm.

Deep-brown eyes, wide and fuckin' wild with want, stare into mine, never breaking contact as she drops to her knees in front of me, her shirt instantly soaked and stuck to her skin.

"I did this," she practically fuckin' purrs with a hint of anger as she runs the pads of her fingers along my hard-on. "Me." She tugs on my wrist, tossing it to the side when I relent and let go. Her mouth closes around the tip and she flays me with a glare, sliding her teeth along it until I groan. "What comes next is mine too."

I think I'm yours…

My cock twitches and her eyes close as she slides forward, taking all of me, deep and full into her throat. She fucks me with her mouth, working hard for every ounce of cum I'm about to give her.

My toes curl and her hands plant firmly on my hips as mine fly to the sides of her face.

I hold on, letting her keep her pace, and what a perfect fucking pace it is.

She pulls back, keeping only an inch past the head in her mouth, and her tongue rolls around me.

I growl, my head tipping back as my muscles lock. "Fuck, Beauty. Mm." I jerk between her lips. "Goddamn."

I give her what she's worked for, coming inside her warm, silky mouth, but she doesn't just sit there and take it.

Victoria fights for it, keeping her suction strong as she takes me in from head to base, her lips stretching along my skin so not an inch is left untouched, and begs for more, making sure she's been given all of me before slowly drawing away.

My body shakes, the pads of my feet curling from the heated tile beneath them and balancing on the edges, muscles fucking worked.

My eyes move to hers, finding them closed, her features smooth, lips even plumper and wrapped tight around me, swollen from the work she's put in.

I groan, twitching in her mouth, and a hint of a smile manages to cross her face. I slam my eyes shut as she grows closer to the tip, savoring the last glide inside the smoothest silk. My cock pops free, and just as quickly as she releases me, her talented tongue flicks along the head for a quick and final taste. It's as if she can't handle it, as if she's already hungry for more.

Needs more.

Craves more.

Are you starved like me, baby?

My eyes peel open, and the scene's almost too much.

Soaking wet and perched on her knees before me, staring at my cock with satisfaction.

A worshipper kneeling before her chosen king.

A rumble reverberates from deep within my chest and my breathing picks up again when she rises to her feet.

Her eyes make their way to mine, and my jaw flexes as I fall into the brazen brown, deeper and fucking deeper.

She leans forward, her lips dropping to my chest. She slides them across, moving up on her toes to better reach my shoulder.

Suddenly and without my knowledge or permission, my pinkie is pushing back the dripping strands of hair that dare threaten to hide her from me.

I want to keep you.

Something flashes in her eyes, but mine lower to her lips when a gentle kiss meets my left pec, where the weight of my world lies, deep within a heart that's torn.

It's too tender, too meaningful.

Too fucking necessary.

A gentle brush of her lips shouldn't calm me so easily.

Should it?

My eyes clamp closed, and I drop my head to the tile behind it.

She understands my internal struggle, doesn't fight or push, but steps out.

When the shower door opens and closes, my eyes open.

It's a clear, thick glass, fogged from the heated water and maybe from my own heavy pants. Regardless, it's distorted my vision of her, only allowing me the sight of her neck and face, and she knows it.

With her back to me, she holds my gaze through the mirror as she kicks off her wet underwear and tugs her solid shirt over her head.

It would be so easy to shove the door open, learn the depth of what she hides, force her to give me something real, but I don't move. I stay beneath the spray until she's back in her room, closing me off inside the bathroom.

I'm in no rush as I dry off, giving her the time she needs to dress, hoping she's tucked away and hiding every inch of her when I enter so I can grab my shorts and go back to my room.

But as I toss the towel in the laundry basket that's yet to be emptied and wrap my palm around the door handle, I freeze.

My eyes fall to the floor only to jump right up as it clicks.

Holy shit.

CHAPTER 18
CAPTAIN

It's a little over an hour later when Victoria finally creeps around the back door, through the billiard room toward the front foyer, and attempts to pass the kitchen only to freeze the second she realizes what awaits her.

Four angry Brayshaws.

When I threw the door open to her room, she was gone.

I woke Royce, who woke Maddoc and Raven, while I searched the property, but there was no sign of her anywhere.

So here we fucking are, waiting.

She's slow in her approach, her knuckles flexing as they tighten at her sides, a way to keep her muscles from going stiff on her.

Once she's out of the shadow the dark entryway provided, she snaps out of her surprise, leans against the wall with her arms crossed and a single dark brow hiked high.

"What is this, an intervention?" She gives a slow blink, working really hard to show her annoyance.

Always a damn brat, can't hold it in when she should.

"Sit." Royce kicks a leg out, finishing off his drink.

"I'll stand, thanks."

"It wasn't a question."

Her eyes fly to mine and hold a long moment before she kicks off the wall and drops into the open chair on the opposite side of the table.

She leans forward, her zip-up sliding off one shoulder as she rests on her elbows, meeting each of our gazes head-on.

Her tongue peeks out, and my eyes follow.

Her lips are puffed up, a deeper shade of red than normal, courtesy of my cock.

Thankfully, Raven catches her attention as she comes from around the counter, four shot glasses hanging from her left hand, two bottles of Don Juan in the right. She sets one bottle and glass in front of Victoria and the others in front of me, steps back into the kitchen, and returns with a fresh-made hot chocolate for herself.

She lowers into the seat beside Maddoc as I twist the top from the bottle, looking to Victoria.

Her eyes tighten, holding mine a long moment, before she opens and pours hers as I pour ours. My brothers reach over, neither waiting to throw back the amber liquid.

I spin mine between my fingers, unsure if she's bluffing or not, but then Victoria purses her lips, brings her shot up, and downs it.

Slowly, I take mine, lick my lips, and pour us all another.

And then another.

She keeps up, not so much as a grimace crossing her stony face in the process.

She's completely closed off, and I'm almost impressed at her ability to hide behind a sheet of nothing, but that talent is what blinded me, blinded all of us, so I focus on my anger instead.

Time ticks by in weighted silence, but finally, five shots and fifty-four minutes in, a low chuckle makes its way past Victoria's lips.

She locks her eyes with mine, throwing back another shot, and a slow smirk follows.

My muscles clench when she carelessly goes for more.

I reach out, about to take the damn bottle, when she shoves herself back, a loud, heavy screech echoing around us as her chair goes with her. In the same move, she lifts the fucking thing to her mouth and goes for a long swallow.

I jolt from my seat, and it's like a chain reaction.

My brothers and Raven fly up with me, Victoria on her feet in the same damn second as us.

"Put the fucking—"

"Try to act concerned right now and I'll finish this fucking thing," she swears, cutting me off. "This is what you set this up for. Don't play like it's not."

Raven masks her expression, shifting her eyes between the two of us.

Victoria slams into her seat, tipping her head back on a mocking laugh. "Man, I expected so much more," she drags out, cutting a glare to Raven as she speaks to me. "This is juvenile, a trick from my own act, in fact. Of course, I was on the other side."

There's a bite in her tone that has me curious, and I glance at Raven right as she lifts her chin at Victoria.

"Fuck you talkin' about, VicVee?" Royce asks.

She blinks hard. "I'm here, I'm buzzed. Should we move along?"

"You should be on your ass." Maddoc glares.

Exactly.

"Wanna ask me why I'm not?" She smirks, tucks her hair behind her ear, her eyes moving to mine. "Oh, I forgot, questions are hard to come by," she says, calling me out.

Anger cuts through me, but like a shard of glass dipped in poison, it stings of betrayal when I wish it would burn with hate.

"And loose lips'll get your ass beat," Raven snaps.

Victoria's glare flies to her. "As do lies, right?" she challenges.

Raven goes to step closer to her, but Maddoc shoots back to his feet, glaring down at her pregnant belly.

Raven's jaw ticks. "I never lied to them."

"Whatever you have to say to convince yourself to feel better."

What…

Raven gapes at Victoria, a laugh leaving both her and Royce at the same time.

Victoria's eyes snap toward Royce before landing on me.

Hold on…

It takes me a moment, but then it hits, and a heavy frown covers my forehead. I lean forward, planting my hands out on the table to get as close without moving my feet as possible.

"Are you fucking kidding me?" My eyes move between hers. "You want to sit here and question her loyalty?"

She doesn't speak.

Holy shit.

I straighten my spine, brows lifted high as I stare at her.

"You really think Raven didn't come home and tell me, tell us, what Maria told her? That I don't know the woman who helped keep my daughter from me, your mother, held me as a baby because she couldn't hold you?

"My father was gracious enough to take pity on her, an outcast Graven maid, before and after her pregnancy, gave her a home when she had nothing, and still she took me, separating me from my dad and my brothers like you were separated from her and with no care for anyone else's feelings but her own. I know he spent weeks searching so he could bring me back home, where I belonged, with my family, and instead of killing her like he easily could have, he let her live."

Her brows draw in.

"Unlike you, Raven came to me, to us as a group, like a true Brayshaw would and shared what she learned, what she knew I'd not only want to hear but need to know. She understands loyalty isn't always easy."

"Yet you looked so surprised to learn Maria was my mother."

"Not surprised she was your mom, Victoria. Surprised you knew she was. Maria made it seem like you had no fucking clue. She acted as if you were out roaming and none the fucking wiser."

Victoria says nothing, her eyes remaining just as hard as she tips her head back, drowning herself in more liquor.

I dart over, yanking it from her, and grip her wrist. "What the hell is the matter with you?"

"Apple juice," she seethes.

I tense and she uses that second to tear her arm free.

She pushes to her feet, walks around me, all eyes following her as she picks up the bottle we were drinking from and sniffs.

She nods, setting it down and looking across the four of us, arms out at her sides, only to let them fall with a hard slap to her thighs. "So what was the plan here, exactly? Get me drunk while you pretend to drink, obviously, but what was to follow that?"

Anger—pure, heated bitterness blisters in her eyes.

She's completely closed off, and a girl I've never seen, don't know or understand stands in front of us.

Suddenly I regret everything that's just taken place, want to wish and wash it away, and I want it to take the black look she gives me with it, and I have no clue why—nothing even happened.

She drank; we didn't.

Why does this upset her?

Why do I care?

A trick she called it, from her own act. What fucking act?

"Tell them, Victoria," Raven suddenly whispers.

Reluctantly, I pull my eyes from Vee to glance at Raven. Her shoulders have fallen, eyes are sloped around the edges. There is no pity but there is regret, pain.

Understanding?

"Tell us what, RaeRae?" Royce sits forward, leaning on his forearms.

"What wasn't mine to share," Raven adds.

My eyes move back to Victoria.

She focuses on the floor, cheeks clenching as she works her jaw over. Tension builds across her forehead, but then she draws her shoulders up, her head jerking slightly before it's gone. She stands to her full height, her features smooth as fucking butter.

"You guys think I haven't earned the right to be here. Well, you haven't earned the right for a trip down memory lane. You're sitting here for a reason, so get to the fucking point."

Shock has my eyes widening, and while this from anyone else would warrant a nasty reaction, my brothers laugh, and fuck me if I don't give a slow chuckle myself.

She tries but cracks the slightest bit, hiding it by licking those lips. She looks across to the four of us.

"Lemme get us started off since this shit got off track," Royce says. He leans forward, removing the lid from the crystal bowl in the middle of the table, and picks up what's inside.

He looks at Victoria and lifts his hand.

Between his two fingers is a small piece of paper.

Her face falls instantly. "Oh shit," she gasps.

Yeah, oh shit is right.

VICTORIA

Oh shit, oh shit, oh shit.

"Ah, so the little liar recognizes this, then." Royce sits back, cocking his head.

This, in part, is what I've been waiting for, but I wanted Captain to ask me directly. There's no getting around it now.

The truth is all that's left.

Still, with nerves running through me, I delay.

My eyes move to Captain. "You went through my things."

"That should have been a given," he replies.

It was.

"Didn't think anything of it at first," Captain admits, an almost imperceptible hint of hope threaded in his tone. "But once it clicked, it all clicked."

Not all of it, or this conversation would have started much differently and without the game before it.

I look to Captain, at the strain around his eyes, and my pulse hammers against my temples. Everything will set in and quickly—he's only had a moment to wrap his mind around what this actually means, after all; it was just a bit ago my lips were wrapped around him.

I'd been waiting for this, so why do I suddenly feel as if I'm not ready for it?

I don't know why I ask myself this; the answer is clear.

He's giving himself to me in small pieces, and I don't want him to take any back, but I said I'd tell the truth if asked directly, and I will.

"All those times I thought you had eyes on Chloe or Mac, I was wrong," Cap says. "It was Tisha you were staring at. You knew she was getting beat. You knew she wrote for the school paper and knew what Jason drove. You bought a toy car and newspaper, tore off the corner, and waited for an opportunity to place it in front of us."

I run my tongue along the backs of my teeth, not denying a thing.

Cap's eyes bore into mine, and I see him working through this as he speaks the words aloud. Tension builds across his face and he licks his lips.

"The town, our people." Captain's eyes slide to his brothers, who clearly haven't moved beyond this moment either. "Issues of all kinds used to go through head of security, shared with us only after things were handled, so we stayed aware but out of the trouble. Until we got to Brayshaw High. We were ready for more, wanted more, and all of a sudden, little hints and tips were being dropped left and right. We were able to take control by being a step ahead."

I swallow as Royce says, "People started to come to us because of it."

"No..." Captain disagrees, his tone low, an achingly obvious sting of realization and single thread of awe, feared hope, burns in his eyes, now solely locked with mine. His brow furrows as he takes a step closer. "No…right?" he whispers.

My heart hammers in my chest.

Go on, Cap.

"The girls being treated wrong at school, the women abused by their husbands, daughters ruined by their fathers, the assholes abusing their power in our name…" Captain turns his head to his brothers, waiting until the last second to take his eyes from me and only for the briefest of a glance. "I'd go as far as to say helping those people, our people, is how we earned the respect, when at first it was given to us because of who we were."

"You earned the love of your town."

"And you made that possible," he says just as quick. "Didn't you?"

"Whoa, the fuck…" Royce slowly pushes to his feet. "Are you saying she…that there was never…"

"It was one person all along." Maddoc glares.

Raven's eyes widen.

Royce looks to Captain.

And Captain, he shuffles closer, never breaking eye contact. "Why?"

"Because she felt it," Raven whispers, but only her husband turns toward her.

Her gaze lands on me, and she gives a small smile.

Captain's knuckle presses below my chin, guiding my face to his.

His eyes search mine, repeating, "Why, Beauty?"

I answer his desperate plea. "Because all my life I listened to the filth people had hidden inside them. I was the shadow behind their ugly, an unseen threat, felt and feared, but the second I realized secrets didn't exist solely for blackmail, as I was told, my purpose shifted. I sought out every secret I could find and did what was needed to right the wrongs."

Captain blows out a low, ragged breath, both hands lifting, sliding along my cheeks and holding my head in place.

The others watch on, not a word spoken, not a breath heard.

Captain's eyes, a gut-wrenching, glorious green tonight, beg for something, but I don't think it's me they want something from—it's himself.

To believe in the words the little liar before him speaks when he so gently and torturously asks his one-worded question. "Zoey?"

Moisture builds in my eyes and I swallow, giving a curt nod, clenching my teeth to keep my jaw from trembling.

He shakes his head, coming closer, his forehead dropping to mine while his eyes keep mine locked in. "Say it out loud. Tell me you are the one who left me proof. Tell me you snuck those hospital records into my bag. Tell me you are the one who led me to my baby girl."

My lips part on a sharp exhale.

Please, his eyes implore.

"Yes," I whisper. "I put them there for you to find."

His hold on me tightens, shakes, and then suddenly it's gone, and just as quickly, he is too.

I'm left standing at the head of the Brayshaw table, Raven, Maddoc, and Royce staring right at me.

Raven catches me off guard when tears roll down her cheek, but she doesn't swipe angrily at them, doesn't fight the emotions she normally hates to show.

I look away, meeting Royce's gaze as he takes three steps toward me.

"Three years, VicVee." Royce's words are coated with a heavy gravel. "You were here for three fuckin' years, quiet as a mouse but as slick as a fucking fox." He grabs my hand, pulling me into him. His lips find my ear as he hugs me. "Should we be proud or pissed, baby girl?"

"Did you know foxes hunt smaller prey than wolves," I whisper. "And in return the wolves look the other way?"

He chuckles, releasing me and perching against the edge of the table.

Maddoc slides his arms around Raven, laying his palms across her stomach, and hers lift to lace into his. He asks, "Are we fools for not seeing? You lived on our property. Went to our school. How'd we miss this?"

"Rich people see no threat in those who have nothing. You were taught to stare past a girl like me, not through. I was taught to focus where no one dared. I see what you can't. You see what I want you to."

"But you fucked up," Maddoc says, adding the obvious.

A scoff leaves me, and I nod. "Yeah, well. It's been a hell of a couple weeks."

Raven's lips twitch.

Captain's voice cuts through the room, and our heads snap his way.

"We have rules." He swallows beyond the strain in his words, and an airiness makes its way through my body.

Brayshaw rules.

I nod, and he continues.

"No one is allowed here, but you know that already. No drugs are allowed in this house, but the weed in your bag will be fine once it's where my daughter can't reach." He eyes me a long moment, then adds, "We eat dinner together every night, no exceptions."

"Oh shit," Royce whispers with a small chuckle, and Maddoc smacks the back of his head.

Captain doesn't look away. "If you can't cook, we can teach you." He pauses, and the tight pull at his shoulders eases some as he fights to let go. "Raven sucks, so don't ask her for help."

She laughs, and I find myself letting a small smile slip as his does, but he quickly clears his throat and walks away, only to come right back again.

His glare is hard, but his words are much, much more. "Unpack your shit, Victoria. Now. Tonight. All of it. And sleep under the covers, not on top."

And then he's gone, and a dangerous, risky sensation runs through me.

Hope.

"Hey, uh, RaeRae, you should loan me your headphones tonight."

My eyes fly to Royce's, and he pops a brow.

Raven laughs, dragging her man from the kitchen, and Royce follows them out.

I take a moment to breathe and then I head up to the room I was given and do exactly as Captain asked.

For the first time, I settle into my new home.

CHAPTER 19
VICTORIA

The sun is just coming up when my door opens and closes.

I stay facing the wall, waiting to see what he'll do, having expected him hours ago.

There's a light shuffle and then silence.

Several minutes go by before he speaks. "What did you mean earlier? What filth and ugly did you see? What kind of life did you live? Where did you live?"

A smile finds my lips.

Sweet Captain, stepping from behind his shield.

Slowly I flip over, finding he's on the floor, his back positioned against the bed, head propped on it.

"I lived here until I was ten years old, in this town. After Donley stole me from Maria at the hospital, he basically put me in a room on the Graven estate and left me there. I guess I was fed and taken care of as a baby because I lived, but I don't exactly have anyone to ask about it."

"What was the room like?" he asks.

"Big, almost like an apartment, I guess. It was cold and bare, with a bath and small fridge, microwave when I got a little older and was trusted to use it."

"No school?"

"Like with other kids?" I shake my head. "No. For one hour a day, I had a teacher, but I think she was just another employee of the house, not a real one, and she wasn't exactly a ray of sunshine.

She was emotionless and wouldn't look at me. Not once in six years did she meet my eyes."

I remember, when she'd leave, I'd stand in the center of the room with my eyes closed, a nasty little thing called hope in my naive heart, all for it to be crushed day in and out when then the lock on the other side would click, confirming what I already knew and expected—I was trapped inside. Alone.

The crazy thing—or maybe it's not so crazy, I don't know—was I didn't even care she left. I just wanted to see what the world looked like outside the door.

"Stop."

My eyes fly to the back of his head, but before I can speak, he does: "Stop thinking in your mind. Think out loud. Tell me. Talk to me."

My chest tightens, and I nod even though he can't see.

"I would talk to the walls, louder when I saw shadows beneath the door, but nobody ever opened it."

"You were alone."

"Yeah," I whisper. "But I didn't hate it. I had a million dresses and nightgowns, a TV, and..." I trail off, wishing I could see his face. "A garden."

His head snaps right, but he doesn't look at me, instead choosing to watch me in his periphery.

"I was bored more than anything, so I would go out into the little yard attached and daydream about climbing the wall, until one day I heard a couple kids playing somewhere near and said 'fuck it' and tried. I tried every day for years, but I never even got halfway up. The wall, it was blanketed in thorns and ivy."

He swallows but says nothing.

"The man who would clean my room and bring my meals found me digging holes in the yard a few times. I was punished—no school for a week, which meant no human contact." I smile into the pillow. "Naturally, I dug deeper."

Captain's shoulders bounce with a quiet, huffed laugh.

"A couple days later, when the man found it again, he walked right out, and the morning after that I woke to my door being thrown open, and pallet after pallet of flowers were carried in, dropped onto the patio with a hand shovel and two pairs of gloves." I smile into the darkness, tapping my fingertips along the satin pillowcase. "My time there sucked a lot less after that. Getting those, planting those, that's when my life actually began. With a purple flower."

"Purple..." he rasps.

Yeah, Cap. Purple.

He's quiet a long moment before he says, "Thorns and ivy, purple flowers...your tattoo."

"My tattoo."

"Tell me more." His command is gentle.

I roll to my back, looking up at the giant chandelier above me. There's no way Maddoc had that hanging in his room when this space was his. Captain must have had it put in for me.

It's gorgeous, too expensive, I'm sure, but...gorgeous.

It's a large glass circle, a line of silver at the tip-top, and encases several dozen stringed diamonds. The center point hangs the lowest, the others surrounding creating a perfect point as they grow smaller and disappear behind the glass around it.

"I never really understood what a birthday was. I saw them on shows and things, but I didn't know when mine was or if I had one, and then Mero showed up. I'd never met him, never seen him before. Later that day he dropped to his knees and smiled." I squish my lips to the side. "He said, 'Happy tenth birthday, sweet girl,'" I whisper. "I left with him the day he came, left everything I'd ever had, ever known behind. The crazy part is I was happy to. In my mind, this handsome man with the greenest of eyes had saved me.

"I had a new room where the door wasn't locked, a new yard that didn't have a wall trapping me in, a swing, and...a friend. Someone to talk to, and he loved to talk." My eyes close, a frown forming. "For hours he'd sit and listen, ask questions. We'd play games and he taught me to cook—I'm really good at it by the way."

Despite the mood, he gives a light chuckle, his head falling back on the mattress, and I wish I were allowed to reach over and brush the golden blond back. "Did he hurt you?"

I pause, following a glimmer from one of the long strands above me, shimmering color down the wall until it slowly begins to fade, as my innocence did.

A wilted flower.

"If I think about it, he was hurting me from the beginning, but I didn't see it. I was groomed, a perfect blank slate to build from. I didn't know about the world; all I knew was what he told me. *There's bad out there, sweet girl, and you're the princess sent to make it right.*" I frown. "That was one of his favorite lines. He taught me how to read body language, how to get a glimpse into a stranger's soul."

Never cower, sweet girl. Your eyes are your power.

"It started small: get the kid at the ice cream shop to admit he stole from the tip jar, convince the guy at the park to steal his mom's car. But I was really good, and suddenly I was twelve but passed for seventeen…and I learned there really was a lot of bad in the world. Mero said my job was to find it, and making him proud became the most important thing in my world. So I did what he asked, always. I found new ways to get smart, powerful people to give up their secrets, and in return, they gave Mero money."

"Blackmail."

"Yep."

"Did you have to sleep with these men?"

I run my tongue along the backs of my teeth. "Did someone force me to a bed and take what I didn't give?" Shame weighs on my chest, and I inhale, the ache only growing. "No, never. Sex wasn't always necessary, but when it was, when I had no other way to get the answer I was sent for, it was."

I was disgusting, craved the approval of a man who I thought was my savior, even mourned his death as I made my way back to this place, and then it was like a switch went off in my mind. All at once, everything clicked, and I realized what I had never seen before: I wasn't his princess; I was his prisoner.

"When I got to the Bray house, I studied everything around me, and it didn't take me long to realize where good met the evil, but your family had no reason to trust me, so I found another way."

Finally, Captain shifts his head, meeting my eyes in the dark. "You found us."

My stomach muscles tighten, and I nod. "Yeah, Cap." *I found you.*

"Why didn't you tell me?" he whispers.

"I was a stranger who knew what she shouldn't." I shrug. "I was basically a stalker."

Captain chuckles, but it quickly dies on his lips.

His hand comes up, pushing the hair from my cheek, and he holds it there a moment. His eyes fall to my mouth, his tongue peeking out to wet his own, but then his swing back to mine and a look I can't decipher flashes across his face.

He stands.

"Sleep, Beauty." He trails his fingertips as they skim along the expensive comforter. "And when you wake up…show me who you are so I can forget the rest."

A spark of expectation fires within his gaze as it meets mine, a glint of impatience just behind it.

He's ready for me.

And then he's gone. A heavy twist takes over my stomach in his wake, and I close my eyes, pulling in a full, deep breath.

Please.

Whoever listens to the desperate whispers of a lonely girl in the dark…

Please.

Let him be my Brayshaw.

CHAPTER 20
CAPTAIN

"The hell you doin', brother?" Royce comes around the corner, joint in one hand, water bottle in the other.

I look to the hose in mine and take another step left. "Soil looked a little dry."

The joint freezes at his lips, his eyes narrowing. "Soil looked dry." He laughs, taking a long drag. "Fuck you know about soil?"

I chuckle, but a sigh quickly follows. "Fuck, dude. Nothing. Looked, I don't know, like the flowers were dying or some shit."

It's been three days since we found out Victoria is the one who gave me the proof my daughter existed, shared a little about her story with me, and I haven't been able to think of much else since.

Haven't talked to her much since, but my eyes hardly leave her when she's near.

Like I told her to, she's made sure to be around for dinner every night, something that my brothers and I have always done since before I can remember, but she hasn't jumped right into normalcy, and while I appreciate her trying to ease in slowly, it's also frustrating as fuck.

Royce bends down, gently brushing across a few of the flower petals, and shakes his head. "Nah, man. Sun's just not hit 'em today yet."

I hike a brow. "The fuck do you know about flowers and the sun?"

He laughs, pushing to his feet with a grin. "Hey, I'm right, fucker. Remember when Ms. Maybell had us start doing outside chores? Mine was the planters on the porch." He shrugs.

I look to the sun and back to the flowers.

"Also learned overwatering kills 'em even faster."

"Fuck." I drop the hose, glaring at the garden.

The purple garden…

A part of Zoey.

A part of Victoria?

Did she give my daughter a garden just as someone gave one to her?

"You good, man?" Royce eyes me.

I run my palms down my face. "Yeah, I'm just—"

"Horny?"

I laugh, my brows lifting as I nod. "Yeah, actually." That's part of it.

"Won't be much longer, brother." He smirks. "By the way, Mac says still no sign of douchebag Mike. Think he got the picture."

"He came and asked to see her. You really think he'd go without saying bye?"

"Yeah, man," he chuckles. "I think taking your brass to his chin might have convinced him to."

"Daddy!"

We turn as Raven and Zoey walk around the house.

"Fuck." Royce quickly stomps out his joint and then jumps in front of her.

She pretends to juke him, spinning around, and he lets her pass so she can run to me, fully believing she evaded his hold.

I pick her up, tossing her in the air, and then kiss her cheek. "Did you have fun on your walk?"

"Uh-huh! We saw five birds." She holds a hand up. "One was a hawk, RaeRae said."

We laugh when she tries to say RaeRae, the nickname Royce uses for Raven, but it comes out as WayWay.

"That's awesome, Zo."

"Zoey," Raven calls. "Tell Uncle Bro what the baby needs."

"Oh!" Zoey spins in my arms, looking to Royce. "Uncle Bro! Baby needs donuts, okay?"

Royce laughs, wraps an arm around Raven, and kisses her temple. "What baby wants, baby gets, Zoey Bear."

I grin from him to her. "Maybell's got all the food ready. We just gotta grab it from her as we leave. As soon as Maddoc's out of the shower, we'll head out."

"I had to go and get sick, delay us by an hour," Raven says, making a face.

"For real, RaeRae, your uncontrollable morning sickness is gettin' real inconvenient." Royce gives a dramatic eye roll, and she slaps his stomach, making him laugh. "Careful, or I might puke on you like you puked on Madman earlier."

"Fuck off." She laughs, then slaps her hand over her mouth. "Oh shit." Her eyes widen, making us laugh.

"You're fine," I tease her.

Her shoulders fall, and she throws Royce's arm off her and sludges past us. "I'm literally a lost cause. The worst."

"Ah, not the worst but…" Royce grins, dodging her punch, and runs ahead of us.

"Uncle, wait!" Zoey squirms, so I set her down and she chases after him, Raven and me on their tail.

We follow them into the house, my steps slowing when we round the entryway to find my dad and Victoria in the kitchen.

They chat with ease as he hands off the butter, and she begins cutting small pieces into the bowl on the countertop, my eyes falling to her lips as she pulls them in, concentrating on whatever it is she's making. She steps back, grabbing her hair in her hands, lifting and twisting it on top of her head. Untying the bandanna from her wrist, she uses it to tie her long locks up.

"Rora!" Zoey barrels into the kitchen.

My gut twists, torn between conflicting emotions, and I'm not sure what to make of it.

My daughter is running for her, and while I'm still anxious and unsure, all I'm thinking is *goddamn.*

Red lipstick on already rosy lips might be my favorite fuckin' shade of her.

Thick, black, winged liner and deep, dark-brown eyes find and hold mine, strings of loose hair framing her face.

Zoey reaches her then, pulling all her attention.

Victoria's eyes leave mine and she dips down, now completely hidden from my sight.

Her warm words follow. "Good morning, Mama," she says.

My heart beats double time.

I can't see her face, can't see Zoey's, both blocked behind the bar. I can see my dad's, though, and his eyes are zoned in on the hidden moment—soft yet studying.

I move forward.

"Morning, Rora," Zoey says. "I had a good sleep."

My lips twitch, my dad's doing the same.

"Girly, I know." Victoria teases with ease. "You were snoring like crazy."

"No!" Zoey laughs, and Victoria's follows.

My dad sets his coffee cup down, bending at the knees. "Guess what I talked Rora into making, Zo?"

Rora?

"What?" she asks, excited.

"Cinnamon rolls."

"Yay!"

I walk around the corner right as Zoey throws her arms around Victoria.

As quick as she celebrates, though, Zoey's face falls, and with it my stomach bottoms out. Her eyes lower to the floor, Victoria's shoulders dropping with them.

Zoey reaches out, running her fingers over the image of a half-bitten heart on Victoria's shirt, mumbling, "One for the tummy…"

"One for the road," Victoria responds, her happiness quickly fading as Zoey's has.

The road?

Victoria drops to her ass right there in the middle of our kitchen and brings herself to my daughter's level, lifts her hands tight into hers, and looks her straight in the eyes.

Something pulls beneath my ribs, making it hard to breathe.

"ZoZo." Victoria's smile is full of tenderness, but she can't quite hide the pain my little girl's sadness causes her. "Rora isn't hitting the road today."

My skin heats, the sorrow in her tone too fucking earnest.

She means leave her; she doesn't have to leave her today.

Zoey doesn't want Victoria to leave her.

My eyes find Maddoc's as he comes around the corner, then slide to Raven's, Royce now on her other side.

He gives a curt nod, and I think I nod back.

I drop to one knee beside Zoey.

"Hey, Zo," I say, gently finding her hips, turning her to me. My pulse throbs in my neck. "You wanna help Victoria make cinnamon rolls before we go?"

"Yes! And eat them?" Her little eyes light up, the green within them a bit brighter today. "Can Rora come too?"

I look to the blond before us, at the promise in her eyes and understanding in her small smile.

"Yeah, baby girl," I quickly throw out before my airway closes on me. "She can come."

As quickly as she lets me go, I'm on my feet, out of the kitchen, and I don't stop until I'm inside my room, pen in hand with the next blank page in my journal staring at me, but all I can manage to write is a single, solid word.

Mine.

The minute we climbed from the SUV, Zoey wanted to play with the rocks in the stream. The water hardly runs this time of the year, just barely brushing over the tip of the rocks, enough to darken the shade and nothing more.

We made shapes with the palm-size rocks and spelled Zoey's name out with the little ones, but that's as much as we got to do before Zoey was hungry, so we head over to rejoin the others.

Maddoc sees us coming and stands, moving over to my SUV that's pulled right into the plush grass. He opens the back, dragging out the ice chest and mini table.

Royce pops up to grab the table, quickly unfolding it while Maddoc digs out some drinks and starts passing them around.

"Uncle D, can I have a juice box?"

"You can have whatever you want, Zo." He smiles, tossing a juice box in the air and catching it behind his back without taking his eyes off her.

She giggles, running over to him to grab it, Raven smiling at the two as she does.

"Go on, keep trying, dick," Royce coughs to disguise his cuss word. "I'm still her favorite."

Raven laughs, pushing to her feet to check out what Maybell packed for us. "Vee, come eat."

"I'm not hungry," she tells her.

Raven pauses, a slow smile spreading across her lips. "You actually ate the cinnamon roll, didn't you?"

I eye them curiously.

"Duh." Victoria chuckles, looking out over the little pond ahead of us.

I go back to helping Zoey pick out what she wants, and once we begin to eat, Victoria quietly rises, walking a few feet away. She sits in a soft spot in the grass, picking at the weeds lining the water.

It doesn't take long for Zoey to notice, and then she's on her feet.

She dashes across the blanket, but I quickly lean forward, catching the hem of her top, and she falls to her butt, looking back at me, mustard smeared across her cheek, strawberry juice on her chin.

I chuckle, grab a napkin, and quickly wipe her face, but she jumps right back up, ready to take off again.

"Zoey," I call her.

She spins, smile wide, little hand pushing back her loose curls. "I wanna go play."

My throat grows thick, eyes snapping to Royce's when his hand grips my shoulder.

"We're right here, brother," he whispers, and Raven grins up at him.

I let my hold on Zoey fall.

She turns and runs for Victoria, her laugh sharp into my soul.

Zoey gives her no warning, but Victoria's head snaps this way just in time. Her arms fly out, and Zoey dives for her, knocking them over.

They both roll onto their stomachs, laughing, elbows in the grass as they stare at each other.

They're talking, I couldn't guess what about, and I smile when Zoey drops her head to the grass, her hand coming up to cover her mouth like they've just shared a funny secret.

I study Victoria's face and I'm struck. Once again, it's not one I've seen, not an expression I know her to have. She's smiling and laughing and…free.

No hidden pain or callous facade.

It's as if, with Zoey, she's someone else.

Herself, maybe?

Suddenly Zoey's head pops up and she stands, tugging on Victoria's hand excitedly, but Victoria pushes up, a hand lifting to her throat as torment blankets her features, creating the same with mine.

She licks her lips before they begin to move, and seconds later, Zoey is running this way.

I set my drink down, ready for her to come back to me, but she doesn't so much as step onto the blanket.

"Um, I want to make a necklace. Can I?" she asks, a little confusion in her tone, as if she doesn't understand her own question.

Can she make a necklace?

"Dandelions," Raven says.

My eyes move to hers, only to jump to Royce when he speaks.

"They ain't close, Cap."

I canvass the area, spotting a small patch about a hundred feet away. I swallow, my eyes moving to Victoria, who stays seated on the grass, waiting.

Maddoc frowns, unsure, his hold on Raven tightening.

"Zoey," I begin, sliding my gaze to hers, the heavy beat of my pulse ringing in my ears.

As if she can sense my denial, her shoulders fall, her head slightly tipping to the side. It's too fucking much.

I swallow. "Don't run off, okay? Stay beside her no matter what."

She smiles, nods, and takes off.

Victoria stands before she meets her and the two race across the grass, both falling to their knees. They waste no time and begin pulling the small weedlike flowers from the ground.

Without climbing to my feet, I reach across the blanket, grab the garbage bag, and start filling it for something to focus on, trying for a deep inhale, but all it does is create more pressure.

This shit isn't fucking easy—sharing Zoey, trying to trust Victoria, forgiving.

"You know..."

My head snaps toward Raven.

Slowly, her eyes peel from where I'm trying not to look. She grips Maddoc's shoulder, using it as leverage to push herself to her feet as she eyes me. "Victoria hates cinnamon rolls."

My brows crash together, and I watch as she makes her way to the girls.

For almost an hour, my brothers and I sit in the same exact spot, not once removing our eyes from them, not a single word spoken.

Once each of them has a flower crown and necklace on, they head back and we snap out of it, hopping to our feet and quickly packing up our things.

"I say we play a game of hide-and-seek before we go; loser cooks all week," Royce suggests, clapping his hands, and then Zoey is in his arms. "Zoey Bear will be my buddy. Not it!"

They run off, making us laugh.

Maddoc grips Raven's hands, tugging her in with a hard jerk. "You wanna hide behind a tree with me, baby?" His intentions are clear in his growl.

Raven, though, she laughs and shoves him away. "And risk Zoey walking up on Uncle D giving D? I don't think so." She quickens her steps as she walks away to hide. "You're it, Big Man. Let's see if you can find me wherever I go."

"I'll find you across the fuckin' world, Mama."

Her steps falter a moment, and if I didn't know Raven better, I'd swear she blushes, but she quickly turns away, disappearing into the brush around us.

I look over and Victoria shrugs, rushing off just the same.

"Should we say you lost? You'll get the kitchen and be able to control the menu a whole week." Maddoc laughs.

"Yeah, Royce didn't think that through." I chuckle.

"No cheating, asshole!"

"Oh, Uncle!"

"My bad!"

I shrug and take off to hide. I head across the pond, ready to slip between the small bush and rocks when a wall catches my eye a few feet down. I move straight for it.

I push a few branches to the side, stepping past the ferns lining the outer edge, and there she is.

Eyes closed, back at the white-petaled ivy, palms flat against it.

As soon as my feet crunch against the fallen leaves, her eyes pop open.

While she doesn't move, a cutting laugh escapes. "The irony, right? I didn't even notice it, slid behind a bush, and here it was. Like fate. Like I needed a reminder of what I'd never forget."

I can't focus on what she's saying—all I see is Victoria, buried in a bed of ivy, white flower tips framing her, like a fucking gift for a god.

Before I can stop myself, I'm against her, the opening of her flannel between my knuckles. I drag my hand down until I can't reach anymore, quickly moving my grip to her waist.

When I squeeze, her head falls farther into the pillow of leaves.

All the things I could give you, Beauty...

"Maybe it's a good thing to be reminded." My chest rises with a heavy inhale. "You can't run from your past."

"How about my future?"

"What's your future look like?"

"You tell me," she dares.

"I've got an idea." I trace the curve of her body with the pads of my fingers. "But I'd be lying if I said I knew for sure."

Victoria doesn't close herself off at my words. She's not a needy girl who wants promises, likely doesn't even believe in them anyway.

Instead, she finds my belt loops and tugs me closer. She leans in, the rise and fall of her chest matching mine as she pushes to her toes, her lips now on my neck.

She tastes me, and her body quakes, causing my groin to tighten. Remembering my rule, she swallows her moans, eyes glossed over and begging.

Heat runs up my veins, and before I can stop it, my hand is sliding into her jeans, past her underwear. "Warm and wet," I groan, my forehead falling to her shoulder. "Just the way I like you."

"So." A harsh breath comes from her nostrils as she fights away her whimpers, pushing into my hand. "You like me, huh?"

A chuckle makes its way up my throat, but it quickly cuts off as she begins riding my hand.

I let her set her pace, not moving an inch, but applying pressure where she leads me. I'm straining in my jeans, aching.

But all I want right now is to drown in her raspy hums, to force the filth I've denied myself into the air.

I want to hear her screams, feel her screams like a pulse beneath my skin, but before I can beg her for them, before I shred my own rule, a not-so-swallowed moan breaks through our little shelter, a deeper, heavier one following, and we both freeze.

My head pops up when Maddoc groans, "Fuck, Snow."

Victoria's eyes fly to mine, but she doesn't laugh or pull away.

She keeps chasing what she wants, intruders be damned. Her pussy clenches around me, so I shift the slightest bit, letting her play on the tips of my fingers instead of my palm.

"Cover your ears," I demand, not wanting her to hear the sounds of another when I have her like this. "Your orgasm belongs to me."

That has her eyes rolling back, her muscles squeezing.

I push two fingers inside her, keeping my thumb up to push against her clit, and she starts to shake, the ivy beside her quivering with her, alerting the others they aren't alone either.

She comes, biting her lip as her eyes slam shut, her walls flexing against me, and I press my hard-on into her leg, my thigh muscles tightening to chase some relief.

Heavy steps against dead leaves follow, but she doesn't hear them, and I don't dare pull out of her—not yet, not when she's still riding out her orgasm.

And when her eyes finally open, they're focused over my shoulder.

She doesn't get embarrassed, tug away, or bury her face.

She gives a hard, bratty blink, a heavy eye roll following as her body begins to sag.

"Raven wasn't kidding," she pants. "There are literally no secrets between you guys."

I shift my head, looking over my shoulder without moving.

Royce and Maddoc are standing there.

"I'll admit." Royce nods his head, crossing his arms as he looks from Maddoc to me. "Hide-and-seek was a shit idea with a kid."

"Hide-and-seek is for kids," Victoria corrects him.

"Yeah, okay." He scoffs and starts walking away. "And chocolate syrup was made for ice cream!"

CHAPTER 21
VICTORIA

Chloe dashes by, grabs my arm, and yanks me close with a wide smile and red cheeks.

I tear free from her. "What the hell?"

She grins. "If my dad asks, I was with you!"

"What—"

"Chloe!" is boomed in the empty hall, echoing across from one end to the next, and she clamps her lips shut with a laugh, yanks her loud-ass heels from her feet, and disappears into the bathroom the second Mr. Carpo steps around the corner looking full-on mob boss.

He skids to a stop. "Ms. Vega."

"Mr. Carpo."

"Did you see my daughter come this way?"

"Yeah, we were in the bathroom, but she left a few minutes ago," I lie.

His eyes narrow, so I add, "I pissed off a Brayshaw. She was, you know, taking a minute to rub it in."

He frowns, nods, and then the poor guy apologizes, and I have to fight back a laugh. "She's working on…"

"Manners?" I suggest. "Yeah, I noticed."

He chuckles, running a hand down his face. "Well, I guess that's a good thing. Lunch is in fifteen minutes. Go back to class, all right?" He turns toward his office.

Suddenly Mac pokes his head out of a door down the hall,

grinning when he sees me standing there, his hair a tangled mess on the top of his head, pink lipstick on his neck.

I cross my arms, and he laughs as he saunters this way.

He nods his chin. "Vee."

"Mac."

Chloe comes out, hair back to perfect, and wraps an arm through his. She smiles. "Thanks."

And off they go.

I make it back to class just a few minutes before the lunch bell rings.

"I'm starved." Raven stands, waiting for me to pack up my things.

"That's news to absolutely no one," I tell her.

She laughs, and we make our way from the room, finding Maddoc waiting just outside as always.

He pulls her into him, kissing her neck as we walk down the hall.

My steps slow as Amber plants herself right in front of Captain at the end of it, where he, Royce, and Mac stand waiting for the rest of us.

"Here we go." Raven smirks, shaking her head, and I don't miss Maddoc's scoff at her side. "You've been on his arm, at his side, and in his bed for weeks. She's testing your status."

"Let her."

Raven's head jerks toward mine. "For real?"

We keep moving forward with slower steps than normal.

"She wants to get under my skin—fuck her."

"She wants to fuck your man." Raven side-eyes me.

"And won't even get close."

"How can you be sure?"

"You just called him mine, right?"

Maddoc shakes his head. "Stay out of it, Snow," he warns with a kiss.

"Oh, I am." She turns to me with a grin. "You want to let her think she can touch him and get away with it, that's on you."

"Then why are you laughing?"

She only smirks and looks ahead.

Chloe steps up right before we do, rolling her eyes at the pretty girl in booty shorts and a tank top.

We catch the tail end of the conversation, right as Amber slinks closer, allowing her hip to pop out as she says, "It's going to be fun, but it would be better with you there."

Captain's eyes shift, meeting mine over Amber's head, and he lifts his arm, casually sliding it right past her, his forearm brushing her shoulder as he does she's so close to him.

She must think he's about to wrap her up, pull her in, and accept her invite because she leans into him.

The second she does, though, I'm shoved from behind, landing right in Captain's large and waiting hands.

I'm pulled, spun, and planted right in front of him. In the next second, his long fingers slip into the front pockets of my jeans, pushing my body into his.

I look at Maddoc, finding a smirk on his lips.

Shithead.

"Sounds like a good time, Amber," Captain finally replies. "Maybe we'll be there."

Amber is only inches from me, her mouth agape as she slowly shuffles backward, a forced partial smile finding its way back to her lips. She lifts her bag higher on her shoulder and nods. "Yeah, okay."

My eyes fall to the purse she grips tightly. "New purse?"

Her glare is instant and on me, but she says nothing, spins on her heels, and walks away.

Chloe and I laugh, while the others look at us, confused.

It lights a small flare in my chest.

How about that? An inside joke I'm on the inside of.

As the group makes their way into the cafeteria, Cap holds me back and turns me in his arms to face him. An unquenchable warmth stares back as his hands begin to trace my ribs, something I've noted he likes to do.

My shape—it's one he likes.

His knuckles lift my chin, and he leans forward, planting his lips at the curve of it, then on the hollow of my throat, his dirty whispers moving to my ear.

"I thought of you last night," he shares, his heated breath making my toes curl in my shoes.

"Before or after you left my bed?"

He squeezes my ass with his free hand, the one under my chin now teasing the skin of my neck and collarbone. "Before, during, and after…long, long after, Beauty."

I lick my lips and wait for more.

"You rolled over and whispered in my ear," he tells me. "Do you remember that, or did my baby talk in her sleep for me again?"

His baby?

Oh God.

My chest falls to his, and he drops his shoulders to the wall behind him.

"Yeah, you talked in your sleep." He nips at the skin beneath my ear, his other hand joining the one on my ass and pushing me against him. "You told me you wanted to roll me on my back so you could climb on top and show me what I do to you. You said you'd ride me slow, drive me mad… That what you want, Beauty?"

I swallow, my eyes closing as he rubs against me, pressing his now-hard cock into my hip. "If you'd have woken me up, I would have given you what I promised," I admit. "Gladly."

"Oh, you did…"

I tug my head back to look at him.

His eyes blaze, pupils dilated beyond belief. "I went to my bed, locked my door, and lay flat on my back. I closed my eyes, and there you were."

He thought of me…

"You rode me slow, as you said you would, clawed at my chest when you learned I liked it, and ground into me at a torturous pace." He unveils his late-night fantasy. "I leaned against my headboard, and suddenly your nipples were in reach, and you were all about it, Beauty. You pressed the taut little pebbles into my mouth…and so I bit."

I suck my stomach in as a heavy need grows throughout my body, clenching my core to seek some relief, and the corner of his mouth tips up.

He sees it, knows what's happening inside me, but he keeps talking.

"When I bit down, you went wild, picked up speed, and begged me for my cum." He hides his face in my neck again, sucking on the skin there, and my hands fly up, latching on to his biceps. "My cock was in my hands, my cum in my own palm, but you earned every drop, and I can't fuckin' wait to give it to you for real."

He lets me go, slips right by, and disappears into the cafeteria.

I'm stuck standing in the hall, ridiculously turned on, and there's nothing I can do about it, so I suck it up and follow.

I probably look like I was just thoroughly fucked, red and wanton, but I don't care.

Especially not when Cap hears my footsteps behind him and pauses. He flashes a devastating grin as he reaches for my hand—he knew what he was doing.

With a light chuckle, I slide my palm into his, and just like that, he stands a little taller.

All eyes are on us the remainder of the day. Sure, he's had me on his lap and his hands around me dozens of times since he deemed me his Bray girl, making me untouchable to others, but today it's different.

The few days that follow even more so. Captain's touch has gone from controlled to possessive, his hands constantly roam my body, and his lips are never far from my skin.

People notice the shift, and I'm more than here for it.

They might see a difference in their beloved Brayshaw, but I can feel it.

His eyes linger longer than his touch, and he does all he can to make sure they're forever on me.

He likes me close, which tells me we are so close.

So after school on Friday, when I spot Amber pulling her shiny, little silver car beside Captain's as he, Maddoc, and Raven stand at his hood, waiting for me and Royce, I'm annoyed.

She climbs from the driver's seat and props her ass near the headlight as she plays with her hair, smiling up at Captain as he blandly stares at her.

This chick, I swear.

She's gorgeous, but she needs to back up.

"Aw shit, I know that face." Royce chuckles.

"She's something else."

"Girl's a power-chasing hoochie mama with your man in her sights, VicVee." He grins.

My eyes narrow on the scene, and I slip my arms through both straps of my backpack, securing it on better.

Maddoc and Captain are both looking at Amber as Royce and I grow closer, but Raven spots us coming from the front seat.

Her eyes follow our steps.

"Pop the back for me?" I ask Royce.

He laughs and runs ahead.

CAPTAIN

The soft click of my trunk opening has both my and Maddoc's heads snapping that way.

Royce comes into view first, a wide grin in place, but then Victoria whips past him, her arm at her side as she makes her way around the silver Audi.

Amber follows my line of sight, spotting Vee coming from the other side.

What—

Suddenly she lifts a bat, bringing it down across the windshield in one hard, full swing.

"Oh my God!" Amber jumps back, her hands in the air.

The glass shatters but doesn't fall in, so Victoria hops up on the hood and stomps through it, kicking it in completely until the glass covers the inside of the car.

And I just fucking stand there, staring.

She jumps down, both feet planting at once, one of them an inch from Amber's.

Without looking, Victoria bends her elbow, tosses the bat up, and catches the barrel. She casually drapes it over the back of her neck, her free hand coming up to grip the stem. She cocks her head but says not a damn word.

And she doesn't have to because there it fucking was.

My girl's public claim.

Amber gets the message, her eyes falling to the ground as she rushes through the crowd that's gathered a few feet back and disappears who the hell knows where.

'Bout damn time, Beauty.

Maybe it makes me soft, but I can't pretend I wasn't waiting for it.

I push off the car, moving toward her, and reach over her shoulders for the bat.

She lets me take it with ease, slips past me and into the open door Maddoc holds for her with a smirk.

Royce laughs, knocking his shoulder against mine as I go to put the bat in the back where it belongs, and before I close it, Raven spins in her seat, smiling at her sister. "That's what I thought."

The girls laugh as I climb inside, and then we head home.

Later that night, after dinner, when everyone is settled in—Maddoc and Raven in their own room, Royce on his computer in his—Zoey and I knock on Victoria's door.

It opens on its own, having not been fully closed, and her head pops up, eyes widening at the sight. She sets her textbook aside, lowering her pencil with it. Her gaze moves from mine to Zoey's.

"Hey, ZoZo," she says easily.

"I got new jammies. Wanna see?!" She smiles, tugs free of my hand, and runs inside.

I'm stuck in the doorway, watching as Zoey climbs on Victoria's bed with her and pulls at the bottom of her shirt. "It's got rainbows and this." She points to rain clouds. "You like 'em?"

Victoria giggles. "I do, and guess what." She lowers her voice as if she has a secret, and like a child eager to learn, I find myself leaning closer. "I have some jammies kind of like those."

Zoey gasps. "You do?!"

She nods with a small smile. "Wanna see?" she mimics Zoey's question.

Zoey laughs, rubbing her hands together in excitement, and I can't help the chuckles that escape.

Victoria's eyes slide to mine as she climbs from her bed and pulls a pair of cotton pants from her drawer, somewhat similar to the ones Zoey has on.

She shows them to her, and Zoey laughs, counting the little rainbows as she falls back on Victoria's pillows.

Pressure fills my chest, but for the first time, there is no added worry behind it.

Vee's eyes find mine. "Everything okay?"

I nod, leaning against the doorframe, and her focus falls to my bare chest but quickly comes right back.

She drops onto her mattress, her hands anxiously gliding along her thighs as she studies me.

An ache forms in the pit of my stomach as I watch her and the curious look that takes over her face as she tracks the pensive expression on mine. I can't deny what I've been trying to say when the clarity of the matter burns so bright, and she sees it.

"Cap…"

"She wanted to say good night," I tell her. "But I don't think I'm ready for bed yet."

She waits.

I walk inside, lift Zoey from the mattress, and move back into the hall, pausing to turn to her.

With slow steps, she meets me where I stand, follows me into the media room, and when I drop onto the couch with Zoey on my lap, she lowers to my side.

We sit and watch *Coco* for the fifteenth time, Zoey playing with Victoria's hair, my arms wrapped tightly around them both.

CHAPTER 22
CAPTAIN

Zoey stands beside me, Easter basket dangling from both hands as she stomps her feet excitedly, not so patiently waiting as my dad takes off his suit jacket, giving her something to sit on the grass with.

He lays it out beside the only two picnic tables we could find that weren't crammed with a dozen others here at the festival.

As quickly as he's stepping back, she's falling to her knees and pouring everything from her basket. She stares at all the sealed plastic eggs with a bright smile.

"Is there candy in them?" she asks.

"I don't know. Open and see."

"Maybe there're stickers!"

I grin. "Maybe."

She gasps, looking to me. "Maybe there's a frog!"

I start laughing, the others following suit.

A frog?

"I don't know, Zo." I chuckle. "But we're about to find out."

One by one, she starts to open them, finding something new each time.

We may have gone a little overboard, but being her first holiday at home, my brothers and I wanted it to be special, so we stayed up half the night decorating the house and hiding eggs from the mansion to the orchard.

We got the biggest, fluffiest bunny we could find, setting it in the center of the room, but when it came to her basket, the big, overflowing one we brought home and the mountain of toys to go with, it didn't feel right, so we tossed it in the back of Royce's SUV. He drove the stuff over to Mac to make sure someone who might need it would get it in time, while Maddoc and I called Maybell in a panic. She laughed and asked us to come down to the Bray house.

When we got there, she was on the porch, bag in hand.

She knew we'd need a little help in the end, and what she had waiting was perfect for Zoey.

A strong, white wicker basket, one she could hold in her hand that wouldn't drag along the floor as she carried it around, was the perfect little fit for her.

It has a purple ribbon that weaves in and out of the edge and small pink flowers strategically sewn along it. With white grass, a small pink bunny, a chocolate duck, and four tie-dyed plastic eggs, it was perfect, as was the look on her face when she found it this morning.

We never even told her about the eggs we hid outside; she was too happy with the few she got, but after seeing her face hunting eggs out here, I might.

"Place hasn't changed at all, has it?" Royce looks around.

I glance from the food carts to the bounce houses and game stations. There are booths lining the area, vendors selling homemade signs and jewelry and other random items you might not find every day.

Every year, as kids, Maybell would bring us here for Easter.

It's two hours outside of town and held on someone's farmland, but there are still a shitload of attendees, while it still remains a place free of Brayshaw townspeople. Since I haven't shared that I have a daughter, it's what we need.

"I'm going to grab a soda or something," Victoria says as she stands and heads toward the food carts.

"Wait up, I'm starvin' too." Royce hops up.

That gains Zoey's attention, but she doesn't even have to ask. Royce picks her up, and off they go.

My dad makes his way around the front of the tables then and drops down beside me.

"How you doin', Son?" he asks, beginning to roll up the cuffs to his button-up.

I nod, dragging my eyes from my brother and focusing on my dad. "I'm good."

He studies me a long moment and then turns away. "You know, you don't have to do what others think is right, what the world, what our world, says is right? In the end, Cap, you're the one that has to choose, to decide, if you want this life or not—the decision is yours. It has to be one you can be proud of, not one you wish you could change." He looks to Maddoc, who stands beside Raven. "That goes for you and your brother. You shouldn't have to drive two hours just to have a place to take your children to play," he says, a shadow of guilt crossing his face.

"So we won't." Raven shrugs. "Next time we have something in town, let the kids of Brayshaw come—all of them, not just the ones with a trust fund."

Maddoc drops his head, kissing her neck, and when he stands, it's a little taller than before. He looks our dad in the eye, speaking for all of us as he knows he can. "We decided a long time ago who we want to be, and that's not changing. It's time the town catches up."

"That's what I had hoped to hear." He nods, a smile on his face as he stands, moving back to the side he was sitting on as the others return.

I raise a brow at Royce, Zoey at his side with a cotton candy twice the size of her on a funnel in her hand.

"She's the boss, Cap!" he shouts with a grin.

I shake my head, looking to Zoey as she tears off a piece and holds it out for Victoria.

Victoria smiles, taking it as she steps up, choosing to sit on top of the table, her soda nestled between her legs, feet planted on the bench seat.

"You don't have to eat that, you know," Raven teases.

Her glare flies to Raven, but then a low laugh follows. "Shut up."

Curious, I study her, noticing the creases now framing her eyes as she purses her lips at the candy.

"You don't like sweets," I realize.

Her eyes fly my way, but she quickly glances down, preparing to stick a piece in her mouth, but I shoot my hand out, snatch it, and toss it behind me.

Victoria's head tugs back, and Zoey gasps, having caught me.

"Daddy, oh no!" She jumps to her feet and tries to hand Vee another chunk. "More for you, Rora. Daddy can't have some."

"Zoey, did you ask Victoria if she wants more?"

Zoey frowns, her eyes moving to Victoria, who clenches her jaw.

"Do you want to have some?" Zoey asks while pushing it toward her.

Victoria's shoes slide against the metal bench, and she rubs her lips together while keeping a smile on for Zoey.

She can't tell her no.

"Zoey, come look at the butterfly." Our dad pulls her attention away.

She runs off, candy-coated sugar still in her hands.

"We have to tell her no sometimes," I say.

Victoria slides her tongue along her teeth, frowning.

"Have you?" she challenges.

My glare is instant, and she sighs, looking away with the shake of her head.

"I can't," she admits. "I've tried and I just…can't."

"So you eat cotton candy and cinnamon rolls instead? Things you don't like?"

She shrugs. "Pretty much, yeah."

Yeah, for Zoey, she means.

My stomach muscles tighten, and I slide over on the bench until I can grab her right foot, lifting it up and over my body so one foot is planted on each side of me.

Her wrist curls, tucking her drink into her chest as she pulls the plastic back into her mouth and bites. "What are you doing?"

"Whatever I want."

She chuckles, leaning forward. "And what is it you want, Cap?"

"I kinda wanna pull a Raven and vomit," Royce jokes.

She laughs, and when she attempts to lean away, I grip her by the shirt and tug her right back.

She smirks, tipping her head to the side, but then her eyes cut over my head, widening in the same second. "Oh fuck."

CHAPTER 23
CAPTAIN

Panic floods my veins as the color drains from Victoria's face in a single second. Slowly, she pushes to her feet, standing above me on the bench.

"Cap," she warns in a deep, desperate tone.

I quickly swivel around, only to freeze. My blood runs cold, my body numb, and I don't remember standing, but suddenly I am, and not ten feet before me…

Mallory.

Her eyes lock on mine, brow furrowed as she glances from me to the girl behind me and back.

The worst fucking thing follows.

Zoey laughs, soft and innocent and way too close.

Mallory's eyes fly past mine, and her face falls. Slowly, she begins to look around, but my family snaps out of their shock, jumping to their feet to block her view.

Raven darts forward, but Maddoc grips her by the wrist, forcing her to his side.

"You have her?" Victoria's whisper is almost silent.

I dart forward, rage boiling my blood.

Mallory's eyes snap over my head to Victoria and hold.

I growl, getting in Mallory's face. My body is shaking, dread building like acid in my gut, burning and eating away at everything inside me. "Leave. Now."

She tries to see beyond me, but I jerk to the side. "Stop fucking looking. Royce."

"On it." His footsteps pound along the pavement in the same second as he goes to make sure Zoey is taken farther away.

Away from the girl who gave her away—who didn't want her.

How could she not want her?

My jaw is so tight, I can hardly crank it open enough to speak. "Get the fuck out of here before I flip out and scare every person in this fucking place."

"Talk to me," she pleads, her palms on her stomach, where our daughter grew.

My eyes are glued to the soft pink fabric there, the same color my daughter is wearing today, and I can hardly fucking breathe.

"Just for a minute, a few seconds even. Please." Her hands lift, and I follow.

The wind chooses that moment to blow her hair forward, and it whips me across the face, a scent I know well and wish I could forget.

"We can…go the other way, away from…" Her eyes slant, moisture building within them.

"Your tears won't work with me, Mallory, but if it gets you away, fine," I force past clenched teeth. "Turn around and walk until I tell you to stop."

Her smile is weak, and she quickly walks backward, her eyes snapping over my head and hardening a moment before she spins and walks away.

I stand there, heaving, un-fucking-sure and gut twisted.

I look to Maddoc, who shakes his head, urging me not to go, to Raven who glares after Mallory, her hands in fists, but I don't look at Victoria.

I can't, and I don't even want to think about why.

I follow Mallory out.

I don't yell for her to stop until we're halfway into the parking lot, but she's quick to whip around, big crocodile tears streaming down her face.

"I said your tears won't work, so turn them off."

"I can't. I just..." Her eyes move behind me.

I growl, getting as close as I can without touching a single speck on her. "Stop fucking looking!"

She nods, her blue eyes coming back to mine. "How long have you had her?"

My chest caves at the question.

I'm standing here in front of the mother of my daughter, who apparently didn't even know Zoey was finally where she belonged.

I should be screaming in her face, telling her what a piece of shit she is, and how she gave away the most precious person in the world, but looking at her...

The creaminess of her skin, the slope of her eyes, the small peak of her nose and soft crimson cheeks...the golden curls framing her face and the way she keeps lifting her left hand to move them away.

Mine flies out, gripping her wrist to keep it still because I can't take it.

It's too fucking hard.

Too fucking much.

I'm standing in front of the one person in the world I should hate more than any other, deep in my soul and with every fiber of my being, but looking at her all I see...is my daughter.

Our daughter.

Half her and half me.

Fuck.

I swallow, my hold on her tightening, shaking. "You've got a lot of nerve approaching us like that."

"This is the last place I thought I'd see you. I was just... shocked."

"I don't care. You should have run the other way when you did."

"You won't hurt me, Captain," she whispers, her free hand coming up to wrap around mine. "You're good, even when you don't want to be."

"Stop," I rasp through the burn in my throat. "What do you want?"

She swallows, a small smile lifting the corner of her lips, and she dares shuffle closer. "Can I say hello?"

"What the fuck?!" My head tugs back. "No. Fuck no. Are you crazy?"

She ignores me, and my pulse beats harder, the blue in her eyes bright and on mine. "What's she like?"

I throw her hand away, yanking back with a shake of my head. "Don't."

"Please."

"Mallory," I seethe, dragging my hands down my face before pinning her with a hard glare. "Go. Stay the fuck away from me. From all of us."

I turn on my heels and rush off.

"You don't have to tell her who I am!" she shouts.

I freeze, but I don't turn around.

"You can say whatever you want. I won't even speak."

When I don't immediately keep walking—why don't I keep fucking walking?—she adds, "I can…be a stranger at the store or…something. Anything."

I bite into my cheek, squeezing my eyes shut.

"I just want to look at her. Just once. Captain, please."

My pulse beats heavy against my ribs, and my head throbs, an instant migraine forming.

My vision fogs, my mind is muddled, which must explain the stupidity that follows.

"You know my number," I rasp when I shouldn't.

She'd never dare to call.

My phone vibrates in my jeans twenty minutes into the drive and again fifteen later, but I don't pull it out.

Not a single word is spoken on the drive.

It helps that Zoey fell asleep within minutes of being on the road, but the silence plays as a broken whistle, forever screaming into my ears and threatening to blow the drums.

Maddoc slid into the driver's seat, knowing I would need to sit in the back. He keeps trying to meet my eyes in the mirror, but I can't look away from Zoey.

My phone beeps again, and my eyes close.

Goddamn it.

My brothers' phones have yet to ring; that can only mean one thing.

It's her.

Begrudgingly and with a grip so tight my knuckles are white, I pull my phone from my pocket and glare at the screen, at the name I haven't seen glowing across it in years and never wanted to again but would have given everything for at one point in time.

When I loved her and swore she loved me back.

One day she was here, and the next she was gone.

I wigged out, searched for her, only to find nothing. The girl I was in love with had vanished into thin air, but as quickly as the worry came, it was replaced with resentment because in our town, there is no such thing as gone at random.

To be gone with no trail to follow meant one thing—she made the choice to go and had help.

When she popped back up eleven months later, she was no longer a Bray girl but weaseled her way into Graven Prep.

To turn your back on a Brayshaw was like a stamp of approval for Graven; they welcomed traitors to their family with open arms and promises, but by that point, I didn't care in the slightest.

That's because I didn't know the reason she had left was to hide her pregnancy, to have and discard my child, to try to pretend she didn't exist and hope I was none the wiser.

I wouldn't have been if it weren't for the documents given to me, sharing the hidden news.

Victoria.

My head snaps over my shoulder, to the third-row seat where she's pushed against the window farthest from me, staring straight out it with a wretched expression, elbow perched on the doorframe, thumbnail sliding across her chin.

Slowly her eyes make their way to mine and hold.

A deep chocolate brown.

Not blue.

Not blue?

My head flies forward, my eyes closing.

Fuck.

My stomach twists even more.

I shut off my phone, not opening the six-message thread waiting for me.

"Pull over," I rasp, and all eyes are suddenly on me.

"Cap?" Maddoc frowns from the road to me.

We're still a good twenty minutes from home, but I'm suffocating in this fucking thing.

"Pull over, man."

He does, and I climb out into the fresh air, nothing but a two-lane highway for miles. I take a deep breath, ready to close the door, when suddenly Royce's shoes hit the ground beside me.

I look at my dad, and he gives a curt nod, shifting closer to Zoey's car seat, so I close the door, and off they go.

It takes us well over an hour to get home, not a word spoken the entire time.

That's one of my favorite things about my brother: his silent support, always there and never pushing.

As we walk up the steps, he turns to me with tension in his eyes, but he only clamps my shoulder and nods, disappearing inside while I drop onto my ass and look out over the driveway, at the orchard and the long road between the trees.

I pull my phone from my pocket, turn it on, and read through Mallory's messages.

My shoulders fall, and then Zoey's voice flows through me, her sweet little call and gentle laugh.

I look over to find her running my way, Easter basket overflowing with eggs, my dad, Raven, and Maddoc trailing her, eggs in all their hands, a trail of some dropped behind them.

I laugh, and it tugs at my insides.

"Daddy, hu-mon!" She smiles.

Right then, her little hand lifts, brushing her curls aside.

Something her mother does.

Exactly the way her mother does.

How did I not connect the move sooner?

How could she share anything with a person she doesn't even know?

A lump forms in my throat, and I swallow past it, my eyes falling to my phone again. I hold my breath, responding with a single two-letter word.

I turn, set it down, and hop off the porch with a smile. "I'm coming, baby girl."

Daddy's coming.

VICTORIA

Two days have come and gone since Easter, and while he keeps me at his side at school and pulls me close when home, Captain's lost in his own mind.

Each night that's passed, his footsteps pad against the floor, my chest rising with each one that grows closer, only to leave me in knots when they disappear, but tonight, the shadow of him hesitates beneath my door.

He stands there, right outside, and I hold my breath, waiting.

He steps inside.

He doesn't bother closing it behind him, doesn't speak, but his eyes find mine in the dark, and slowly, he slides beneath my covers, lying on his side so he can face me.

His eyes are rimmed with dark circles, proof he hasn't slept, and his body sags with the weight of the world, but he doesn't let anyone into his.

As far as I can tell, he's held it all in so far.

Captain reaches out, and I force myself not to frown as his knuckles bypass my jaw when they normally glide along it, and instead his fingers slide into my hair.

My blond hair.

He kisses along my jaw, down my chest, until his lips are settled on my breastbone. When my legs fall open for him, he climbs between them.

I run my hands along his skin, letting him take what he needs, feel what he wants, and kiss wherever he chooses, wishing he'd finally kiss my lips.

His fingers slip beyond my shorts and underwear, slowly sliding into my pussy with no hesitation. He pumps torturously slow, nipping at my chest as he pants against it.

I reach for him, but he presses his upper body into mine more, locking my hands against the mattress, his fingers interlacing and squeezing me tight as my walls clench around him.

He groans, whispering words into my skin that I can't make out, and I break out in goose bumps.

His fingers hook inside me, and he drags his lips to my ear. Suddenly his thumb is swirling along my clit, and my back arches right as he whispers, "Come."

I do.

My body quakes against his, trying to suck him in farther.

He waits for me to ride it out, for my breathing to settle, and then he sighs, shifting us both so once again we're on our sides.

Within minutes, his eyes begin to close, and only then do I

realize his hold on my hair never wavered, never loosened or let go, instead burying deeper as he falls asleep at my side.

I try not to wonder what it means, but sleep becomes the enemy.

And in the back of my mind, I know it won't be the only one.

CHAPTER 24
CAPTAIN

We needed a day away after how last weekend played out. My mind has been so heavy I could hardly focus in school, let alone at night when all I had was time to think.

This morning was the first I felt calm, and I knew instantly what I wanted to do.

I needed another chance at a first with my daughter, since our first Easter, unbeknownst to her, was tainted. So we ditched school and loaded up in my SUV and went to our family cabin in the woods.

It's decades old but has been kept fresh and refurbished on the inside.

It sits high in the mountains, other mounds of rock and hillside surrounding it with a creek running through.

There are several others surrounding it, all owned by other students at Brayshaw High and even a few from Graven, from back when they weren't the enemy, way before our time.

It's a fun party spot for all the teenagers to go to get away from the city, but on weekends like this, when no one else is around, it's peaceful, nothing but the sound of birds and water against rocks to be heard.

That and the echoes of Zoey's laughter as Maddoc helps her try to climb a tree.

"Daddy, look at me!" She smiles, waving. "I'm waaaay up!"

Maddoc is holding her up completely; she only has a foot and single hand touching the oak, but to her, she's climbed a tree.

I smile, opening the lid to the barbecue. "Dang, Zo, watch out for chipmunks way up there!" I tease her.

She turns her attention back to Maddoc as Raven steps up beside me, eyeing the hot links on the grill. "I'm so starved." She eyes them.

"You're always starved."

She laughs, bumping my shoulder, but then she grows quiet a moment. "Not to cloud your happy mood, but…do you ever wonder what it was like for her?"

She doesn't say her name, but we both know she means Mallory.

I frown at the food in front of me, flipping over the meat. "Might make me shitty to admit, but I hadn't. Not once until I saw some things change in you."

"Yeah," she whispers. "Shitty you couldn't be a part of it in some way. I hate her for you, but I imagine your hate isn't so simple."

She looks up at me, but it takes me a second to meet her eyes, allowing her to witness the struggle in my own. "Nah, Raven. It's not."

"'Sup, RaeRae." Royce is suddenly beside her, throwing an arm over her shoulders as he shouts, "Wanna go play at the Graven cabin again, Madman?"

Maddoc's head snaps our way, and he mouths *fuck you* while flipping him off.

Royce laughs, kisses her temple, and walks away. "Going to find that blond who ran off the second we got out here."

"She went up the hill!" Raven shouts.

And off he goes.

To find my blond.

A heavy sense of unease fills my veins at the thought.

Damn it.

VICTORIA

With a deep breath, I close my eyes and wrap my palm around the spiked greenery, exhaling when warm liquid glides along my skin, dripping down my forearms in slow, heated trails.

"The fuck!" is shouted, and my eyes fly open to find Royce a few feet in front of me, his eyes wide, yet somehow still he scowls.

"I'm fine."

"Let go."

"I will."

"Now!" he snaps.

My hands tighten, driving the thorns deeper before I finally let go, looking at the heavy strips of red coating my tan skin.

He grips my wrists, pulling each hand to his face to inspect the damage, but all he gets are smears of the mess I made.

"It's just a little paint."

"Paint?" he deadpans, dropping my hands, and his eyes fly to mine. "Are you for real some secret psycho?"

A laugh flies from me, and I shake my head.

He already knows blood is a wicked tool meant to paint a picture of pain, revenge, and hate—of death.

I, for one, have never been a fan of art.

Royce tugs the shirt over his head, patting at my hands until the tiny holes are visible.

"Fucked yourself up pretty good here."

"Eh, it'll only sting for a couple hours."

He scoffs, sitting on a large boulder to the right.

He crosses his arms, staring at me. "You wanna tell me why you're uglying up your hands?"

"Depends."

"On what?"

"You wanna tell me what you're trying to pull behind your brothers' backs?"

His glare is instant. "Fuck's that mean?"

"Come on, Royce. We just went over this…" I tip my head back and forth teasingly. "Secrets are my thing, remember?"

His eyes narrow, and he licks his lips, kicking his feet out. "So it's not some kinda 'this person has a big mouth and the word spread to me' shit? You legit fuckin' see what others don't?"

"It's almost a curse." I shrug. "Makes me question everyone and everything. Most people don't make random moves, you know? Especially in worlds like the ones we live in. I mean shit, there are four other families, three now that the Gravens are out, that run towns just like yours. There're secrets everywhere and always someone scheming. Nobody wants a seat at the bottom; they want to climb that invisible ladder to the top."

"I'm not scheming," he rushes out.

I smirk, bringing my eyes to his as I push off the rock. "I know."

I walk by and the bushes rustle behind me, alerting me he's done the same.

"Hold up. How do you know?" he asks, jumping beside me and holding the branches out of the way so we can make the short descent to the cabins.

"You've spent a lot of time on your phone lately, and anytime I pass your room with you inside, you have your computer out."

"So fuckin' what? Maybe I'm watchin' porn."

I laugh. "Maybe…but I've also seen you chatting with Maybell."

"And? She's basically my fuckin' mom. That don't mean shit."

I nod, stepping onto the little bridge that carries us across the tiny stream below. "True."

"VicVee!" he snaps.

I turn to him with a grin. "You're tailing someone and not someone the boys are aware of because you're not using your main PI. I also know you took a little road trip with Mac right after Raven and Maddoc got married, but it wasn't to see the person you're having watched. You have a master plan that's about to be put into motion, but it's a self-serving agenda, and before you get all mad and snap at me, there is nothing wrong with that when it doesn't hurt your family any."

Royce gapes at me. "Mother of goddamn, VicVee, that's some scary shit right there." He chuckles lightly, but then he leans forward, his mask slipping over his eyes, darkness taking over. "Say a word and I'll…"

His threat never follows. He gauges me, and when he nods, I decide he might just trust that I won't.

But I can't be too sure.

He moves by me, but before I can turn to follow, a warm body is behind me, locking me against the railing.

Captain's arms come around me, loosely holding me to him as his head falls to my shoulder, seeking out the skin of my collarbone. He plants a small kiss there, and he doesn't lift from the spot. He hugs me to him, so I allow my body to relax, giving him the weight of mine, and he accepts it with a heavy inhale.

We stand there, my eyes closed, as I think his are too, listening to the creek below us, neither of us letting go until, somewhere behind us, Zoey calls for her dad.

That night, Captain lays blanket after blanket on the balcony and pulls me outside with him. He turns off all the lights, nothing but the stars above us to light the area, and settles into the pallet, tugging me down beside him.

We lie there, staring up at the sky until we fall asleep, and in the morning, we pack up and head back to the unknown reality awaiting us.

CHAPTER 25
VICTORIA

"And that, right there, is the best lasagna you'll ever eat in your life, Zoey Bear." Royce winks at her, picking up his and Raven's empty plates on his way to the kitchen.

Zoey laughs, licking her fork, little feet swinging beneath the seat.

The others roll their eyes playfully, and when I look at Captain with a grin, I find his frown focused on the screen of his phone.

Before *I* frown too, I clean my mess and step out onto the porch for some fresh air. Raven follows. She drops beside me, pulling a blanket over her legs.

I look at her stomach, which seems to be growing a little more by the day.

She catches me, and a side grin takes over her face. "There's a human inside me. Weird shit, right?"

I chuckle, but it dies off on a sigh. "Yeah. It's a crazy process."

"How much do you know about the process, Vee?" she asks instantly, her eyes sliding back to mine.

I glance across the yard. "Too much, Rae. Can we leave it at that?"

"For now." She frowns. "Is he okay?"

My eyes fly to hers. "How would I know?"

"He spends his nights with you, Victoria."

"Does he?"

Restless thoughts spin in my head as, for the millionth time, I try to weigh the events of the last few weeks. Is he with me when he's in my bed?

Raven glares, but it's not for me, and then the front door opens and closes, and Captain barrels down the steps.

"Packman," she calls.

He skids to a stop, whipping around with his phone in his hand. His eyes fly between us.

"I'll be back," he says, quickly looking away. "Zoey's in the media room with Dad and Royce."

"Where are you going?" Raven asks.

"To grab somethin'."

Only when his taillights disappear does she turn to me with a scowl. "Why do I get the feeling he just lied to me?"

"I think he did."

"Maybe it's because you're right here."

A laugh bubbles from me, and she joins in, dropping her head back on the seat.

"Yeah, Raven." I sigh. "Maybe."

It doesn't take long for Maddoc to come for his girl, so I follow them inside and up the stairs. The two continue down the long hallway, following Royce's and Zoey's laughter into the media room while I disappear into mine.

I must fall asleep because I'm woken hours later when Captain comes inside my room.

He kneels at the side of my bed. "You awake?" he whispers.

"I am."

"Go on a drive with me."

My brows pull in, but I nod, climb from my bed, slip my shoes on, and walk over to where he now waits for me.

He holds my eyes a long moment and then takes the hoodie from around his arm, pulling it over my head. It swallows me whole, of course, but I don't care.

Captain inhales, long and deep, his hands coming up and pushing the hood down, his fingers slipping around my neck to free my hair from beneath the expensive cotton. He leans in, skimming his lips along my cheek, kissing where my jawbone meets my neck.

My eyes close, my palms lifting to his chest, and he reaches up and holds my hands a long moment before dropping one and tugging me along until we're out the front door and he has the passenger door open for me to climb inside.

We drive in comfortable silence for hours, going nowhere, simply around the town and up and down the country roads outside it, his hand latched tightly with mine the entire way.

Only when the moon is ready to rest does he pull down the long dirt road to the mansion.

Inside the house, he pauses in the hall near his door. Once again, he pulls me to him, his eyes a deeper blue, the green a thin hidden ring around them, and he leans in, kissing the same spot as earlier before he lets me go, stepping into the bathroom.

I stand there, listening as the shower is turned on, the soft vibration of the glass door opening and closing.

Before I can stop myself, I'm in his bedroom, standing right in front of his nightstand.

My fingers graze along the brass handle of the drawer, readying to open it and pull out the journal I know sits inside, but then his phone vibrates right on top, the screen lighting the still-dark room with a message not meant for me to see, from a name I wish I didn't.

My Mallory: when?

No.

My stomach bottoms out, dread digging deep within my chest and knocking me back.

I fall onto his mattress as the inevitable coils in my gut, stripping me of what I thought was our start.

But here he was, reaching for a completely different one.

I push my feet into my shoes, bending to pull the back up over my heel when Raven comes around the corner, fanning herself. "Where are you going?"

"To get some air," I tell her as I walk out, shutting the door behind me and starting down the dirt road toward the Bray houses.

The girls are scattered around, coming in and out, as are the boys from their house, all getting their daily required chores completed.

"Need a hand?"

Nira turns around and shrugs, getting back to pulling the weeds. I drop to my knees beside her, digging right into the dirt, and damn if the feel of the cool soil doesn't calm me.

Nira laughs. "You want some gloves?"

She holds out a box, but I shake my head.

"I'm good."

"Right," she scoffs. "If you were good, you wouldn't be spending your Saturday morning on your knees in the dirt at the group home you used to live in when you now live with a bunch of rich kids in a fancy-ass mansion."

"Meh." I shrug. "It's not that fancy."

When I look up, we both laugh.

"For real, though. If you don't want people to think you're miserable, maybe don't look like you are." Her eyes lift to the messy ball on my head held back by a green bandanna. "And try brushing your hair."

I fight a grin. "Shut up or you can do this by yourself."

"I don't need your help."

"No, but I have a joint we can smoke once your chores are done."

She looks up. "Okay, you get the right side; I'll get the left."

I smirk. "Deal."

We're done quickly and hiding out on the opposite side of the house, smoking.

"So I ran into Mike," she says casually as she takes a hit, missing the way my muscles lock.

"Oh yeah?" I spin the bandanna around my wrist. "When?"

"Couple days ago. I went into the Chinese place downtown to use the restroom, and when I was coming out, he was walking in."

He hates Chinese food. He followed her there. "What'd he say?"

"Asked how I was, how it was going at the house, and about you, duh."

I nod, rubbing my lips together. "What'd you tell him?"

"That if he was smart, he wouldn't go around asking about Captain Brayshaw's newest Bray girl." She shrugs, passing me the joint.

Bet he just loved hearing that.

"He just laughed," she continues. "Saw him leave a few minutes later. He got a new car."

My brows pull and I look at her. "Yeah?"

She nods. "Must have found himself a nice gig wherever it is he took off to. That sucker couldn't have been cheap."

I nod but don't comment.

What are you up to, Mike?

Nira takes one more hit and passes the joint back again, slowly pushing to her feet. "I've got to take a shower before the rest of the girls get done with their chores and hog the hot water. See you around."

Just like that, the other half of the day is left for me and my jumbled mind.

I make my way around the front of the group home, glancing from the girls' to the boys' home just across from it and out at the street ahead.

Fuck it.

I drop onto the grass where I stand and pull my phone out, flipping it around in my hand.

I take a deep breath, glaring at the screen.

I decide to try Maria again, but again there is no answer, and her voicemail is full. It's annoying, and to be honest I don't even know why I keep trying. If she doesn't want to talk, that's fine. I shouldn't care.

I don't care.

But why the fuck can't she answer?

What if it was about Zoey?

Where's Captain?

And why the fuck is Mike still here, and how the hell did he buy a new car?

I scoff at myself.

He's here because he hasn't had a chance to say bye to me yet.

Maybe I should go find him? Maybe I'm just bored out of my mind.

"What are you doin', girl?"

My shoulders fall, a sigh leaving me as I glance over my shoulder, shielding my eyes to see beyond the sun. Maybell comes down the steps, a town car pulling in in perfect timing with her feet hitting the walkway.

"Getting some sun." *Getting away from the Bray house.*

She eyes me, her lips pursed. "Mm-hm. Come on now, get on in."

I frown. "Why?"

Her dark brows lift. "'Cause I said, child. Get in. You can use a distraction. Getting some sun," she mocks with a scoff. "Girl, please."

A chuckle leaves me, and I'm tempted to ask how she would know, but that's a fool's question. She knows everything, so I push to my feet. "All right."

The car doesn't stop at the main grocery store she would normally go to; I know because I used to help her carry them inside. The driver continues down the road a little farther and around the corner where another, smaller store sits in a neighborhood.

We get inside and start checking off items on Maybell's long-ass list—it takes a lot to feed ten to twelve teenage girls.

"I heard you made your cinnamon rolls," she says, pointing to a large bag of rice.

I bend down to grab it, dropping it into the cart before bringing my eyes to hers. "Gee, wonder how Rolland was aware I knew how."

Her smile is small as she continues to push the cart farther down the aisle. "I wonder…"

When I shake my head, she chuckles and nods toward a case of flour.

"You know, that's my recipe."

My eyes slide to hers, and slowly I set the item into the cart.

"Made those for Raven's mother when she was young, for Rolland and the boys' biological fathers, for the boys as they grew…"

For everyone but Zoey.

I frown, my hand shooting out and gripping the metal cart, and her eyes come to mine. They're gentle and knowing, and it pisses me off more.

"Why tell Rolland knowing he'd ask me to? That wasn't my memory to take," I say. "Hasn't she lost enough family firsts and traditions?"

Maybell's smile is kind, maybe a little sad. "You've been making those for her for some time, Tor."

My heart shakes.

And there it is. She did know.

"Why would you teach me how to make them?" I didn't mean to whisper, but that's how my words come out.

I don't even know why I asked. The answer is obvious.

Because she knew—she knew where I was disappearing to each day and what Zoey was missing out on already, so she gave me something she trusted I'd give her. A piece of home I never knew existed. Sure, it's a damn recipe, but it's their recipe.

I let go of the cart and face forward again.

We get halfway around the store, the cart already half full, when her usual helper from the group home finds us, deeming me useless.

I could stay, but she's aware I'm not fond of others and would use this lady's arrival as my escape anyway, so she turns to me before I can.

There's a shadow in her dark eyes, one that has me pausing, but instead of voicing what's crossed her mind, her hand finds my bicep and she squeezes. "Go on," she orders quietly. "You know the way home."

For some reason, I feel compelled to say, "I'm good, Maybell."

She nods, the corner of her lips lifting. "You are, Tor. You will be."

I pinch my lips together, nodding, and get out of the aisle as quickly as I can.

I hate when she gets all crypto like that.

On my way out, I buy a drink, taking a second to open it and breathe before cutting across a small park beside the building. I get halfway through the open field when my steps slow, only to come to a full-on halt seconds later.

Across the road a sexy, sleek, black SUV I'd recognize anywhere is parked, and sitting right inside, with the driver's window rolled halfway down, is Captain.

His chin is dropped to his chest, and I can't tell from here, but I think his eyes are closed.

Panic wraps around my ribs, squeezing like a tight rope, and I'm ready to run right for him, to make sure he's okay, conscious and breathing, when suddenly his head pops up, the window rising with it.

His door is shoved open, and he slams it closed behind him just as quickly. Phone in hand, Captain takes quick steps up a long, curving driveway, and right as he reaches the end, where the cement meets the stone steps leading to the front door, it opens… and all the air is forced from my airway as Mallory is revealed on the other side.

As if my blood has turned to stone in my veins, the unexpected weight threatens to collapse my lungs and snap my ankles.

I'm frozen in place, unable to look away, traitorous eyes glued on what may very well be the end of our beginning, on Ken and his Barbie, flawless, gorgeous—made for each other.

He says something, and I wish I knew what, as she answers with a smile.

Mallory steps from the doorway but keeps one hand inside, wrapped around the doorframe.

The ice that froze me here must have fully taken over, numbing other parts of me, because I feel nothing when she grips his shirt as he likes to do with mine, gently pulling him closer, and it doesn't sting when she angles her mouth to his and he does nothing to stop her.

She's cautious, almost slow motion in her advance, or maybe that's how my mind decides to torture me, by slowing this nightmare down to make sure I can replay it with no moment left out.

Her pink lips lock with his.

Thick, full lips I crave but am not allowed to touch.

That refuse to touch mine.

What's worse than the kiss itself is Captain's response—or lack thereof.

He doesn't pull back, doesn't tear away or shove her off.

Her lips mold to his, and he accepts them, accepts her.

Her feet begin to shuffle backward, her lips still aligned with his, fists still tight on his shirt as she leads him up the two steps from the porch to the entryway.

She stares up at him, and he stares down at her as his foot makes the final move, officially placing him across the threshold.

Blindly, Captain reaches behind him, closing them inside.

As if the seal of the door shook the ground beneath me, cracked the earth to its core and released molten lava right at my feet, the ice in my blood melts, and I'm flooded with everything at once.

The ache and the burn and the venomous sting threaten to take me to my knees, but I refuse to fall.

It's a deserving pain, after all, so I welcome it, embrace it.

"Fuck you doing, VicVee?" Royce's voice suddenly meets my ear, and then he's beside me, staring at the same door I can't seem to pull my eyes from. "Go get your man." I must shake my head because he asks with a heated undertone, "He not worth the fight, or are you too weak, not up for a challenge?"

"He's worth every hit, Royce. Every battle." I'm surprised by the hollowness of my own voice, and he must be too, because his head snaps my way. Slowly, I meet his eyes. "I'd fight for what I want, and I can sure as shit handle it. I'm not too weak or afraid or anything else you might think or want to believe, not in the slightest."

He turns his body to face me better.

"I'd go up against anything or anyone for him."

He frowns, whispering, "Except her."

I nod, and I'd go as far as to say he feels bad, not that I want him to.

Royce looks away, heavy tension lining his forehead. "That's fair, but that girl, she don't deserve him."

If only he knew how true a statement that was.

His footsteps carry him away, and then he calls, "Come on, girl. Let's go home, huh?"

Translation: Let's not sit here and see how long it takes him to come back out.

"Did you know?" I call out.

"That Cap is fucking his baby mama, who I'm half tempted to feed to the gorilla at the zoo?" he snaps. "Nah, can't say I did."

He slips inside with a hard slam to his door, so I make my way over, climbing into the passenger seat of his SUV.

He puts it in gear, but before he presses on the gas, his dark eyes swing to mine. He opens his mouth to speak but then shakes his head and off we go.

Only once on the drive back do I realize the timing was no accident, none of it. The trip to the store, Cap's arrival, Royce and the ride home—Maybell knew what she was doing.

She always does.

The rest of the afternoon is a wasted pit of time, like staring at the sun at the peak of day wishing for the moon to show himself.

I'm about to give in and look at the clock I've forced my eyes not to touch when an engine dies out front, alerting us Captain's finally back.

The door flies open, and he rushes inside, quickly tossing his keys on the coffee table.

"Hey," he says, stiff and to no one in particular, his feet carrying him directly through the living room, right past us. "I talked to Dad. He said he just now convinced Zoey to leave the zoo."

Royce's eyes stay locked on me as he talks to Captain. "Season pass is gettin' its use, huh?"

Captain chuckles, and it serves as the phantom of my dying opera. "I know, right?" His left foot hits the first stair, his gaze never even flicking in our direction. "Let me shower, and I'll do dinner tonight."

A shower… Why a shower?

My stomach turns.

Royce's eyes tighten, moving between mine.

I wait for him to call Cap out or at the very least put me on blast for spying, but all he does is reach beside him for a bottle of Crown, twist off the lid, and take a swig. He passes it to me, answering Cap's question even though he didn't stick around to hear one, "Sounds good, brother."

I take the fucking bottle, knowing I'd have to consume more than this thing can hold in order to get drunk enough to hide from the visions in my head.

I swish the golden liquid, eyes on Royce's. "Got anything stronger?"

CHAPTER 26
CAPTAIN

My tires crunch against the gravel, rocks flying around when I slam my brakes, but I don't wait for the gate to be opened for me. I throw it in park, keys still inside, and hop the fuck out.

Andre meets me halfway through the crowd, but I don't stop to let him talk, and as quick as he was in front of me, he's behind me.

"She's as bad as your brother's girl. Don't listen for shit," he shouts above the roar of the crowd.

"I'm aware." I shove the door to the Wolves Den the rest of the way open, but I'm not seeing her or my brother anywhere.

"I wasn't worried much since your boy is with her," he says. "And she seemed good when she got here, but, uh…I don't know about now."

My head snaps toward his, and Andre slips in front of me with his hands raised, nodding with a tense look in his eyes. "Right-side room, my man."

I rush for where he mentions, the room where Victoria poured a drink on that Amber chick, reaching it right as the dude who makes drinks in here comes out with empty hands. He quickly disappears.

I tear inside, and all heads fly my way—except Victoria's.

"Out," I snap, eyes on my brother, who is laid out on the couch, legs spread and arms draped along the back of it, joint in one hand, Victoria in the other.

The stray girls and guys rush by, and then it's just us three and the music.

Victoria's head is dropped back, so when she opens her mouth, Royce's arm is able to curl right around. He cages her in as he slips the joint between her lips.

She inhales, holding it in as she leans forward, leisurely pushing to her feet, and takes the few steps to me. She blows the smoke into my face on a slow blink.

"What are you doing?" I grind out.

The corners of her mouth lift with her hands, and suddenly she's dancing, eyes closed, goofy-ass fuckin' grin in place.

"What's she on?"

Royce tilts his head. "A pill or four to do the job alcohol couldn't."

"And you didn't think to call me? Why?"

He chuckles, dragging his ass to his feet as he stumbles toward me. "Because she asked me, that's fuckin' why. I wasn't so sure you'd care, brother. She's just a little liar, betrayed you, right? Broke trust? Showed no loyalty? Did one of the worst fuckin' things she could do?" He eyes me a moment. "That's why you spent the last month fighting how she makes you feel, right? Why we spent the last fucking month hating her, ain't it?"

My head tugs back. "That's why you brought her here?"

"To see if you'd come for her?" He lifts his arms out, head swaying a bit. "Yup, and you did."

I study him, finding no hint of humor or sense of pride, nothing that shows his purpose for tonight was fulfilled by my showing up.

A sharp twinge shoots up my spine, stiffening my neck. "What's wrong?"

He laughs, but it's hollow, his hand coming down hard on my shoulder as he steps directly beside me, our heads turned toward each other. "Nothing, bro." He eyes me. "Not a fuckin' thing."

His shoulder knocks mine as he makes his way out, and worry pulls at my brows, but I shake it off, turning to Victoria.

The lighting is low, the glow of the room a soft red and likely heightening her high.

I move toward her, and with every step, my heart hits harder against my chest.

She sways in ways I've yet to see, a snakelike rhythm I didn't know she had.

My stomach aches as I watch her, a sick and twisted pain that plays a lot like guilt.

Beauty…

Her eyes pop open, meeting mine, and all her movement stops, her hands fall to her sides like deadweight, and her head begins to tip, too heavy for her to hold up any longer.

That's how med cocktails work, in spurts of energy, and then you're like a fucking zombie to the outside world while living in your own twisted one.

With a frown, I wrap my arm around her middle, scooping her in my arms, and glance over my shoulder.

Andre rushes up, talking into his earpiece, and as quick as he's called, more men are in front of us, clearing a path. Head after head turns our way, but nobody stares long and not a word is spoken.

She laughs at nothing along the way, her eyes snapping around as if following a butterfly only she can see.

Andre opens the gate wider so I can easily exit and pulls my passenger door open for me, disappearing just as quickly.

I lay her in the seat, reclining it so she's able to lie back, and reach across to buckle her in.

She snaps from her little trance, a hand shooting out to cover mine on the seat belt.

I turn my head toward her, and she tilts hers.

"My sweet Captain," she rasps, her fingers coming up to skim along my jaw. Slowly, the pad of her thumb drags along my bottom lip, only to come back to the center. She slides it down until my mouth is free from her touch and subconsciously my chin dips with her, fighting to keep the connection. "And his sweet, poisoned lips."

My brows pull in, and I touch her flushed face with the back of my hand. "You feelin' okay?"

She hums, her eyes closing as her hands leave me completely.

I glide my knuckle along her jaw, my palm opening to brush across the silk of her skin, but she doesn't move.

She's asleep.

My sleeping beauty.

I sigh, step back, and close the door.

The second I turn, knuckles come down across my chin, and I fall back against the door.

My head whips around, my body setting into fight mode in the same second, but I freeze when I find Royce standing there, his hand still in a fist at his side.

He glares but says nothing, and for some reason neither do I.

I stand there, silent, as he tears the back door open and throws himself inside.

It takes a minute for me to collect myself, and then I call Maddoc.

He answers on the first ring.

"I got 'em."

"Why didn't he answer?" he snaps.

I shake my head, walking around to my side. "They're fucked-up. I don't even know if he has his phone or not."

"Any trouble?"

"Nah." I climb inside, frowning, glancing at Royce over my shoulder. "They're both already passed out. Guess they wanted to get fucked-up."

Maddoc pauses. "Without us?"

"Maybe 'cause I'm a baby-carrying buzzkill," Raven offers, letting me know we're on speakerphone.

"Yeah." I nod, tension lining my gut as I look at the small cut on my lip in the mirror.

Maybe.

VICTORIA

When my eyes peel open, I freeze, close and reopen them, but when I do, he's still here, in my bed.

Slowly, I sit up, and my head pounds instantly.

A hangover? Seriously?

I lick my lips, realizing how dry my mouth is, and climb from the bed, all my clothes from last night still on, minus the shoes.

I tiptoe to the bathroom, and right as I'm about to close the door, my eyes move back to the bed.

Captain lies flat on his back, shirt off, staring right at me.

The shit from yesterday comes crashing back like a truck into a tree; everything inside me bends and breaks on impact, reshaping what was never formed right in the first place.

He kissed Mallory, probably had sex with her, and here he is, just-fucked hair and worn-out eyes to match, but there was no action in my bed.

"What's wrong?" he rasps.

"Nothing."

"You're lying."

"Oh, now you can tell when I'm lying or not?"

His eyes narrow and he pushes into a sitting position.

I lean against the frame. "You should go."

His frown deepens, but it's the confusion in his eyes forcing mine away.

"Go, before Zoey comes looking."

"I told you before…" He trails off, clearly attempting to gauge me. "Let me worry about her."

I nod, and slowly he drags himself to his feet, but he doesn't walk out; he makes his way to me, and with every step, my ribs ache.

My throat thickens as his knuckles find their way under my chin, lifting my head to his. His steady scrutiny momentarily steals my thoughts, and I sag against him. "Next time you want to go out and get fucked-up, don't."

He holds me there, in his palm, under his spell, and then he lets go, and the hole it leaves inside me is a sign I need to prepare to do the same.

The plan was to make him mine.

Plans change.

CHAPTER 27
VICTORIA

After a long, scorching shower, I make my way downstairs, my foot hitting the final step at the same time Captain's carry him out the front door.

I look to Zoey sitting at the bar with Raven, a plate of cut-up strawberries and a cup of milk in front of her.

The second Captain is gone, Raven hops up to grab a can of whipped cream from the fridge and shakes it up. "Okay, Zo, let me show you how to eat a strawberry."

Maddoc scoffs, coming around the corner with his gym bag over his shoulder. "Keep pouring all that white into your mouth, baby, and I'll—"

"Yo!" Royce shouts, throwing a couch pillow at Maddoc, but it falls in the middle of the floor. "Sweet little baby girl ears."

Raven laughs and nods her chin at Zoey, who follows her lead, leaning her head back so Raven can spray some right into her mouth.

Zoey laughs, but then her eyes widen. "Oh no! I have to tell Papa something!"

Raven quickly spins, flicking her cream-covered tongue along Maddoc's lips, and hurries after her. "Tell Captain we're out back."

Maddoc tries to frown at the shit on his mouth, but he can't completely hide the smirk as he licks his lips. "You sure you don't wanna shoot some hoops? Mac and a couple other assholes are gonna be out there."

Royce shakes his head, pulling his eyes from his phone to Maddoc's. "I'm good."

"You mean you feel like shit?" he tosses out.

Royce nods. "Yup."

"That's what you get, dick," he snaps. "Watch Raven."

"I know the drill, brother."

Maddoc nods, tipping his chin toward me in acknowledgment as he walks out.

I grab an apple, biting into it as I lean across the counter.

Royce stares right at me, and I can tell he has something on his mind, but before anything can be said, the front door opens and Captain walks in.

He glances around, his eyes landing on me.

I cover my mouth to speak with my mouth full of apple. "Zoey's outside with your dad and Raven."

It takes him a moment, but then he nods, and off he goes.

I wait until his footsteps can no longer be heard and push up on my palm. My eyes lock with Royce's. "Will you take me to Maria's?"

His glare is instant. "Why you askin' me?"

"Because anyone else will want to know why and ask questions along the way. You won't."

He pushes to his feet, coming to stand across from me. I'm sure he'll say no, tell me to fuck off, but he doesn't. He steps back, pulls his keys from his pocket, and presses a button on the little black fob. "Get in. I'll meet you out there."

I toss the apple in the garbage, doing as he asks.

Five minutes later, he's sliding in his seat right as Raven starts walking down the porch steps, headed right for us.

I sigh, looking at Royce.

"I'm on babysitting duty." He grins.

I can't help it; a small laugh leaves me. I go to open my door, but Raven catches it, slamming it shut, and climbs in the back seat.

"If you guys don't stop acting like I'm fragile, I will show you real fuckin' loud that I'm not. I can sit in the back seat of a giant, luxury-ass car." She chuckles, closing her door and getting comfortable. "There're even ass warmers back here. I'm good."

We laugh and Royce pulls out of the driveway onto the dirt road.

"So." Raven sits forward. "Where we going?"

My head snaps toward Royce, who smirks at the road.

"Go on, VicVee, share with the class."

Damn it.

I sigh, spinning in my seat to face her. "We're going to Maria's."

Raven's mouth opens only to clamp shut as she meets Royce's gaze in the mirror, quickly moving it to mine. "What are you doing, Vee?" she asks, shaking her head. "You don't ask one to do something the others wouldn't like. Trust me, I've done it. It pisses everyone off, but that's not the part I'm trippin' on." Her eyes narrow. "You asked him to take you somewhere, and he said yes. Something happened, and he knows about it."

I don't say anything, but whatever she sees staring back has her dropping against the seat with a small, almost unnoticeable nod. "Turn the music up, Royce, and stop for ice cream on the way."

He chuckles. "You got it, RaeRae."

A few minutes into the drive, Raven asks, "You think Captain would be mad at you for wanting to see your mom?"

"She's not my mom."

"Even if you don't claim her, she's still your mom. Just answer the question."

I glare out the side window. "Should I care if he was?"

"I wouldn't if it were me," she admits. "I hated my mom, yeah, that was common knowledge, but she was mine to decide what to do with, no one else's. No matter what she did or didn't do."

I hesitate before sharing, "Maybe it makes me fucked-up, but I don't want a relationship with her. That's not why I'm doing this."

"I'm sure you do, you just haven't realized it yet," Raven says. "But either way, if that's not the reason we're temporarily hiding our little trip from Cap, then why?"

"Zoey lived with her almost since birth. She cared for her day and night, and as far as I know, she hasn't reached out to anyone once since Zoey came home. That's… I'd expect more from her. I've called her a few times and nothing."

"Goddamn, VicVee," Royce grinds out, his glare coming back. "You think something's up. That's what this is about."

I shrug.

"You should have fuckin' said somethin'," he barks.

Meaning when trouble is or could be involved, his brothers should be too.

The rest of the drive is filled with music and pulling over once so Raven can throw up the ice cream she ate on the way. When we get to the long country road leading to the home Zoey spent her first few years of life in, a chill runs down my spine.

Royce turns into the driveway, drives through the sky-high bush line, and then we reach the iron gate. He presses hard on his brakes, bringing us to a screeching halt.

The sudden stop sends dust into the air, the small gust of wind stirring up the ash and creating a scorching, black rain.

"Holy shit." Raven leans forward in her seat.

I reach for the handle, and then the doors lock, and my eyes fly to Royce.

He glares at Raven.

"Keep that ass in this car. I fuckin' mean it, RaeRae. Move and I will tape you to the seat. I don't give a shit. Got it?" He tips his chin, but it's in fear and love for the girl who broke through his heart.

Surprising us both, she nods and sits back. "But you only get five minutes."

Royce gives a curt nod, and the lock sounds. Both of us step out into the yard.

I reach for the fencing, but Royce's hand flies out to stop mine.

"Hold up. We need to make sure the electricity is off."

"It is," I tell him, glancing where the little red light normally blinks.

I push, and it begins to slide along its track.

We walk down the driveway, toward the pile of burned wood and black powder, and then I see it: the garden on the side, the perfect curve and bright purple flowers, untouched and soaking in all the sun has to offer.

But it's the new piece to the property behind it that has my airway closing.

A wall, built strong and tall and wide, from one end of the flowers to the next, a heavy ivy draped thick and full from top to bottom, identical to my once-was prison.

My chin unexpectedly wobbles, so I bite into my bottom lip. "For eighteen years she hid away, all to get caught in the crossfire in the end," I breathe.

Royce's head snaps my way, his eyes widening as trickles of red spill down my chin.

His shoulders square, and he glances across the acreage, coming to his own conclusion. "Graven."

Before I can blink again, Royce is dragging me to the SUV, shoving me in through his door, and climbing in behind. "Call Maddoc," he tells Raven as he peels out, flying down the road.

"He's on the court." She shakes her head. "His phone has to be on the bench."

A few seconds later, she curses, shaking her head. "Cap's not answering either."

"He's home. He should."

"He was getting in the pool with Zoey. His phone must not be on him either. Talk."

"The house is ash, burned down," Royce says.

"Eye for an eye?" Raven wonders.

Of course, that would make sense, considering it was on her word that one of the other council families came in and burned Donley's place, my once home, the Graven estate, to ash.

After he betrayed the system built over hundreds of years ago with his lies and greed, he was cast out by the heads of all five families, a mutual decision among them all.

But that's if you look at this at face value.

This isn't about the fire or revenge or a home for a home. This is about the beautiful, familiar wall built in its place and the memories it's meant to trigger, the promises made alongside it.

"I promise you. It'll be you and me forever one day, no matter what."

The only person this was meant to speak to is me.

Message received.

"We're going to Maddoc," Royce announces, as if there was any question.

I sit back, closing my eyes the rest of the drive, knowing one thing for sure.

He's watching.

"You good, RaeRae?" Royce asks a few minutes later, as the last time Raven came down this road, she was crashed into by a Bray-hating psychopath. "Baby's good?"

He reaches back, and Raven grabs his hand, giving it a light squeeze.

"Yeah, Ponyboy. We're good. Let's get to Maddoc."

"Couple more minutes."

Once we're a couple of streets from the park, I unbuckle my seat belt. "Let me out. I'll walk home."

Royce's head snaps my way. "Fuck no."

"Come on. I need some air."

"You're 'bout to get some fuckin' air when we get out at the park."

"You pass the street on the way to the courts anyway."

He says nothing.

"Let me out or I'll just walk away the second we stop."

“Then walk the fuck away when we stop,” he growls. “I’m not pulling over.”

I shake my head, throwing myself against the seat.

“Let her out, Royce,” Raven tells him.

“What?!” he shouts. “This is already my fuckin’ ass here. I—”

“You saw how I was after everything with my mom,” she reasons with him. “Come on, Royce,” she whispers. “She only wants to walk home, not run off like I did.”

Royce’s jaw ticks, but when we come around the corner, only a turn or two from the Brayshaw mansion he should be passing to get to the courts, he pulls to the curb, pops the lock, but doesn’t look over.

I don’t hesitate, climb right out, and walk a single block up, where I plant my ass on the curbside.

With a deep breath, I grab my phone, trying Maria once more, but this time it doesn’t even ring, and I hang up before I can be told the mailbox is full.

I don’t know why I even tried; I know she’s gone.

The flowers and the wall made just for me are confirmation.

I drag myself to my feet, attempting to stuff my phone in my pocket as I spin on my heels to head home, but it falls to the cement when suddenly I’m staring into a pair of ocean-blue eyes.

Fuck.

CHAPTER 28
VICTORIA

I'd swear minutes tick by and neither of us speak, so I decide to be the first. "I knew you'd find your way to me."

"I had to."

I lick my lips, looking to the side, only to come right back. "No, you didn't. You should have stayed away. You should walk away now."

"I've been trying to get you alone for days. I'm not going anywhere."

I scoff, shaking my head, careful not to bump shoulders as I step past.

"What, can we not even talk?"

No. We can't.

"Damn it, Victoria. Please."

My teeth clench, but I keep moving.

"I'm scared!"

I freeze, squeezing my eyes closed.

Don't fall for this.

The self-reminder fails, and my shoulders drop.

I spin around, my hands flopping out as if to say *okay, you got me*, but the longer we stare at each other, the clearer it is one of us is out of the loop, and that one is me. "Scared of what, Mallory?"

"He didn't tell you."

I don't allow myself to swallow and manage a calm and clear voice. "Tell me what?"

"He's letting me see her," she says, gauging me.

My heart drops, my entire world—a world that never belonged to me—crashing at my feet.

My Zoey.

Her daughter.

I can't stop them, my tears building without permission.

She zones right in on the moisture in my eyes, a heavy glint of something shining in her own.

I know what I want to say to her right now, and that's to back the fuck up and get the fuck out, not to play games she's not strong enough for, but I can't.

Calling her out on her bullshit will only backfire, and I'll be the one who takes the heat.

If I want to be Brayshaw, on my own merit and at my own hand, I have to be brave, selfless, even more so in a situation like this.

I have to let the green monster inside her out.

So I rub my lips together with a nod, fighting beyond the acid coating my throat, begging me to keep the words buried, to stay silent.

"You shouldn't be afraid of seeing her. She's… God, Mallory." A shuddered cry steals my breath. "She's perfect. Beautiful."

She cries, the back of her hand coming up to the edge of her nose as tears roll down her pink cheeks.

"I made a mistake," she whispers. "Lots of them, really."

Boulders, heavy mounds of them, fall onto my chest, crashing into my lungs and crushing my ribs along the way, or at least that's how it feels.

"I thought I could do this, but I can't. I—"

"Wait," I rush out, pulling air into my aching body. "What are you saying? Can't what?"

"I knew you'd be at that festival," she admits.

My brows slam together. "How?"

"It doesn't matter." She shakes her head, a barren look taking over her. "I didn't… I panicked that day. I was hurt." A small glare forms through her cloudy eyes, and guilt adds to the pressure in my head. "Confused. Victoria, you—"

"Stop," I cut her off.

"Tell him I can't come, that I don't want to see her."

My head tugs back, a broken laugh escaping as I subconsciously move away from her. "No."

"You have to," she snaps.

"Fuck you, and fuck no." I look at her hands she nervously pulls at. "No way."

Her mouth opens only to close a second later, a bitter, lost laugh leaving her. "He's with you, isn't he?"

"You have no place to question me."

"Don't I?" she throws back. "Are you in love with him?"

More pain, more pressure.

"You have to tell him," she demands, and now it's her who begins to back away, a cautionary flash in her eye. "Unless you want him—want them—sitting and waiting, all for no one to show up."

My shoulders fall, another round of tears flooding my sight.

I shake my head, turning my body away from hers. "It's like you don't know him at all, Mallory." Somehow, I force my eyes back to hers. "I can scream it in his face, record this, and play it back for him to hear with his own ears, and still…he will be wherever he promised he would. He has to see to believe. It's who he is."

It's almost as if she didn't hear a word I said, like this entire conversation never happened, as a lost look blankets her.

"What happened, Tor? Why'd you—" She cuts herself off, her fear of the answer keeping her from asking the question.

And for a moment, I'm grateful she's too weak.

Her eyes travel over me, settling on the ground beneath my feet, and she swallows.

She walks away, and I'm left to head home and break the dam built by the enemy. I've said it all along: No matter who you are, hope is a dangerous beast; it sinks you and…

When you drown, your hope floats, but it's not strong enough to pull you up with it. So like a body chained to a brick, down you go.

I don't remember the short walk to the mansion, but suddenly I'm standing in the driveway and then stepping inside the house.

Not thirty seconds after I close the door, Zoey is skipping down the stairs, Captain at her heels. Only when she reaches the bottom step do I notice the little bow in her hair today, the same soft shade of blue as the tiny Vans on her feet.

She spots me first, running over with a smile.

"Rora! I got new shoes."

I lower onto one knee, so she and I are eye level, and let her interlace our hands. "I saw."

"Do you love them?"

I love you, pretty girl.

"I do." I swallow, releasing her, and she runs off.

My eyes trail her as she goes, catching a flash of pink as she does, and slowly, I turn my head toward Captain.

He pats at his front and back pockets, his eyes bouncing around the room until they land on the counter where his phone is plugged into the charger. Once it's in his hands, he's searching around again, a small frown wrinkling his forehead.

"Hey," I say, slowly pushing to my feet.

His eyes briefly meet mine, and his lips rise into a small smile. "Hey."

"Looking for something?" I ask, walking farther into the room.

"My keys."

"They're in your hand, Cap."

He freezes, opening his palm with a scowl.

"Leaving?"

He hesitates, but then his shoulders seem to grow wider as he opens his stance. In that one move, his decision, if ever he questions himself, was cemented. "Yeah, I am," he says.

This is what I meant when I told Mallory that Captain has to see with his own two eyes. He has to read a situation, understand it for what it is, feel it in his gut. He would drive himself mad with what-ifs, forever question me if I were to even hint at that thought.

So I smile as real as I can muster. "You painted her nails."

His eyes move between mine, and he nods. "Took me a couple tries."

A small laugh leaves me, and at first, his lips lift, but then he glares at the floor, and his feet start moving. "Captain—"

"I have to go," he says, cutting me off. "Zo."

Zoey runs right in, a fluffy, basketball-shaped, mini-backpack on her back, and slips her hand right into Captain's.

They walk out the door, leaving it wide open, so I step out onto the porch.

"So much, Rora!" Zoey calls just before Captain closes her door, climbing into his own.

Each roll of the tires has my pulse growing stronger.

So much, ZoZo.

The second they get onto the dirt road, Royce's SUV flies by, passing Captain's, and when Captain keeps going, Royce slams on his brakes, sending dust flying all around.

Maddoc's and Royce's doors are thrown open, and they both pop out, leaning over where the hood meets the open door.

They look down the road and to me, both coming closer.

"He left?" Royce shouts.

I nod.

"You didn't tell him." Maddoc's frown deepens. "Why?"

He holds my eyes, doing his best to read mine, only looking away when Royce is suddenly standing beside me on the porch.

He waits for me to look into his eyes, understanding. "Why would she?"

In other words, why would I think he'd care?

He hated Maria and would have no other reason to give a damn.

Right?

CHAPTER 29
CAPTAIN

"Daddy, look!"

I follow her little finger, spotting the squirrel right before it runs up the tree trunk. "I see, baby girl."

Zoey taps the little stick against the root of the tree and then sets it down and runs back over to me. "Can we go home now?"

I turn her toward me, and she puts her little hands on my cheeks. "You ready to go home now? See your papa and your uncles, Raven?" My eyes move between hers. "Rora?"

She smiles, squeezing my cheeks until my lips are pinched. "And my bestest friend?"

A small chuckle leaves me, but with it comes pain in my ribs.

"Ready, Daddy?"

My eyes canvass the area once more, and I pull out my phone to check the time. Two hours late.

I give Zoey a little shake and she laughs, wrapping her hands around my neck as I lift her from her feet and head back for the car.

"How about we go see a movie and then we go home?" I ask her. "Does that sound like fun?"

"Yes!"

I get her buckled in and drive us to the movie theater, but the second the SUV is in park, Zoey's eyes close.

Only then do the events of tonight hit me.

I don't know what I expected, what I had hoped for.

That might be a lie.

I've spent almost three and a half years hating Mallory.

First for leaving and breaking a part of me I never meant to give to her, then for hiding my daughter from me, and later, when I no longer gave a single shit about her myself, I hated her for our daughter.

How dare she abandon our little girl.

The second she asked to see her, my instincts told me *no, fuckin' never*, but the guy she left behind was confused, and he and the father I am now, who doesn't understand how she could leave, blended together. Millions of questions ran through my head.

What if she didn't want to leave me but was forced?

What if she never planned to give Zoey away but felt helpless?

What if she did what she did for our little girl?

What if it was honor and selflessness that took her from me, from us?

A decision a Brayshaw would make?

If there was a chance, even the smallest of one, what kind of father would I be if I didn't try to take it, if I didn't try to give my daughter a mother she deserves?

Mine was taken from me. I could never take hers from her.

Not that Mallory gives a shit; she didn't even have the guts to tell me she wouldn't be here.

With a deep breath, I pull from the parking lot, intending to head home, but end up driving around for who knows how long.

Maybell is sitting on the porch when I turn onto the property, but as she sees me, she stands and walks to the edge of the driveway.

I slow to a stop, rolling down my window when she makes her way to it.

"Ms. Maybell, kinda cold out tonight to be sitting on the porch."

Her eyes are heavy with understanding. She was waiting for me. "Tough day, boy?"

I'm unable to hold in the frown that takes over, and she gives a sad smile, her hand coming up to touch my cheek.

"Go on," she whispers. "Get that baby girl tucked in bed."

I nod, waiting until she's inside the house with the door closed, and roll the rest of the way down the road to do just that.

Zoey wakes up as I carry her into the house, and I'm surprised when there's no one sitting around in the living room.

"Baby's sleeping, Daddy?" she whispers with a yawn.

"Yeah, Zo, I think everyone is sleeping. Let's give you a quick bath since you're awake now, okay? Get you nice and warm for your bed."

She nods, shifting in my arms.

I set her down on her little stool in the bathroom and run the warm water, adding a few bubbles so she doesn't get too cranky, and help her inside.

As I start washing her hair, she begins to sing, "Wash, wash the baby…wash, wash the baby."

I grin and she smiles too, blowing at the bubble in front of her. "That's a good song."

She yawns, tilting her head back and closing her eyes so I can rinse the soap out. "I'm gonna sing it to my bestest friend."

I grab her hand, so she can stand, and lift her from the bath, wrapping a towel around her. "I think that's a good idea. Raven will love that song."

I carry her to her room and help her into pajamas.

She grabs the little brush from her dresser and runs it over to me, and I gently comb through the blond curls, and with each swipe, my chest tightens.

She may never know where her curls come from or that the golden shine in her hair isn't only from me. I stop brushing and turn her in my arms, tucking her hair behind her ears. "Want to bring your pillow and blanket and sleep in Daddy's bed?"

She shakes her head, glancing at her own. "My train and my bunny and my other toys missed me, see?"

On her bed, there must be six stuffed animals along with her favorite one, the stuffed train Maddoc had ordered for her when she was first set to come home.

A chuckle leaves me. "Okay, baby."

I kiss her cheek and stand, following as she climbs into her bed, tucking her blankets to her chin.

She reaches up to grab my face, so I lower, and the vessels attached to my heart pump fiercely, to the point of pain, when she rubs her little nose along mine.

Victoria.

What the hell did I do?

I swallow, kiss her forehead, and whisper into her ear, "I love you, Zo."

She yawns, wraps her arm around her little train, and closes her eyes, her soft words finding me right as I begin to close the door, "Love you, Daddy."

Daddy.

Something I am because I was gifted with the position, and not by one girl but two.

I go to step into my room, but when I spot Royce's door open, I move to his instead.

I need advice, help.

I need my fucking brothers.

We don't hide from each other, never lie or go behind the others' backs, and I've done all of those in the last few days.

Betrayal burns deep into my core, and it's coming from every angle, but I suck it up and step inside his room, ready to give every last detail…only to find it empty.

I move inside, sitting on the edge of his bed, and drag my hands down my face.

I could easily go down to get Maddoc, but I won't wake up Raven when I know she's having an even harder time sleeping than normal.

They'd both be pissed if they knew I even paused for such a reason.

I decide to text Royce, asking where he's at, and he sends back a single word.

Royce: *out*

I sigh, toss my phone to the floor, and tug at my hair.

He's pissed, and I am such a dick.

I replay the day, and it's not the disappointment or anger I expected that I get stuck on. A second round of burning abandonment eats at me as I remember the way Victoria laughed when I admitted I messed up painting Zoey's nails and had to try again.

It was so soft, even her eyes smiled, as if she could picture it or wished to, like she wanted to be there to see it.

I bet she'd have recorded the sight rather than tried to step in to do it herself.

Forcing my thoughts to keep moving, my mind goes to the long drive I took with a sleeping Zoey in the back seat. Only then do I realize it's the same one I took Victoria on.

I was chasing the comfortable silence she gave me, the sense of ease and clear mind she provided. Having her beside me erased the millions of thoughts that were plaguing me only minutes before.

Zoey was home safe with my family, and my girl was safe with me.

My girl?

My lungs deny me a breath as guilt eats at my betrayal like a feast for the wicked, tearing at my insides and reaching for the gut, the one part of me I've always been able to follow. To trust as I was taught, but everything that's happened lately was a result of my decision.

My instincts left me blind.

Nothing Victoria did was to harm.

Victoria changed my world when she left those hospital records for me to find, and then she came into it and changed it again and again, for the good and then the bad, and the truth followed, and with it, I was struck.

I am struck.

She was loyal to me when she had no reason to be.

The second the thought hits, a heavy sense of desperation floods my veins, and I'm on my feet pacing.

What the fuck did I do?

I need her.

Her hands and her skin and smile, her glare and the bratty little attitude she loves to give when she's pushing back.

I want her to push back.

I want her.

My feet carry me to her bedroom, and I lay my knuckle against the wood of her door, slowly pushing it open.

The light of the moon is a little brighter than normal tonight and peeking through the edge of the curtain. It hits the chandelier above just right, illuminating her figure beneath the comforter I picked out for her, in the bed that I put together myself because I trusted no one else to do it right.

Her chest rises, rustling the sheets and alerting me she's awake, that she knows I'm standing here in her doorway.

As I grow closer, she shifts to lie flat on her back, the blankets moving with her and falling a bit from her body.

My left knee hits the mattress first, and I climb up along her body, between her open legs, until my palms are flat beside her shoulders.

I can see her face now.

She watches me, a softness in her eyes I don't see often, but the slight lift of her lips is sorrow filled, and the pain cuts into my own skin.

Every night she waits up for me, expecting nothing and

accepting the little I give, and I gave even more to a girl who wasn't her.

My hands start at her ribs, gently sweeping along her top and down her naked thighs until I can reach behind her knee. I tug, bringing it up to my side, my eyes closing as the heat of her blends with mine, bringing her core closer.

I dip my head, slowly kissing along her collarbone, and her chest inflates, sparking a fire in my own.

My hand comes up, fingertips trailing the length of her arms and up over her shoulder until I can grip her neck. I pull my head back, kissing her chin and then the corners of her mouth, and I freeze there.

Her shuddered breath has my eyes peeling open, and finally her palms land flat on my chest.

I drop my forehead to hers, soaking in the feel of her.

When her fingertips curl, my hands sink into her hair, and I do what I've wanted for so fucking long.

I tip her mouth to mine, my lips falling onto the softest fucking pillows—

"I lied before," she breathes.

My eyes fly open, our mouths touching.

Raw sorrow washes over her, and I'd swear a cloud of moisture sneaks into the deep, hypnotic brown of her gaze. Her hand leaves my chest, sliding along my arm until it's tethered with the one in her hair.

My fist tightens, and I press against her, but then she pulls it back, taking mine with her, and cold, hard dread seeps into me.

Her eyes avoid mine, seeking out the night surrounding us as she repeats in a whisper, "I lied before… I'm not okay with pretending to be her."

Ice.

My body turns to ice, stuck, fucking frozen.

I try to pull her to me, but the hand she left on my chest is a barrier, pushing me away.

The dark of the night aches behind her words, coating my throat, threatening to suffocate me.

"What…no. Beauty, no—"

She shakes her head, and then the light hits just right, capturing the tear that falls from her eye, and I fly from the mattress, toppling over my own feet and almost falling to my ass.

The knob of her door stabs me in the ribs as I stumble into it, my back hitting the frame as I race backward from her room on unsteady feet.

She knows.

She fuckin' knows.

My pulse beats out of control, and I can't breathe. I fall to the wall, sliding down it until my ass crashes to the floor.

I bury my head in my hands, and then a pair of unlaced black boots are in my vision.

I look up at my brother.

Royce shakes his head, anger in his eyes, but it's gone in a blink.

He came home for me.

"You fucked up, brother," he whispers.

"I did." I nod. "And you knew."

"I did." He drops beside me with a sigh. "At least we know you're as human as the rest of us now."

I scoff and a heavy chuckle leaves him.

"Wanna know something that might make you feel even shittier?" he asks.

My eyes slide to his, but he looks away before he speaks.

"She's okay with losing," he says. "Or, shit, she thinks she is anyway."

Okay with losing, as in losing me to someone else.

Raven was right—she's serious about her place here, and she plans to take it with or without me.

"What are you gonna do, brother?" Royce asks.

"I guess it depends on what she does," I tell him. "But probably nothing good."

His eyes cut to mine, and I shrug.

"Can't let her lock me out, won't let her go." I face forward again. "Guess I'll force her hand."

"That's kind of fucked."

"Yeah." I nod. "It is."

Everything is.

CHAPTER 30
VICTORIA

Morning comes too quickly and with it the smell of breakfast.

Today I can't hide from what's been happening.

The boys gave me a small pass last night, but they'll fill their brother in on everything with Maria today, and I'll have to face him—and what he and I are not.

I drag my ass from the bed and into the shower, but I don't linger. There's no point.

I'm out and dressed within fifteen minutes. I part my hair, braiding back one side, and pull it up into a messy bun on my head, tie a white bandanna around it, and skip the eyeliner for today.

Downstairs, Zoey sits on the couch watching cartoons with Maddoc, while Raven chats with Rolland in the kitchen.

Royce makes his way in then, and I'm a little shocked when he kisses my cheek as he passes, moving to do the same to Raven before grabbing the hot chocolate already made and waiting for him on the countertop.

"Thanks, RaeRae," he says as he takes a sip, walking out.

Captain comes around the corner next, his feet stopping when he spots me.

"ZoZo, you replaced me with Uncle D?" Royce teases her, sitting down and scooting her into his lap. He kisses her cheek. "Cartoon time is for Uncle Bro, 'member?"

Zoey just laughs and snuggles in to get comfortable, the little dog ears on her slippers flapping all over.

But I caught it and so did Captain—Royce called her ZoZo. Not Zo or Zoey Bear.

The corner of Captain's mouth lifts, and he keeps moving toward me, but then Maddoc pops up from his seat.

"Captain," he calls, and slowly Royce's head lifts. "Outside."

He spins in an instant, meeting his brother near the door as Royce gently moves Zoey off, whispering something in her ear before calling on Rolland. "Sit with her?"

Raven meets my eyes, coming over to lean against the counter as Rolland exits the kitchen.

He drops beside Zoey, and the three disappear out the front door.

As soon as they're gone, Raven sets her coffee cup down and moves for the coffee machine. "You look like shit. I'm guessing you didn't sleep?"

I sigh. "Nope. Not much anyway."

She sets a half cup of coffee in front of me, a glass flute full of creamer beside it. "I'll never understand why they pour it from the bottle it comes in into this heavy thing. Why choose to dirty an extra dish?"

I chuckle but frown at the cup. "You know they've been giving you decaf, right?"

She smirks, stepping back so she can lean on the counter without hitting her belly against it. "Course I know. It makes him feel like he's 'protecting me' or what the fuck ever..." She shrugs, then nods her head at the mug she gave me. "That's from the pot he made after he gave me mine."

I pull it over, and she laughs, but it's quickly cut short when the door opens.

"Oh shit," she hisses but full-on grins as she not so casually moves to the other side of the counter to watch.

Behind me, Rolland makes an excuse to get Zoey up, and the two run off.

Suddenly Captain is in the place she just left, glaring down at me with too many emotions in his eyes to count.

"What?"

"You didn't tell me."

I take a slow sip, letting the warm beverage ease my dry throat. "When exactly was I supposed to do that?"

"When you first got home." He glares.

"And you'd have, what? Stayed?"

His frown deepens.

I lick my lips, lifting my shoulders, and give a simpler answer: "I didn't think you'd care."

His brows jump high in surprise, but anger quickly replaces everything else. "That's how we're playing things now?"

"Did we miss something?" comes from Maddoc.

We answer at the same time.

"No," I say.

"Yes," he booms.

Cap glares. "My room. Now."

My head jerks back. "Kiss my ass."

"Let's go."

My lips smash together, and I look to the caramel-colored liquid in my cup. "I don't think so, Cap."

When he doesn't move, doesn't speak, I force myself to meet his frown.

Guilt lines his eyes, heavy and loud, screaming at my own.

He should feel none; he promised me nothing, and he has every right to go after whatever it is he wants. He should feel no guilt.

"Stop."

"Stop what?" he rasps.

I shake my head, looking away, but he gets right back in my line of sight. Closer, right in fucking front of me close, my knees now against his thighs close, I can smell his aftershave too fucking close.

"Stop what?" he repeats, the tenderness fading away as his frown deepens. "There are no secrets here."

Okay, fine.

I lean forward.

"Stop looking at me with shame in your eyes because you can't help but want to give the mother of your child a chance to be everything you wish she was," I snap. "That is your choice. I am not a rock in your way or a complication or anything else for that matter. Your life, your choice."

Let her fuck you over if you have to, to see.

Captain chokes on air, his Adam's apple stuck up high as he tries to swallow but is denied.

Silence surrounds us, and I'd almost say Captain looks embarrassed.

"So much for no secrets, Cap." I glance around the room at the glares of three Brayshaws, all directed at the one before me. "Seems your family didn't know about that."

I slide off the barstool, taking my coffee with me, and at first, I assume he allows it, but then the cup is snatched from my hand and I'm spun around.

"You came in here yesterday knowing where I was going, didn't you?"

"Yes."

"How?"

I open my mouth to speak but close it.

"How?" he shouts.

I square my shoulders, letting out a long breath. "She told me."

Captain's body goes stiff in front of me. "Mallory. She told you. When? What did she say?" He can't hide the dreaded hope in his heart, and it continues to murder mine.

He hears it, his family hears it, and everyone's shoulders drop a little lower.

"She wanted me to tell you not to wait for her, that..." I trail off when heavy creases form around his eyes. "She changed her mind."

Captain studies me a long hard moment, his hand flying from my elbow in the next. He jerks away.

A switch is flipped, and suddenly his guilt and embarrassment are too much, clouded with anger and resentment and confusion.

He has no clue how to channel all the emotions flying at him at once, and he knows it; the realization only makes this harder for him.

He deals with it the only way that makes sense to him in this moment: by pointing a finger at someone else in hopes it dulls the ache building inside him.

"You think I trusted her?" he asks with disgust, and I get the feeling it's directed at himself. "I would never trust a word she says, not that I believe a fucking word you're saying either."

Fair enough.

His words are lies, though; it's why he's coming undone in this exact moment—hearing the truth, that she didn't simply get caught up or have an emergency she couldn't get out of. She chose not to meet her daughter, turning her back on her for the second time—that's how he sees it and it's killing him.

"What did you do, go looking for her?" he asks, shaking his head spitefully, but doesn't let me answer. "You knew I was with her the other day. You been following me again?"

He throws the coffee cup, sending it shattering into the sink, but I don't jump like I imagine he wanted me to.

"You need to mind your own fucking business," he barks, stepping back only to creep in again. "Stay out of things that don't concern you, especially something like this. You don't know what's best for her. You're not her fucking mom!" he shouts.

My muscles grow stiff, and as if I swallowed a lump of flour, I fight for air I can't get.

He keeps going, and in my peripheral, both his brothers move closer, fearful their calm and collected brother might be losing his balance.

"She might like you, Victoria, but she's three! She likes everyone!" His voice carries across the house, echoing along the halls and ricocheting against my temples. He drives it home, pushing a hard finger into my chest as he tips his chin, staring at me through his lashes. "You are not her mom."

I never tried to be her mother; I only wanted to make sure she forever had someone in her corner when he couldn't be, but I can't say that to him now.

So instead, I nod my head and say, "You're right. I'm not."

But my surrender to his words has a triggering effect, and the anger and pain he was trying to push off onto me soak inside his own soul. Naturally, as one does when they're consumed with more than they can handle, drowning with no sight of the surface, he pushes harder, cuts deeper.

I see it in his eyes, the resolve, the cut of the cord he was barely hanging on to.

His shoulders square, eyes narrowing as his lip curls. "Maybe it's good your mother was murdered," he growls.

"Captain!" Raven snaps.

He ignores her, creeps closer, bending so we're eye level. "My dad might have shown your mother mercy when she fucked up and stepped over the line, but I won't be so kind with you."

That burns a fire under my own skin, and I punch him clear across the fucking jaw.

"Oh shit" comes from Royce, but nobody moves in.

Captain's head snaps to the side, the corner of his lip busting, but I wait until he drags it back to speak.

"Fuck you, dick. I would never do a damn thing to take her from her home, and I don't give a flying fuck if you believe me or not. At this point, I almost hope you don't just so you feel like a helpless little bitch a time or two when you realize I'm not the fucking bad guy here." I push at his chest, but he doesn't budge.

"You have no idea how fucked what you're saying is," I force past clenched teeth. "But if I have to be the bad guy to make you feel better, fine. Consider me warned, Cap. And fuck right off."

I shove again, pushing past him when he calls, "Try to leave and I'll lock you in that room like a proper fucking princess."

A laugh bubbles out of me, and slowly, I spin to face him.

"Typical broken-boy bullshit," I snap, and his brows crash in the center. "Can't hardly look at me but can't stand to see me go."

Head cocked, he glares through thick lashes, his tongue sneaking out to dab at the blood in the corner of his mouth. "Say what you want. I'm not fucking joking."

"Do you really think I would give up my place if you don't come along with it?" I ask, shaking my head. "Because I won't. So go ahead, fuck Mallory some more, asshole. You never said you were mine, so you've got every right, yeah? But don't do it expecting me to be sitting on the sidelines or crying in the fucking background. I won't. I said I wanted you to be my Brayshaw, Captain. I never said a damn thing about needing you to become one."

I walk away, but I only make it to the door.

"Victoria." The urgency and panic in his tone are the only reason my feet don't carry me outside.

I take a deep breath and turn around, my throat closing at the sight.

Captain is on his knees, shoulders dropped as low as they can go. He opens his mouth, but I cut him off.

"If you say sorry right now, I'll punch you again."

"I'll take it," he rasps. "Every one you've got. I'll take 'em, Beauty."

I look to his brothers, both stuck with frowns on their faces, pain on Raven's. None of them have a single idea what to say—rare for a Brayshaw, let alone four.

"Come to me." The words leave him on an empty breath.

I shouldn't, but I let my hand fall from the knob, allow my

feet to carry me to the broken boy on the floor as his family stands back watching.

I don't get to decide what to do once I reach him because his hands shoot out to grip my shirt, and I'm tugged against him.

His arms wrap tightly around me, and he yanks me down, his legs swinging around so he can drop to his ass, placing mine in his lap.

He doesn't say a word, but he holds on to me like he can't imagine letting me go.

Minutes pass, and I find my hands lifting, my palms flattening on the sides of his face, and his head lifts.

Regret buries the blue in his eyes, giving me only a murky green to stare into.

He grips my face in his palms, staring deep into my eyes, and says what I had no idea I needed to hear.

"I didn't fuck her."

CHAPTER 31
VICTORIA

Raven knocks on the doorframe, coming in slowly. "Damn, Vee. Tryin' to make me look bad?"

"Please." I chuckle, fastening my belt. "They fell in love with you when all you wore were cheap sweats and a two-dollar tank top."

"Eh, it was less. Got that five-finger discount," she teases, making her way to my bed and sitting on the edge.

I laugh. "Right."

"The boys haven't said much about what they think happened out at Maria's," she offers, assuming I was curious as to what conversations were had when I wasn't around.

She assumed right.

"They have their PI looking but…"

But she wasn't all that important to them, so a manhunt isn't something she's afforded. Not that one would be needed. They must figure it has nothing to do with them but simply her past catching up to her, as it does in places like this.

She leans back on her hands. "You sure you're up for this?"

"It's a concert with thousands of people."

"And we'll be in a mid-level suite, each of us at arm's length with no escape."

"I told you last night and the night before and earlier this morning, Raven: I'm going. I'm fine. Stop." I slide my eyes her way.

She nods, picking up my phone only to toss it to the side. "Have you guys talked?"

"Nope. He played the part at school all week, as you saw, but as soon as eyes were away, his hands were too. I'm leaving it alone."

"You think he's talked to Mallory again?"

I shrug, moving to the closet to grab my shoes. "I can't see him reaching out after he gave her what she wanted and she bailed, but her…I'm not so sure about."

"Yeah, me either."

I sit down, glancing up to find her frowning.

"What?"

Her lips purse a moment, and then she sits up. "If I ask you a question, will you tell me the truth?"

I hold her eyes a moment and then bend to zip up the side of my leopard-print boots. I stand, adjusting the shoulders of my top, letting one side hang. "I'm done hiding, Raven. You can ask me whatever you want, and I'll tell you the truth."

"I keep going back to why Mallory would stop to talk to you at all, to trust a stranger of a girl she saw with her ex to relay any kind of message."

I meet her gaze.

"A stranger wouldn't do that, would they?" she asks.

"No," I answer instantly. "A stranger wouldn't."

Before she can say anything else, Maddoc walks in.

He glares around the room, his eyes lifting to the chandelier. "For real?"

I chuckle. I knew that thing had to have been added for me after Maddoc moved out of this room.

Raven looks up, laughing, and then drops onto her back on my bed. "That would have been fun."

Royce is suddenly inside too, and throws himself right beside her. "Oh, yeah." He grins. "With the right reflection, proper positioning." He spreads his hands out. "That's like twenty ass cheeks, at least."

She laughs, letting Maddoc tug her up, and right as Captain appears, leaning against the doorframe.

His eyes bounce across the room, landing on me. "Ready?"

I nod, turning away to grab my phone off the charger, frowning at the long lock of hair that falls over my shoulder, into my face.

I should have put it up.

Hid it.

I should cut and dye it.

I must delay too long because suddenly I'm barricaded between strong shoulders and Cap's hands land on mine.

He pulls one behind me, helping me tuck my phone into my back pocket, and laces his fingers through the other.

I turn my head as he lifts our clasped hands to his mouth, running his lips across our knuckles, only to let go.

Royce's arms are around us both in the next second. "Glad the class is getting along and all, but, uh, baby girl's asleep, the concert starts in an hour, and we're all still sober. It's a damn shame, really."

"Fuck you guys. Are you really getting drunk?" Raven asks.

I scoff, rolling my eyes as I walk toward the bedroom door. "Please, like your man would allow himself to be anything but stone-cold sober at a concert with his pregnant wife."

"She's gettin' it." Maddoc eyes me as he passes us, waiting for us to follow.

She laughs, shoving me to the side and stepping out before me. "True dat."

My eyes travel over her as she descends the stairs ahead of me. About six months pregnant, and you'd never know by staring at the back of her.

She's trim and hourglass shaped, still wearing her own low-rise jeans and Timberlands. Her black tank top almost blends with her long, sleek black hair. If it wasn't for the deep purple tips and streaks, it would.

She looks over her shoulder, her gray eyes shining and popping against the heavy liner on her lids. "Seems he's in a touchy mood tonight, huh, Vee." She winks.

"Raven."

She laughs, facing forward again. "My hands are on the railing, Big Man, and you're right in front of me. I'm good."

I chuckle and Maddoc groans.

Within an hour, we're walking into the arena.

Of course, they got a suite with private security and table service, and no one asks for proof of ID.

The waitress comes back as quickly as she left and with a tray full of shit. Royce grabs the hand of a girl right behind her, pulling her inside with us as if he ordered her from the menu too, but then Mac and Chloe and a few others I recognize from school enter right behind them.

I glance around at the newcomers, seeing a girl for each guy who's entered.

Royce catches my eye and he winks. "I got you, VicVee."

I chuckle, shifting in my seat.

Captain leans against the black box railing, drink hanging from his fingers, eyes on me.

I didn't get a chance to fully look him over earlier, and I'm glad because this exact position, posture, and lighting all make for a hell of a fantasy. His sandy-blond hair is perfectly swept, but not in a preppy-boy way, more tycoon, dark and dirty businesslike.

Black on black, sleeves rolled halfway up his forearms, tattooed knuckles screaming at me as he lifts the amber liquid to his lips, leaving nothing but ice in the bottom of his glass.

I push to my feet, and his smirk slowly grows, but then the crowd goes wild, the last opening act stepping off the stage, having just announced it's time to get the party rolling.

It's like nothing I've ever heard before.

My eyes fly around the arena. Thousands upon thousands of people are on their feet, screaming and cheering. The lights go off, and it only gets louder, and then a single light above the stage kicks on, smoke following, and there he is.

G-Eazy takes the stage, and when he does, Raven practically leaps from her seat.

Maddoc rolls his eyes, but he can't hide the grin—anything to make her happy.

"He make you think about that punk bitch, RaeRae?" Royce shouts over the crazy of the crowd's shouts behind us.

Raven's head snaps his way. "Bass Bishop was no punk, Ponyboy." She turns to him, but her eyes soften as she reaches out and Royce tethers his hand in hers. "He was good to me, but never as good as you." She winks.

He holds her gaze a long moment, nodding slightly as he lets her go.

Bass is the guy who used to run things at the warehouses; he helped her out, breaking his loyalty to the boys in the process.

It pissed the boys off, but in the end, he saved Raven, and Maddoc was grateful—Royce, not so much. He felt like Bass came in and tried to take a place he hadn't earned.

The joke is Bishop—with his sleek black hair, swept back or messy, leather jacket, and torn-up jeans—looked like G-Eazy. That mix of hood and rockabilly.

"Love you, RaeRae!" Royce shouts with a grin, and she yells it right back.

Maddoc slides behind her right then, whispering who knows what in her ear, and she giggles, her hand coming up to wrap around his neck, and the two start grinding to the beat.

Suddenly, Captain is at my back.

"Red's your color, Beauty," he says into my ear as his fingers run along my ribs, stopping where the stretchy shirt disappears into my high-waisted black jeans. His eyes fall on my lips, painted a heavy red, five shades darker than my natural color and the same exact shade as my top.

He licks his own. "But I knew that already." His gaze comes back to mine, softening as he stares. His hand comes up to grip the side of my face, a sadness suddenly clouding his. "Victoria," he whispers, and my lips pull in, a heavy crease forming above his brows. "The shit I said about Maria…that was fucked-up. I didn't mean it."

I nod. "I know."

He shifts, bringing us closer, and my heart rate spikes. "I'm—"

"Victoria!"

Captain's hand falls, and my glare flies to Chloe.

"I need to find the ladies' room. Come with me?" Her smile is bright and annoying, and I'm ready to tell her to go the hell away, but the longer I look at her, the more I see.

Her eyes are pleading.

Her secret slaps me in the face, and even though I don't want to walk away right now, she might just need me to, so I nod, slipping away from Captain, but he quickly grabs my arm.

"You're not going to the bathroom by yourself," he snaps.

Mac knocks his elbow with Captain's and points up a long set of stairs, where massive body after massive body lines every three to four steps and leads to a glass hallway, a private bathroom just at the top.

"Maddoc picked this box for that reason," he tells him.

"And you think he'd let Raven go alone?" Captain questions.

Mac laughs, shoving at Captain playfully. "Fuck no. If my girl were pregnant, I wouldn't either."

My eyes snap to Chloe, and she frowns.

"Ready?" I ask her and she nods, leading the way.

As soon as we're inside the glass building, she moves to the side, staring down at the others below, dancing and laughing, Mac and Captain staring right at us.

"Don't judge me," she says.

"I'm not."

She whips around, angry glare but heavy moisture in her eyes. "I went to the doctor. I'm only six weeks along. The threesome with Royce was well before that. It's Mac's."

My lips pucker as I almost speak but quickly pause. "Okay… so why are you crying?"

"Because now it's real." She laughs nervously, shoving open the door into the bathroom, me right behind her. "I'm pregnant, and my dad is probably going to have him murdered."

"Doubtful."

She disappears into the stall. "You don't know my dad!"

I roll my eyes, waiting for her to come out.

The door shoves open, and her four-inch heels carry her to the sink to wash her hands. She runs her fingers through her hair and turns to the side to inspect her figure.

"Why haven't you told Mac?" I ask her.

She sighs. "Because once we're finally done with school, he wants to take over as head of Brayshaw security. He says all the time how dangerous it is. Add a kid into that, and he'll give up what he's been working toward. It's all he wants." She looks my way, her lipstick in her hand. "Mac comes from nothing, earned everything he has, and he's worked so hard to earn their trust, to get to where he is—a place where he'll have a chance. I can't take that away."

"Who says you're taking anything away?"

She laughs as if I'm the most naive person on the planet, and her words confirm the thought. "You have so much to learn."

I shake my head. "Did you ever stop to think that maybe he wants those things so bad because they'll make him feel worthy of you?"

Her eyes fly to mine, and slowly she puts her makeup back in her purse.

"Your own dad was head of security, Chloe, and now your boyfriend is going for that spot, wants it, as you say, more than anything." I shrug, pushing out of the bathroom door. "Sounds like, in his mind, the key to keeping you is to become one of them."

We stand there, inside the closed-off glass, staring down at the guys staring up at us.

"I don't love him because he's Brayshaw."

"Does he know that?"

"He better," she says. "I can't believe this, but you're so right, Vee."

"Let's keep it at Victoria. We're not even friends yet."

She laughs. "Yet. Nice."

Together we head back for our seats, but just before we get there, her hand grips my arm, holding me back.

Fear lines her eyes, so I spin around and grip her shoulders. "You're Chloe Carpo. You're strong and determined and honestly kind of a bitch, but..."

She laughs, tension rolling off her. "You suck at a pep talk, but thanks." Her eyes slide by mine, and she whispers, "I'm telling him. Now."

My brows jump. "Now?"

"Right now."

"Baby?"

I look over my shoulder to find Mac standing there, his hand extended for Chloe to take, so I slowly squeeze by, giving them the whole two feet of privacy this place allows.

As I look around, though, I notice Captain is gone, Maddoc and Raven too.

I turn to Royce right as he grips me by the wrist and yanks me from the suite with angry, jerky movements.

"What the hell—"

"Come on," he hisses, his steps urgent.

"Royce, what's wrong?"

"We gotta get over there. You need to put this bitch in her place."

"What are you talking about?"

We come around the corner and I skid to a stop.

Mallory stands there, laughing and drinking with a group that must be her friends.

"Fuck," Royce seethes, dropping my arm as he darts forward, and it all happens so fast.

Raven is suddenly in front of her, swinging full force and hitting Mallory square in the nose, sending her stumbling onto her ass.

Maddoc has Raven in the same second, keeping her back with his chest, hands holding her wrists to keep her from falling.

He's furious.

Mallory adjusts her crop top. "You're pregnant, you psychopath!"

Raven tries to haul herself at her again. "Oh, you care?! The girl who gave away—"

Maddoc's hand swiftly wraps around Raven's mouth, the look in his eyes enough to get her to completely give in. Her forehead caves, her eyes falling to the ground.

Mallory stands, moving over in an attempt to shield herself at Captain's side, and that's when I realize I was moving closer, when her eyes lift, locking with mine.

She drops her arm instantly, and his gaze slices my way.

"You're a piece of fucking work, you know that?" I keep walking toward her, and she frantically looks across the room.

But before I can get any closer, security is there—Brayshaw security.

Maddoc slips in front of me, glaring. "Not the fucking place."

He's right; it's not.

This is some serious Brayshaw dirt. Zoey is still a secret to their world.

"Let's get the fuck out of here. Now," Maddoc shouts.

We turn to follow the men down the hall and through a private one that leads to the back lot, where we parked.

It's not until we're outside, under the dark night sky, that I realize Mallory followed.

"Captain, wait. Please!" she yells, and I jerk to a stop, swiveling around to look at her.

She eyes me, and tension lines her brow, but she forces her gaze away, quickly looking to Captain.

He continues to ignore her, his face a blank slate as he quickly keeps walking, but she runs after him, high heels, tiny skirt, and all.

When she realizes she can't keep up, her eyes fly to mine. She opens her mouth only to close it a second later.

Captain happens to choose that moment to reach for my hand, and Mallory begins to nibble at her lip.

And then her eyes close, and she shouts, "She told me not to go!"

Everyone stops.

Captain stops.

Time fucking stops.

But I rush her, my fingertips an inch from gripping her by the shirt and yanking her to me, when mine's caught from behind and I'm held still, Royce at my back.

"Let go," I force past clenched teeth, but he continues to pull me back, farther away.

The crunch of gravel beneath Captain's shoes echoes in my ear as he turns to face her. "What are you talking about, Mallory?"

Captain's voice is low and lethal, leaving no room for lies. Demanding the truth.

"She did this." Mallory moves a few slow steps back, rushing out, "All of it."

Oh my God.

I jerk forward again, but just as I do, Royce is there, blocking me.

Giving her the motherfucking floor.

"She came to me, the other day, and…and before. She's the one who told me to leave, that it wasn't safe here for me."

The vessels around my heart tug and pull, tangling around until I'm sure no blood can flow through and I'll fall to the ground any moment.

It wasn't safe, but she was the least of my concerns.

"She said that you couldn't protect me, Captain. She took your daughter—"

"Are you fucking kidding me?" I shriek, managing to make it around Royce, but he has my hands behind my back in the same second, and in the same move, Mallory has slid behind Captain.

"It's true," she shouts, tears in her eyes.

"Mallory—"

"You did this!" she shouts again.

"I was—"

"You—"

"Shut up!" Captain barks, spinning out of her grasp and glaring down at her. "Shut the fuck up. Why would I believe you?"

"Why would you believe her?" she counters, and goddamn it if those weren't the perfect words for her to choose.

Slowly, his head swivels around to mine. "Is it true?" he asks. "Did you tell her to leave? Are you the reason I lost Zoey, lost them both?"

My gut twists, tighter and tighter, like a boa forcing the life from its prey as I stare at the pain in his eyes, but that's not the hardest part.

Somehow, despite everything, he still has hope she's good, maybe even needs her to be, if not for himself then for his daughter.

For their daughter.

It almost kills me where I stand.

He's in my face so fast, I can't brace for it, stumbling back until my hands meet the rocky ground. Small pebbles cut into my palms as Captain's always-quick hands let me drop.

I push to my feet.

"Yes or no," he growls, and I don't miss the small crack in his voice. "Are you the reason she left?"

I'd swear in this moment, it's possible for bones to break from emotional pain. My ribs ache as if snapped, my chest caves as if my lungs have been punctured as I stare, the moonlight playing vicious painter, sharpening his features and darkening his eyes.

The lost boy in front of me, so desperate for answers he doesn't understand as the girl at his back left him with none.

Am I the reason she left?

The simplest answer…

"Yes," I whisper.

The cords in his neck stretch to their brink, his throat sinking in as if he's swallowed molten metal and the burn is too fucking strong, too much.

I don't even recognize the voice that follows. "Leave. Now."

I attempt to swallow, but my body denies the request, so I nod and turn away, but he's not done.

"You take nothing," he seethes. "Leave with the clothes on your back, never look back. Be invisible or I will make you disappear."

"Captain…" Raven says but trails off.

My eyes slide to hers, watching the array of emotions as they flash across her face.

She takes a step toward me, but with my arms still at my side, I lift my fingers where only she can see.

It's okay. Stand with them; they need you most.

I can't possibly glance toward him, but slowly her features smooth, her hands slipping into both Maddoc's and Royce's as she slowly licks her lips, an almost unnoticeable nod following.

My stomach twists.

Cross one, cross all.

"Victoria, wait!" Mallory frantically cries. "Don't leave! Please, I—"

I stop but don't look her way, and as I expected, nobody follows.

My feet can't carry me away fast enough. I cut through the cars in the parking lot, walking as quickly as I can until I'm far enough away they could never see. I drop my back against the nearest car, my hands coming up to cover my face as I try to catch my breath.

"Finally."

The air gets lodged in my throat as a shiver runs down my spine.

Slowly, my hands fall from my face, and there he stands: black hoodie and jeans. Gloves and a pistol.

My body sags, and I shake my head. "I expected you sooner."

His eyes fall, but his smile is the last thing I see before everything goes black.

CHAPTER 32
CAPTAIN

Numb.

I'm fuckin' numb. From the roots of my hair to the soles of my fuckin' feet, I feel nothing, have felt nothing for three days now.

The only time anything breaks through is when I look at my daughter, and even then, it's the most fucked-up, off-putting emotion that consumes me and, on top of that, the least expected.

Deep, bottom-of-the-pit betrayal.

She has no clue I sent her friend away, yet still, in her eyes, my mistake stares back, but I'm not so sure I made one.

Victoria brought this on herself. My daughter only knew her because Victoria manipulated her way into her world, stole something a little girl should never lose—her mother. She tried to take Mallory's place.

Victoria said she wanted to be Brayshaw, and in the grand scheme of things, she was well on her way, gave herself two options—as mine or as a selfless hero. She covered both bases.

She fucked with my head over and over, and each time I proved to be weaker than the last. Blind to her.

Why her?

"Captain, did you hear me?"

I push off the bench, shaking my head. "I can't do this right now."

As soon as my hand wraps around the handle of my SUV, she calls my name, and it takes everything I've got to turn and face her.

"Why are you leaving?" She measures me. "What's wrong?"

I was five minutes from happy, and then you showed up and ruined it all.

I lift my hands, letting them fall back to my sides.

Her skin flushes, eyes narrowing the slightest bit. "You're in love with her."

Victoria.

She's none of her fucking business, but I'm not looking to argue, and a response like that will only bring more questions.

I keep my face blank. "She lied to me."

Her body rocks the slightest bit, a small frown written across her forehead. "So did I, yet here you are."

"I gotta go." Yanking the door open, I slide in.

"Captain!"

I hold in a groan, glancing at her through the closed window.

She gnaws at her bottom lip. "I'll see you tomorrow, right? You're coming?"

I give a curt nod and get the fuck out of there.

I head straight for home, but something has me pulling around the side of the Bray house and parking. I climb out, dropping onto the old swing behind it.

I grab my brass knuckles from my pocket, slip them on, and make a fist.

A perfect fucking fit.

My Brayshaw token.

Strong and solid, unbreakable and whole. Threat without words, fear without movement.

I pull them close, reading the words scrolled beside them.

Family runs deeper than blood.

Proof of these words are my brothers, my father. Raven.

My family, none by birth.

My fist tightens.

We all serve a purpose.

Maddoc is the lead; he holds the key but never steps ahead.

Royce is the warrior; he bears the crest but never tries to rule.

I am the anchor; I hold the brass knuckles, the loops signifying the fusion of our family—full circles, never one stronger than the other, a reminder we are equals. Always.

But maybe our dad got it wrong.

Maybe he saw what doesn't exist.

My family trusted me to make the right choices, fell in line with me, and I let them down. More than once.

I'm not sure how long I sit before the back door opens and Maybell steps out.

I go to stand, but she calls out, "Don't go gettin' up, boy. I can make it down these steps just fine on my own."

A chuckle leaves me, but a sigh quickly follows.

She makes her way over, sitting on the small stone wall framing the swings in. "I knew, when all the girls were suddenly dying of thirst and needed to be in the kitchen, one of yous was back here."

A small grin forms, and I shake my head, glancing at the kitchen window a moment. Slowly, my eyes slide to one of the most important people in our lives.

"She's gone and your journal isn't working," Maybell guesses correctly, understanding softening her eyes. "Tell me what's on your mind, boy."

I look at the sand at my feet. "What you said to me before, about how once we choose, that's it, there's no going back, no changing our minds."

"Sealed in the heavens and etched along the walls of hell."

I nod. Yeah. That.

"I chose Mallory first," I say. "Isn't that the answer to all this? The glue. Where my anchor fell?"

A wolf only has one mate in his lifetime.

She sits silently for a long minute, only speaking once I force my gaze to hers.

"The way I see it, that's where the anchor broke from the chain, crashed to the deepest part of the sea where only one person will be brave enough to go. That person will dive headfirst into the dark waters, not caring to make it back to the surface, because to fix what's broken in you is worth the risk of losing everything, even life."

I open my hand, twisting my wrist, and study how the sun reflects off the brass. A golden rainbow.

My jaw ticks.

"And that glue you speak of? That's classic Captain right there, my nurturing, loving, deep-thinking boy." My eyes find hers again, and she gives a small smile. "You hurt, are confused about the girl who doesn't deserve it—the struggles of a man who loves his daughter with the sun and moon, the air and the fire of the earth. She may have done what she did, but that will never take away from how this girl gave you the most important person in your world. You may hate her, but you're grateful, and it tears you apart, and sorry to tell you, boy, but it will never stop tearing you apart. It's proof of your heart, Captain Brayshaw. It's what makes you, you."

A hint of ache sneaks into my frozen body, and I welcome it.

I lean forward, elbows on my knees. "I wish I were as sure as you, Maybell, 'cause right now all my mind is telling me is to fix what's broken, but I have no clue where to start, no idea what I should attempt to fix first or at all."

She pushes to her feet and comes to stand in front of me.

I lift my head, meeting her deep-brown eyes.

"Tell me this, boy. If there are two bleeding souls and only enough thread to mend one, who do you heal?"

"What if neither of them deserve it?"

She nods. "What if I told you one of those souls was yours?"

A desperate, selfish ache forms in the pit of my stomach at her words.

Suddenly she's holding out a small envelope addressed to her.

My brows snap together. "What is that?"

"Don't know." She pins me with a steady, strong gaze. "It's not mine."

She points to the very edge where a small anchor is drawn.

It's for me.

My chest wall expands out, and slowly, I push to my feet, now towering over her.

"It came in the mail a couple days ago. I thought it was odd it was in the lockbox, but then I looked at the back."

I grab the manila envelope from her hands and flip it over.

Written in cursive on the back flap, it reads:

I'm trusting you as you trusted me.

Only if she's gone.

Something stirs in my gut, twisting and turning at the emptiness inside.

Maybell's hands come up to pat my cheeks as she's done so many times in my life. "Go on home, my sweet boy. Someone wants you to see what's inside that envelope."

"Who sent this?"

"I have an idea," she says, but nothing follows, and with an encouraging smile, she walks back into the Bray house.

Thankfully, my dad has Zoey in the pool house watching movies this afternoon, so I'm able to rush right home, up the stairs, and into my room. I slam the door closed behind me and tear open the envelope, pouring its contents onto my comforter, and then I freeze.

A single folded piece of paper.

One rounded diamond.

I stare at the items, and my throat tightens with uncertainty.

I tug at my hair, scrub my hands down my face, and in the end, I can't fucking do it.

I yank my phone from my pocket and press number three.

It rings once before she answers.

"I need you."

"I'm coming."

My phone falls to the floor, and I wait.

A little less than a half hour passes, and then my door is thrown open.

Maddoc enters first, his eyes flying around the room before settling on me, and then he pushes the door open farther, stepping aside so Raven can slide past him.

"Cap." She rushes over, and the door closes right as she plants her feet in front of me.

Before Raven, it was only me and my brothers, and while we have always been enough for each other, understood and listened as a team, had the others' backs no matter the situation, even if we were the fuckups, adding Raven to our family was a necessity we didn't know we were missing.

I can be weak in front of my brothers and not be judged, but there's something about having a female to confide in that settles us a little differently. Not better or more, just…different.

"Sorry it took a minute." She hugs me. "We had just climbed out at the warehouses, Maddoc had to drop off something, but we jumped right back in the SUV and came home."

I squeeze my eyes shut as she pulls away, dropping my head back.

Her hand comes up to brush along my hair. "What happened?"

I jerk my chin toward the bed.

She follows my line of sight, a frown instantly forming. "What is that?"

"Can't bring myself to look."

Her eyes come back to mine.

I'm fucking terrified, Raven.

She sees it, understands as she always does.

Her Brayshaw item is a knife, and I think I understand it now.

Her blade, it holds the pain.

She's the true strength between us all.

Her hands fall and she steps away, moving to my mattress.

She lifts one leg, sitting half off the edge, her gaze meeting mine as she first picks up the envelope. She reads the writing there before flipping it over and seeing the message on the other side.

Her chest inflates. "It's about Zoey, isn't it?"

"I think so."

Her eyes find mine once again as she blindly grasps the thin piece of paper, her other hand reaching out for me.

Anxiety tugs at my muscles, and at first, I don't move.

Raven slowly shakes her head, her chin tipping the slightest bit. "Come on, Cap."

Slowly, I make my way over, sitting on the opposite side so we can face each other, and her hand slips into mine as she holds the paper open between us.

We look at the same time.

Captain,

If this is in your hands, my daughter is not.

This means she's everything I hoped she'd grow to be, everything your father once promised she would be, despite the ugly life she lived and the little chance the world gave her.

You may know, if she allowed herself to open up at all, she saw the darkest parts of it but in a light she didn't then understand. Maybe that's what molded her, her ability to see beyond the obvious, into someone's soul.

I never got a chance to earn her love, and if you're reading this, I never will, but that's not why I write you this letter.

I write to give you a gift—a gift I stole.

It's not mine to offer, I have no right, but it was created for you, so I have no reservations.

It is my hope that this will ease your soul, give you peace, and relieve you of the guilt your heart holds.

Zoey gave me this, she mended all that was broken inside me, and while I know her being in my care when she should have been in yours caused you grief, I am grateful for my time with her.

I wish I could watch her grow, but fate has other plans and beautiful, bright ones for her. And you.

If you are wondering if my daughter knows of this letter, the answer is no.

I have placed all my faith in Maybell, in her trusting my words, and that you are only reading this now because she is gone.

So here, sweet Captain, is my gift to you.

All my love, Maria

Raven's hand is shaking, so I grip her wrist and gently take the paper from her fingers.

Our eyes meet, and the moisture in hers has me swallowing.

She reaches for the large, fake diamond, and as she spins it in her fingers, her thumb pushes along the edge, and a flash drive pops from the other end.

Both of us freeze.

"Cap…"

I grab it from her, flipping it over to find the bottom is flat silver.

She jumps up, searching my TV for a way to turn it on but she has no clue what to do next.

I stand, pulling it from the wall a bit to slide it in the open space behind it, and instantly, the screen turns a bright blue.

I hold my breath as I grab the remote, my eyes on Raven.

She grips my elbow, towing me back to the bed, and together we sit.

It is my hope that this will ease your soul…

A shaky breath leaves me, my eyes on the ceiling.

Without a word from me, Raven stands, exiting my room only to come back with my brothers' hands in hers.

I swallow, nodding as they enter, tense and unsure.

They drop onto the bed behind me, and Raven comes right back to sit at my side.

She takes the remote from my hand and presses play.

What's only seconds aches like hours, and then…

"You're so annoying. Do you have to do this every day?"

My muscles lock when Mallory's voice fills the room before the picture comes into view.

You can't see her face, like the camera is behind her as she sits against a headboard on a bed I don't recognize.

The wall in the background of the shot is a large open window, overlooking…a garden.

"Stop complaining. It's not for you."

Victoria.

"Oh shit" comes from Royce.

Suddenly she's lying on her stomach, right beside Mallory. As she does, Mallory shifts, her body coming into full view.

Her stomach round and…

My ribs constrict, everything in my body tightening.

Zoey.

My eyes fly to Raven's belly and back to the screen.

This. This is what my daughter looked like growing safely inside her mother.

Raven's hand squeezes mine, and we watch as Victoria pulls something from behind her.

A book.

She opens it somewhere in the middle, like she's already made it through the first half of what must be three hundred pages, and begins to read out loud.

She reads to my baby girl, and my family and I sit here and listen.

Victoria shifts on the mattress, her long blond hair falling over her shoulders and blocking her face from the camera's view, and right as I think how I wish I could push it aside, how I need to see her lips as the words leave them, a hand slides into view, doing exactly that.

Victoria looks up, and in her eyes, I see pain, fear, and it aches within my own chest.

What were you afraid of?

She quickly stands from the mattress, the camera shutting off right as Mallory calls her name.

It rolls into another video and then another. In each one Mallory is there, and her belly grows bigger.

In the next, the wind blows Mallory's hair around as she stands in front of a bed of flowers.

She must hear something I don't because she turns, frowning at the camera.

"How do you feel?" Victoria asks her.

Mallory's shoulders fall. "Like someone is playing soccer in my stomach."

Raven chuckles, her free hand moving to her own baby bump, and Maddoc slides closer to her back.

"It's kind of annoying," she says to Victoria.

Raven says the exact words that leave Victoria next, and at the same time, "It's not annoying."

Mallory rolls her eyes and moves closer to the screen.

She reaches out, and then the camera is dropped but not turned off, the frame tilted and only giving a view of half their bodies.

She grabs ahold of Victoria's wrist and drops it onto the curve of her stomach.

Victoria's muscles seem to freeze, but then she relaxes, and with slow, gentle movements, she opens her palms wider.

Seconds tick by, her airy laugh following, and my pulse runs wild, kicks harder.

"Basketball," she whispers.

We were on her mind right then.

I was on her mind.

The father of the baby she's watching grow, whom she didn't know and had no reason to link herself to.

But she did it for the innocent little life beneath her palms.

The video rolls into the next, and I shoot to my feet, moving closer to the TV.

A hospital…

Holy shit.

Mallory's cries fill the room.

"I can't do this. I don't want to do this." A shuddered breath leaves her. "I should have had the abortion like I was going to before you dragged me out of that office and talked me into this."

No…

I swear my ribs snap one by one.

"No, you shouldn't have, and I didn't stop you. I offered another way, and yes, you can, just…breathe," Victoria tells her.

"Get that stupid camera out of my face," Mallory snaps.

"I can't. This isn't for you."

Suddenly Mallory's cries grow louder, and my heart starts to pound in my chest, breaking away the final layer of ice the last few days created.

Tears fall from her eyes, and she frantically pushes her legs around beneath the blanket covering her.

"Oh fuck," Raven rasps, but I can't look at her.

My eyes are glued to the TV.

"Just a little longer," Victoria whispers.

Mallory's breathing starts to smooth out, her eyes sliding toward the screen. She cries, "It hurts."

There's a moment's hesitation, and then the camera is set down.

My eyes are locked on Mallory's as hers move around the room, trailing Victoria, I think, and then Victoria's at her bedside, a cloth in one hand, her other sliding into one of Mallory's.

My lungs allow a full breath as she pats at Mallory's face with the small towel.

Mallory sits up as much as she can until her forehead is against Victoria's, and Victoria lets the cloth fall, her hand coming up to gently move Mallory's hair from her face.

"Why haven't you left, Vee? I'm awful to you."

"You're alone, fifteen, and having a baby. I might be awful too if I was in your shoes." Her eyes move between Mallory's a moment, and then she sits on the edge of the bed. "Are you afraid?" she whispers.

"Not for reasons you probably think," Mallory admits. "Only of the pain." When Victoria doesn't respond, Mallory says to her, "You think I'm making a mistake."

"I'm not here to judge you."

"But you have an opinion."

Victoria slips behind her, pulling her hair back and beginning to braid it. "Only you know if you're not ready to be a mom. That's your decision, and if you're not and you know it, then…I think admitting that makes you stronger than anyone I know."

Victoria's words twist and turn inside me.

Strong. She called her strong.

Was she?

"But?"

Victoria sighs, her arms falling to her sides. "But it's weak and wrong that the father is out there, someone who would want and love her in a heartbeat, and you don't want to give him the chance."

Mallory looks over her shoulder, meeting Victoria's eyes. "He'd kill me."

"And your life is more important than your child's?"

"I don't want to be a mother, and I don't want the reminder that I am anywhere near me. You said if I stayed locked in this damn place, had this baby, you'd keep her away from me, hide her, and set me up. That I could go on with my life like this never happened—and worth a hell of a lot more."

I swear moisture builds in Victoria's eyes at the foul fucking words spoken by Mallory, but she blinks them away.

You lying bitch.

My chest tightens, my pulse hitting against my temples as she readies to speak, but Mallory's face pulls tight, and she cries out right as a doctor comes in.

The woman lifts the blanket from Mallory's legs and looks up with a smile.

"It's time," she says.

"Maddoc," Raven breathes behind me.

Mallory pants, shaking her head, and right as I think it, my words are voiced.

"You can do this," Victoria whispers.

"Okay, Mallory," the doctor says. "Time to push."

My heart beats wildly, emotions I can't control taking over and stealing the air from my lungs as I move to stand directly in front of the TV.

Victoria holds her hand as Mallory screams and cries and pushes, and then I hear her.

The softest scream, a fresh, brand-new cry.

Her first second in this world.

Her first breath.

Moisture fills my eyes, and my jaw shakes as my baby girl is lifted into view. My feet jerk to the side when suddenly I can no longer see her.

"Congratulations," the doctor says. "It's a girl."

The nurse slides back into view a few torturously slow minutes later, and in her arms, wrapped tight in a tiny cocoon of teal and pink, a little striped beanie on her head, my baby girl cries. With the sound, my heart fucking sings.

The woman leans over, prepared to hand her to her mother, and my ribs ache as Mallory denies her, closing her eyes and looking away.

My stomach hollows as her hand slowly rises, pointing straight to Victoria.

The nurse offers a small smile, and with a shaky nod, Victoria walks around the bed. She wipes her hands on her jeans and welcomes my newborn daughter into her open, steady arms.

Her cries begin to soften, and when Victoria pulls her in tight, they stop, her little hands tucking in as her eyes begin to close, the warmth and comfort she needed having been given to her with zero hesitation.

My baby girl, so tiny.

"Does she have a name?" the nurse whispers.

My core tightens, and I look to Mallory as it does, but she keeps her eyes closed, shaking her head as if she knew the question was directed at her.

Again, the nurse looks to Victoria, who stares at Mallory a long moment before moving her attention back to my baby in her arms.

Her smile is soft and a little sad as her knuckle comes up to rub along my daughter's cheek. "She almost never made it to the world, was almost never given her sweet little life."

A knowing smile finds the nurse's lips, one that I don't quite understand, and Victoria nods.

"Zoey," she whispers. "Her name is Zoey."

The video cuts off, and I stumble back, falling to my ass on the comforter, my hands burying into my hair.

Oh God. Oh fuck.

No, no, no.

I try to swallow, but my airway is coated with the painful knowledge of my mistakes, of all I felt deep fucking down that Victoria was and weakly allowed another to taint.

Fuck, I—

"Look, ZoZo."

My head snaps up as another video begins to play, but Victoria can't be the one who turns it on.

Zoey sits in Victoria's lap, drool falling from her lips as she chews on her little fingers.

Zoey giggles and Victoria smiles wide. "You know him, huh?"

She taps her hands on a picture frame, my sophomore basketball photo locked inside it. "That's your daddy, and look at this one." She swaps out the image, and suddenly it's one of Mallory.

Victoria holds it up for my daughter. Zoey smiles at this image too, like she's seen it before. "There's your mom."

Her mom.

Solid fucking proof, if I were to still need it, she never tried to replace Mallory, but in fact wanted Zoey to have all Victoria felt Zoey lost—or was losing.

Before anything else can be said on the camera, Victoria spins around, frowning at whoever is there, and the screen goes black.

I spin, scrambling for the remote when suddenly it's lifted into my face.

I look up, meeting Royce's sorrow-filled eyes as I grab it from him, ready to turn it off, to breathe a minute, when once again laughter fills the air.

I look at the screen, and this time I can't hide my emotion, can't fight it off, as Victoria sits on her knees, and across from her, my baby girl takes her wobbly first step.

Steps I missed and hated myself for, a memory I would never get back but desperately wanted plays before me.

"Oh my God." Victoria's voice cracks. "Come on, Mama. Come see me."

She holds her hands out, a light chuckle leaving her as she smiles wide at my little girl.

Zoey laughs, clapping her hands as she takes another and then another before she falls into Victoria's arms.

Victoria laughs, holding her to her chest and clapping her hands for her.

She stares at her, at the little girl she clearly loves with all she is, as if she didn't save Zoey but Zoey saved her, blessed her life and gave it meaning.

"You did it, ZoZo!" she says softly, but something shifts in her eyes, and she gently sets Zoey down, setting a little toy in her lap. "You did it…and your daddy missed it," she whispers, pulling her lips in.

I bite into my cheek as she grows closer, and right before she reaches the camera to turn it off, guilt washes over her.

I quickly press pause, stopping anything else from coming onto the screen.

I want it all, all the memories, all I missed, but I can only take so much at once.

Defeated, fucking wrecked, I turn to my family.

"You didn't know, bro," Royce stresses.

"I need a minute." I swallow, looking away from them.

Without hesitation, they walk out, closing my door behind them, and I fold my hands behind my head, dropping my chin to my chest.

This is why.

This is fucking why.

The pull, the goddamn noose around my neck, tugging me toward her, cutting off my air until she was near or in sight, finally allowing me to breathe.

She didn't even fucking know me, and she felt for me, hurt for me, fucking fought for me. She was the voice I wasn't given, protected what I didn't know needed protecting, and preserved what I'd thought I lost.

My daughter's journey to birth, her first breath in this world, first step, and who knows what else is on that video, whatever she could share with me.

Victoria gave my life meaning.

And I couldn't even give her the benefit of the doubt.

Mallory pointed the gun, and I pulled the trigger, just like that.

Blindly.

And what did Victoria do?

Maybell's words slam into me so hard I fall to the wall, smacking at my chest for the air I can't find, that my body denies.

That person will dive headfirst into dark waters, not caring to make it back to the surface, because to fix what's broken in you is worth the risk of losing everything…

She let me turn her into the devil when she was the saint, and all so I could have whatever it was I was chasing after.

A fool's dream.

A naive man's thoughts.

I was wrong.

My eyes fall on the remote again, so I pick it up and press play, fast-forwarding through a few clips I will be watching on repeat later, until I find a place to pause.

Victoria sits on a brown suede couch, Zoey tucked into her side, a little blanket draped around her as they sleep.

There they are.

My baby.

My girls.

My sleeping beauties.

Fire builds in my gut, and I toss the remote to the ground, charging for my door, and tear it open.

I freeze in the doorway when Maddoc, Raven, and Royce are still standing right there, waiting for me.

Royce nods his chin. "Now we find her?"

"Now we find her."

CHAPTER 33
CAPTAIN

"How the fuck can we not find her?" Maddoc glares.

"It's been three days. How far could she get?"

"China," Royce scoffs. "Antarctica. Fuckin' Transylvania."

I swing my scowl to him.

"Just sayin'." He shrugs.

Raven sits forward. "You think she'd go out to Maria's, sleep on the property or whatever?"

"Doubt it," he says, pushing to his feet. "Nothin' there but ash and flowers."

"Flowers?" Maddoc frowns.

Royce nods, looking between us. "Them and that wall's the only thing that didn't go down in flames."

"What wall?"

"You know." He lifts his hands, looking up as he draws it in the air. "Big ugly thing, leaves and shit all over it."

I yank my phone from my pocket, scrolling through old photos until I get to the ones my PI sent me of Maria's property before I had ever seen it. I pull up the one that shows the garden, shoving it toward him.

"Yeah, those flow—" He cuts himself off, his hand wrapping around my wrist and bringing it closer. "Where's the wall?"

"There was no wall." I shake him off, my frown moving from Maddoc to him. "When she was little, Donley Graven kept her locked in a studio, a garden outside the doors and stone wall surrounding it, covered in thorns and ivy."

Maddoc frowns. "Donley Graven got a bullet to the back of the head months ago. He's six feet under, and Collins Graven took off to Europe. His every move is tracked, hasn't looked back since."

Raven's hands slide along her belly, tension in her eyes. "Yeah, but knowing about the wall and considering everything else, how I had their shit burned, the fire screams Graven to me."

"She might have different enemies, Raven. She ended up here; she didn't start here."

"Didn't she?" she challenges. "You said she was born here and kept locked away."

"Yeah, but she had no human contact then, not until Mero—" I cut myself off. "Wait. She did talk to one person there."

"Who?" she asks.

Royce flies from his seat right then. "Incoming."

We jerk around to spot a black car rolling up the driveway.

Nobody comes down this road.

Maddoc pushes Raven behind him, but she shoves him, gripping his arm to see best she can.

The door opens, and none other than Connor fucking Perkins, our old principal, our father's once friend, and my biological father, steps out.

What the fuck?

I'm down the porch steps, freezing him in his before he has a chance to close the door behind him.

"The fuck are you doing here? You were told to leave this place."

"Where is she?" he rushes out, ignoring me completely.

Anger builds in my gut and I move closer. "You are not seeing my daughter."

"Not her, Captain. Victoria." He shocks me.

My muscles grow stiff.

Royce pushes forward, eerily slow. "Why you care?"

Perkins's shoulders fall, his eyes moving across us. "You sent her away like you sent me away, didn't you?"

Maddoc pushes forward. "Why wouldn't we?"

Perkins's head tugs back, his eyes flying between ours. "Maybe I made a mistake. I guess I thought..." He closes his mouth, nodding. "Never mind."

"No, no, no." Royce slips by him, yanking the keys from his hand, putting them in his pocket. "Say what you came to say. Why do you care about a poor little group home girl?"

"I think she's in danger," he says.

My gut twists. "Why?"

"I went to Maria's. It's gone."

"We know," I snap. "If that's all, you can go now."

His mouth falls open the slightest bit, and he shakes his head, eyeing me. "Was I wrong to believe Victoria means more to you than she does?"

My jaw ticks, but I give him nothing.

"Did she explain anything to you?" he asks. "Why she came?"

"Let's pretend she didn't," Royce snaps. "Fill us in, Perkins. Now."

"All right." He swallows with a nod. "I guess I'll start at the beginning. Victoria was born but never held, stolen from her mother, and taken back to the Graven estate," he begins. "She was raised but never spoken to, fed and clothed but left alone."

All shit I already know but is news to my family, so I let him continue.

"She had a garden she cared for and nothing else. Not even a name, no identity whatsoever."

"Until Mero," Raven guesses, reaching out for Maddoc's hand.

Perkins nods. "She'd never even seen beyond the walls she lived in until Mero Malcari showed up and bartered for her. She went from being invisible to being adored. From having her small garden to her own greenhouse. Mero was everything to her, so she followed him blindly. It wasn't until she came here that she began to question everything she ever knew.

"After years of coaching her, he was finally ready to come home, back to Brayshaw. He asked his precious tool to come first." I glare, and he moves his eyes to the ground a moment. "Her job was to find one secret, something nobody else knew. She started with who she saw as the weakest link."

Weakest link?

He must see it because he shakes his head. "Not you, Captain."

"Mallory," Maddoc guesses.

Perkins nods. "He set her up in a hotel for a week, but it only took her twelve hours. She knew everything there was to know about this town, the Brayshaws and her bloodline, the Gravens, or at least Mero's version of the truths, so she knew what he would do with what she'd found out.

"For the first time, Victoria was faced with a moral decision, and she chose right. She waited out her time here and went back to the man who gave her a purpose in life, the man she idolized until that moment, and lied straight to his face. She let him down for the first time in her life to save a baby she had no ties to."

"He knew she lied."

Perkins nods again. "And he punished her for it, severely, but she was his future, as he saw it, so he made sure it was nowhere anyone could see."

Her scars.

He cut her up, blended his marks with the marks left by the thorns from the ivy tower she was once locked inside—a reminder she was not free, though she might have felt like it.

"As I said, Mero saw her as his future, so from the moment he had her, he began making sure she was ready for what that meant."

"He taught her how to defend herself," Raven whispers.

"Yes," Perkins says. "She fought back and won."

She killed him.

"Victoria was on my doorstep, bloodied and frail, not twenty-four hours later. I was ready to send her away, thought she was some crazy looking for a payout, when she threatened to expose me as your biological father," he tells me, a small smile finding his mouth. "Still not sure how she figured that one out."

"She's smart." My body aches.

He nods. "I didn't know what to do with her, so I leased a small place on the edge of town and put her inside it. Mallory disappeared a week later."

She didn't convince Mallory to leave me like Mallory twisted the situation to make me believe.

She convinced her to keep Zoey, and the only way to get Mallory to agree was to hide her away. She'd have the baby and walk away like nothing happened, and nobody would ever know.

"She moved her in."

"I didn't learn that until later, but yes," he confirms. "During the pregnancy, she made her way to you guys. She convinced me to get her in contact with your dad and went to see him. I was surprised when he so easily gave her a safe place in the girls' Bray house and had Maybell help enroll her in school. From that day, she spent every day giving back to your family the only way she knew how."

"Finding and giving us secrets." Maddoc frowns.

"You said Mero bartered for Victoria."

Perkins's chin lowers the tiniest bit as if he was waiting for me to ask.

"Why would he do that? Her being Graven blood meant nothing; they didn't claim her. Why did he want her?"

I look across at my brothers, swiveling around when my dad's voice interrupts.

He steps through the doorway, farther out onto the porch. "Go on, Perkins." He gives the man permission to tell what he must have hidden. "He asked you a question. Answer."

Slowly, we look back to Perkins.

"Mero could have taken any girl and turned her into his little revenge machine, but he wanted to add insult to injury." Perkins glances over our heads once more and then back to us. "He wanted the daughter of the Graven maid, the innocent infant girl your dad tried to save, when he refused the innocent son of a maid of his own, a son of Brayshaw."

"What…" Royce draws out.

Panic and anger knot in my chest.

Refused a son…

Perkins locks his eyes on mine.

"Victoria came here, found out what she needed to know, and went back, lied to Mero," I repeat what he told us. "How did he know she was lying?"

Perkins nods his head in confirmation. "She had a shadow."

"Who did he have watching her?"

Our dad makes his way down the porch, stepping around us to stand at Perkins's side.

The four of us turn to face him.

He licks his lips and says, "His son."

VICTORIA

I swallow the last drop of water from the bottle I've been sipping on for the last hour right as the door opens and in he walks.

"I've gotta say, I've missed your lavender scent, Garden Girl." His smile is soft, and I don't doubt his words for a minute. "It's been three days," he says gently. "Ready to talk to me yet?"

"You left those gloves for me, didn't you?" I ask him. "The ones in the planter's box at the park?"

He nods, eyes bright with pride. "You should never have to dig in the dirt like that again."

"You built the wall. Did you kill Maria too?"

He tenses. "Man, straight for it, huh?"

When I say nothing, he gives a curt nod. "I'm sorry, but I promise she didn't feel a thing. I needed you to know I was here, that I was waiting for you, but it took you longer than I thought it would for you to realize."

I eye him a long moment, and in the end, I have to look away. "You shouldn't be here."

Confusion is in his voice. "I'm here for you. You said you needed time to save the little girl. I gave it to you. Time is up."

"Don't be a fool." I shake my head. "I told you I was staying. Get out of here before they find you."

His chuckles have me turning toward him. "Nice try. I know you're on the outs. Don't forget, I exist to watch over you. From the start, my life was spent protecting you."

I push the hair from my scalp, raising a brow as I force him to look at the small gash the fore-end of the gun left, and shame covers his face.

Suddenly he's on his knees in front of me, gripping my hands in his. "I never wanted to hurt you, but I knew if you yelled, they'd come running, if for no other reason than to know why."

"You didn't want them to spot you."

His brows lower in a deep scowl. "I'm not afraid of them."

"You should be. They'd cut you into pieces and fry you up for the wolves if they knew who you were."

"I heard what he said, what they think of you." His animosity toward Captain is front and center. "He told you to go. He doesn't care."

"I didn't say they'd do it for me."

He shakes his head. "Another reason for us to take off now."

My head tugs back. "I'm not leaving."

His forehead tightens and then he nods. "And I'm not leaving without you. Victoria, he didn't choose you."

"He's angry."

"He doesn't deserve you."

My shoulders fall. "And I don't belong to you."

His eyes harden, his grip on me following, but I don't show him the sting it causes. "We came into this together. For years, they overlooked you, and then she came in and became God. She didn't even have to work for it, Vee."

"You have no idea what she did and would do for them, but this isn't about her. This is about me, what I want. You've known from the minute you followed me here I had every intention of staying. Nobody asked you to come back."

"I came back for you! Everything I have ever done has been with you in mind." His lip curls, his hands trembling on mine, and I wince when a knuckle cracks. "I have loved you all my life."

"I wasn't yours to love."

"You were supposed to be. When I found you, when I led him to you, he promised you'd be mine and she'd be his. But he took you as his instead."

"He manipulated us, both of us."

He throws my hands away, shaking his head as he stands and begins to pace. "I want… I can't leave you here. Mero is gone; I'm here. We have the money, what you didn't give Mallory anyway. Let's go."

"You're forgetting I've had the money all along. I don't want it."

"Come with me."

"You don't need me. Just…go."

He shakes his head, dragging a hand over his mouth. "I never should have allowed things to go this far."

My eyes narrow and he steps closer, his hands sliding along the base of my neck, eyes falling as he runs his fingers down my shoulder before flashing to mine.

"He doesn't want you," he whispers, flicking my hair. "But I do. We'll help you see."

My muscles freeze, and it doesn't go unnoticed.

His smirk is slow, and my pulse hammers out of control.

"We?"

His arms wrap around me, pulling me against him, and I'm too shocked to stop him. "Don't look so nervous, baby. I've got it all worked out."

My throat begins to close. "What did you do?"

"What I had to do to make sure you have everything you need to be happy." His fingers run along my cheek, and he leans closer as my body grows heavy. "Go to sleep, sweetheart," he whispers as my vision begins to blur. "And when you wake up, we'll be a step closer."

CHAPTER 34
CAPTAIN

"His son," Maddoc draws out slowly, his feet carrying him closer to our dad. "What fucking son?"

Our dad's eyes soften, regret heavy within them. "We should go inside, sit."

"No," I say, looking to Perkins. "He doesn't get to come inside."

Our dad nods. "You boys know I tried to save your fathers the night Brayshaw was ambushed eighteen years ago. You know my brother was with us during that attack, and I left his body behind, believing he was dead. We all know now that wasn't true."

"Enough with the backstory." Royce crosses his arms. "What are we missing?"

"Mero knew our plan was to raise you boys as our successors. Three boys, from Brayshaw's top three men—a new future for this town." Our dad looks to Perkins and back to us. "A few weeks before the murders, my brother came to me to tell me he was expecting a son."

"He wanted him to have a place with us."

"Yes." He nods. "But the timing had me questioning my brother's motives. He'd never spoken of a child, you three were already born, and suddenly he had a woman none of us had ever seen him with before, conveniently five months along."

"He waited to find out it was a boy before he told you," Maddoc says.

"Exactly." Our dad shakes his head. "I didn't believe him, but he expected that and had a DNA test to prove it. He thought that would be enough, that he was my brother, so that meant his son would be promised all you three were, but it wasn't that easy."

"Why not? The kid wasn't even born yet. He'd have come in as we did, just a baby."

"From a relationship I'd only just learned of and with a mother I didn't know. I denied his request."

"But you were the lead," Raven says, studying him with narrowed eyes. "You couldn't give him what he wanted, but you did love him, so you couldn't give him nothing either..." She trails off, shaking her head.

He eyes her a long moment, and shame shadows his face as he looks to us. "When Maybell sent Maria my way, pregnant and homeless, I knew the father of her unborn baby had to be a Graven. I just didn't know who. It just so happened—"

"Your brother's wife was having a boy and Maria was having a girl." Raven glares. "You made a promise that wasn't yours to make."

"You're wrong, Raven," he says, his eyes moving to mine. "I gave my word to protect the life of Maria's child with all my ability, to bring her into the Brayshaw world where she would be safe, raised alongside you all, and in return, Maria gave me permission to promise her daughter to my nephew."

My face falls.

Victoria.

He continues, "Your fathers and my brother died not long later. Maddoc's mother and I took the other two of you and your mothers into our home, and I offered the mother of Mero's unborn son a position. A month following that, Maria went into labor, and after she was born, Victoria was taken."

"So Maria lost her meal ticket," Royce says.

"I had no intention of firing her or sending her away," he tells us. "But yes, that baby was her security, and suddenly it was gone."

"Maria was afraid."

Our dad looks to Perkins a long moment, and when he brings his eyes back to ours, distress shines through.

"Dad?"

"In her eyes, Mero was gone, her baby was gone, and it was only a matter of time before I'd send her on her way. I couldn't protect an unborn little girl as I promised, and with that failure, any trust she had in me died too."

"I don't understand." I shake my head. "Mero was Brayshaw, was he not? He died as one, didn't he?"

"He did." Our dad nods.

"So she didn't trust you—who cares? Her son was Brayshaw, innocent. He could have grown like us, with us. He deserved to be here." I glare at him. "Why would you turn him away?"

"Holy shit." Raven connects something we haven't as our dad's chin falls to his chest. "You wouldn't, not unless you had to protect your family, your sons." Her shoulders fall, pity in her gaze. "You gave her a job, trusted her to live and work in your home, and it was your biggest mistake, became the very reason you hold the earning of trust so highly."

Our dad's eyes cloud with guilt. "Every boy grows into a man, but not all are meant for this, not all are strong enough to let go of the past and be the difference in the future."

"Stop," Maddoc draws out, a calm to his tone that has all eyes moving to his. "No more bullshit. Say it."

Our dad nods. "When Mero died, I hired his mistress as our maid."

"A maid," Royce repeats, turning to us.

A maid…

All at once, realization hits us.

"You gave her a home because you loved your brother, and she murdered your wife, murdered our mothers."

Our dad swallows, moisture building in his eyes. "She could have killed you all, but Maybell heard the screams. She got there just in time."

"That's why you sent her to prison instead of killing her yourself, because she was pregnant."

He nods. "I couldn't murder my nephew, even if his mother murdered my wife and the wives of my best friends." He clears his throat. "A couple months later, a woman was on my doorstep, an infant boy in her hands, and without a blink, I sent her away. I would not have him grow up in my home, with my sons, and come home to find you all dead as I did your mothers."

"He was innocent."

"As was she…until she wasn't. I put her away for life; she had nothing to lose. I have no doubt in my mind she'd find him as an adult and do all she could to turn him against our family."

Perkins steps forward. "Mero must have known his son would be denied."

Our dad sighs. "I assume so too."

"This is why you allowed Victoria into the group home. You knew it was her. You knew Maria was her mother."

He doesn't deny it. "Yes. I led her there myself, but I didn't tell her. She figured it out on her own."

I drag my hands down my face, turning to Perkins. "What made you come here today? Why'd you assume she was gone?"

I'd swear he was waiting for my question.

"Mero Malcari's offshore account has been sitting idle for almost three years." His eyes move between mine. "It was cleaned out yesterday. Every penny."

My gut twists.

No.

"How much was in the account?" I force my voice steady.

"Just over twelve five."

My soul begins to ache, and slowly, I turn away from my family.

I lick my lips, trying to ease the sting threatening to knock me on my ass.

This is on me. I asked her to leave, and so she did.

Twelve million five hundred thousand dollars.

I'll never find her, never get to thank her for what she did, let alone grovel over what I have done.

I swallow and take a deep breath, turning back to Perkins.

Raven lets go of Maddoc's hand and walks over, looking up at me with tense eyes. "She wouldn't take a dime of Donley's money when it should have been hers. She wanted me to give it all to Bass Bishop," she whispers, looking at my brothers as they step in closer, closing off our circle.

"Maybe that's 'cause she was sittin' on millions, RaeRae," Royce says quietly.

Raven shakes her head. "She didn't take from that account. There's no fucking way."

Royce looks back to Perkins. "How did you know the account was emptied?"

My head snaps left, and it hits. "She left you a clue," I say before he can answer. "Didn't she?"

"I got an email," he shares. "There was a contingency on the account. The moment funds were withdrawn, it autosent."

"Why you?" Raven asks.

"Because I was the first person she forced herself to trust when she had nowhere else to run," he tells us.

I step toward him. "Show me."

He pulls the phone from his pocket, handing it over.

My eyes fall to the screen where no words lie, only a clip-art image.

A single, outlined anchor.

My chest caves.

She trusted Perkins to understand what it meant, to tell me something was wrong if she was gone, because she swore she'd never leave.

"She didn't take the money," I croak.

"Keep scrolling, Captain. There's one more. One I couldn't figure out."

With shaky fingers, I drag my thumb up the screen, and every muscle in my body locks when the second image stares back.

"A bird?" Royce whispers, shaking his head in confusion.

Holy shit.

Her friend. The boy from the Graven estate.

He found her for his father and then spent his life watching her, following her…and now he's come back for her.

Beady eyes and a red neck, white painted wings, rimmed in black feathers.

A fucking vulture.

"It's Mike." I shock them all, my pulse pounding double time.

"Whoa, are you for real?!" Royce runs a hand over his hair.

"I knew something was off with that motherfucker. I had that damn feeling and I did nothing about it." I drop the phone and drag my hands down my face, folding them around the back of my neck as I clamp my teeth together.

Fuck!

"She told me her damn self to basically watch his punk ass, that he didn't belong here. She knew he wasn't like us. Fuck, man, she told me to make him go!" A deep ache sets in as a scalding fire lights in the pit of my stomach. "He's Mero's son. And he never fucking left."

Maddoc yanks the phone from the ground, glaring at the screen, but slowly his eyes lift to our dad. "You turned your back on a fucking baby, and now he's here, fucking with our family."

"I had no clue, son," our dad whispers. "If I had, I would have told you."

"You should have fuckin' known. She was burned by a Brayshaw, for fuck's sake! The burned always turn to Graven!" Maddoc jerks away, turning to us. "We fuckin' had him."

Raven reaches out to grip Maddoc's wrist and pulls him toward her, but her eyes slide to mine. "We have to find him."

My temples throb, and I clench my jaw to refocus the tension.

I look from Perkins to my dad, to Raven and then my brothers. "I've got a feeling he'll find us first."

"Why would he do that? If he has her, why not leave, take her with him?"

"She's not his prisoner." I shake my head. "The tower was a message, a fucking…grand gesture or some shit he thought she'd appreciate, making his intentions clear. He's twisted in the head, but he's bettin' on her agreeing to leave. She won't."

"You sure about that, brother?" Royce asks. "You told her to go."

"It doesn't matter." My eyes meet his.

"Cap," Raven whispers, pulling our eyes to her. She gives a sad smile. "If it comes down to a threat against you or her leaving, she will go."

I gently place my hands on Raven's forearms. "I know you did what you had to to help us, to save us, and we love you for it, but she is not you, Raven. She said she won't go, and I believe her." I nod, meeting my brothers' eyes before looking back to hers. "I trust her."

Raven studies me a long moment, and then with a deep inhale, her smile grows until a small laugh leaves her. "And there it is."

Maddoc slides up, wrapping his arms around her, and she leans against his chest. "Okay, Cap. Tell us what to do."

"If Mike came for her, he wants her to want to go. He won't hurt her, there's no way. If he planned to do that, he'd have done it a long time ago," I tell them, the only reason I'm not fully losing my shit right now. "I have no doubt he's been watching; he's seen her with me. He knows what she wants. He has no choice but to persuade her."

"He wants to convince her she isn't wanted here, that she means nothing," Raven guesses.

I nod, thinking.

What I have to do becomes clear, a wince following.

Fuck.

I turn away, rubbing my palm along my chest, my shoulders set.

Before I can think too hard on it, I pull out my phone, scroll, and hit call before bringing it to my ear, speaking the second the line is picked up. "I hope you're home because I'm coming over." I hang up as quickly as I dialed.

Royce frowns, looking from Maddoc to me. "Cap."

"You're not gonna like it. I fucking hate it."

"We're with you."

"Captain," Perkins interrupts, stepping closer, eyeing the four of us but settling on me. "He's a smart young man. All he's ever known is trickery, and all he has ever had is her. If push comes to shove, he won't hesitate to do whatever he has to. He loves her."

"She's not his to love."

She's mine.

CHAPTER 35
VICTORIA

My tongue smacks against the roof of my mouth, my lips parting with a bit of a sting as I peel my eyes open.

Mike sits across from me, elbows on his knees, holding out a water. "Thirsty?"

It takes serious effort to lift my foot and knock his hand, and even then, it doesn't do a damn thing. "Ambien in all the water bottles?"

He nods, a small grin on his lips. "In case you reached to the back of the fridge. Just like old times." He stares at me a moment, and it's as if he feels the distance the last few years have placed between us, a heaviness settling over him. "Remember we'd slip it to my good old dad so we could stay up together?"

I try to clear my throat, but it's too dry, so I nod, rasping, "Yeah, Mike. I remember."

He nods, looking away, only to swing his eyes right back, and this time they're focused. "You are leaving with me, Victoria."

My blinks are so heavy, my eyes begin to close again. "Where are we?" I fight to stay awake, glancing at the lavish bedroom.

"Least suspecting pit stop." His smile is sad as he grabs a remote, turning on a little monitor and stuffing the controller into his jeans. "I didn't want to do this, but you need to see."

"See what?"

"Reality, so you can leave this place without doubts," he whispers, lowering to his knees. "I told you, I'm giving you everything you need to be happy, baby, so there'll be nothing left for you here."

Tension pulls in my gut, my eyes bouncing between his. "Mike…"

"Shh." He pushes my hair back, setting a water bottle in my lap. "The seal's not broken on this one. No more meds."

There's a sound in the background, and a voice follows, but sleep calls.

"I'll be back soon, Tor, and with a surprise."

A loud ring has my eyes opening, a clinking sound following, and I push into a sitting position.

"Hi."

My muscles tense, but I focus on the voices.

"You got here fast."

Mallory.

My eyes fly around the room, landing on the monitor Mike turned on, and I pull myself up, squinting at the tiny screen.

Several small squares make up the monitor, a live-stream surveillance system like the one Mero had.

"You asked me to come see you today, and here I am."

A sting shoots through my body, making my feet throb.

Captain?

Mallory is hesitant with her backward steps, but just then he slips inside with confidence.

He's with her right now?

My hand flies to my chest as he wastes no time pushing against her, his hand grabbing at a piece of her blond hair he seems to love so much.

"Now I want to hear you beg." He leans in and as his mouth slides across hers, a metal taste coats mine. His hands slide along her collarbone as he tips his head. "You know how much I loved that…you begging."

Oh my God.

I try to look away but can't.

My eyes refuse to leave the pair who match so perfectly, a cloud slipping over my sight as Captain lifts her chin, his strong gaze holding hers.

The mother of his child.

The girl he believed over me.

He leans down, placing his lips on hers in a slow, gentle kiss that turns my blood to acid, burning my soul as it eats away at my insides.

Her hand comes up, her fingers lacing into his on her face.

"I need to feel you, Mallory. Show me how bad you want me, remind me what it's like to have a girl like you."

As if a blow from a world-class boxer slams into my chest, all the air in my lungs is forced out with a single, harsh, burning breath, leaving me gasping.

You really do want her.

He wastes no time, tugging his shirt from his body and walking her backward.

They disappear from the screen, showing up in the next little box as they make their way through what must be her house.

"Where are we going?" she asks him.

"Outside, on the patio."

She attempts to stop his forward advance. "Why?"

"So your neighbors can see what I'm about to do to you."

Mallory gives a hasty nod, but then her eyes cut left, and suddenly they're staring right into mine through the monitor.

My muscles freeze as my head tugs back as I realize she knows I'm fucking watching.

You little bitch.

She's in on this with Mike…but who manipulated who?

"Wait," she suddenly whispers, pulling away, and then she grips his hands, shifting and leading him to the right. "I have a surprise for you, Captain."

He yanks her into him. "You're the only prize I want."

Hot, angry, dumb-girl-devastated tears fill my eyes, but still, I can't look away.

"Trust me," she dares to say, and I want to strangle her where she stands.

But the anger is nothing compared to the rip of my organs as he places his lips on hers and whispers back, "I do."

I fall onto my ass, staring at the stupid black-and-white screen and wishing for a sudden power outage because there's no way I can turn it off.

As her dress slips from her arms, my tears follow, falling with the same amount of ease.

She kicks the fancy material to the side, left standing in nothing but a matching bra and panties and soft pink heels to match.

"Open the door, Captain. Take me inside, and then we can go outside if you'd like."

He makes no move at first, and then a tight nod follows, his eyes closing as his hand comes around her waist, pulling her nearer, his other wrapping around the door handle.

I squeeze my eyes closed.

And then a lock turns.

It happens so fast.

The sound of a door clicking open hits, but I realize it's not coming from in front of me and the monitors but behind me.

My eyes fly open, my body jolting upright in the same second as my attention stays glued to the wreckage.

Cap and Mallory stumble inside the room I'm locked inside.

I shuffle back, the lack of air in my lungs forcing me to bend at the ache's will.

Something behind me falls, crashing to the floor, but the

impact is nothing compared to when his eyes lift, slamming into mine.

His arms tighten, but around her, as he tilts his head, his mouth gaping open only for no sound to come out.

"Surprise," Mallory whispers, the word curling off her tongue like a taunt. She grabs his hands, pulling them from around her body.

He stands there, frozen in place, his eyes flying across the room, landing on the screen on the small table.

They narrow as he pieces it together, realizing I watched every move made, heard his every desire.

"No," he breathes, shaking his head frantically.

He darts forward, but Mallory slips in front of me first.

"What the fuck is going on here?" he asks, but his voice is just above a whisper.

I've lost, that's what.

He stands still as a statue as Mallory turns to me.

Wild, crystal-blue eyes meet mine as her clammy palm flattens on my cheek. "Mike thinks he knows what you want." She leans forward, sliding her lips across my cheek until they meet my hair in a move that is purely for show. "But I know you better, don't I?"

"What the hell are you doing?" I breathe brokenly.

Her soft chuckle fans across my skin, and I force myself not to shove her back. "You made me think we were friends. You pretended to be there for me. You lied to me, Vee, and for what? Him? You must feel like such a fool now, seeing how easily he gave you up."

"You're a crazy bitch," I hiss. Realization slams into me: She actually feels betrayed by me in some way. As though my protecting an innocent child at any cost was somehow wrong.

Captain frowns, unable to hear our quiet words, and unease creates heavy creases across his brows.

Mallory grips my chin in a hard hold, forcing words past clenched teeth. "You gave me no choice. I am controlling this party, Victoria, so play along." Her voice is so low, there is no way he can hear, but she might as well be screaming in my ear when she says, "Play along, you worthless little toy, and take what you want, Vee, because this will be your one and only chance to have him."

My only chance.

Because he chose her. And she's taunting me, punishing me for what she thinks I did to her.

My chest caves as I stare at Captain, and even more so when his focus switches to the beautiful, near-naked blond in front of me.

Maybe she's right...

Despite what anyone wants, I have no intention of leaving this place, no matter the girl on his arm or the obstacles that may follow. This is my home, and it will stay so, and she's making it clear, in case it wasn't, that no matter what she does, she'll always have a part of him I won't, and she plans to use it as a weapon against me because I'm her enemy now.

She'll always stand in my way, even when she doesn't want him, if it means keeping him from me.

With that thought, I stand perfectly still as her hands lower to my jeans, and when she unbuttons them, I allow her to push them down.

She bends over, picking them off the floor, and spins on her heels, resting her ass on me, nothing but the thin line of her G-string and my thong between us.

She tosses my jeans to Captain, who catches them with a tight frown.

Mallory grabs her hair in her hands and drags it all to the opposite side of her, tilting her head, and like a robot, I give her what she wants—my participation in this strange punishment she's crafted for me.

I lean closer and press my lips to her shoulder.

Captain's eyes follow the movement, and slowly my pants fall from his hands.

"Come here," she whispers to him.

Of course, he listens.

My pulse beats heavy in my throat, vibrates deep within my ears, and only grows louder with each slow step closer he takes.

"She's gorgeous," Mallory says to him, and his features tighten, gaze flying between mine only to cut to hers. "Isn't she?"

Her fingers suddenly slide along my outer thigh, and he follows the contact as he gives an almost unnoticeable nod, and her hand dips beneath the band of my underwear.

It takes everything inside me not to wrap my arm around her neck and choke her on the spot, but then I'd have to sit back and break a little more as he comes to her rescue.

So as she begins to pull my underwear down, pushing them along my thighs, I allow it. They fall to my feet.

Captain's eyes fly to mine, a twisted expression taking over his face.

She blocks my exposed body with her own, and asks him, "Are her eyes on yours?"

His features pull, but he nods, and then her hand slides behind her.

I grind my teeth together, fighting back tears as she violates me, and right here for him to see.

Her hand slides along my center, and shame colors my neck and cheek as my body reacts to the sensation. My core heats without permission, and I can't stop the shuddered exhale from escaping, but it helps hide the slight cry that slips out in the same second.

Mallory's chest inflates with a heavy inhale, proud of her piece-of-shit self, and her blue eyes lock with mine over her shoulder. A wicked glint glares into me as she lowers her hand, now cupping me completely.

Her smile is slow and then she quickly spins to grip me better, still hiding me from him. She brings her lips a fraction from mine, and my eyes fly over her shoulder.

Captain doesn't stop her, but why would he?

He didn't come here to sleep with me.

He came here for her.

"Touch me, Victoria," she commands in a quiet purr, hatred and victory woven in her tone.

Fear and fault make for a heavily polished gleam within his eyes.

If I can't kiss your lips, Cap, I'll settle for the travesty of tasting you on hers.

My hands lift, landing on her naked ribs, and I yank her to me, wishing it were her throat I was squeezing instead.

Her eyes fire with a taunting glow, a low, purposeful "yes" following.

I take her mouth as he did, and when she releases a fake moan into mine, my heart cries.

I tear away from her, swallowing back pitiful waterworks that threaten to expose just how much this hurts, how fully she's won.

I'm strong, but not this kind of strong.

Mallory's palm finds my outer hip, squeezing as she grips the hem of my shirt, and begins dragging it up.

"No, wait!"

We both freeze when Captain finally speaks, and in a loud, panicked tone.

One that gives him away.

Gives us away? Is he as tortured by this as I am?

Slowly, Mallory pulls back, her eyes falling to the floor, shifting to him in the next second.

"So you have touched her," she says quietly, my shirt still tight in her grasp. She looks at her finger, at the proof she touched me staring back at her, and glides it along her lips. "But have you tasted her?"

Captain's eyes snap to mine, widening and then narrowing in the same second as he realizes what I did after they stumbled into the room: the girl standing between us, the one he once loved, isn't after him—she's here to get back at me.

CAPTAIN

If I could speak, I wouldn't know what to say.

Mallory and Victoria.

The girl I thought I loved and the girl I now know I do.

I look into Mallory's eyes, at the burning jealousy staring back, and for the first time, I realize she's not doing this in a deluded attempt to win me.

She's hates the loyalty that Victoria has shown me.

All of this, the lies, the manipulation, her trying to slide back into my life, our daughter's, it had nothing to do with me or us or Zoey.

It was about Victoria and the ache losing her leaves behind—a feeling I know good and fucking well.

I look to her, and everything shifts into place.

My life, all the ways I was tested as a boy, as a man and father, all led me here. To her.

Victoria came into my town to ruin my family but felt a moral obligation in her gut to save it instead. She turned her back on all she ever knew, the man who gave her a chance at life—even if it wasn't a good one—for me, a guy she'd never even spoken to but felt inclined to help.

Victoria convinced the girl I so frivolously loved to give my daughter the gift of life, forever changing mine in the process. She had to make Mallory believe she was doing it for her own good, because Victoria cared for Mallory, and in the end, it enraged Mallory that it was all a lie.

Victoria was born, raised, and ruined, all so, in the end, she'd be right here today.

Five feet from me, staring into my eyes with such fervor, a heavy, burning need for her king—happy to be nothing more than a peasant when she deserves a crown of her own.

Willing to participate in whatever this messed-up situation is with a girl she thinks I've chosen over her if it means she'll have a single piece of me, if only for a moment.

She came here and protected our name without being asked, without permission, and without pause.

With selfless intent and a pure heart.

My Beauty.

My Brayshaw.

I watch as Mallory gently nudges Victoria, my eyes glued to Victoria as she scoots back on the mattress, lying flat on the plush pillows, her lower half bare.

Mallory climbs up beside her, lying at her side, her fingertips running along Victoria's thigh, and Victoria tenses.

"She deserves more than she's been given," Mallory whispers, but it's not enough to hide the venom in her tone, and my eyes tighten, darting to hers and quickly back to Victoria's. "Doesn't she?"

"Yes," I rasp instantly, and Victoria's features twist, but I lose her expression when Mallory's hand comes up, forcing her face and attention toward her.

I want it back.

"Let us have you," Mallory murmurs, but the edges of her eyes crease. "Say goodbye, have closure." But the way she says it sounds more like "Let us ruin you all over again."

I don't want closure.

I want today, tomorrow, always.

But then Victoria's eyes meet mine, no hesitation shining within them, and damn if it doesn't fucking sting.

Does she want this?

I swallow, my lips flattening.

How can I deny her a single thing after the shit I've put her through?

I can't.

I have to give her whatever she needs, and then I'll take her home and give her more.

So when Mallory calls me over with a crook of her finger, tugging on my arm, I climb onto the mattress, lowering my body on Victoria's free side.

"Taste," she whispers, and my eyes fall to the glistening sheen on her lips.

My gut twists, but when Victoria's hand finds mine on the mattress, I take reprieve in her touch, lacing my fingers into hers, and lean across her body, locking my lips on Mallory's, tasting Beauty on her, and a low rumble settles in my chest.

Mallory smirks against my mouth, slowly pulling away.

She leans down, preparing to kiss my girl, but I can't take it and nudge Mallory's shoulder. I want her away.

She doesn't get angry as I thought she might, but a smile covers her lips and she glides her hand along Victoria's thigh until she can grip around the back of her leg, holding on to it as she falls beside her on the pillow.

She's opened her for me, and when I look to Beauty, she silently begs me to take Mallory's place, so I don't hesitate slipping between her thighs, my arms at her sides, shielding her. Guarding her.

There's a heavy strain between her eyes, one that only gets worse when Mallory's hands slide between us, and we allow her to unclip my belt, pop the button on my jeans, and unzip them. They fall open.

Mallory's hand glides across me, and the muscles in my back clench.

I'm about to snap, tell her to get her fucking hands off me, when she pulls away on her own.

"Let her feel," she suggests, but we all know it's a command.

This is her show and we're just fucking stuck in it.

She lies back, watching Victoria watch me.

I lower my body, applying the slightest pressure to Victoria's center with mine, and she gasps, but she doesn't touch me, and fuck, I wish she would.

I want to feel her hands on my skin—I need to feel her hands on my skin.

Her warmth.

Her forgiveness.

Her heart.

But right now, I'll settle for her heat if it's what she wants.

Anything for you, Beauty.

I take my knuckle, feathering it along her panty line and straight down until I meet her clit. I barely touch her, the smallest, shortest of grazes, but still she gasps, those thick, red lips parting.

Mallory hums beside her, her own hand disappearing between her legs. "She likes that."

"I know what she likes."

"So show her. Give her what she needs, Captain."

My body shakes.

Victoria's hands on me shake.

Do we shake in rage or fear or more?

Am I really about to fuck the girl I'm in love with for the first fucking time with the girl I thought I loved right beside us?

"She's ready for you," Mallory taunts, her shuddered breath fanning over us both.

Anger builds in my chest.

Who is she to tell me?

Victoria is mine, not hers as her twisted mind is trying to convince her.

A shadow falls over me, one that seems to blanket Victoria the same.

"Go get us drinks," the demand flies from my mouth before I can stop it, and everyone freezes.

My eyes meet Mallory's.

Ever so slowly, her frown slips in place, her body pulling away from us both as a gauged gleam slowly fills her eyes.

"Please." I force the word out, doing my best to keep my tone calm when I'm about to lose my shit.

I can't do this. I fucking can't.

At my side, Victoria squeezes and then lets go of my hand, and my attention snaps to her.

A dark, tortured demand of acceptance she's granted herself burns in her eyes, one that has me holding my breath.

Victoria's left hand slides into Mallory's hair, tugging her close.

White-hot jealousy threatens to blur my vision as Victoria's tongue, a tongue I haven't thoroughly tasted, disappears into Mallory's mouth. With each passing second, a heavy tension carves deeper and deeper into her forehead until she finally pulls back to meet Mallory's eyes, a dead look in her own.

"Make us a drink?" she whispers.

Her approach is much different from mine and more effective—making Mallory the center of the attention, making her feel like she's the important person in this room, just like she wants. And it's working, because of course it is. All she wants is the power in her palms, to feel like she's winning whatever game this is, and Victoria just gave it back to her.

"You want a triple, Vee?" she asks her.

Victoria nods, and just like that, Mallory stands from the bed and walks out.

It's us now.

Me and her.

My eyes fly to hers, and I open my mouth to speak, but her hand quickly comes up to cover it.

"Not a sound," she rasps my own stupid, fucked-up rule, sadness lining every inch of her.

Instantly, I feel like even more of a piece of shit.

As far as she's concerned, I gave her so little of me and took even less of her. I touched her, but only if she was quiet.

She touched me, but my lips were off-limits.

I took away as much emotion as I could.

She must think I did all that to show her how little she meant when that's so far from the truth.

I did it to keep as much of myself as I could, as long as I could, because I knew if I wasn't careful, everything inside me would quickly be hers, and I wasn't ready for it.

I was fucking terrified of it.

Of her.

Of us.

Not anymore.

Never again.

I have to show her.

I lower until our bodies are flush against each other, pelvis to pelvis, heart to fucking heart, and her bottom lip starts to tremble, but she pulls it between her teeth to try to hide it.

She thinks this is goodbye.

She's so wrong.

Any wall I was trying to keep between us falls from my eyes, leaving them as open and honest as ever before and locked with hers.

I gently press my forehead to hers.

Slowly, with sweaty palms and a shaky grip, I place my nose beside hers, gently gliding it back and forth.

Every single muscle in her body locks as her eyes flutter, flying between mine.

Instant, hot tears build, and she lets out a broken breath.

"Yes, baby," I rasp, swallowing.

It's you.

"But you…you're here." Her tears spill over, soaking the hair above her ear as she shakes her head. "You were about to…"

"It's not what you think, I promise," I whisper, pushing her hair back. "I saw you, and all I wanted was to be, to do, whatever it was you needed or wanted, but I can't. I'm sorry, but I can't. Not like this, baby. You deserve so fucking much more."

Her tears roll onto the pillow behind her, and she shakes her head. "I don't want this." She both soothes and shocks me. "I just wanted you, no matter how it had to happen."

My heart breaks looking at her.

"Why are you here if you didn't know I would be?" she whispers.

"We know about Mike, about everything." I slide my hand along her cheek. "I came to set him up, catch him trying to catch me acting shitty to make you think I didn't care, make you want to leave, give up on me, and then suddenly you were here and..." My brows lift and I shake my head, lowering my voice when something clinks in the other room. "My brothers are outside waiting for him to show—"

She flies into a sitting position, shoving me back in the process, her stare bouncing around the room frantically. "Everything I could want to be happy..." Sheer panic-stricken eyes fly to mine. "Zoey."

"What—"

"Oh my God! Go!" She scrambles from the bed, grabbing her pants off the ground as she runs for the door, but I grip her elbow.

"What?!"

"Go! He knew!" she cries. "He knew what you'd do, knew they'd follow!"

It takes a half a second and then it clicks. "No..."

My phone is in my hand in the next second and right as Mallory comes around the corner.

Her eyes narrow. "What—"

In one quick motion, Victoria, still naked from the waist down, grips her by the neck, kicking her feet from under her, and slams her to the floor with a hard thud.

The glasses in her hands shatter on the floor as she cries out, and I rush right past, fastening my jeans. I yank my shirt from the floor, throwing it on as I run for the door.

"You psychotic bitch! Did you know?!" Victoria screams at Mallory behind me.

I've already dialed Royce, and I'm throwing the door open right as he answers.

I don't let him get a word in, shouting, "Get home! He's coming for Zoey."

I dash outside, briefly glancing behind right as Victoria screams, a vase full of white roses in her hand. She slams it down, shattering it into a million pieces directly beside Mallory's head.

I'm halfway in my truck when she breathlessly reaches the door, tugging her jeans up her thighs. "Hurry!" she shouts as I'm already reversing from the driveway and racing home.

I dial my dad, but he doesn't answer, so I try Raven next, and it goes straight to voicemail.

"Fuck!" I scream, punching the steering wheel.

Maybe Maddoc was calling her?

Maybe he reached her?

Maybe Royce talked to Dad.

I growl, trying one more person.

He answers on the first ring. "Captain?"

"Are you still at my house?"

"I left ten minutes ago. What's wrong?"

"Fuck," I swallow. "Perkins, he's coming for Zoey."

Time ticks in slow seconds and then the line goes dead.

I scream, throwing the phone across the car. "You useless piece of shit!"

I bite into my cheek as my vision clouds, and my chest fucking knots until I can't breathe.

Please.

Please no.

Please. Let me get there in time.

I'm coming, Zoey.

Daddy's coming.

CHAPTER 36
VICTORIA

I get my pants over my ass, quickly buttoning them and spin on my heels as Mallory pushes up into a sitting position, her hand going to the back of her head.

She gasps, shaking when she feels the blood there. "Oh my God." Angry eyes fly to mine, tears big and bright. "What the hell is the matter with you—"

"Shut up," I shout, grabbing her purse from the table and pouring it out. "Where are your keys?"

"Victoria, what's going on?"

"Where the fuck are your keys, Mallory?!" I scream, rubbing at my temples as the ache there doubles.

"Oh my God, you didn't know."

My head snaps up to hers.

"He said you knew." She shakes her head frantically. "That the three of us were leaving together." She points to the corner, and my eyes zone in on a set of suitcases, tucked away in the corner. "Mike said he had a few things to do before we could go and that he'd drop you off with me today so we could talk once he was gone, but he didn't go until just before Captain got here, so there was no time. I was going to let you have her so you would see I forgive you. We would be friends again. Victoria, I met with Captain yesterday, asked him to come today for you, so you could say goodbye."

My jaw flexes. "Keys."

She points to the fireplace, and I dash across the room.

"He set us up," I tell her, grabbing the keys. "He's going after Zoey."

"Why set me up? We wanted the same thing. Why go after her?"

My glare swings her way. "Because he knows I love her and that I would never leave her," I all but growl, rushing for the exit. "And he knows you're a psychotic bitch who manifested some sort of relationship in your head when there never was one, which meant you'd be easy to control and even easier to toss out in the end."

"Victoria!" she shouts as I step out the entryway. "Did you ever care about me?"

I freeze a moment.

She doesn't deserve my answer, not after all the shit she's pulled, yet still I find myself looking into her eyes for what I hope will be the last time.

"No." I slam the door shut, jump into her car, and head home.

CAPTAIN

As the mansion comes into view, I spot my brothers jumping from one of their SUVs, but as I slam on my brakes, dirt flies around, blocking my view.

I jump out, running straight ahead.

Maddoc's feet hit the porch as Royce's meet the side of the house and our dad's voice shouts out, "Boys!"

For a split second that plays out in slow fucking motion, as if time has stopped, Maddoc's gaze meets mine, and the panic and fear are mirrored in his. I swear to fucking God, our hearts hit the dirt as unimaginable images flash before us.

We make it around the house to find him pushing to his feet, dirt and blood covering the lower part of his dress shirt.

"Raven?!" Maddoc shouts.

"Pool house. Zoey too," he calls with a cough. "Mike got away."

Fuck!

We cut right, dashing straight there.

I reach it first, throwing the door open, and we shove inside.

A large iron skillet comes swinging from the right, smashing right into my face, and I stumble into my brothers as her body swings around, a gun in her right hand and pointed directly between my eyes.

Raven's eyes widen, blood dripping from a small cut over her left cheek.

Her body slumps as she realizes it's us, and Maddoc flies by just in time to catch her in his arms. Tears pour from her eyes in an instant, and she drops the gun, wrapping her hands around Maddoc's neck as her eyes snap to mine. "In the closet," she cries.

I snatch a throw blanket off the armchair and wipe the blood from my nose and lip with it as I head down the hall and into the room.

I throw the closet door open. "Zoey..."

She doesn't answer.

"Zoey!" I panic, pushing clothes around. "Zoey, baby girl, where are you?"

Fuck, fuck.

No, no, no...

"Zoey!" I boom, shoving shit around until I get to the back corner.

My chest caves as I push aside the last row of clothing, and I swallow, glaring at the blanket tucked back beneath them.

I grab the heavy cotton and pull.

And my body grows a thousand times heavier, too fucking heavy, my head falling to the side.

There she is, headphones covering her little ears, Raven's phone in hand, a video playing on the screen.

I collapse, hitting my knees against the hardwood beneath them, and her little head snaps up. My baby girl.

She smiles, but it quickly falls from her face and she pushes the headphones off. She reaches out, gently placing her soft hand on my cheek, and my eyes pool with tears. "You got owies, Daddy?"

I choke on my breath, clenching my teeth as tears fall before I can stop them.

I nod. "Yeah, ZoZo."

I grab her under the arms, pulling her into my lap, and fall back against the wall. "Daddy has an owie." I hug her to me, breathing her in as my emotions take over.

I hold her tight, blowing out long, shuddered breaths as I try to settle myself.

In the next second, Royce slams against the door, his eyes bouncing around until they land on her, and his head falls to his chest in relief the same second he's shoved to the side, Victoria now standing in the doorway with a tearstained face.

Her cry is loud, her hand pressing to her mouth to hide it as she turns away.

Royce grabs her, pulling her into his chest, his arms wrapping around her, and her body shakes with silent sobs. He whispers something to her and slowly turns her toward me.

Eyes full of guilt find mine, unsure, afraid, and all I want to do is wash it away.

I hold a hand out, and she rushes right for it, slipping her fingers into mine as she lowers herself to her knees beside me, beside us.

Zoey looks to her with a sad smile on her face as she tucks her head into my chest. She reaches out, and Victoria gives her her free hand.

"Did you see Daddy owie, Rora?"

Victoria inhales a choppy breath, nodding as she licks her lips. "I did, ZoZo, but he'll be okay."

"Can you make him better?" she asks her.

Victoria's eyes slide to mine; she's waiting, hoping.

I squeeze her hand, and she nods.

"Yeah, Mama." Her eyes move to Zoey again. "I think I can," she whispers.

As Zoey slides her headphones back on, none the wiser about what's happened here, Victoria drops her forehead to mine.

"I'm so sorry—"

"Victoria!"

She freezes.

I freeze.

Our eyes lock.

Mike.

"Fuck." Royce dashes from the room.

Before I can grab her, Victoria yanks herself away.

I quickly set Zoey aside and jump toward Victoria, but she slams the door, something heavy hitting it from the other side.

I shake the doorknob, banging my shoulder into the door as fear grips my throat. "Victoria! Open the fucking door! Now!"

"Stop," she rushes in a whisper. "Don't scare her."

My head swivels around to find a little frown marring Zoey's forehead as she looks right at me, ears still covered.

I turn back, my palms and face pressed against the white wood.

"Vee, baby, Beauty." My breathing speeds up. "Open the door."

I wait, but silence is all that follows.

Fuck!

VICTORIA

I walk through the living room, glancing at the other three as they argue about how to approach.

Their eyes snap to mine and slowly narrow.

"VicVee..." Royce drags out, turning his body toward me. His eyes take in the direction I'm headed and then quickly snap up to my face.

I dart forward as he hops over the couch, but he only manages to grab my shirt as I swipe the gun from the floor, tearing away from him, the sound of my top shredding at my back.

"Victoria!" he shouts, rushing behind me, but I don't stop.

I walk right out the front door.

And there he stands.

Dark hair matted and twisted, blood dripping from his mouth and arms, soil across the front of his shirt with a gun in his hand. "There she is," Mike coughs, staggering. "There's my girl."

My eyes fall to Rolland, flat on his back beside him, bleeding from who the hell knows where.

"Oh, him?" Mike glares, turning toward him. "Yeah, he got me, but he made a mistake and left me breathing." In one swift move, he pulls his leg back and skips forward, kicking Rolland in the gut.

Rolland groans, rolling on his side.

"Let's go," he says to me, jerking his head as if to tell me to hurry.

Only then do his eyes go to my hand, following as I lift the gun and point it right at him, but the motherfucker smiles, proof someone got him good, painting his teeth red too.

"Come on, Garden Girl." He chuckles, walking toward me. "You could never shoot me."

"I have before."

"By mistake." He lowers his gun to his side. "I taught you how to shoot, remember?"

I put my finger on the trigger. "So you know I won't miss."

"You'd never hurt someone you love."

"I stabbed your father in the gut with a kitchen knife."

"After he used it on you."

My lips smash together. "Don't make me do this, Mike."

His smile grows, and he takes another step, closer to me, closer to Captain.

Closer to Zoey.

I pull the trigger, shooting him in the thigh.

"Fuck!" he shouts, dropping to one knee, his hands hitting the grass.

He groans, hunching over as he squeezes at the wound. "Damn it, Vee," he grates.

Suddenly, I'm grabbed at the elbow and thrown back, the gun falling from my hand and dropping into the flower bed as Captain, Maddoc, and Royce rush forward.

In one solid line, they move for him, but Mike is quick, and just before he's within their reach, the gun is back in his hands and he's on his feet, the barrel pointed right at Captain's head.

They freeze where they stand, and Mike quickly shuffles backward.

"Cap…" Royce stresses.

Tension lines their backs, wrapping around their shoulders, and their hands ball into fists.

Mike chuckles, spitting blood as he smirks at Captain.

"You guys." He chuckles. "You're all pathetic, can't protect your women for shit."

Maddoc takes a step forward, and Mike swings the gun to him.

"I almost got yours, didn't I, Madman?" he mocks, but his gaze narrows slightly as Maddoc keeps moving forward. "The little cut on her cheek." He smiles. "Yeah, she got me right here, though." He pats at the blood patch on his shirt growing larger near his abdomen. "What kind of pregnant chick keeps a knife tucked in her jeans?" he mocks with a coughed laugh.

"You're not leaving here alive," Maddoc grounds out.

"I'm leaving with Victoria or you're burying your brother alongside me."

The gun swings back to Captain.

I jerk forward, only to have Raven dart a hand out the door and grab me by my wrist and fling me back.

She's shaking with anger, but dread is clear in her eyes. "They're out there for you."

"And the people who need them most are inside this fucking house," I force past clenched teeth, yanking free of her hold as I quickly shift my gaze back to the scene, returning them to her just as fast.

Her brows cave and she wraps her arms around her middle. "Don't you get it? You're one of them, one of us. They will die for you."

"Don't you get it?" I whisper, tears clouding my eyes. "I can't let them."

She opens her mouth and then closes it, shaking her head frantically. She growls. "Goddamn you, why are you so stubborn?"

"Because I'm your sister." I quickly squeeze her hand, turning away.

I walk out onto the lawn as quietly as I can, but the second Mike spots me behind them, all heads fly my way.

Mike uses that to his advantage, darting forward to knock Captain in the head with the gun, like he did to me, and he falls to his knees.

His brothers fly around, ready to attack, but I shout, "Wait," and they all freeze.

"Victoria, don't," Captain growls, pushing to his feet.

I walk out in a wide arc so they can't reach out and grab me, and Mike slides his feet my way, forcing them to curve the other way.

Mike's breathing begins to settle as I grow closer.

"It's okay, Cap," I tell him softly, not taking my eyes from Mike's. "He won't hurt me."

Mike's lips twitch, an almost unnoticeable nod leaving him.

"I won't let him leave, and never with you," Captain says.

My blood pumps fiercely, and I nod and then slide between them all, right in front of Mike, but he keeps his eyes on them, gun raised and pointed high.

His free arm comes down around my waist, and he yanks me to him.

"Don't fucking move!" he shouts, and I know Captain has stepped closer.

"Mike," I whisper, sliding my hands up to his face. "Mike, look at me."

His eyes tighten, and he jerks slightly, so I press tighter, move in closer.

A heavy line forms between his brows, and he licks his lips.

"Mike…baby, look at me…" I glide my thumbs back and forth in slow sweeps. "Please, look at me," I whisper.

His jaw flexes and then his eyes briefly cut to mine.

I smile, gliding my hand down. "Hi."

His nostrils flare, his eyes bouncing between mine and over my shoulder in rapid, constant motion.

"Let's go, let's leave this place," I tell him. "You were right. There's nothing for me here. I saw what you wanted. I saw him with Mallory. He doesn't want me, and I don't need him."

"But the girl, she's still in there."

"We don't need her," I rush out. "We can…we can have our own."

He swallows, and his head tips to the side with a slight nod. He lowers his mouth to my ear. "You will love me," he murmurs, kissing my hair, and I squeeze my eyes shut. "I swear you will."

I nod, dropping my hands to his chest, my heart seizing when a click rings in my ear. "But only if you can't love him."

I gasp, shoving at him. "Mike, no!"

But it's too late. The gun has already gone off.

I whip around, screaming as Captain's body falls to the ground, Connor Perkins on top of him.

Everything happens quickly from there. Royce tackles Mike to the ground as Maddoc picks up the gun, points it right at Mike's head, and without so much as a blink, he pulls the fucking trigger.

I dart toward Perkins and Captain, screaming when I see blood running down Captain's head.

I grab Perkins, and he groans. "I'm sorry," I cry as I roll him off, scrambling closer to Captain.

Royce falls right beside me as my hands move to my mouth.

"No, no, no..." He panics. "Brother, no!"

"Oh my God," I croak, my eyes falling to his soiled shirt, blood dripping down his side.

Raven runs out the door as Maddoc spins and drops with us.

"Cap." Maddoc smacks his face lightly. "Captain!"

I cry, pushing up his shirt to apply pressure to the wound, but freeze, my palms searching along his stomach, smearing the blood in search of the bullet hole, but I don't find one.

I quickly move to his head, shaking as I inspect the gash there.

Not a gunshot wound.

"He hit his head," I whisper. "He hit his head," I say louder.

They look at his stomach and then his head.

Maddoc quickly feels for a pulse, nodding with a glare. "He's knocked out."

"Thank fuck," Royce croaks.

"Guys," Raven whispers.

All eyes slice to her, and slowly she lowers to her knees beside Perkins, who holds a hand over his gut, blood pouring from him, the color having drained from his face.

Oh my God.

Maddoc and Royce glance at each other, whipping around when footsteps sound behind them.

Rolland drags himself closer, falling beside Raven and Perkins.

He looks to his sons and then slides behind the man.

Raven helps him push his upper body from the grass, and Perkins hisses, his head falling back on Rolland's chest right as he settles himself there.

Dad grips Perkins's hands. "I've got ya, old friend," he says.

Perkins's face tightens, and he blows a hard breath from his nose. "He's..." He tenses in pain. "He's okay?" he asks, his eyes on mine.

I look to Captain, whose eyes begin to flutter behind closed lids.

I nod and Perkins nods back. "Good." He swallows, his blinks slowing. "It, uh…" He stretches his leg out. "It's cold out here, huh?"

I look at Maddoc when he drops beside him. He nods lightly, hanging his head as he props his arms on his knees. "Yeah, man. It's cold."

It's not cold.

Royce lowers next, sitting at my side, but nobody says a word.

Perkins gives a small laugh, but it turns into a wheeze and then a small cry, and I force my eyes to the grass.

"It might…" Our stares fly to Perkins. He tries to swallow, tears falling from his eyes, beads of sweat rolling down his forehead. "It might mean…mean nothing to you but I…I'm proud—" His voice cracks. "So proud of who you are."

We follow his line of sight straight to Captain.

Captain, whose eyes are open and cloudy but locked directly with Connor Perkins's, the man who just gave his life to save his, a boy who vowed to never claim the man as his father.

They hold each other's gazes, father and son, as Perkins takes his last and final breath.

He dies in Rolland's arms.

CHAPTER 37
CAPTAIN

Raven pulls the sweater from over her shoulders and drapes it over Perkins's body as my dad lays him on the ground.

My attention moves to the pool house entryway, and Royce pops up, jogging inside to check on Zoey.

My head falls back into Victoria's lap, and she offers a broken smile.

"I'm so sorry," she whispers.

I shake my head, and her forehead comes down to meet mine. "This isn't on you, baby."

Her eyes fall.

"Maddoc," I call, lifting my hand.

She pulls back, pushing to her feet as Maddoc yanks me to mine, holding me there a moment until I'm steady.

"You good, man?" He eyes me. "He knocked your ass out with the gun and then you hit your head on a rock when you went down."

My eyes slide to Perkins's lifeless legs beneath the thin cotton covering him, and I swallow, looking away. "Yeah."

I let go of him, walking over to Mike's body, my eyes zoning in on the gunshot right between his eyes. I look at Maddoc, and he nods.

He pulled the trigger.

Tires squeal around the front of the house, and Maddoc's face falls, but Royce rushes out, shouting, "It's Maybell!" He jogs over to us, his eyes moving between the bodies. "She's coming to play with Zoey, keep her busy inside while we…clean up."

Dad pulls his phone out. "I'll call James. He has men for this."

"No," Victoria says, and our eyes swing to her. "James isn't in charge anymore." She looks at Royce. "The boys have someone to call."

Royce frowns, but then a nod follows, and his cell is in his hands. "Hey, Siri, call Mac," he says as he walks away.

It takes less than twenty minutes for Mac to roll up, Andre and a couple others just behind him.

They wait at the edge of the grass as Mac walks over, but he doesn't look to us. He walks right up to Mike's dead body and slips an all-black ski mask over his head.

Mac stands and moves to Perkins to do the same, but I find myself sliding in front of him, and his eyes fly to mine.

"I, uh." I swallow. "Him, we'll bury."

Mac gives a curt nod. "I'll make sure he gets where he needs."

I nod and slowly move away, watching as he pulls Raven's sweater from his face and slips the mask over.

Only when he stands, having hidden the proof of who these men are, do the others come forward. They look nowhere but at the bodies, lift them, and carry them away without a word.

Victoria sighs, her hands moving to her head as she lets out a heavy breath.

"What the hell?" comes from Raven, and we turn to find her staring at Victoria. "What is that?"

Victoria frowns and then her eyes lower, and ours follow.

My muscles freeze, and we look at each other.

A deep crimson rushes up her neck and her hands lower, prepared to cover what we've now already seen, but then they drop.

Her shoulders square, and with a deep breath, Victoria grabs her shredded shirt in her hands and pulls it over her head.

"Holy shit," Royce whispers.

Scar after scar lines her abdomen in no particular pattern and of no common size, cut after cut, but none so deep the skin is bubbled, though each is lifted enough to touch.

But that's not what Raven saw or where our eyes are frozen.

Just beneath her bra line, in the most elegant of cursive, a line is engraved into her skin, thick, solid letters, each word as clear as the next.

It starts on the far right, and like a wave, it rises and falls perfectly with her curves, stopping at her breastbone.

Family runs deeper than blood.

My eyes move to hers, my feet subconsciously pulling me closer.

Her smile is small and tight, unsure.

She licks her lips. "When I was little, I had no knowledge of who I was or why I was alive. The maid who cleaned my room and my teacher called me Girl; Mike called me Garden Girl." She laughs, but it's sad.

"He was the boy, the friend you had there who talked to you through the wall, wasn't he?"

She nods. "I didn't know until later, but Mero had planted Mike at the Graven estate, hoping he'd find me, and he did, came to live with us a couple years later, once Mero was sure he had all my trust," she says. "Even when he did, he still called me what he knew me as."

"Perkins," I say. "He said before Mero you had no identity..."

She licks her lips. "The day he came for me, on the drive back to his house, Mero said to me, 'Everyone has a place in the world, and you've just found yours.'" Her eyes gloss over, and she lifts them to lock with mine. "He told me his name, and then he gave me mine."

"He was Brayshaw when he left..." Maddoc draws out, looking from her tattoo to me.

"In Mero's mind, that's all he ever was." Her eyes bounce between mine. "Even when he pawned off his own son to Graven for them to raise. Even later when he tied himself to them even more by taking me."

Everyone has a place in the world, and you've just found yours…

"Brayshaw," I whisper. "He gave you his name, our name."

She nods. "He said I had to earn it for it to be true, so I did, and then I came here and realized I was everything opposite of what it meant to belong in a place like this. My purpose changed overnight, and nothing had ever felt more…right."

Suddenly I'm in front of her, my knuckle on her chin, but I don't have to lift; she does it for me, staring me straight in the eyes.

"I knew you were meant for me," I rasp, my fingertips skimming across the tattoo.

"It shouldn't have been so hard to get here," she whispers, her palms flattening on my chest.

"Yeah." I nod. "It should have. We don't love without a little bloodshed."

Her muscles tighten, and I push closer. "Guess you don't want me to be your Brayshaw anymore?"

She smiles, shaking her head no.

"Good." I sink my hands into her hair, my eyes falling to those lips I've fucking missed. "I don't want to be your Brayshaw. I want to be your man."

She pushes onto her toes, aligning her mouth with mine. "But, Captain…we can't always have what we want," she whispers my words. "Now can we?"

"We're Brayshaw, baby. We want, we get."

No exceptions.

I fill the cup to the brim, slowly pouring it over Zoey's head, and she laughs.

"Waterfall!" She smiles, reaching across to grab the floating baby doll from the water, and stands.

"You ready to get out, princess?"

She nods, so I set the cup on the counter, grabbing her towel and wrapping it around her as I lift her from the bathtub.

I kiss her hair as I carry her into her room and get her dressed in her pajamas.

"Rora!" she shouts.

I look toward the door, and there Victoria stands. She leans against the doorframe, her eyes on us.

Zoey sits at her little vanity, handing me her brush.

Victoria chuckles, but her breath seems to lodge in her throat when I hold the light-blue brush in the air. Slowly, Victoria walks into the room, taking it from my hands as she steps up behind Zoey, and I step behind her.

My hand covers hers, one on the brush, the other on the tiny chair, and my head falls into the crook of her neck.

She guides, and together we brush my daughter's hair.

"Rora, you know what?" Zoey asks her.

"What, ZoZo?" she responds, resting her cheek against me.

"Ms. Maybell said we can make cookies tomorrow, with M&M's. Want me to make one for you?"

"Can I have extra M&M's?"

She laughs, picking up the plastic brush in front of her and brushing the giant Barbie head on her vanity. "Okay, Rora."

I smile, sliding my head back slightly so my mouth can graze along Victoria's collarbone, and she inhales deeply.

I drag my lips to her ear. "At some point, we'll sit her down and tell her…that you don't like sweets."

An airy chuckle leaves her, and she pulls back, but only far enough to where our eyes can meet. "Not a chance."

I lift my left hand, pushing her hair from her shoulder, and her eyes close.

"You, uh, want me to take her for the night?"

We look to the hallway where Royce stands, freshly showered, brow raised.

I chuckle, bending down to kiss Zoey. "Nah, man," I say to my brother, looking to Victoria. "I need my girls tonight."

I look his way, and he nods, understanding in his eyes, but then a grin quickly spreads. "Hey, Zoey Bear."

"Hey, Uncle Bro!"

He chuckles. "Let's go make some popcorn and hot chocolate, taking as absolutely long as humanly possible to do so, and then we can meet Daddy back upstairs?"

Victoria laughs, shaking her head, and Zoey jumps up.

"Can we put cheese on it?" she asks him, running off and snagging a stuffed animal on the way.

I glance at Royce, who puts a hand over his heart as if he's wounded, but he drops and swoops her in his arms. "Cheese. Like Uncle D?"

Zoey nods. "Yep. Lots and lots of cheese."

They disappear.

Victoria sets the brush down, and I push to my feet, staring at her.

I grab her by the hand, walking backward from Zoey's room, into the hall, toward hers.

She doesn't question me, says not a word as she blindly follows where I lead.

Once inside her bathroom, I finally let her go, but only so I can get the water on to let it heat.

I step around her, closing and locking the door, and I stay there when her hands land on my back, gliding up and around my shoulders, massaging the muscles there.

My head falls to the door, my breathing deep and full as I focus on her touch, memorizing the span of her fingers and the sound of her breath.

She shifts closer, her lips pressing against my shirt, and I quickly spin to face her.

Her eyes heat at the sight of mine, and slowly she steps back, unbuttoning her jeans, so I follow, both our bottoms hitting the floor together.

She tugs her top from her skin as I do mine, but I dart forward as she attempts to unclip her bra and do it for her.

I haven't seen her like this, bared for me, so with slow movements, I graze her shoulders, my dick twitching against her as she moans from nothing but the feel of my knuckle on her shoulders.

I drop my lips, running them along her skin, kissing as the last piece of clothing hiding her from me hits the floor at our feet.

Her nipples are hard, and she shifts the tiniest bit, sliding them along me, and I groan against her.

She turns her head toward me as I do, and when I lift, her lips are right there, mere inches from mine.

My stomach twists in anxiousness, but I force my eyes closed, blindly reaching for her hand and tugging us into the shower, directly under the spray.

I spin her, blocking her body from my view, but it doesn't work.

Her ass stares right at me, and then my cock is pressing against it, my hands coming around to cup her pussy and pulling her into me even more.

Victoria moans, her head falling to my shoulder, harsh breaths turning to a warm, smoky mist above us with the help of the heated shower.

Her feet shift, legs opening wide, and I don't wait, I push a finger inside, and then another, and she gasps but quickly swallows it down.

I growl, nipping at her neck, and she shakes.

"Sound. Every fucking sound, every word, every need…" I flick my tongue along her skin. "I want. Hold nothing back. Ever. Never. I want to hear what I can do to you. Always."

A heavy, breathy moan follows, and my dick fights for entrance.

I glide along her ass cheeks as she makes circles on my hand, and she pushes back against me.

"I need to feel you," she begs. "Not your hands, not your mouth." Her palms slide down her own body, and she pulls at her nipples, gasping and tightening around me as she does, but her hands quickly come around, slip between her ass and me. She grips me, squeezing. "This. I want this."

"I'm gonna give it to you, baby, so fucking soon, but let me take care of you, and then wash you, and then I will fuck you, properly, and in your own bed."

"Mm," she hums, stroking me. "As long as I get to come on your cock, Cap, I'm good with that."

Fuck.

I push into her palm, locking her hands there as I reach forward and pinch at her clit, vibrating my hand as I barely move in and out of her, focusing on the little nub instead.

"Finish me. Get me to the bed." She shakes, her breasts pushing into the air, tempting and teasing me to face them full-on. To grab and squeeze and play with what's mine and mine alone.

I moan.

And hers follows, her pussy pulsing around my fingers as she trembles in my arms, choked whimpers flying from her mouth to my groin, and I pump into her hand, the veins in my dick throbbing in her palm.

I pull back from her heat and her hand, and she falls against me.

As her breathing slows, I gently wash her hair, carefully avoiding the small wound on her left temple, and as my hands go down, I close my eyes, grabbing both her breasts in my palms and gently massaging the soap along them. Her nipples harden once again into sharp little peaks.

I can't help myself; I grip them between my fingers and squeeze.

She moans. "More."

So I tug and twist, and when her legs begin rubbing together, I release them, ready to move farther down, but freeze.

I don't know why, but a hint of fright stings my fingertips as I ready myself to feel along her belly, her scars. Scars I'm not sure she cares to hide but hides to protect the words scrolled along her skin, just under my right palm.

"Captain," she whispers, her hands coming up to cover mine. "Every piece of me is yours."

My heart hammers in my chest as she glides our hands slowly along her stomach.

Graze after graze scrapes along my palm, and with every one, a promise locks in my head.

For every sting she felt, I'll feel.

Every cut she took, I'll take.

Every pain she suffered, I'll settle.

She holds our hands just above her abdomen, letting hers fall as I slide slower, washing her between the legs.

I bend, nipping at her ass cheeks as I massage along her thighs and calves.

I stand, moving from the water completely so she can rinse easier as I quickly wash my body.

My eyes fall to the drain as the blood that was matted deeper into my hair, the blood that didn't come off with the quick rinse I took before I could go back to Zoey, washes away.

Victoria sees it too and turns.

She looks up at me, stepping closer with a soft smile on her lips. She pushes onto her toes, wrapping her arms around my neck.

She hugs me to her body as my arms do the same, and for the first fucking time tonight, maybe in days or weeks even, the nails hammering me down are removed, a weight lifted.

What a couple fucking months of trials.

I thought I was tested to the brink when I learned I had a daughter I couldn't find, let alone see, and again when I did locate her and was forced to leave her where she was until I could get her home, until it was safe enough for her to come home.

I was so fucking wrong.

That was nothing but the lead-up, the training for the finals.

In the back of my mind, I knew I'd have to face Mallory in some way at some point, but I buried it beneath rage and disgust, when really she deserves none of that.

Not my hate, not my anger.

Not a fucking thing.

She made a decision, one I'll never understand, but it was hers to make, and I get that now.

Some people aren't meant to be a parent—or maybe they are, but they're ready in their own time, should that ever come.

Deep down, though, an active parent or not, there's love there. I didn't believe it before, but I can't deny it now.

Conner Perkins, a man I would have been happy to never have seen again, the man who gave my mother a son when her husband could not. Cancer took his ability, and though it happened all wrong, Perkins gave my parents me.

He didn't claim me, not even when he died, and I have to admit it was the most selfless thing a man could do. I had a family, a purpose and place in life, and he allowed me to keep it when the world was ugly.

But the man showed up today, concerned for a girl he had come to know, ready to help. I thought he turned his back and ran when I reached out for help for the first time in my life, but he showed up, giving his for mine.

I'm standing here because of him.

And Zoey came into this world because her mother allowed it.

They loved what they let go, if even only a little.

Will my daughter grow up and wonder why her mother left her?

I imagine the answer is yes, but I'll do all I can to make sure she never hurts because of it. I'll love her with all I have, and I have no doubt the girl against me will too.

I've watched them together, and I tried to refuse what I witnessed, but today, everything came into perspective.

Zoey has no idea what a mother is, but everything my brothers and I got from Ms. Maybell, time and attention, love and comfort, she's gotten since before she was born and from the most unsuspecting person.

The girl from the group home.

The feisty, rebel blond I might have missed had she not put herself in front of me, but the second she did, something in me stirred.

Zoey will love her like a daughter loves a mother, confide in her when she can't me, fight with her when she doesn't get her way, and she won't always.

Together, we'll protect her and love her and show her how to be strong and independent and watch as she grows into who she's meant to be, whatever she wants to be.

The water begins to chill, so I reach out and shut it off, and Victoria pulls back, looking up at me.

My hand sinks into her hair, dripping wet and slick to her back, her brown eyes so fucking soft and open.

I tilt her head, and her lips part, gaze bouncing between my eyes.

My thumb runs along the plump edge of her mouth, and her eyes close on a slow blink.

When they open, her pupils are dark and dilated.

"These lips," I rasp, dipping down to drag mine across them. I groan. "I've dreamed of them, imagined them sliding along mine, opening for me, for my cock and my tongue."

Her hand comes up to grip my wrist, eyes wild.

"They're mine."

"So take them."

My dick twitches at her words.

My free hand comes up, gripping her jaw as my other pulls her closer, my feet shifting in as she tips her head back more, begging. Ready.

Mine.

My pulse is out of control, my heart pounding against my skin, against hers.

I close my eyes, and my fucking toes curl into the puddled water at our feet, anticipation racing up my spine in an exhilarated zing.

I inhale as she does, and my lips press into hers.

She sighs, her lungs seeming to expand, taking in more and more air as I close my mouth around hers, my palms squeezing tighter, and then her back hits the wall, and my tongue dives into her mouth, hers fights back, pushing and twisting and rolling with mine.

I groan, and she jumps up, wrapping her legs around mine, letting her ass slide down until she's aligned with where she wants me.

I grind against her, memorizing her mouth, her sounds and motions.

I reach around, squeezing her ass, and she gasps, her head falling back.

And that's it.

I fly from the shower to the bed.

With her still latched tight around me, I push the comforter down, burying us beneath the sweet satin, knowing I'm about to enter an even sweeter one.

Her legs stay locked around me as her head pulls away, her hands gliding into the hair at the base of my neck.

She lifts, kissing me with slow full strokes, as she shifts her hips, aligning me at her entrance.

Her eyes pop open, locking with mine, and I push inside.

My mouth opens, my forehead creasing as I sink into the softest fucking heat, my body shaking as hers opens, welcoming me fucking home.

"Goddamn, baby," I moan, pushing in farther, and her head falls back.

I take advantage, my mouth trailing kisses down her throat, and with each one, her back arches more, driving me deeper, my kisses lower until I can pull her nipple into my mouth.

"Oh, fuck," she croaks, rolling her hips as she grips and squeezes her free breast the same way.

I bite, and she twitches; I flick my tongue, and she pulls the other tight between her fingertips.

My baby likes her nipples played with.

I pull out slowly, sliding back in, and she moans, her legs coming up to her sides. I do it again and again, and she starts to pant.

"Oh my God…Captain, mmm," she whispers, her hands gliding across my back and pulling my body down on hers.

She begs for my weight, so I give it to her, her moans now right in my ear, lighting me up.

"Mm," she whimpers. "Harder. More."

I swiftly squeeze my hand behind her and yank her up more so she's halfway up the headboard and scoot with her.

My hand comes down, using her ass for leverage, my other hand on the wall behind our heads, and her legs fall open.

I shove inside to the brink and she gasps, a slow smile forming along her face as she pushes back.

I fuck her into the mattress, both our moans filling the air around us.

Fire spreads through my groin, my muscles tightening, and I move faster and faster, until she's attempting to force me still as it becomes too fucking much, too damn good, but I keep going and her features pull tight, her orgasm right there, ready to set her free.

I thrust in farther, grinding, and she falls apart, her moan loud and airy in my ear.

I groan, twitching as I fill her, my forehead falling to hers. "Fuck, mmm." I push in more and she gasps.

Slowly, her muscles ease, and I go to climb off her, but she quickly wraps her arms around me, holding me there, perfectly fitted against her, the final piece to my puzzle.

Her hands draw small circles along my back, her breathing going back to normal.

"Hey, Cap?" she whispers.

"Beauty?" I kiss her neck, tasting the sweat I earned.

"I love you."

My tongue freezes on her, my muscles right there with them, but her touch never slows, her fingers continue to draw on my skin.

I pull back, meeting her eyes.

So sure, so honest and open and infinite.

My baby.

My Beauty.

I smash my lips into hers, and she slides her hands into my hair, smiling against my lips.

"I think there's a little girl waiting for you out there," she says when it takes me two seconds to get lost in her all over again.

"No, baby," I whisper, kissing her lips quickly and pulling away, tugging her up onto her feet with me. I push her hair from her face. "She's waiting for us."

She inhales deeply, nodding.

"But first, pajamas."

She laughs, moving to her drawers while I grab a towel to wrap around my waist and move for my room.

As I reach for the handle, I glance back at her, and her eyes are already on mine.

"In case you weren't sure or had any doubt, don't," I tell her, opening the door. "I love you with all that I am, and I'll never stop."

Tears fill her eyes, and she nods. "See you in five, Cap."

"In two, Beauty."

She laughs, turning away as I head to my room to get dressed.

The second I step back in the hall, Zoey and Royce step off the stairs.

She runs past, spotting Victoria right as she comes out of her room while Royce pauses beside me.

He holds up the popcorn and thermos full of what I'm sure is hot chocolate, a pack of foam cups hanging from his mouth.

I laugh, yanking it from his teeth, and he grins.

"What do you say, brother?" He nods his chin.

My smile is soft, and I nod, hitting his back, and he grins, walking ahead of me, following the girls into the media room.

Victoria grabs the remotes while Royce sets the items on the table and begins pouring small cups.

I drop onto the couch, and Zoey climbs up beside me, Royce lowering beside her while Victoria moves over to my free side.

The moment she gets the TV on, Maddoc and Raven walk in, hand in hand.

I look to Maddoc, who shrugs, and the two walk around, sitting beside Victoria.

Raven bumps her in the shoulder, and Victoria laughs, glancing Raven's way.

Royce smiles around the room and leans forward, pouring a couple more cups.

"Got one more?"

All eyes snap to the doorway when our dad speaks.

He holds up Zoey's blanket, and she gasps, her hands lifting and waiting for him to toss it over.

Royce nods, revealing one last cup in the bag.

He pats the seat open on his other side. "Come on, Dad."

Our dad sits down, and the six of us look at Zoey.

"What are we watching, ZoZo?"

Everyone laughs as she shouts, "*Trolls*!"

The answer was expected, and any other night we might try to convince her to pick something different, but not tonight. Tonight, we take whatever we're given, all taking comfort in what each of us clearly needs right now—each other.

Our family.

Brayshaw.

I run my hand along Zoey's head, and she swings her smile to me, climbing onto her knees to grip my face.

She rubs her little nose on mine, smiling when I do the same back.

“Baby kisses, Daddy.”

And butterfly hugs, baby girl.

With ease in my mind and a full heart, I smile at the TV screen.

This.

This is what life is about.

CHAPTER 38
CAPTAIN

"Daddy, who's that?" Zoey asks as I place a framed photo on her little vanity.

I stare at the man's face, at the smile I never got to see in real life but that shines bright, youthful, in the photo my dad gave me. "That's your other grandpa. His name was Connor."

"Can he come to the zoo with me and Papa too?"

I swallow. "No, ZoZo, he can't."

When her little shoulders fall, I bend down, kneeling in front of her with a small smile, and pull her into me.

Her little hand comes up, and she sticks it in the small pocket on my T-shirt, her eyes slowly lifting to mine again.

"He might not be able to go places with you, Zo, but when you go to sleep at night, before you close your eyes, you can tell him all about it." I offer her all I can of the man who gave his life for mine. "If you want."

"Okay!"

"Okay," I whisper. "Grab your backpack. You're gonna go play with Mac and Chloe for a little bit, remember?"

"Yep." She grabs her bag and runs ahead of me, not stopping until she meets Royce outside, who has his back door open and ready for her to climb inside.

The others walk out then too, Maddoc and Raven taking their own car as well, our dad and Maybell riding with them.

"Meet you out there?" he asks.

"Right behind you."

I watch them drive off, pulling my phone out as soon as they're gone and forwarding the email that just came through to Victoria's phone.

She steps on the porch right as her phone pings.

She opens it, looking at the screen with a small frown on her face as she reads the opening.

Captain,

As asked, here are the final recordings from Maria Vega's voicemail. I find it an odd request, a ten out of ten from you.

My best, James

Victoria's eyes fly to mine, and she shakes her head in confusion. "I don't understand."

With a small smile, I wrap my arms around her, pulling her against me.

"The day I found out she died, I was an asshole to you, and yes, a lot of that was because I was angry something so huge in your life happened and you didn't think to share it with me, but I was also angry that you were so sure I didn't care."

Her eyes move between mine.

"For the last two years, I went to bed listening to a voicemail left by Maria. Every single night, she'd call me and tell me about Zoey's day. What she did, the things she said or discovered. Every detail she could remember, and it wasn't given like a list or a chore," I tell her. "Maria would laugh, and sometimes I thought she might have been crying when she'd share little things, and then Zoey came home, and the voicemails stopped."

"You started calling her," she whispers.

I swallow. "Every night."

Her eyes fill with moisture, and she smiles. "You have a big heart, Cap, and despite all the bad shit you felt she was a part of, you knew what it was like to have to go to sleep every night without Zoey."

I nod.

It couldn't have been easy. Maria had already lost two children, if I count myself, in her life, and she'd just lost a third. She helped take care of my daughter from infant to toddler too. She loved her, and I know Zoey loved her back.

"She listened to them, all but those last ten," I tell her, reaching for her arm and pulling her close. "I want you to be the one to listen to those."

She swallows. "Why?"

"So you know what I was feeling when I acted like I felt nothing."

"You told her about us?" Her voice breaks.

"I did, Beauty. I was lost and angry, but I have no doubt she died knowing you'd be safe with me."

She pushes against my chest, bringing her lips to mine for a slow, soft kiss. "Thank you."

"Thank you," I tell her. "I was a piece of shit. I hurt you, and I'll never forgive myself for that. Ever."

"I know. You've told me a million times, Cap," she whispers. "But you should forgive yourself."

"I won't, but thank you for wishing I would, for forgiving me. For giving me more than I knew I needed and for going with me to this thing today."

The softness she reserves only for me covers her eyes as she leans in. "Always."

The corner of my mouth lifts, and I slide my lips along hers. "Remember you said that."

She laughs, allowing me to tug her along, and the two of us climb into my vehicle. We make the twenty-minute ride to the Brayshaw memorial park.

I'd never been to an actual funeral before today, and I'd be happy never to again. I don't like when people cry, and there were tears all over this afternoon, most from people twice my age, people who knew Connor Perkins a hell of a lot better than I ever did.

It's been exactly two weeks since the man gave his life for me—his son. The son the world never knew he had.

I think we gave him a goodbye my mother and Connor would be proud of. I think him getting peace after death would mean a lot to them.

He had a handcrafted casket with his last name engraved along the top, and as a family we decided to give him a place in the Brayshaw cemetery.

If I had to guess, I'd say half the town showed up to pay respects to the man I had no clue so many were connected to.

The last thing I expected today was for sadness to creep inside me, but it's there, nonetheless.

I didn't want to know the man as a dad, but it's funny the thoughts that run through your mind when the possibility is stolen from you.

The service ended about an hour ago, and we've been sitting at a small circular table just big enough for us for the last hour, picking at the plates of food in front of us ever since.

My head rises when Maddoc and Raven push to their feet.

"We're heading back. Cool if we pick up Zoey on the way?" Maddoc asks.

I nod, sitting back in my seat. "Yeah, man. Thanks."

He clamps a hand on my shoulder, and they start to walk off, but Raven pauses.

"Royce, you comin'?" she asks him.

His eyes never move from his phone. "Nah, but I am leavin'."

He hops up, kissing Victoria's forehead and clasping my hand before he follows them out to the parking lot.

My dad catches my eye and jerks his head, so I look to Victoria.

She smiles. "Meet me in the truck?"

I nod and she runs off, catching up with the others as I make my way to my dad, and the two of us walk along the edge of the pond.

"Mallory got on the plane?" he asks.

I nod. "Mac escorted her across the fucking country, took her passport and IDs when she got there."

"Big of you to set her up like you did."

I shrug. "A condo and a few sets of zeros is nothing for the peace of mind that comes with knowing I won't have to see her again. She wanted nothing to do with this place anyway."

"And if she had?"

"I'd have to find a way to be okay with it, but not for her sake."

He nods, stopping to face me. "I know something else is on your mind. Don't make me ask questions. Talk to me, Son."

I scoff, licking my lips as I glance away. "I was never supposed to be here," I say for the first time. "My father wasn't one of you, like Mike's was. I can't help but think Mike was right to try to take what was mine. I took what should have been his—his place in this family, the place his dad left behind."

"You're wrong. Mero was a man of Brayshaw, as you have men at the warehouses and around this town and under you and your brothers' influence. But your father, the man your mother married, my best friend, he was Brayshaw. He was you as you are to them, as you stand here today. With or without you, Captain, Mike would never have been given your place. He'd have had to earn it as he grew. I have no doubt in my mind he would have failed. He was weak-minded, as my brother was."

"Maybe he wouldn't have been if he'd grown up with us."

"Maybe, Cap, but we have no way to know. What I do know is I've seen more strength and growth in this town, in this family, in the last several months than I saw in a lifetime of serving this place. That's no coincidence. That's Brayshaw at its finest."

I swallow, nodding as I move my eyes to his. "Thank you. For everything you did for us, for taking us in, giving us a home, and for being a father to Royce and me when only Maddoc was yours to care for."

"You were all mine, and I love you equally."

"And I'll love my nieces and nephews as they come, just the same. Like my own. Like you do."

His eyes gloss over, and he glances away. "Go home, Captain. Today is not the day I cry in front of you."

A light laugh leaves me, and I wrap him in a hug.

"Thank you for allowing me to be your father, Son," he whispers as he pulls away, quickly walking toward Maybell on the other side of the park.

I meet Victoria at my truck and head home.

Her eyes slide to mine when I don't get out right away, and I smile, lifting her hand and kissing along her knuckles. "They took Zoey for ice cream," I tell her.

She smirks, leaning over. "That right?"

"That's right. Go up to my room, Beauty. I'm right behind you."

"Aye-aye, Captain," she teases as she hops out.

I wait a couple minutes, leg bouncing all the while, and then head up, taking the stairs two at a time.

Okay, Beauty. Here we go.

Life.

I rewatched the videos Maria left me, for the fifth or sixth time, and then I typed in Zoey's name and learned what I didn't know.

Zoey means *life*.

And full of life, she is.

She smiles with her heart and cries from her soul, loves with all she is and listens with all she has. She's strong and intuitive and perfect.

As is the girl who helped assure she was brought into this world.

This girl, she's stubborn, bratty, and doesn't listen for shit, but I like her that way.

Love every piece of her.

But if she keeps pretending to like candy to appease my little girl, I might throw her ass out.

"What the hell?" she whispers, only to yelp when I sneak behind her, squeezing her hips.

She whips around, laughing, and shoves me in the chest.

"I knew you couldn't handle seeing it open without reading," I tease her.

"Well, you left it open." She pushes me back, falling on top of me.

"I did." I push her hair over her shoulder. "Keep reading, Beauty."

Her eyes narrow, and I reach behind her, dragging it to my chest, my eyes on hers as hers fall to the paper.

Did that get your attention, baby?

I hope so, and I also hope you know how wrong that is.

I know there is still so much to learn about you, and I need you to understand I'm here for it. All of it.

I want all your past and every minute of your future, and not just for now, Beauty.

I want to be the king of your kingdom.

Today.

Tomorrow.

Always.

I want you to wear a ring that says you're mine.

Her lips part, her eyes popping up to mine as she chokes on her own words.

"Turn the page, baby," I whisper.

She does, and taped to the center is a white-gold band with a single amethyst flower in the center.

I push her shirt up, tucking it into her bra so I can trace the tattoo hidden there.

She doesn't run around showing her stomach, but she no longer goes out of her way to hide it either. Her shirts are no longer constantly tucked in or half past her hips, and if she's self-conscious about her scars, you'd never know it.

It was all about hiding the words etched into her skin, the ones she felt she hadn't earned and couldn't explain, not the battle wounds beneath them.

"I'm the anchor." I run my fingertips along the tattoo. "You're the waves, and this is our ocean."

"I suck at swimming," she whispers.

A chuckle leaves me, and she sinks against my chest. "That's what my chain is for. For you to climb when you feel weak, for you to hold when you feel alone, for you. All for you."

I sit up, pushing my hand into her hair, and her eyes move to mine. "You said you felt your life started with a purple flower; it's only right your future starts the same. As mine. As ours," I whisper. "Me and Zo."

Her tears fall with her next blink, and I reach up to catch them.

"It's tradition in this family to marry young, but even if it weren't, I'd ask you for this, for your word. Be my wife, Beauty. It can be later, I don't care, but wear my ring, make me this promise."

Her eyes fall back to the page.

As her fingers lift, tracing along the single question just above the ring, I read the words out loud.

"So what do you say, baby? Will you be my Brayshaw?"

She slips the ring from the paper, placing it in her open palm, and waits. A small smirk curves her lips, eyes following as I wrap my fingers around her wrist and shift closer.

I dip my head down to grasp the custom piece between my teeth and position her ring finger to my lips. Ever so slowly, I glide the proof she'll always be mine into its place, and as I slide my mouth up, my eyes lock with hers.

A deep brown, darker than ever.

A little soft and a lot wild.

Victoria's lips part, and with my grip still strong around her wrist, she gently falls back on the comforter, her thighs rubbing together.

I shift on the bed, smirking down at her. "Oh, my baby wants to play."

She chuckles, a deep husky sound as her hands slide along the comforter, until her fingers meet. "She does." She blinks slowly. "This is our first time alone in this house."

My abdomen tightens, heat spreading through my body, and my cock hardens.

I stand from the bed, slowly kicking off my shoes, my eyes trailing over my girl, ready and waiting for me.

"Yeah?" I rasp, licking my lips while watching her bite into hers. I tug my shirt over my head, letting it fall to the floor.

Her eyes land on my chest, her back curling, courtesy of her own memory of what she knows I can do to her.

She trails my every move as I undo my belt and jeans and kick them away.

I climb onto the bed, caging her in.

Her chest inflates with a deep breath, only for it to leave her on a harsh hiss when I lower my pelvis to hers, my hard-on now pushing against her.

"And how's my baby wanna spend our first hour alone?"

Suddenly her eyes snap to mine, a raw urgency boiling within them. "Tear my clothes off, Captain, and don't be gentle."

I groan and don't fucking dare make her ask me twice.

I sit up, straddling her body, and start with my hands at her hips.

I push the thin material up and over her ribs, scooting back so I can add my tongue to the trail, but in the center of her stomach. When I get to the tattoo beneath her bra line, my cock twitches.

I dip down and bite.

Mine.

She gasps but presses her body firmer against me.

My hands glide to the center of her top, and as I bring my eyes to hers, I shred the fucking thing.

Her tongue slips between her teeth as she smiles, her fingers clawing into the blanket.

I lean forward, sinking my teeth into the threaded material of her bra, and with a tight grip to the left side, I rip through it.

Her breasts fall with a heavy bounce, swollen to their fullest and peaked to perfection.

I can't help myself and flick her rosy, pebbled nipple.

She moans, her hands coming up to clench my sides.

Her pants already have a few holes in the thigh, so I slide my hand inside, massaging her inner thigh until she twitches, and then rip them straight the fuck open, all the way up to the crotch of the jeans.

I lower and her chest rises and falls, faster and faster with each inch closer to her pussy my mouth grows.

Her legs fall open, half covered in jeans, half bare.

Pussy's bare.

I bring my lips to the center of her but don't touch, allowing my heated breaths to drive her mad.

Her legs jerk, and right as they settle, I pull her clit into my mouth and suck.

She moans, her feet lifting from the mattress.

"Oh, yeah," I groan. "My baby wants to fuckin' play..."

I stand, grab her hips, and lift her from the mattress.

She's dazed and almost falls, but I'm right here to catch her.

My fingers wrap around the back of her leg, and I glide my hand up as I rid her of the rest of her bottoms.

Her hands leave me, and I look up to find her rubbing and tugging on her nipples as she watches me, my face even with her pussy, fingers teasing against the hole of her ass.

Her legs open farther, hardening my cock even more.

I press against the sensitive, virgin piece of her.

Something I'll take when she's ready for me.

I push to my feet, leaning my head down toward her, and her chin lifts to close some of the distance. She waits for my lips to meet hers, but seconds before my mouth meets my favorite fucking pillows, I quickly dip into the crook of her neck.

She lets out a little groan, and I hold in my laugh, kissing her along her throat.

But she doesn't allow it.

Her fingers glide into my hair, grabbing a handful, and she tugs until my eyes meet hers.

Dark and demanding, just as they should be.

She shifts, now holding me still with a firm grip on both sides of my face, and her eyes narrow.

Victoria opens her mouth to speak, but I don't give her the chance.

My lips come down on hers in a hard, eager kiss, and she's desperate for it.

She drives her tongue inside my mouth, her left leg coming up to wrap around me, and I grip her behind the knee to hold her there.

Victoria stretches onto her toes, shifts her hips, and drops right down on my cock.

I growl, my hand flying to grip her ass, and she cries out, her head falling back, breasts pushing up against me.

She grinds her hips, and my toes curl.

"Fuck," I rasp, swooping down to grab her other leg, and swiftly spin us, setting her ass on the edge of the windowsill.

Her legs leave me, widening, sticking straight the fuck out behind us as she wraps her hands along the edge of the wood, pushing against me thrust for thrust.

I push in more, driving my cock into her, and she quivers around me.

"So fucking good, Beauty." I lean forward, pulling her nipple into my mouth, and she pants.

"Yes, mm." She holds my head still. "Keep—" she gasps, clenching around me. "Keep doing that."

I flick my tongue along the swollen peaks, and her fingers twitch against my scalp.

She changes her mind, slamming my mouth to hers, and kisses me wild, bruising and begging, only to rip away just as quick, her lips landing on my chest.

I lift her again, keeping me inside her, and take us to the bed, but she has other ideas and scrambles along the mattress.

She turns around and gets up on all fours.

Meeting my eyes over her shoulder, she slowly lowers until her tits are touching the blanket, nothing but a tanned and toned ass in the air.

My pulse is out of control as I slip inside again, my head falling at the feeling.

All the way in.

Pure fucking heat races through my veins, and slowly I pull out, sliding right back in.

Victoria's moan has my eyes lifting.

I run my fingers up her back until I can grip her hair in my fist and tug.

Her head snaps to the side until she is once again looking at me.

"Eyes on me, baby," I tell her. "Watch me fuck you. Watch what you do to me."

I fuck her harder, faster, nothing but the sound of skin slapping skin, her heady whimpers and rich moans filling the house.

She starts to shake, her legs damn near giving out, so I wrap a hand around her stomach and lean over her.

I fuck her from behind, my lips pressed to hers, eyes locked together.

"I'm so close," she gasps. "Right there."

I pump shorter, harder, and faster, my fingers coming down to cup her pussy, and a heavy crease forms above her brows as her pleasure threatens to tear her apart.

"Come with me, Captain," she moans, pushing her ass into me. "Look me in the eyes and come for me."

I jerk and do just fucking that.

I come hard and long and as loud as she does.

Both our bodies collapse, but I spin her and slide back in, and she shakes beneath me.

I pump slowly, the feeling almost too much to handle as my body is still on its high, but I'm not ready to let go yet.

Not of this.

I skim her neck with my lips, and she sighs, a sound that settles into my soul.

Beneath me, her legs lax at our sides, hands now trailing along my back.

"That was a hell of a yes, Beauty."

She chuckles, her hands coming around to rub along my chest.

I lift until I can look her in her eyes.

My Beauty.

My girl.

My future.

EPILOGUE
VICTORIA

"Hey, ZoZo," I whisper.

"What?" she attempts to whisper back, but there is no way she didn't gain the attention of the entire car.

It's confirmed when I'm not the only person who laughs.

"ZoZo, is Rora trying to get you to tell her our secret?" Captain asks from the driver's seat.

I peek through my fingers, making eye contact with her, and shake my head with a grin.

Her little jaw drops. "Rora! That's bad! Daddy said no peeking!"

Her hands come up to cover my eyes for me.

"She can't see, Daddy. I fixed it."

Royce laughs at my side, and the sound of a body shifting on leather lets me know Raven has turned in her seat to look back as well.

"Good job, Zo. Almost there, Beauty. Keep those eyes closed a couple more minutes," Captain says.

As Captain said we would be, only minutes later he announces we're pulling off the highway, and then the ride grows a little bumpy.

"Keep them closed," he says as the roar of the engine quiets, and the doors around me begin to open.

I listen as he unbuckles Zoey's seat, hearing her little shouts as she tells her Uncle Bro to "wait up."

Captain chuckles, his hand skating along my thigh until he reaches my seat belt and unclips it. "She's becoming a mini Royce. I'm kinda scared," he jokes.

I laugh, pinching my eyes closed tighter as he drags me across the seat by my hips until my legs are hanging out the door, his body between them.

"Don't open them yet. Just listen," he tells me as he grips my hands. "All your life you had what others gave you, did what others told you, and then you came here, and every move you made was for someone else. Never you."

His forehead falls to mine, and I soak in the feeling, lacing my fingers with his. "Cap…"

"Today, I want you to look around and find what you love, what speaks to you, and I want you to have it."

My mind begins to race as I try to imagine where we are and what exactly he's talking about, and then he helps me step from the truck, the door softly closing behind me as he places himself at my back.

His lips find my ear, and at first, he teases, blowing hot air only to kiss me on the skin just beneath. His airy chuckle tells me my soft moan and involuntary shiver are what he was after. "My baby, always needy."

"You make me this way," I rasp, my head falling to his shoulder.

"I'll keep you this way."

"Promise?"

"Open your eyes, Beauty."

I don't hesitate, and as they fly open, I freeze.

And then the slightest bit of wind blows toward us, and with it an array of scents I couldn't pinpoint if I tried.

Row after row after row, tower after tower…flowers as far as I can see.

Every shape, color, and kind and more.

Large greenhouses sit on each side, holding who knows what inside.

People walk all over, wheelbarrows in tow, picking the perfect florae.

Picking what speaks to them.

I swallow, and he spins me in his arms, his knuckles sliding under my chin to lift my eyes to his. "Purple was given to you, it's been good to you, but if you got to choose, what color would you pick?"

My mouth opens, but nothing comes out, so I shake my head.

His smile is soft, as are his lips when they brush along mine. "Come on, baby. Let's go find you."

I nod, turning in his arms to find Raven, Maddoc, Royce, and Zoey now standing a few feet ahead of us, a wheelbarrow for us at their feet.

"Ready?" Raven grins, her belly round, almost at full-term now.

I nod and grab Captain's hand, and off we go.

We needed more than a wheelbarrow.

Thankfully, the nursery has delivery trucks, which we filled to the brim, but not just me.

I can say with complete certainty none of the boys have ever been to a nursery before, not that I had either. They went overboard.

Any and everything Raven, Zoey, or I stopped to look at for more than a second, they snapped their fingers and had someone load up. Eventually, me and Raven shared a look and stopped pausing completely.

Naturally, they noticed and got mad about it.

All we did was laugh, though.

Here we are, four days later, sitting on the back patio looking out at all the added life around the property.

"So, pink, huh?" Raven turns toward me. "I figured you for more of a…I don't know, not girly."

I laugh, my eyes moving to my garden.

A large, white marble bench with plush black cushions sits in the center, matching stones that lead to the seat trail in front of it, all cased in by bright, fluorescent-pink flowers of every kind.

"He went a little overboard, didn't he?" I laugh.

But Raven only smiles. "Nah. He did good, Vee."

I smile, stand, and walk over to the added "piece of me," as Cap called it.

He had it built just outside my window, said so I could look out at it anytime I wanted and see something that would forever be mine.

That's the part that got me.

This is my home, my future.

My purpose.

All the bad shit along the way had to be to lead me here today. To them.

To him.

Any other time, be it sooner or later, and things wouldn't have happened as they did, Zoey might not be here.

Everything went as it was supposed to.

"Hey."

I smile, glancing at Captain over my shoulder.

He hides something behind his back.

"Hey." I grin, spinning to him. "Whatcha got?"

"It's not for you." He tips his head, smiling at me as he brings a dozen white roses around for me to see. He leans in, kissing me softly, but as soon as the kiss deepens, he tugs away.

"Come with me," he whispers.

"I mean, I'm trying, but…" I tease.

He laughs loudly, throwing his head back, and grabs my hand, leading me to the truck. "Later, baby. Promise."

I grin, following him. "I thought we were going swimming?"

"We are when we get home. Just a quick stop." He opens the doors of his SUV.

Zoey already sits inside, buckled and ready to go, a small purple bouquet in her grasp. "Rora, look what I have."

"Those are so pretty, ZoZo."

She smiles, smelling the center of them, and looks out the window.

Captain slides inside, and we're on the road in seconds.

Not long into the drive, I realize where we're going, and then we're pulling into the Brayshaw cemetery.

Once we're parked, the three of us climb out, and Zoey runs right for where she knows Connor Perkins was buried.

Captain and I catch up, and she waits for him to remove the other set of flowers that couldn't be more than a week old and quickly places the new ones inside the built-in vase.

"Hi," Zoey says. "I bringed some from home today. I hope you like them."

I glance at Captain, who wears the softest smile as he stares at his little girl.

Sensing my stare, he turns to me.

"Aren't you going to put those in too?" I ask him.

He shakes his head, his knuckles coming up to slide along my cheek. "No, these are for someone else."

I watch him curiously as he walks off, but he only makes it a few feet before glancing back in indication for me to follow.

I grab Zoey's hand, walking alongside her as we trail Captain about fifty yards over, to a large wall made up of stone and gray swirled marble.

He stops, turns to me, and lifts Zoey into his arms. He licks his lips, seemingly nervous, and hands over the bouquet.

"Thought you might like to place these."

He leans forward, kissing my cheek, and Zoey follows, rubbing her nose along mine.

The two step back, and I watch as they head for the SUV.

Slowly, my eyes move to the wall in front of me. Right there, in an open square, sits a beautiful brass vase and, beneath, a small golden plaque.

In loving memory of Maria Vega.

Tears fill my eyes before I can stop them, and my hand comes up to cover my mouth.

He did this. For me, for him.

For us.

With shaky hands, I lift the soft white roses and set them inside the holder, stepping back to look over the small cube dedicated solely to her, a place to remember the mother I didn't know much about, the woman who loved and cared for the little girl we love and will forever care for.

She was kind and gentle and never pushed when I continuously pulled away.

I'd go visit Zoey, and she'd leave us alone, though sometimes I'd catch her recording me, but I never asked her why.

It was always a little awkward being around her, as if I was supposed to speak or ask questions, but for whatever reason, I never did.

Maybe it's because the man who taught me what it meant to trust ended up being the biggest, most untrustworthy manipulator of all.

I guess I didn't want to find out if she'd end up the same way. It was one of those situations where it was better to assume than know for sure.

Now, in her passing, I can look at Zoey, at the healthy and strong little girl she is, and say the woman who gave birth to me had a hand in making her this way.

I can remind Zoey of the woman who tucked her in at night when her dad and I couldn't.

I reach up, running my fingers along the engraving.

I will remember you, Maria Vega.

I make my way back to Captain, who stands outside his SUV, a small smile on his lips, eyes soft and bright as he pulls me into his arms, his lips instantly falling to mine.

He kisses me slowly, with such purpose I lose my breath, and

I realize, in this moment, it was never about this place, and my subconscious knew this all along.

My drive to stay here, it was all to end up standing right here, right now…with him.

He is my purpose.

My home.

And Zoey, she'll be our everything.

"So much, Beauty."

I grin against his lips, whispering, "I love you too, Cap."

Always.

"Daddy, can we go swim now?!" Zoey calls from the back seat.

Cap pulls away with a grin, and the two of us climb inside.

"Of course we can, baby girl."

Captain calls his brothers, letting them know we're on our way back so they're ready to swim when we get home.

As we're pulling onto the property, Captain comes to a stop.

A girl with short, almost silver-colored hair is climbing from an old white Camry, staring up at the girls' Bray house with a scowl, a duffel bag hanging from her hand.

My mouth drops open, a laugh escaping before I can stop it, and Cap's eyes fly my way.

"Holy. Shit." I laugh again. "He did not."

I look to Cap and he frowns.

"Beauty…"

I grin, shaking my head, and hit the dash. "Get to the house."

"Victoria."

"Cap, come on. Give it maybe ten minutes." I raise a bratty brow. "Trust me, this is too good."

His eyes narrow farther, and then he scoffs, lacing his hand in mine as he continues to roll forward. "With my life, baby," he whispers, kissing my knuckles, right where the single tidal wave tattoo sits, matching the anchor on his.

I'm the wave, he's the anchor, and this life is our ocean.

We get to the house right as the others are opening the gate to the pool.

I practically skip from the car, a grin I couldn't hide if I tried on my face.

Captain chuckles. "Man, it must be good."

"Oh, baby, you have no idea. Just wait."

He shakes his head with a grin and joins the others, helping Zoey take off her cover-up and into her life jacket. He strips down, and my eyes instantly fall to the tattoo now covering the left side of his ribs.

It's an anchor splashing into the ocean, wrapped tight in barbed wire, each spike representing a single scar on my stomach. There are forty-two.

My man said he had to bleed as I did, as many times as I did.

He catches me staring and winks, jumping right into the water, making a big splash that has Zoey laughing and jumping right after him.

I smile, my eyes moving to Raven as she drops in the chair beside me, the other two boys hopping in with Cap and Zoey.

Raven grabs my hand and places it on her belly. Right as my skin lands on hers, the baby kicks.

My eyes fly to hers, and she grins, looking to her stomach.

"Playing basketball," she whispers.

"I can't believe you haven't found out the sex yet."

"I'm not finding out," she tells me, looking back to the boys.

My eyes widen. "Why not?"

"I want to be surprised…like you were," she says quietly, briefly meeting my eyes, and something inside me settles.

Zoey.

"But I talked to Maddoc about it, and we did make an appointment." She smiles at the boys. "Only 'cause someone else needs to know, needs something for himself…something to help bring him back when I can tell he's feeling a little lost."

"Royce."

She nods, then hits my side with a grin, and my eyes fly to the pool.

All three climb the steps at once, trunks riding nice and low, and at the same time, both Raven and I sigh, chuckles quickly following.

"That's a lot of steam for one family."

I nod, my eyes grazing over every inch of Captain's physique. "Yep."

Mine.

The boys prepare to jump in, ready to make a big splash at a smiling Zoey's request, when Royce's phone rings.

He darts for it, and I sit forward in my chair, unable to hold in my grin.

Here we go…

Cap meets my eyes, nodding his chin, and I wink.

Royce hangs up as quickly as he answers, and what do you know? He starts pacing, running his hands through his hair.

"Royce?" Raven notices right away.

He freezes, looking her way, his eyes growing wide as if he's just been caught and I can't help it—a loud laugh leaves me.

His glare is instantly on me and grows deeper by the second.

That has all eyes shifting to mine, and I only laugh harder.

"You little shit," he drags out. "Always a step ahead, huh?"

"What the hell are we missing?" Maddoc eyes us both.

"Hey, Raven," I say, eyes on Royce. "Did you know there was an opening at the Bray house?"

All eyes fly to Royce.

Raven frowns, confused. "Nobody moved in after you left, so yeah, I guess. Why?"

"Spot's been filled."

"Wait, what?" She looks from Royce to me. "By who?"

I grin, and Royce tries hard to keep his frown in place but ends up laughing.

"Yeah, VicVee. By who?" He saunters over, acting like he's

ready to share the juice and play along with me, but then I'm scooped into his arms, screaming as he jumps into the pool.

We pop up, and I splash at him, swimming to the edge as he grins. We laugh as I pull myself up to the edge, sitting there soaked, still in my clothes.

"So." I hold my hands out teasingly. "You wanna tell them who the new girl is, or should I?" I tilt my head.

Royce's smirk is slow.

And then he drops the bomb they never expected.

I smile, lean back on my hands, and stare as the others gape at their brother.

I look across my family, a calm in my soul and humor in my eyes.

Captain hops onto the ledge of the pool beside me, Zoey splashing around near our feet.

He leans over, kissing my neck, and one thing is agreed on.

Summer is about to be a whole lot more interesting.

Playlist

"ocean eyes"—Billie Eilish

"Tempt My Trouble"—Bishop Briggs

"Hate Me"—Ellie Goulding & Juice WRLD

"LockDown"—Destiny Rogers

"2 Souls on Fire"—Bebe Rexha feat. Quavo

"Talking Body"—Tove Lo

"Burn Slow"—Jaira Burns

":((sad face)"—Bahari

"Worth It"—YK Osiris

"Play with Fire"—Sam Tinnesz feat. Yacht Money

"Rock Bottom"—Hailee Steinfeld feat. DNCE

"I'm a Mess"—Bebe Rexha

"We Can Make Love"—SoMo

"Lights Down Low"—MAX

"Let You Down"—NF

"Hate U Love U"—Olivia O'Brien

"Apologize"—OneRepublic

"White Flag"—Bishop Briggs

"Saints"—Echos

"BRN"—AViVA

"Just a Man"—SoMo

"Bless the Broken Road"—Rascal Flatts

READ ON FOR A LOOK AT THE FINAL STEAMY INSTALLMENT IN THE BRAYSHAW SERIES,
BREAK ME, BRAYSHAW

CHAPTER 1
BRIELLE

He thinks he's sly, lying back in the seat of a car that can't possibly be his, playing PI and sucking at it.

I mean, come on. He sits in plain sight, laughing and chatting with the guy behind the wheel, smoking something he definitely didn't buy here, while he waits for what? Me? For some sort of grand exit, where I'll flip my hair over my shoulder and push my chest out, paint my lips bright, and do my best dirty work to draw him right in, all the while he'll be laughing in his mind, planning the move he'll then make on his friend's little sister?

No, that's not it.

He's parked directly in front of my aunt's house with the windows rolled down and doing nothing to hide the sound or smell coming from the vehicle.

He doesn't think he's sly.

He simply doesn't care because he *knows* he's untouchable—it's written in the way he pushes the passenger door open and steps out into the murky air with the ease of a rebel.

This guy, he comes from a place so far from this one, it's not even funny.

Here, teenagers get drunk on tailgates at dirty riversides. They camp out and are welcomed home the morning after by loving mothers and fathers, with smiles and biscuits and gravy. They fight over girls or guys or whose fault it was that their rival teams scored at the night before's game. Simple, everyday stuff.

In the world he comes from, teenagers are a thing of the past, the parties at mansions, parents irrelevant, and the fights far crueler. It's a town founded and run by an ethically challenged power family, void of a justice system.

No, that's wrong too.

There *is* a justice system, and it consists of three rough and ruthless eighteen-year-olds.

Three adopted siblings born for a purpose greater than those on the outside could ever understand.

The brothers of Brayshaw.

One of whom is sitting outside my house this very instant, waiting.

It won't kill him to wait a little longer…

ROYCE

Scanning the fenceless houses of the tattered block, I step into the large, open grassy area and bring myself closer to the one with the rickety back door and busted-ass blinds.

There's a random bench dropped in the center of the yard, so I plant my ass on the old, splintered wood.

"Why are you sitting in my backyard staring at my house?"

I hop right the fuck back up, spinning to glare at the mini-chick raising her brows at me.

I don't say shit as I eye her, and she crosses her arms, popping a hip out while she waits. The girl can't be more than, fuck, I don't know. Five feet max. Maybe.

Fucking tiny.

Kinda mousy, with sunglasses hiding her eyes.

I hop over the bench, pushing toward her, and her chin lifts to the sky—the only way she's able to keep hers on mine—but she doesn't inch away.

"Why are there no fences around to keep people *like me* out? To stop me from staring at *your* house?" I counter.

"Because this place is as safe as safe can be."

"No such thing, baby girl."

"The worst that happens here is Tom Marvel down the street waters his yard on even days instead of odd." Her mouth gapes as she mocks shock, tilting her head.

So she's a brat.

I glare. "Sounds like a good time."

"Bunches."

"You said *you* live here?"

She slips her thumb around the straps of her backpack. "I did."

I flick my gaze over her form. "All five feet of you?"

She straightens her spine, gaining a whole extra inch, but before anything else can be said, the heavy creak of old metal followed by the quick slam of a screen has both our heads snapping toward the sound.

A slow smirk spreads across my lips as I take in the sight.

Thick, dark hair, long and lengthy, with pasty-ass skin.

There she is.

The picture of payback.

The perfect knockoff of her punk-ass brother.

"Ah, *now* it makes sense," the short chick says.

"What, how you're cramping my style, wasting my time and your breath?" I ask, not taking my eyes off the target as she lights a cigarette, bringing it to her red-painted lips.

Her head turns this way the second she pulls it from her mouth, and slowly she blows out a long line of smoke, zeroing in on me and the mouse.

She waits, but so do I.

Here, kitty, kitty…

She pretends to be chill but can't handle it and forces herself to take slow strides this way.

"You can go now," I tell the girl at my side, but she doesn't move, and quickly, my mark is stepping in front of me.

"Cousin," she drags out, but neither of us bother looking her way. "Who's your friend?"

Her sexy smirk makes its appearance.

It's a good one too. Little too confident, but it's all good.

I can kill that, easy. Besides, this would be a lot more difficult if she were unsure about herself—groundwork would have to be laid before the girl could be.

"Not my friend," short girl shares, her tone all peppy and shit as she adds, "He's here for you, actually."

At that, a saucy grin grows as if she already figured as much.

This shit will be too fucking easy.

I shouldn't play with my food, but what am I to do when it so clearly wants to play back?

I push closer, coming almost eye level with her, and her focus falls to the tattoos on my neck. "I got an hour before reality comes crashing down, *Brielle*. What are you gonna do with it?"

She studies me a long moment and then turns to the cockblocker.

Her demeanor shifts, a small twist edging her lips. "Think you can keep yourself outside a little longer?"

The animosity isn't missed.

"Do I ever come in when you take over?" short chick replies.

Brielle grins and, just like that, leads me right where she wants me.

Toward her bedroom.

The house is neat, almost sterile, and a huge fuckin' contrast to her room, which is a damn mess. There's shit all over, and the bed's unmade.

I glare at the mattress sitting on the floor, about ready to walk out and drag her ass with me, but then the girl starts to strip.

So I plant my ass, and I let her put on a little show.

I may be a guy, one who loves to fuck, gives as good as he gets and all that, but I don't do desperate, and it seems she's borderline just that.

I came here for a reason, though, so I lean back on my hands and let her do as she pleases, which happens to be me.

With her breasts hanging bare, tight-ass pants still on, she steps toward me and drops to her knees. She frees my cock from my jeans and wastes no time pulling me deep into her throat.

It's not the way I like it. I need a little lead-up, like to build that heavy tension that gets my blood pumpin', cock twitchin', and mind racing. Need my girl wet and ready, desperate for the first touch of the night and ready for more, fuckin' needy. Greedy.

This girl allowed time for none of that, so all I can do is watch her work.

A minute or two ticks by, and then she's moaning around my shaft. Finally, my hard-on grows just shy of a full salute.

I tether my hands in her hair to give her a bit more drive, and it works. She picks up some speed, tightens her lips around me, and I tip my head back a bit, trying to fall into the moment more, but as my eyes glide by the window, I fucking freeze.

The cousin, as she called her, peeks through the torn blinds, her head dropping when she realizes she's been caught, and suddenly she's gone.

A heavy crash and quiet yelp follow.

"The fuck?" I snap, freeing myself and jumping to my feet.

I'm soft in an instant, quickly shoving myself into my jeans and rushing out the door. "She better not have been recording."

Footsteps pound the linoleum floor at my back.

"Please," Brielle scoffs, hiding her naked chest with her hands as we push out onto the porch.

The girl is hopping up from the ground as we step out, limping a little as she hurries around the house.

"You better chase after her," Brielle pipes up.

I cut my gaze over my shoulder, glaring at her. "And why the fuck would I do that?"

She smirks, walking backward into the house. "Because *that*… is Brielle. I'm her cousin Ciara."

My muscles lock, and she laughs, shaking her head as she closes the door in my face.

Motherfucker!

I leap over the railing, running after the little sneak.

"Yo!" I shout.

The *real* Brielle picks up her pace, bouncing all around as she tries to keep her weight off her left foot, but it doesn't matter now. I'm already right behind her.

"Why'd you let me think she was you?"

She scoffs. "It's not my fault you assumed I was the taller, hotter, *easier* of the two of us."

I grip her by the arm, halting her movement, and she tips her head back, eyes still hidden behind her big-ass shades.

I glare, opening my mouth to tell her I don't know the fuck what when she crosses her arms again, catching me off guard.

"I know who you are."

I shoot up straight. "Yeah, and who am I?"

She doesn't miss a beat. "Royce Brayshaw, of the Brayshaw family."

I run my tongue along the backs of my teeth. "And who are you, so we're clear?"

She reaches a hand out, and I frown at it then her.

"Oh, sorry, right. You're silver-spooned." She tips her head. "*This* is called a pleasantry; many people use them."

"Your name, smart-ass."

Her hip pops out. "Shake my hand."

I hold in a growl, slapping my palm against hers, and she gives it a good, solid squeeze.

"It's good to finally meet one of you in the flesh." She passes her tote over to her other shoulder with a slight shrug. "Anyway, you already know who I am." She pauses. "Well, *now* anyway."

"Your name, from *your* lips, not that…whoever the fuck that was."

My jaw ticks as I wait for her to speak.

She doesn't, so I creep closer.

"Don't play games with me, girl."

"Right…" She pulls her lips in, nodding. "'Cause *Brayshaw*."

My head tugs back, and even though I can't see 'em, I imagine this little shit rolls her damn eyes at me.

She looks to her watch, and my annoyances are about at the *fuck shit up now, figure the rest out later* level.

"Whatever," she huffs. "I'm Brielle Bishop, and I'm late."

She turns around and walks away.

Leaves.

Yeah…I don't fuckin' think so.

I chase her ass.

BRIELLE

Oh my shit, one of my brother's psycho bosses is following me and not just *any* of his bosses.

It's the hot, kind of scary, *I'm going to liquefy you with my dark and daring eyes and maybe even by accident*, playboy one I've heard so much about but have never actually stood toe-to-toe with before today right freaking behind me, watching as I hobble around like I'm lame, probably picking me apart from his place at my back as he does.

So, okay.

To be fair, I look nothing like someone who met my brother first would expect, and considering he's been living in the group home on Royce's family's property for the last four-ish years, while working for them just as long, it makes sense this guy showed up with what he thought was a clear idea of what he'd find—the exact opposite of yours truly.

My brother, he's an easy six-foot, pasty-looking rebel with ink-black hair and crystal-blue eyes. He's tall and trim and has a natural edge to him, an aura people are drawn to despite his unapproachable, at first glance, appearance. He's sort of the best of both worlds and can pull off his chosen persona with zero effort.

I, on the other hand, am legit barely scraping by five foot, as Royce oh so typically teased, and my sunglasses hide my eye color, so he couldn't look there for resemblance—not that he would find any even if he could see through the giant reflective lenses. My hair is on the shorter side and so platinum in color all I have to do is add in a little purple shampoo and bam, solid silver.

I have an actual ass, which I'm sure he's not used to, either. It's nothing like Ciara's high and tight one. Mine's more plump and peachy, full and round, but I happen to like how it gives shape to my waist, so if he is judging, I don't even care.

That doesn't mean I like him trailing me as he sums me up with a glance, though…if that's what he's doing.

Why is he still following me?!

A sudden sharp ache zings up my leg, forcing a wince from me, but I keep moving.

"Stop walking," he commands, as if I'm supposed to listen.

I pick up the pace. "Can't. Like I said, I'm late."

"For what, Bible study?"

"Funny," I quipped, internally cursing the awful school uniforms we're forced to wear here. "A little disappointing, considering your reputation for quick wit, but maybe everything

I heard about you is wrong. After all, you were unexpectedly… insufficient."

I trip over a small hump of grass, but before I'm forced to catch myself with my injured foot, large palms wrap around my upper ribs and I'm lifted off the ground, only to be lowered right back, my bag falling to the crook of my arm.

My head snaps up and to the side, allowing me to meet his aggravated eyes over my shoulder.

"Come on now, girl," he whispers mockingly. "If you wanna spin stories, try one I can't prove wrong where we stand."

"Go for it, Slick Rick."

He gives a half shrug, and something tells me he totally will, so I retract, rushing out "No, don't" before he can make a move.

Okay, so my bad. I lied.

As far as I could tell from the angle of my little peep show, he lacked in no facet of the word, but I would swear Ciara was just that to him—lackluster, unexciting. Far from his type, should this prominent playboy have one.

Not to judge my cousin or anything—she has issues and it's her choice to use sex to make her feel better—but she jumps right to it like a dog in heat. I hear the tales time and time again, how she cuts the sensuality out of it, a self-proclaimed quickie queen.

Give them more than your body, B, and they'll shit all over it.

Words of wreckage from her.

With a guy like this one, though, I imagine that's the worst way to be.

I'd bet you've got to awaken the chef to be served the five-star delight from this too-tall, too-gorgeous, tattooed brute of a boy.

You'd only be shorting yourself to not do so.

It's like cocoa without the whipped cream—lacking the full, glorious experience.

The corner of his mouth lifts, but his eyes seem to narrow more. "Far from a boy, short stuff."

My nose scrunches, a small ripple running across my ribs. "I said that out loud?"

"You did."

"Like…all of it? Or, you know, just the boy part…"

I swear he's about to chuckle but swallows it, and just like that, the hint of embarrassment warming my blood fades.

"How 'bout," Royce starts, "you repeat *all of it,* and I'll tell you which part you already shared?"

"That sounds like a horrible idea."

He raises a single brow, and I'm instantly drawn to the tiny scar above the thick, dark curve.

Once I've allowed myself to focus on a part of him, I'm unable to stop, so from there, I search for more—for proof of struggle and pain, for signs of a life lived, and for the dark I've heard so much about but can't seem to find staring back.

I spot another small marking on his cheekbone and a ghost of one on his jaw, but my focus falls to the thick, full bottom lip he drags along his upper teeth.

He's perfectly flawed…and still holding on to me.

"Why are you here?" I lift my gaze to his, though he can't see beyond my frames.

A small wrinkle forms along his forehead, but his question doesn't match the one his eyes provide.

He wants to know how I know who he is and, even more, if I do, why I'd ask such a question, but those queries go unasked as he decides another is more important. "Why'd you let me think your cousin was you?"

Because I'm tragic and eager to please.

"She seemed more your type."

A shadow flashes across his face, a burn I recognize—one that ignites when met with judgment and personification. But did he not do the same to me?

He's the one who saw her and, boom, his mind was made up.

It's only natural, though, allowing what's on the surface to settle all.

It's humanity's biggest downfall—judgment. Expectation.

"My type, huh?" he bites out, blatantly aggravated. "How you figure?"

"I mean…you're basically wearing the same pants, so…" I joke. "Peas in a pod, Tweedledee and Tweedledum…Cheech and Chong?"

That does it, takes him off defense mode, and the corner of his mouth lifts with his sudden and unexpected laugh.

It's not brash and boisterous but a laugh just loud enough to stir the birds in the trees surrounding us.

It's throat-deep and jagged yet somehow still a lively and free sound, one that has me smiling, but the moment my lips curl to their fullest, his expression goes slack.

In a single inhale, the guy at my back morphs, now the bearer of the finest worn mask at the nonexistent masquerade he's forced himself into.

A fake in the flesh.

Or maybe fake isn't fair, but regardless, he chose to censor himself.

I don't need any more of that type around me, those closed off and prone to hiding.

All anyone ever does is hide things from me.

"You can let go of me now," I tell him.

He cocks his head, bottomless, dark eyes piercing mine through a mass of black lashes.

Something in my gut stirs, and I want to look away but don't.

So I try again to get him to be the one to step back, since it seems I'm glued in place.

"Pretty sure I'm no longer falling."

"Who said I grabbed you 'cause you were falling?" His grip tightens, his body shifting closer and closer and leaving no room to twist, no air to breathe that isn't infused with his very scent—weed and wonder. Wind and water.

I frown, blocking out the refreshing aroma, not understanding what he's getting at, and that's when the squeal of old brakes rings in my ears.

My head jerks toward the street to find the little white car that left him behind, the driver launching himself out of it the second it's in park. He rushes around the vehicle, yanking the back door open as he canvasses the area around us.

I don't have to do the same to know this block is quiet and empty this time of morning.

A sliver of panic zips through me, tingling my spine and lodging my breath deep in my throat.

Royce dips down, swiping my legs from beneath me, my body now cradled in his arms, so I quickly latch on in case he decides to try to toss me around.

Before I can wrap my head around what's happening, before I can process any of it, we're stepping from the grass onto the street and sliding into the back seat. The door's slammed behind us, and suddenly we're moving.

This is definitely when I should snap out of my shock and scream, kick, and fight and go full Karate Kid on his ass, but all I can think of is oh.

My.

Shit.

A Brayshaw just kidnapped me.

And I straight up let him.

About the Author

USA Today and *Wall Street Journal* bestselling author Meagan Brandy writes New Adult romance books with a twist. Born and raised in California, she is a married mother of three. Coffee is her best friend, and words are her sanity.

Website: meaganbrandy.com
Facebook: meaganbrandyauthor
Facebook group: facebook.com/groups/130865934291300/
Instagram: @meaganbrandyauthor
TikTok: @meaganbrandyauthor
Merch: teepublic.com/user/meaganbrandy